Introduction for Children

For Christians the Bible is the most precious book in the world. Some precious things are put up on a high shelf where no one will touch them or break them. The Bible is not like that. Christians show how precious the Bible is to them by touching it every day! They spend part of each day reading the Bible. Little by little Christians get to know and love its many stories and poems. Some parts of the Bible they learn by heart.

The Bible is a precious book, but it is not easy to read. If you have ever tried to read the Bible, you know that it can be hard to understand. Without a guide, it is easy to get lost.

We hope our book will guide you in reading the Bible. We've included a short Bible passage for every day of the year and also some of our thoughts about the passage. Even though we have both been reading the Bible for a long time, we don't pretend to understand everything in it. The Bible is like an ocean that is so big and deep you can never reach the bottom. But this book will introduce you to many of the best known and best loved parts of the Bible. This book will also help you connect the Bible to your life, both the good parts and the bad parts. We hope you will spend your whole life exploring the Bible—there is always more to discover!

If you have ever tried to pray, you know that it can be hard too. Sometimes you aren't sure what to say, and you wonder if God really hears you. Sometimes you feel too angry or sad or tired or silly to pray. Sometimes you listen for God's answer, but you don't hear anything. But praying is important, because it is a way for us to speak to God and for God to speak to us. So in this book we wrote a short prayer for every day of the year. Reading the Bible and praying go together. Both of them help connect us to God. The prayers in this book are only beginnings; you may add to them or make up your own.

We want you to know a little bit about us. Both of us are Christians, who pray and read the Bible in our own lives of faith. And both of us are professors, who teach people preparing to be leaders in the church. We have dedicated this book to our children—Clara, Andrea, and Emily Pauw, and Laura and Kate Garrett—because we want them to grow up praying and reading the Bible too.

May reading this book strengthen your faith; writing it has certainly strengthened our faith!

Making Time for God

MAKING TIME FOR GOD

DAILY DEVOTIONS FOR CHILDREN AND FAMILIES TO SHARE

SUSAN R. GARRETT
AND
AMY PLANTINGA PAUW

A Division of Baker Book House Co
Grand Rapids, Michigan 49516

Published by Baker Books
a division of Baker Publishing Group
P.O. Box 6287, Grand Rapids, MI 49516-6287
www.bakerbooks.com

Printed in the United States of America

Fifth printing, July 2007

Library of Congress Cataloging-in-Publication Data
Garrett, Susan R., 1958–
Making time for God : daily devotions for children and families to share / Susan R. Garrett and Amy Plantinga Pauw.
p. cm.
Summary: Bible passages, lessons, and prayers are presented for each day of the year.
ISBN 10: 0-8010-4505-3 (pbk.)
ISBN 978-0-8010-4505-9 (pbk.)
1. Christian children—Prayer-books and devotions—English. 2. Devotional calendars—Juvenile literature. 3. Family—Prayer-books and devotions—English. [1. Devotional calendars. 2. Prayer books and devotionals. 3. Devotinal calendars.] I. Pauw, Amy Plantinga. II. Title.
BV4870.G34 2002
249—dc21 2002009123

Introduction for Parents or Caretakers

"Recite them to your children," Moses tells the people of Israel after he speaks the Ten Commandments. "Talk about them when you are at home and when you are away, when you lie down and when you rise" (Deut. 6:7 NRSV). Many of us who care for children earnestly desire to do what Moses instructed. We want to give our children more than physical nurture—more, even, than love and security. We want to give them confident assurance that the Creator of the universe knows them by name, loves them, and desires their love in return. We want to give them knowledge of the Bible and instill in them a lifelong hunger to know both the questions it raises and the answers it provides. We want to encourage them to follow Jesus as his disciples. We want to teach them to pray.

But talking about the Bible with children is not an easy task. The Bible is challenging even for adults and all the more so for children. To begin with, it is a big book. Moreover, the language of most published translations is too hard for preteen children to understand, and many parts of the Bible presume obscure cultural or historical knowledge on the part of the reader. Finally, some sections of the Bible are too violent or sexually explicit for children.

Teaching children to pray is also a challenge, especially if the parents or caretakers are themselves out of practice in this area. What should one pray for? How formal must one's language be? And how should one answer the penetrating questions about God and about prayer that children—once they know that the door is open—are prone to ask? These challenges became apparent to us when our own children reached the age of seven or eight, and the simplest bedtime prayers and picture Bibles no longer seemed adequate for a short nightly devotion. So, being theologically trained, we decided to write a devotional book that addresses the difficulties mentioned above. We wanted it to be a guide that would "hook" our own and other kids on the habit of daily Bible reading and prayer. Such a habit, if formed early, can last a lifetime.

The Book of Exodus tells how God accompanied the people of Israel as they journeyed to the Promised Land. But as people of faith we are *all* on a journey. None of us has already arrived at the destination; none of us has all the answers to our deepest questions about God's world and our place in it. *Making Time for God* is not a book of pat solutions to our problems. At points we acknowledge to our young readers that the Bible raises new questions for us even as it answers others. But we also seek to persuade readers that the Bible offers invaluable help as we journey with God. Its words guide us, encourage us, inspire us, and correct us as we press on toward the goal. As the psalmist writes, "Your word is a lamp to my feet and a light to my path" (Ps. 119:105 NRSV).

We hope that the lessons we draw from the Scriptures and the prayers that we base on them will help shape the moral character of children. But not every entry in this book ends with an explicit lesson or virtue. There are no fictitious morality tales here about children who obey their parents, tell the truth, witness to their neighbors, or befriend the new kid at school. The process of shaping moral character, we believe, is sometimes best approached more indirectly—by helping kids to witness the dilemmas and the complexities of life, and by showing them ways that real people of faith have coped with these dilemmas over the centuries. So, instead of telling artificial stories, we draw on examples from the Bible, church history, and everyday life to help kids think about how to live rich and full lives of service for God. We describe successes but also failures; we speak of hope but also of despair; we describe confident faith but also times when faith is tested to the utmost. In doing so, we hope to foster recognition that the Bible is so much more than a book of tidy rules.

One difficulty in reading the Bible with children is finding a suitable translation. Two translations we find generally reliable and presented in language simple enough for children are the *New International Reader's Version* and the *Contemporary English Version*. It is a good idea to purchase a Bible for your child, and we recommend either of these two translations. For most entries in the book, we have used whichever of these two best captures the underlying Hebrew or Greek of the passage in question or best renders a particular phrase or idea that we want to emphasize. But for some biblical passages neither translation proved suitable, and in those cases we used the *New Living Translation*, the *New Revised Standard Version*, or an original translation. At the end of each biblical passage, the translation is indicated by the appropriate initials: NIRV, NLT, CEV, NRSV, and AT (author's translation).

A number of considerations went into our selection of biblical passages and our composition and arrangement of entries. For one thing, we have attended to the rhythm and flow of the calendar year. We have paid attention both to the secular calendar (with entries, for example, observing African-American History and Women's History months, Valentine's Day, and Thanksgiving) and the liturgical calendar (observing, for example, both Lent and Advent). We have also attended to issues that we see as important for children growing up in today's world, including "positive" topics like faith, friendship, and care for the earth, as well as "negative" topics like racism, death, and divorce. We have drawn on nearly all the books of the Bible. In doing so, we have incorporated many of the stories or passages that have been especially important down through the centuries for Christian faith, practice, and self-understanding. But we have also treated some passages that are seldom treated in children's Bibles or devotional books (such as the Song of Songs and the Psalms of lament). Where possible, multiple entries from a given biblical book have been presented in "chunks," so as to help our readers grasp the content and flow of the material as the Bible presents it. Throughout the work, we have drawn on the best of current biblical and theological research, though our dependence is nearly always implicit so as to keep the entries simple.

The prayers we have included with each entry are quite brief and are focused on the topic of the Bible passage and the meditation. Daily prayer can easily grow tiresome and repetitious, and tying prayer together with Bible reading offers a way to keep prayer fresh. The Scriptures offer both new language and new topics to inspire the life of prayer. But you may wish to encourage your children to "pray beyond" the confines of the short prayers that we offer here. One idea is to work with your child to make lists of all the possible types of prayers (praise, thanksgiving, confession, and intercession, for example) and possible situations or people for which or for whom to pray. Such lists can help both you and your child as you decide how and what to pray each day.

We have envisioned *Making Time for God* as appropriate for children aged seven through twelve, but this is only a suggested range. With help, younger children may be able to appreciate some of the entries. Teenagers, especially those new to Christian faith, may also find this a helpful book. Though older children in the target range will likely be able to read and understand it by themselves, there is much to be gained by having them read and discuss the biblical passages and meditations and pray with you. Therefore we hope that you will make a daily practice of reading the book with your child. To that end, we have tried to write it in a way that will make it interesting and inspiring not only for younger readers but also for adults.

Perhaps it goes without saying that there is also much to be gained by teaching children to worship and study regularly with a larger body of disciples. In *Making Time for God* we make occasional encouraging references to church and to worship, and we hope that if you and your children do not already have a church home you will find one and make regular worship a part of your life.

We sincerely desire that *Making Time for God* will give you not only concrete guidance but also confidence and joy as you lead your children into a life of sustaining faith in our Lord Jesus Christ.

We are thankful for the support and encouragement we received from many members of the Louisville Presbyterian Seminary community. President John Mulder and Dean Dianne Reistroffer shared our enthusiasm for the project from the beginning. David Hester, Gene March, Heather Thiessen, and Trisha Tull provided expert counsel. Melisa Scarlott was a tremendous help in organizing all the entries. Brad Wigger, Director of the Center for Congregations and Family Ministries, encouraged us and provided opportunities to present our material in workshop settings. In addition, a number of students gave useful feedback and suggestions as the work progressed.

The Henry Luce Foundation, Inc., awarded Susan a Henry Luce III Fellowship in Theology that made possible a year's study leave. Although the fellowship was awarded to support another research project, the freedom and mental space that the grant afforded were key to the conception and early development of *Making Time for God.*

Katherine Paterson, Fred Rogers, and Celia Straus all gave strong encouragement in the crucial early phase of our project. Bob Hosack at Baker Book House receives our sincere thanks and appreciation for taking the project on. He and editor Sharon Van Houten gave invaluable counsel as the book took final shape. Our families played significant roles all along as readers and unofficial editors. Jim, Laura, and Kate Garrett, and Alan, Clara, Andrea, and Emily Pauw all deserve our special thanks. We dedicate the book to Laura, Kate, Clara, Andrea, and Emily.

JANUARY 1

•

Jesus Christ the Son of God is always "Yes" and never "No." And he is the one that Silas, Timothy, and I told you about. Christ says "Yes" to all of God's promises. That's why we have Christ to say "Amen" for us to the glory of God.

2 Corinthians 1:19–20 CEV

Happy New Year! Have you made any resolutions yet? A resolution is a promise you make. Some people resolve to break a bad habit, or to get more exercise, or to work harder in school. If you've made resolutions before, you know that keeping them is much harder than making them. It is easy to say, "Yes, I will stop fighting with my brother." It is hard to actually do it.

But God doesn't break resolutions the way we do. When God promises to love us and forgive us and heal us, we know we can count on it. Jesus Christ is God's living "Yes" to us. Jesus Christ is our proof that all God's promises to us will come true.

It is good to make your own resolutions and to try to keep them. But it is even more important to trust God's resolutions about you!

God, thank you for saying "Yes" to us in Jesus Christ. Help us trust your promises, and help us keep the promises we make to ourselves and others. In Christ's name, Amen.

JANUARY 2

•

In the beginning, God created the heavens and the earth. The earth didn't have any shape. And it was empty. Darkness was over the surface of the ocean. At that time, the ocean covered the earth. The Spirit of God was hovering over the waters. God said, "Let there be light." And there was light. God saw that the light was good. He separated the light from the darkness. God called the light "day." He called the darkness "night." There was evening, and there was morning. It was day one.

Genesis 1:1–5 NIRV

These are the first words of Genesis, which is the first Book of the Bible. The name "Genesis" means "beginning." It is a good name for this book, which tells us about the beginning of everything in the starry heavens and on our lovely planet Earth!

Genesis 1 is a kind of poem reminding us that God is the one who created everything. God is the one who made light to shine where before there had been only darkness! In the verses that follow this passage, the author of Genesis tells how God created the sky with its sun and moon and stars, the dry ground, and every living thing.

Scientists also tell stories about how the world came to be. We can study their ideas and learn from them. But when we study science, it is good also to remember what we learn from Genesis: *God* is our Creator, and God called the creation *good.*

Creator of all, thank you for the light and the darkness. Thank you for the sun, moon, stars, and planets. Thank you for the oceans, mountains, and every living thing. Thank you, God, that we too may look at your work and see that it is good! Amen.

JANUARY 3

•

Then God said, "Let us make man in our likeness. Let them rule over the fish in the waters and the birds of the air. Let them rule over the livestock and over the whole earth. Let them rule over all of the creatures that move along the ground."

So God created man in his own likeness.
He created him in the likeness of God.
He created them as male and female.

Genesis 1:26–27 NIrV

Do people ever tell you that you have your dad's smile or his eyes? Or are you shy, or cheerful, or smart like your mom? Sometimes kids are a lot like their parents; sometimes they aren't like them at all!

The author of Genesis says that the first human beings, male and female, were created in God's likeness. But in what way were they like God? Was it the way they looked? The way they acted? The way they thought? What made those first humans like God, and what makes us like God today?

One answer is that we, like God, are caretakers of our earth. God created humans with the intelligence and abilities they would need to help in the work of tending or caring for this marvelous creation. We can do this work in many ways, for example, by trying not to waste water, food, or paper. Caring for the earth is a big and very important job! Are you helping to do your part?

Loving God, you care for all your work, and all creation shows your glory! As I grow, teach me how to love and tend the earth and its creatures. Amen.

JANUARY 4

•

The woman said to the serpent, "We can eat the fruit of the trees that are in the garden. But God did say, 'You must not eat the fruit of the tree that is in the middle of the garden. Do not even touch it. If you do, you will die.'" "You can be sure that you won't die," the serpent said to the woman. "God knows that when you eat the fruit of that tree, you will know things you have never known before. You will be able to tell the difference between good and evil. You will be like God."

Genesis 3:2–5 NIRV

God created the world good. And yet, from the very beginning, forces were already at work making things go wrong.

Genesis tells how God had given Adam and Eve all that they needed for a happy life and had commanded them not to touch or eat from a certain tree. But then a voice—the Bible says it was the voice of a serpent—told them to ignore God's command! The rest of the story tells how Eve and Adam listened to the voice of the serpent instead of the voice of God. When they ate the forbidden fruit, they pushed themselves away from God. It was as if they were saying, "We don't want to listen to you anymore."

In this story Adam and Eve were the first ones to push themselves away from God. But what happened to them also happens to us! We too find it easy to stop listening to God. We all need help to hear and obey God's voice.

Dear God, I love your world and all the good things and people in it! But even good people mess up. Help me want what is good. Make me willing to hear and obey your voice. Amen.

JANUARY 5

•

The LORD was pleased with Abel and his offering, but not with Cain and his offering. This made Cain so angry that he could not hide his feelings. Cain said to his brother Abel, "Let's go for a walk." And when they were out in a field, Cain killed him. Afterwards the LORD asked Cain, "Where is Abel?" "How should I know?" he answered. "Am I supposed to look after my brother?"

Genesis 4:4b–5, 8–9 CEV

Cain and Abel were brothers. They each brought a gift to God. God accepted Abel's gift, but for some reason (the Bible doesn't say why) God did not accept Cain's gift. You can imagine how Cain must have felt when God rejected his gift. Cain couldn't control his anger and jealousy, and so he killed his brother.

Anger, hatred, and jealousy can be like loud voices speaking in your head and in your heart. The voices may tell you that if you hurt the person with whom you are angry, you will feel better. But that message is a lie. Hurting the other person won't make any of the bad feelings go away. And the harm that you do will make others feel angry and may lead to more trouble.

Cain could have made a different choice. He could have told God about his anger. When we bring our bad feelings to God in prayer, God always accepts our prayer and works to heal the pain that we feel.

Dear God, teach me not to listen to the voices of anger, hatred, and jealousy. Instead help me to bring all bad feelings to you so that you can heal my heart. Amen.

JANUARY 6

•

When Jesus was born in the village of Bethlehem in Judea, Herod was king. During this time some wise men from the east came to Jerusalem and said, "Where is the child born to be king of the Jews? We saw his star in the east and have come to worship him."

Matthew 2:1–2 CEV

Have you ever watched a sunrise? Everything is dark, and then little by little, light starts to appear in the eastern part of the sky. Today, January 6, Christians celebrate Epiphany, which means appearance. On this day, many Christians remember the appearance of Jesus Christ to the wise men. From far away, the wise men saw the light of Jesus' star in the east and came to worship him. His coming is good news for the whole world!

If you live in the northern half of the earth, Epiphany comes at a time of year when the days are very short and there is not a lot of light. Celebrating Epiphany reminds us that Jesus Christ is the light of the world, who comes to bring us all light and life.

Jesus Christ, you are the light that shows us God's love for the whole world. Shine on me, so that I can share your light with others. Amen.

JANUARY 7

•

"I am going to bring a flood on the earth. It will destroy all life under the sky. It will destroy every living creature that breathes. Everything on earth will die. But I will make my covenant with you. You will enter the ark. Your sons and your wife and your sons' wives will enter it with you. Bring two of every living thing into the ark. Bring male and female of them into it. They will be kept alive with you. . . . Take every kind of food that you will need. Store it away. It will be food for you and for them."

Genesis 6:17–19, 21 NIrV

You probably know the story of Noah's ark. You may have seen artists' pictures of the famous boat with its elephants, monkeys, giraffes, lions, lizards, and other animals marching in, two-by-two!

But the story of Noah's ark is a serious one, about how God judged the people of the earth. A judge decides whether people are following the rules and living right. In the story of the flood, God decided that the people weren't living right. They were doing cruel and harmful acts. The Bible says that is why God sent the flood.

Many people find it scary to think about God as a judge. They would rather talk about how God loves us and helps us! Indeed, God does love us greatly. But because of that great love, God gave us rules to live by and expects us to treat each other right. Can you think of ways that God helps us do that?

Holy God, thank you for loving us so much and for expecting us to live up to your high expectations. Please forgive us when we do wrong. Show us your path and help us to do right. Amen.

JANUARY 8

•

Abram fell with his face to the ground. God said to him, "As for me, this is my covenant with you. You will be the father of many nations. You will not be called Abram anymore. Your name will be Abraham, because I have made you a father of many nations. I will give you many children. Nations will come from you. And kings will come from you. I will make my covenant with you. It will last forever. It will be between me and you and your children after you for all time to come. I will be your God. And I will be the God of all of your family after you."

Genesis 17:3–7 NIRV

God made a promise to Abram. Abram and Sarai would have a son, Isaac. They—and all Isaac's family after him—would be God's people. God would bless them. They would know and love God and must live in God's way. To remind them of this promise (or covenant), God gave the new name "Abraham" to Abram. If you read a little farther in Genesis 17, you will see that God gave the new name "Sarah" to Sarai. You will also see that Abraham asked God about his older son, named Ishmael. Ishmael's mother was Hagar. Abraham wanted to know if God would bless Ishmael and his family. God promised to bless Ishmael too.

Today, people from many nations call themselves "children of Abraham." Jews are his children because Isaac and Abraham were their ancestors. Muslims are his children because Ishmael and Abraham were their ancestors. Christians are children of Abraham because they share Abraham's trust in God, and God adopts them into the family. What about you? Are you a child of Abraham too?

Dear God, you have blessed so many people. Bless me too! Help me to be part of your people. Help me to live in your way. Amen.

JANUARY 9

•

Then the LORD said, "You can be sure that I will return to you about this time next year. Your wife Sarah will have a son." Sarah was listening at the entrance to the tent behind him. Abraham and Sarah were already very old. Sarah was too old to have a baby. So she laughed to herself. She thought, "I'm worn out, and my husband is old. Can I really know the joy of having a baby?" Then the LORD said to Abraham, "Why did Sarah laugh? Why did she say, 'Will I really have a baby, now that I am old?' Is anything too hard for me? I will return to you at the appointed time next year. Sarah will have a son."

Genesis 18:10–14 NIRV

Sometimes we hear an idea that seems so impossible it makes us laugh. "That's crazy!" we might think or say. "That could never happen!"

The Lord told Abraham that his wife Sarah would have a baby. Sarah had wanted a child for a long, long time. But now she was much older than most women who have babies. To her, the Lord's promise seemed a little crazy! That is why Sarah laughed.

But God is the source of all life. And God likes to bring new life and new hope to people who think "That could never happen" or "It's too late!" The Lord's promise would indeed come true: Soon Sarah and Abraham would have a baby boy, Isaac.

Lord, Giver of life, if ever I lose hope or think "It's too late," please remind me of Sarah. Remind me that nothing is too hard for you! Amen.

JANUARY 10

•

Isaac grew. The time came for his mother to stop nursing him. On that day Abraham had a big dinner prepared. But Sarah saw Ishmael making fun of Isaac. Ishmael was the son Hagar had by Abraham. Hagar was Sarah's servant from Egypt. Sarah said to Abraham, "Get rid of that slave woman. Get rid of her son. The slave woman's son will never have a share of the family's property with my son Isaac." What Sarah said upset Abraham very much. After all, Ishmael was his son. But God said to him, "Do not be so upset about the boy and your servant Hagar. Listen to what Sarah tells you, because your family line will continue through Isaac. I will make the son of your servant into a nation also. I will do it because he is your child."

Genesis 21:8–13 NIRV

Abraham and Sarah were now the proud parents of Isaac. But things were not going well. Abraham's other son, Ishmael, and Ishmael's mother, Hagar, were living with them. Sarah didn't like Hagar and Ishmael. (Did you notice how Sarah wouldn't even call Hagar by her name?) Sarah wanted all the blessings to go to Isaac. So she told Abraham to make Hagar and Ishmael go away.

This upset Abraham. Ishmael was his son too! But God told Abraham not to worry about Ishmael, or about Hagar either. God had special plans for them. (Did you notice how God calls Hagar by her name?)

Sometimes we act like Sarah. We not only want blessings for ourselves—we try to keep them from others. God didn't stop Sarah from acting that way, and God won't stop us either. But God wants better from us. God would bless Hagar and Ishmael in spite of the jealousy of Sarah.

God, forgive me when I try to keep all your blessings for myself. Remind me that there are plenty of blessings to go around! Amen.

JANUARY 11

•

Early the next morning Abraham got some food and a bottle of water. The bottle was made out of animal skin. He gave the food and water to Hagar. He placed them on her shoulders. Then he sent her away with the boy. She went on her way and wandered in the desert of Beersheba. When the water in the bottle was gone, she put the boy under a bush. Then she went off and sat down nearby. She was about as far away as a person can shoot an arrow. She thought, "I can't stand to watch the boy die." As she sat nearby, she began to sob. God heard the boy crying. Then the angel of God called out to Hagar from heaven. He said to her, "What is the matter, Hagar? Do not be afraid. God has heard the boy crying as he lies there. Lift the boy up. Take him by the hand. I will make him into a great nation." Then God opened Hagar's eyes. She saw a well of water. So she went and filled the bottle with water. And she gave the boy a drink.

Genesis 21:14–19 NIRV

Hagar's water bottle was empty, and she thought that she and Ishmael would die. But then she heard the voice of an angel! Through that voice God told Hagar of the blessings ahead. Then God opened Hagar's eyes to see a well filled with water that they needed so much.

Hagar's story is important because she reminds us of many women who have been treated badly by those with more power. For example, in America before the Civil War, some slave women thought of Hagar as one who suffered in the same way they did. Even today, Hagar causes us to remember that women are sometimes treated cruelly or violently although they have done nothing wrong.

Dear Lord, open our eyes to see where women—and children and men too—are being treated badly. Remind us that you see and care for those people and show us how to help. Amen.

JANUARY 12

•

In the beginning was the one who is called the Word.
The Word was with God and was truly God.
From the very beginning the Word was with God.
And with this Word, God created all things.
Nothing was made without the Word.
Everything that was created received its life from him,
and his life gave light to everyone.
The light keeps shining in the dark,
and darkness has never put it out.

John 1:1–5 CEV

If you turn to the first words of the first book of the Bible (Genesis), you will see that it starts the same way this passage does: "In the beginning." The story of Genesis 1 is about how the whole world was created by God's word. "God said, 'Let there be light.' And there was light." Every time God says "let there be" in Genesis 1, more of the world is created.

John 1 says that God's Word was there "in the beginning," even before there was a world. This Word is the source of all life. This Word is the light that lets everybody see God.

John 1 is telling a new story about God's Word. This Word, which has been in the world from the beginning, is now in the world in a new way. God's Word has come in person! Do you know who this person is?

God, through your Word, you created the whole world. Thank you for giving me life. Thank you for the light that lets me see you more clearly. I pray in Christ's name, Amen.

JANUARY 13

•

A man came who was sent from God. His name was John. He came to give witness about that light. He gave witness so that all people could believe. John himself was not the light. He came only as a witness to the light. The true light that gives light to every man was coming into the world. The Word was in the world that was made through him. But the world did not recognize him. He came to what was his own. But his own people did not accept him. Some people did accept him. They believed in his name. He gave them the right to become children of God.

John 1:6–12 NIRV

God's Word, the light of the whole world, was coming in person! That was a pretty amazing story! So God sent a man, John the Baptist, to tell people about it and prepare them to believe this good news.

Some people didn't believe it. How could the Word of God come in person? That's impossible, they said. When Jesus came, they didn't recognize anything special about him. They thought he was just an ordinary person.

But some people did believe the good news. They believed that, in Jesus, God's Word had come into the world in a new way. It's still a pretty amazing story. Do you believe it?

God, thank you for sending witnesses to spread your good news. Help me to believe it and to spread the good news to others. Amen.

JANUARY 14

•

Philip found Nathanael and told him, "We have found the One that Moses wrote about in the Law. The prophets also wrote about him. He is Jesus of Nazareth, the son of Joseph." "Nazareth! Can anything good come from there?" Nathanael asked. "Come and see," said Philip. Jesus saw Nathanael approaching. Here is what Jesus said about him. "He is a true Israelite. There is nothing false in him." "How do you know me?" Nathanael asked. Jesus answered, "I saw you while you were still under the fig tree. I saw you there before Philip called you." Nathanael replied, "Rabbi, you are the Son of God. You are the King of Israel."

John 1:45–49 NIRV

Almost all Christians sometimes wonder if what they believe is really true. In a world filled with bad news, the good news of Jesus Christ can seem too good to be true. Having doubts and asking questions are a normal part of faith.

Jesus came from a small town called Nazareth. Nathanael didn't think a famous or important person could come from a little place like that. He had doubts about Jesus. But when his friend Philip invited him to come and see Jesus, Nathanael went anyway. He soon changed his mind about Jesus! Nathanael saw right away that Jesus knew the truth about him. And so Nathanael told the truth about Jesus: He called Jesus the Son of God and the King of Israel.

Jesus praised Nathanael for his faith. Even though Nathanael had doubts, he was willing to come and see Jesus. Jesus promised that Nathanael's faith would grow as he saw even greater things.

Lord Jesus, sometimes I wonder if your promises are true. Make me willing to come and listen to what others say about you, and help my faith grow stronger every day. Amen.

JANUARY 15

•

"I will cause peace to flow over her like a river.
I will make the wealth of nations sweep over her like a flooding stream.
You will nurse and be carried in her arms.
You will play on her lap.
As a mother comforts her child,
I will comfort you.
You will find comfort in Jerusalem."

Isaiah 66:12–13 NIRV

When we look at all the problems in the world around us, it is sometimes hard to imagine how the world could be different. In this passage, God wasn't telling the people of Israel how things were then, but how things would be in the future. In this vision, no one is fighting, no one is poor or hungry, no one is sad or lonely. As a mother comforts her child, God comforts us with this vision.

God gave Martin Luther King Jr. a vision too. He had a dream that one day his country would be a place where people with different skin colors respected each other and worked together. He dreamed of a day when there would be freedom and justice for all people. Our country still isn't like that. But Martin Luther King's vision shows us what God wants us to hope and work for.

God, thank you for giving us a vision for how the world can be a better place. Give us strength as we try to change things. Comfort us as we wait for your will to be done on earth. Amen.

JANUARY 16

•

Jesus said to the servants, "Fill the jars with water." So they filled them to the top. Then he told them, "Now dip some out. Take it to the person in charge of the dinner." They did what he said. The person in charge tasted the water that had been turned into wine. He didn't realize where it had come from. But the servants who had brought the water knew. Then the person in charge called the groom to one side. He said to him, "Everyone brings out the best wine first. They bring out the cheaper wine after the guests have had too much to drink. But you have saved the best until now." That was the first of Jesus' miraculous signs. He did it at Cana in Galilee. Jesus showed his glory by doing it. And his disciples put their faith in him.

John 2:7–11 NIrV

It is embarrassing to run out of food at a party. Part of being a good host is to have plenty of food and drink to offer your guests. But at this wedding in Cana, the hosts ran out of wine.

The bride and groom could have sent the guests home thirsty. But one of the guests was Jesus. Jesus did an amazing and wonderful thing. He took six stone jars, each full of at least twenty gallons of water, and turned the water into wine. You probably know the size of a one-gallon jug of milk. Now imagine 120 of those! Because of what Jesus did, there was more than enough for all the guests to drink.

The wine was a sign of the new life that God offers us in Jesus. Jesus doesn't bring us just a little bit of new life. He brings lots and lots—more than enough for everyone!

Generous God, thank you for the new life you offer us in Jesus. Help us to put our faith in him, like the disciples did. Amen.

JANUARY 17

•

There was a Pharisee named Nicodemus. He was one of the Jewish rulers. He came to Jesus at night and said, "Rabbi, we know you are a teacher who has come from God. We know that God is with you. If he weren't, you couldn't do the miraculous signs you are doing." Jesus replied, "What I'm about to tell you is true. No one can see God's kingdom without being born again." "How can I be born when I am old?" Nicodemus asked. "I can't go back inside my mother! I can't be born a second time!" Jesus answered, "What I'm about to tell you is true. No one can enter God's kingdom without being born through water and the Holy Spirit."

John 3:1–5 NIrV

When you were born, you began a whole new way of life. You breathed air. You drank milk. You saw colors. You were held and cuddled by others. Before you were born, you couldn't do any of these things!

When Jesus talked to Nicodemus about being born again, Nicodemus became all confused. He thought Jesus was talking about being born again just like the first time.

Instead, Jesus was talking about a new kind of birth. This time the Spirit will give you birth. When you are born again of the Spirit, you begin a whole new way of life: a life of trust and love and joy. Do you want to be born again in this way?

God, sometimes it is hard to understand what the new life you offer is like. Thank you for sending Jesus to guide us. Send your Holy Spirit so that we can be born into this new way of life. Amen.

JANUARY 18

•

"God loved the world so much that he gave his one and only Son. Anyone who believes in him will not die but will have eternal life. God did not send his Son into the world to judge the world. He sent his Son to save the world through him."

John 3:16–17 NIRV

John 3:16 is the favorite Bible verse of many Christians. It is a good verse to memorize. That's because it proclaims such good news: God loved the world so much that God gave us Jesus. What an incredible gift!

Imagine getting a really big and wonderful gift and putting it in your closet without opening it. If you decided to do that, your life would go on just the way it had before. You would lose out on all that the gift had to offer.

But suppose you decided to open and enjoy the gift. Your life would never be the same again. That's the way it is when you accept the gift of Jesus. You start enjoying eternal life with God right here on earth!

God, you love the world so much that you gave an incredible gift. Because of Jesus, my life will never be the same. Thank you! Amen.

JANUARY 19

•

"Here is the judgment. Light has come into the world, but people loved darkness instead of light. They loved darkness because what they did was evil. All those who do evil things hate the light. They will not come into the light. They are afraid that what they do will be seen. But those who live by the truth come into the light. They do this so that it will be easy to see that what they have done is with God's help.

John 3:19–21 NIRV

Many people leave outdoor lights on at night after they go to bed. That's because burglars hate the light. They like to break into a house and steal things in the dark. That way no one can see them. If burglars see a bright light, they stay away. John 3 says that all who do evil things hate the light.

But if we are trying to do something good, we come close to the light. We want to see better what we are doing, and we don't care if others see us. We are not afraid of the light.

When Christians are doing good, they draw close to Jesus, the Light. Jesus helps them see and do what is right. Jesus helps them see that all their good works are done with God's help.

Christ Jesus, you are the Light of the world. Without you, I am in the dark. Help me come close to you, so that I will see what is good and have the strength to do it. Amen.

JANUARY 20

•

Just then Jesus' disciples returned. They were surprised to find him talking with a woman. But no one asked, "What do you want from her?" No one asked, "Why are you talking with her?" The woman left her water jar and went back to the town. She said to the people, "Come. See a man who told me everything I've ever done. Could this be the Christ?" The people came out of the town and made their way toward Jesus.

John 4:27–30 NIRV

Sometimes we feel uncomfortable with people who are different from us. Maybe they have a different religion or a different skin color than we do. Maybe they have a lot less or a lot more money than we do.

Jesus had a long conversation with a woman who was very different from him. She was a Samaritan and he was a Jew, and Samaritans and Jews weren't even supposed to talk to each other. Also, in those days, Jewish teachers like Jesus did not talk to women in public. That is why his disciples were so surprised to find him talking to a woman.

Jesus didn't stay away from people who were different than he was. Jesus' good news about eternal life with God was for everyone. The Samaritan woman went back to her town and told everyone about Jesus. After that they wanted to talk to Jesus too!

God, I'm sorry that sometimes I stay away from other people just because they are different from me. Help me remember that the love you showed us in Jesus is for the whole world. Amen.

JANUARY 21

•

A lot of Samaritans in that town put their faith in Jesus because the woman had said, "This man told me everything I have ever done." They came and asked him to stay in their town, and he stayed on for two days. Many more Samaritans put their faith in Jesus because of what they heard him say. They told the woman, "We no longer have faith in Jesus just because of what you told us. We have heard him ourselves, and we are certain that he is the Savior of the world!"

John 4: 39–42 CEV

Faith in Jesus spreads because Christians don't keep the good news of salvation to themselves. They tell others! A person who tells others about Jesus Christ is called a witness. Who are the witnesses who shared their faith with you?

Anyone who believes in Jesus Christ can be a witness. A witness can be a woman or a man. A witness can be young or old, healthy or sick. A witness can be black or white, rich or poor.

The Samaritan woman who talked to Jesus became a witness. Many people believed in Jesus because of her words. Because they believed what she told them, they wanted to meet Jesus for themselves. After they met him, they said, "We are certain that he is the Savior of the world!" The Samaritan woman's good witness helped them become witnesses too!

God, thank you for sending witnesses to tell me about Jesus. Make me a good witness to others. Amen.

JANUARY 22

•

Some years later God decided to test Abraham, so he spoke to him. Abraham answered, "Here I am, LORD." The LORD said, "Go get Isaac, your only son, the one you dearly love! Take him to the land of Moriah, and I will show you a mountain where you must sacrifice him to me on the fires of an altar." So Abraham got up early the next morning and chopped wood for the fire. He put a saddle on his donkey and left with Isaac and two servants for the place where God had told him to go.

Genesis 22:1–3 CEV

God told Abraham to do something terrible. God told him to take his beloved son, Isaac, and sacrifice him to God. (Usually the Hebrews killed animals like sheep and gave them as sacrifices or gifts to God.) God was testing Abraham, seeing whether Abraham trusted God to do what was right. But Abraham didn't know that. Abraham only knew that God had given him instructions. And Abraham obeyed by taking Isaac up the mountain to sacrifice him.

God loves all people and values each one's life. God never wants a child to suffer. So why would God ask Abraham to kill his son? This we cannot understand. For thousands of years faithful Jews and Christians have struggled to answer this question.

Abraham trusted that God was good, and he knew that his life and Isaac's were in God's hands. When they were going up the mountain, Isaac said to Abraham, "Father, where is the lamb for the sacrifice?" "My son," Abraham answered, "God will provide the lamb." And God did. As Abraham was about to sacrifice his son, an angel called out and told him to stop, and Abraham found a sheep caught in the bushes nearby. So Isaac was saved.

God, sometimes it is so very hard to trust you and to follow your instructions. Sometimes it seems as if there is trouble on every side and no way out. Help me to know that my life is always in your hands. Amen.

JANUARY 23

•

One day Jacob was cooking some stew. Esau came in from the open country. He was very hungry. He said to Jacob, "Quick! Let me have some of that red stew! I'm very hungry!" . . . Jacob replied, "First sell me the rights that belong to you as the oldest son in the family." "Look, I'm dying of hunger," Esau said. "What good are those rights to me?" But Jacob said, "First promise me with an oath that you are selling me your rights." So Esau promised to do it. He sold Jacob all of the rights that belonged to him as the oldest son. Jacob gave Esau some bread and some lentil stew.

Genesis 25:29–34a NIRV

Jacob and Esau were twin sons of Isaac and Rebekah. Esau was a few minutes older than Jacob. In those days, the oldest son had certain rights that other children did not have. For example, the oldest son might receive a special blessing. And when parents died, the oldest son would receive more of the property that had belonged to them. Here, Esau bought some bread and stew. He didn't pay with money, but with his birthrights. Now, Esau would not be the one to receive his father's special blessing. That stew came at a very high price!

Esau had been terribly hungry and weak. In order to buy Esau's birthrights, Jacob had taken advantage of his brother's weakness. Later, Esau became so angry at Jacob that he said he would kill him. Jacob had to leave his home in order to save his life. So Jacob also paid a high price.

God, help me not to waste all your blessings but to use them wisely. And teach me not to take advantage of someone else's weakness but to help him or her. Amen.

JANUARY 24

•

So Jacob was left alone. A man struggled with him until morning. The man saw that he couldn't win. So he touched the inside of Jacob's hip. As Jacob struggled with the man, Jacob's hip was twisted. Then the man said, "Let me go. It is morning." But Jacob replied, "I won't let you go unless you bless me." The man asked him, "What is your name?" "Jacob," he answered. Then the man said, "Your name will not be Jacob anymore. Instead, it will be Israel. You have struggled with God and with human beings. And you have won." Jacob said, "Please tell me your name." But he replied, "Why do you want to know my name?" Then he blessed Jacob there.

Genesis 32:24–29 NIRV

Something very strange happened to Jacob one night. A man came and wrestled with him for a long time, and even hurt Jacob's hip. The Bible doesn't say who the visitor was or why he wrestled with Jacob. But somehow Jacob sensed that God was present in this mysterious stranger. Jacob insisted that the man promise Jacob good things for the future. The man—or perhaps it was an angel—blessed Jacob and gave him a new name, "Israel." Things would never be the same for Israel after that. God's chosen people would be named after him!

Sometimes we wrestle with God too. For example, we wrestle with God when we feel angry at God about something, or when we sense that God is trying to speak to us but we don't want to listen. Can you think of other times when we wrestle with God?

Wrestling with God is very tiring work. God is much stronger than we are! When you find yourself in such a struggle, do what Jacob did: Ask God for a blessing. You may find that the struggle was God's way of making you into a new person!

God, you come to me in so many ways. Help me to see how you are present with me even in hard times. Help me always to look and to ask for your blessings. Amen.

JANUARY 25

•

Joseph's brothers saw that their father loved him more than any of them. So they hated Joseph. They couldn't even speak one kind word to him. Joseph had a dream. When he told it to his brothers, they hated him even more.

Genesis 37:4–5 NIRV

Jacob had twelve sons in all. He treated his son Joseph better than he treated his other sons. He even made Joseph a beautiful coat. This made Joseph's brothers feel angry and jealous.

Joseph had a strange dream. He dreamed that his brothers were bowing down to him, the way slaves used to bow down before their master. He told his brothers about his dream, and they hated him even more. They went on to sell Joseph as a slave and told their father, Jacob, that a wild animal had killed him.

One day the people of Israel would look back on the twelve sons of Jacob as their special ancestors. But first many other things would happen to Joseph and his brothers. For one thing, Joseph's dream about his brothers bowing down to him would come true.

Sometimes Jacob and his children acted very badly. They could be hateful and cruel. But the Bible tells us that, still, God was always present with them. God even used the terrible betrayal of Joseph by his brothers to bring good to many people. You can read about it in Genesis 37–50.

God, thank you for being present with us even when we or other people aren't acting right. Thank you for showing us how you can use bad things that happen to bring about good. Amen.

JANUARY 26

•

God wants everyone to be saved and to know the whole truth, which is, There is only one God, and Christ Jesus is the only one who can bring us to God. Jesus was truly human, and he gave himself to rescue all of us.

1 Timothy 2:4–5 CEV

Sometimes good news is only good news for some people. "Latisha made the team!" "Michael won a prize!" Good news for them means bad news for the people who didn't make the team or didn't win a prize. Have you ever felt left out of good news like that?

God's good news doesn't leave anyone out. It is good news for everyone: young and old, rich and poor, male and female, Asian and Hispanic. God wants everyone to be saved and to know the truth about God's love.

That means Christians should welcome everyone, not just people who look and act like them. Christians should not leave anybody out, because God's good news is for the whole world.

Christ Jesus, thank you for bringing me to God. I rejoice that there is no one left out of God's love. Amen.

JANUARY 27

•

Don't have anything to do with godless stories and silly tales. Instead, train yourself to be godly. Training the body has some value. But being godly has value in every way. It promises help for the life you are now living and the life to come.

1 Timothy 4:7–8 NIRV

Many people admire great athletes. Athletes have trained their bodies so that they are fast, strong, and coordinated. This hard training makes athletes beautiful to watch. Who are some of your favorite athletes?

Training your body is good, even though your body will eventually grow old and die. But training yourself to be godly is even more important:

- Train your ears not to listen to gossip
- Train your mouth not to speak lies
- Train your hands not to hurt others
- Train your heart to love even difficult people

This training will make you a beautiful person, not just now but forever!

Holy God, make me a godly person. Help me to run the race of faith and not get tired. Make me strong so I can love you and serve others. Amen.

JANUARY 28

•

Don't let anyone look down on you because you are young. Set an example for the believers in what you say and in how you live. Also set an example in how you love and in what you believe. Show the believers how to be pure.

1 Timothy 4:12 NIRV

Do you get tired of hearing people say, "You're not old enough"? Eighth-graders say it to fifth-graders. Big brothers say it to little brothers. Parents say it to children. Whom do you say it to?

You may not be old enough to drive a car or vote for president. But in what really counts, you are old enough. You are old enough to believe in God. You are old enough to love others. You are old enough to live a holy life. Don't let anyone look down on you because you are young. Even young people can be grown-ups in the faith!

Everlasting God, all the days of my life are in your hands. Help my life be an example to other people, even to those who are older than I am. Help me learn from others, no matter what age they are. Amen.

JANUARY 29

•

People who want to be rich fall into all sorts of temptations and traps. They are caught by foolish and harmful desires that drag them down and destroy them. The love of money causes all kinds of trouble. Some people want money so much that they have given up their faith and caused themselves a lot of pain.

1 Timothy 6:9–10 CEV

Have you ever noticed that the Bible talks a lot about money? That is because money is very important to people. People use money for food, clothes, medicine, and shelter. Not having enough money leads to suffering. When people are homeless or can't afford to buy food and medicine, they are in serious trouble. God doesn't want anyone to live like that. That is why God wants people who have enough money to share with those who do not.

But some people don't just use money—they fall in love with it. They spend all their time thinking about how to get rich, or how to spend their money. Having lots of money becomes more important to them than anything else. Money becomes their god. When that happens, their whole lives become twisted and broken. They turn their backs on God and hurt other people. Falling in love with money causes pain and trouble. God doesn't want anyone to live like that either.

Generous God, teach me the right attitude to have toward money. Keep me from falling in love with money, and show me how to share what I have with others. Amen.

JANUARY 30

•

I remember your honest and true faith. It was alive first in your grandmother Lois and in your mother Eunice. And I am certain that it is now alive in you also.

2 Timothy 1:5 NIRV

Families tend to pass things down. They pass down names. They may pass down traits like being tall or having curly hair. They often pass down special songs or favorite recipes. If you have an older sister or brother, you probably have hand-me-down clothes.

Timothy's family passed down faith. His grandmother Lois had faith. She passed it down to Timothy's mother, Eunice. And his mother passed it on to him. Who passed down the faith to you? It doesn't have to be someone in your family.

If someone has given you hand-me-down clothes, you know that they are usually not as good as new. They may be worn out or stained or missing a button. Hand-me-down faith is not like that! Faith that is passed down keeps growing and getting stronger. Whom can you pass your faith on to?

God, thank you for the people who passed down faith to me. Show me how to pass down my faith to someone else. Amen.

JANUARY 31

•

God has breathed life into all of Scripture. It is useful for teaching us what is true. It is useful for correcting our mistakes. It is useful for making our lives whole again. It is useful for training us to do what is right. By using Scripture, God's people can be completely prepared to do every good thing.

2 Timothy 3:16–17 NIRV

The Bible was written by many different people a long time ago. God's Spirit helped the writers know the truth about God and about the world. That is why we can trust what Scripture says. The Old Testament was first written in Hebrew, and the New Testament was first written in Greek. But Scripture has been translated into English and hundreds of other languages, so that people all over the world can read it and learn from it.

There are many questions that the Bible does not answer: How big is the planet Jupiter? Will my friend with cancer get better? What is 832 times 27? But Scripture does give us true and useful answers to the biggest questions in life. What is God like? How are human beings supposed to live? Will evil and suffering ever go away? We can trust the answers Scripture does give to keep us on the right path.

God, thank you for breathing life into Scripture. Make Scripture come alive in my life. Amen.

FEBRUARY 1

•

For freedom Christ has set us free. Stand firm, therefore, and do not submit again to a yoke of slavery.

Galatians 5:1 NRSV

Today is Freedom Day! On February 1, 1865, the leaders of the United States passed the thirteenth amendment to the U.S. Constitution. This law freed the slaves and said that all slavery in the United States was ended.

Slaves suffered greatly and were treated as if they were not human. But in a different way slavery was also bad for their masters, because it gave them too much power. Having so much control over the lives of other people led many slavemasters to act very cruelly. Fear and hatred grew.

In his letter to the Christians in Galatia, the apostle Paul also talked about the end of slavery. He wrote, "For freedom Christ has set us free!" Never again should we act as if we are slaves. Paul was talking about obedience not to human masters but to all the rules humans follow when they try to serve God. The rules may be good and may help to keep order. But often we make them into slavemasters, by giving them more power than God wants them to have. And so the rules get in the way of our knowing and sharing God's love. Christ brings us into the freedom of that love!

Christ Jesus, you have set me free! Teach me that you are not a cruel master but a brother who loves me and who will guide me into new life. Show me how to live in the freedom of your love. Amen.

FEBRUARY 2

•

You are all children of God by believing in Christ Jesus. All of you who were baptized into Christ have put on Christ as if he were your clothes. There is no Jew or Greek. There is no slave or free person. There is no male or female. Because you belong to Christ Jesus, you are all one.

Galatians 3:26–28 NIRV

What things make people different from one another? Some people have black or brown skin, and others have white. Some people are rich, and others are poor. Some people live in big cities, and others live in suburbs or towns or another country. Can you think of other differences?

Differences aren't bad, but they hurt people when we tell ourselves that one group is better than another. In the apostle Paul's day, for example, many people believed that free people were better than slaves and that males were better than females. They used their beliefs as excuses to treat men and free people better than women and slaves. But Paul said that when we come to Jesus everything changes. Christ Jesus makes us into one people before God. Christ teaches us new ways to live and work together—ways that treat all people well.

Try to think of ways that you can practice being "one in Christ" with those who are different from you. Ask your mom or dad or minister for their ideas, too!

Loving God, although your children are so different, through Christ you have made us into one family before you. Teach us to look past our differences and find ways to serve you together. Amen.

FEBRUARY 3

•

But the fruit the Holy Spirit produces is love, joy and peace. It is being patient, kind and good. It is being faithful and gentle and having control of oneself. There is no law against things of that kind.

Galatians 5:22–23 NIRV

When someone truly loves you, you want to do good things for her. Perhaps you think of ways to make her work easier, or perhaps you surprise her with a gift of something you made. You don't do these things because you have to earn her love—you know that she loves you already. You do them because you want to express your own love in return.

The Galatians thought that if they followed certain rules they would earn God's love, but Paul told them that they had it wrong. God loves us without our having to do anything at all!

But that doesn't mean our lives will be wild or out of control. Quite the opposite. For now that Christ has come, we have new power for living and for serving God. This "new power" is the power of the Holy Spirit. Whenever the Spirit of Jesus is at work in us, goodness grows. And we find ourselves asking, "God, how can I do more?"

Holy Spirit, work in my life! Bring me love, joy, peace, and patience. Make me kind, generous, faithful, and gentle. Teach me self-control. Show me how to serve you better in all that I do. Amen.

FEBRUARY 4

•

Finally, the king called in Shiphrah and Puah, the two women who helped the Hebrew mothers when they gave birth. He told them, "If a Hebrew woman gives birth to a girl, let the child live. If the baby is a boy, kill him!" But the two women were faithful to God and did not kill the boys, even though the king had told them to.

Exodus 1:15–17 CEV

The king of Egypt was worried that the people of Israel were getting too strong and were having too many babies. So he told two Israelite women, Shiphrah and Puah, to do something terrible. He told them to kill all the Israelite baby boys, instead of helping them to be born safely. It was dangerous to disobey the king, but Shiphrah and Puah knew that the king's command was wrong, and they refused to do it. Instead, they protected the lives of the baby boys. Because of what they did, God blessed them.

If powerful people tell us to do something that we know is wrong, we should ask God to make us brave enough to disobey them. That is what Harriet Tubman did in the United States when she broke the law and helped hundreds of slaves escape from their masters. We show our love for God by doing what we know is right, even if it might get us into trouble.

God, help us to do what is right, even if important people are telling us to do what is wrong. Make us brave and strong like Shiphrah and Puah, and bless us, just as you blessed them. Amen.

FEBRUARY 5

•

The Hebrews kept increasing until finally, the king gave a command to everyone in the nation, "As soon as a Hebrew boy is born, throw him into the Nile River! But you can let the girls live." A man from the Levi tribe married a woman from the same tribe, and she later had a baby boy. He was a beautiful child, and she kept him inside for three months. But when she could no longer keep him hidden, she made a basket out of reeds and covered it with tar. She put him in the basket and placed it in the tall grass along the edge of the Nile River. The baby's older sister stood off at a distance to see what would happen to him.

Exodus 1:21b–2:4 CEV

Moses was born in a very bad time. The Hebrew people were slaves in Egypt. The king had ordered that all the baby boys born to the Hebrews should be killed. But Moses' mother put Moses into the river in a tiny boat made out of a basket. Maybe someone would rescue him! Moses' sister watched to see if her brother would be okay.

Imagine what that must have been like for Moses. Do you think he cried when he was in the basket? He surely couldn't understand what was going on, because he was only three months old. He didn't know that God had plans for him.

Perhaps you are a little bit like baby Moses. Things may happen around you that you don't understand. Sometimes you may even be in danger. But unlike Moses, you can look around and see the people who keep an eye on you and help you, the way Moses' sister helped him. And unlike Moses, you are old enough to trust that God has great plans for your life!

God, help me to trust that my life is in your hands. Thank you for the people who watch out for me and help me. Amen.

FEBRUARY 6

•

About that time one of the king's daughters came down to take a bath in the river, while her servant women walked along the river bank. She saw the basket in the tall grass and sent one of the young women to pull it out of the water. When the king's daughter opened the basket, she saw the baby and felt sorry for him because he was crying. She said, "This must be one of the Hebrew babies." At once the baby's older sister came up and asked, "Do you want me to get a Hebrew woman to take care of the baby for you?" "Yes," the king's daughter answered. So the girl brought the baby's mother, and the king's daughter told her, "Take care of this child, and I will pay you." The baby's mother carried him home and took care of him.

Exodus 2:5–9 CEV

Where does courage come from? Are some people born with it?

Moses' sister, Miriam, saw the king's daughter pull her baby brother out of the water. Even though Miriam was just a slave girl and the king's daughter was a very important person, Miriam went right up to the daughter to talk to her. Miriam could have gotten in trouble. But she saw a chance to help her brother.

Because of Miriam's quick thinking and her bravery, Moses' own mother got to keep on taking care of him for a while. Miriam's bravery came from *love*. Because she loved her baby brother, she wanted to help him—even if she had to put herself in danger.

Most people aren't born with courage. But love can make anyone very brave. Love for one's family or one's nation can do that. And love for God can give great courage to people—even shy people. Because, when a person loves God, pleasing God by doing right becomes the most important thing.

God, fill me with love for other people and give me courage to help them when they need it. Fill me also with love for you and with the desire to please you. Amen.

FEBRUARY 7

•

The LORD said: "I have seen how my people are suffering as slaves in Egypt, and I have heard them beg for my help because of the way they are being mistreated. I feel sorry for them, and I have come down to rescue them from the Egyptians. . . . Now go to the king! I am sending you to lead my people out of his country." But Moses said, "Who am I to go to the king and lead your people out of Egypt?" God replied, "I will be with you. And you will know that I am the one who sent you, when you worship me on this mountain after you have led my people out of Egypt." . . . Moses replied, "I have never been a good speaker. I wasn't one before you spoke to me, and I'm not one now. I am slow at speaking, and I can never think of what to say."

Exodus 3:7–8a, 10–12; 4:10 CEV

When was the last time you thought of an excuse to get out of doing something? When it was time to set the table? When it was time to mow the lawn? When it was time to practice the piano?

God had an important job for Moses to do. Moses would lead the Hebrew people out of slavery! Moses didn't want the job, so he thought up one excuse after another. But for every excuse Moses gave, God promised help to solve that problem. Finally Moses ran out of excuses.

God has important things for us to do too—things like loving people who are different from us and being patient, kind, and giving. Even when our conscience is telling us the right thing to do, it is easy to think up excuses. But God has an answer for every excuse we can invent and will help us to do right.

God, thank you for having such high expectations for me. Forgive me for the times when I think of reasons not to do what you want me to do. Help me want to do what is right! Amen.

FEBRUARY 8

•

Moses and Aaron went to the king of Egypt and told him, "The LORD God says, 'Let my people go into the desert, so they can honor me with a celebration there.'" . . . That same day the king gave orders to his slave bosses and to the men directly in charge of the Israelite slaves. He told them: "Don't give the slaves any more straw to put in their bricks. Force them to find their own straw wherever they can, but they must make the same number of bricks as before."

Exodus 5:1, 6–8a CEV

Moses knew that God wanted him to lead the Hebrews out of Egypt. God had even given Moses special powers and a helper, Aaron. But when Moses went to the king of Egypt, the king (Pharaoh) said, "No way!" and he made the Hebrews' job even harder.

Today too, people may not like it when we try to make changes in the way things are done. They may even try to stop us. Why would people do that? Sometimes because they believe the changes we want would be wrong. Sometimes because they don't understand the changes. Sometimes because they (like Pharaoh) would lose money or power if the changes were made.

Moses and Aaron did not give up, because they were sure of what God wanted them to do. They would keep working to reach their goal. If you believe in your heart that God wants to bring about a change in your world, then be prepared to work for it! No one said it would be easy.

God of justice, there are so many things in the world that are unfair. Give me eyes to see how I can work for a better world and determination to keep on working. Amen.

FEBRUARY 9

•

Here is my message for Israel: "I am the LORD! And with my mighty power I will punish the Egyptians and free you from slavery. I will accept you as my people, and I will be your God. Then you will know that I was the one who rescued you from the Egyptians. I will bring you into the land that I solemnly promised Abraham, Isaac, and Jacob, and it will be yours. I am the LORD!" When Moses told this to the Israelites, they were too discouraged and mistreated to believe him.

Exodus 6:6–9 CEV

Can you imagine news that is too good to be true? But what if it really *is* true? Many bad things had happened to the Israelites. The people had been slaves for many years. Lately Pharaoh had made them work even harder than before. They didn't believe Moses when he told them how God planned to set them free. But God really would set them free!

Today too, people who have suffered a great deal may have trouble believing promises of good things to come. Their hearts have become too heavy. They see no reason to hope for the future.

We don't know why there is so much suffering in our world. But we know that God sees the suffering, and that it is not the way God wants it to be. God's promise is that one day all people will be truly free—free from pain and free from slavery of every kind. The news may seem too good to be true. But true it is!

Lord, you see the suffering of your people in the world. Give us courage to trust your promise that one day all people will be truly free. Teach us how to comfort and help those who suffer. Amen.

FEBRUARY 10

•

The LORD said to Moses: "The Egyptian king stubbornly refuses to change his mind and let the people go. . . . Tell him, 'The LORD God of the Hebrews sent me to order you to release his people, so they can worship him in the desert. But until now, you have paid no attention. The LORD is going to do something to show you that he really is the LORD. I will strike the Nile with this stick, and the water will turn into blood.'" . . . Moses and Aaron obeyed the LORD. Aaron held out his stick, then struck the Nile, as the king and his officials watched. The river turned into blood, the fish died, and the water smelled so bad that none of the Egyptians could drink it. . . . The king did just as the LORD had said—he stubbornly refused to listen. Then he went back to his palace and never gave it a second thought.

Exodus 7:14, 16–17, 20–21a, 22b–23 CEV

To change the king's mind, God had planned for some terrible things called plagues to happen in Egypt. After ten plagues, Pharaoh would finally realize that he should let the people of Israel go free. In the first plague, the Nile River turned into blood. People couldn't drink water from it anymore. But Pharaoh was still too stubborn to let the people go!

Why didn't God change the king's heart? Why does God let people go on doing bad things to others? This is a mystery—a puzzle that we will never completely figure out. But when we see cruelty in our world we can do several things. We can try to find ways to convince people to stop being so mean toward others. We can pray for God to change people's hearts. And we can trust that God feels great love for those who suffer, and works to set them free.

God, we don't understand why people sometimes treat others so badly. Help us trust that you are working to end cruelty and injustice, and show us how we can help. Amen.

FEBRUARY 11

•

The LORD had spoken to Moses. He had said, "Pharaoh will refuse to listen to you. So I will multiply my miracles in Egypt." Moses and Aaron did all of those miracles in the sight of Pharaoh. But the LORD made Pharaoh's heart stubborn. He wouldn't let the people of Israel go out of his country.

Exodus 11:9–10 NIRV

Have you ever ridden your bike down a dead-end street? You had a choice about whether to turn onto that street in the first place. But once you did, you didn't have any choice about which way to go. The street goes only one way and then it ends!

Pharaoh got himself into a dead-end situation. God had sent many plagues on Egypt to try to get Pharaoh to change his mind and let the people of Israel go. Each time, Pharaoh could have turned around and listened to God. But he refused, and his heart became more stubborn and harder to change. Finally his heart reached a dead end. It had nowhere to turn, no possibility of changing. When the Bible says that God made Pharaoh's heart stubborn, it means that God stopped trying to change Pharaoh's heart. Pharaoh's heart was so hard that he could not hear or know God anymore. God finally let Pharaoh be the way he wanted to be.

Our actions and attitudes form patterns. At first they may be easy to change. But the longer we keep acting or thinking in a certain way, the harder it is to change. Like Pharaoh, we can get stuck going down a dead-end street. But if we want to turn around, God will help us.

God, do not let my heart become hard. Make me realize when I have made a wrong turn and help me find my way back to you. Amen.

FEBRUARY 12

•

During the night the king sent for Moses and Aaron and told them, "Get your people out of my country and leave us alone! Go and worship the LORD, as you have asked. Take your sheep, goats, and cattle, and get out. But ask your God to be kind to me."

Exodus 12:31–32 CEV

Do you ever celebrate an "Opposite Day" at your school? On this silly kind of day, some kids may wear their clothes inside out, while others walk backward down the hallway. Maybe one of the kids gets to pretend to be the teacher, or maybe the principal comes and sits at a student's desk for a while.

The king of Egypt had an "opposite" kind of day, but it wasn't silliness. Pharaoh thought the people of Israel would always have to obey him—not the other way around. But in the last plague, all the firstborn sons of the Egyptians (even Pharaoh's own son) died. Then Pharaoh realized that he was not really the boss. The God of the Israelites was! So Pharaoh asked Israel to have God bless the Egyptians.

God often surprises us by showing that the mighty aren't as mighty as we suppose and the weak aren't so weak after all. Even those who seem weak may have great power to bring goodness into others' lives. Think of how babies do this! Or think of a loved one who is quite ill. Her illness may bring family and friends together as they love and help her and one another.

Lord of the mighty and the weak, help me not to be afraid of those who seem to be so powerful. And help me to see how even the weak can bring blessings. Amen.

FEBRUARY 13

•

All that night the LORD pushed the sea back with a strong east wind. He turned the sea into dry land. The waters were parted. The people of Israel went through the sea on dry ground. There was a wall of water on their right side and on their left. The Egyptians chased them. All of Pharaoh's horses and chariots and horsemen followed them into the sea. . . . The Egyptians said, "Let's get away from the Israelites! The LORD is fighting for Israel against Egypt." Then the LORD spoke to Moses. He said, "Reach your hand out over the sea. The waters will flow back over the Egyptians and their chariots and horsemen."

Exodus 14:21b–23, 25b–26 NIRV

Finally Pharaoh permitted the Israelites to leave Egypt. But after they left, he changed his mind one more time. He sent his army after the Israelites to bring them back. Imagine how frightened the Israelites must have been! How could they possibly get across the Red Sea? They knew that the soldiers were close behind. All hope was lost. But the Bible says that at the very last moment God took action to save them by sending a wind so strong that the water blew aside. The Israelites walked through the sea on dry ground. When the Egyptian soldiers came after them, God let the water rush back in to cover the soldiers, and they all drowned.

This story of the crossing of the Red Sea shows us that if people trust in God even when the situation looks hopeless, astonishing things may happen. God hears the voices of those who suffer and works to deliver them. Even when we cannot do anything else, we can pray for deliverance.

God, I praise you, for you bring good out of suffering and evil. You bring mighty rulers down and raise up the weak to new power. Rescue those who suffer. Amen.

FEBRUARY 14

•

We don't need to write to you about love among believers. God himself has taught you to love each other. In fact, you do love all the brothers and sisters all around Macedonia. But we are asking you to love each other more and more.

1 Thessalonians 4:9–10 NIRV

Did you give someone a valentine today? February 14 is a great day to think about the people we love and the people who love us! It also happens to be a great day to think about God, who loves us completely and helps us to love others more.

The people in the Thessalonian church had been having a hard time. Some people in their city were trying to make them stop meeting with one another. It would have been easy for the members of that small church to give up their struggle to stay together. They could have gone back to living as they had before they ever heard about Jesus. But they didn't give up. In fact, Paul wrote, their love for one another was so strong that other churches for miles around looked to them as an example to follow. They loved one another so much that it must have been God, and not a human being, who taught them to do so! "You're doing great!" Paul told them. "Now, keep on loving—more and more and more!"

God, your love is too wide and too deep for us ever to understand! Teach us to love each other the way you love us. Make us an example for other people to follow. Amen.

FEBRUARY 15

•

When Jesus saw the crowds, he went up the mountain; and after he sat down, his disciples came to him. Then he began to speak, and taught them, saying: "Blessed are the poor in spirit, for theirs is the kingdom of heaven."

Matthew 5:1–3 NRSV

Jesus was a teacher. But he didn't teach language arts, math, or science. He taught his disciples how to serve God joyfully. The words "Blessed are . . ." begin one of the most famous passages in the Bible. This passage is called the Sermon on the Mount because Jesus is said to have spoken it to his disciples while they were sitting with him on the mountain.

When Jesus said "Blessed are the poor in spirit," he meant that God cares in a special way for those whose spirits are beaten down by cruel people or by hard times. He meant that God feels great kindness toward those who have missed out on the good things in life. He meant that God showers love upon those who are very sad. "These are the ones who have the kingdom of heaven," Jesus said.

In our world, we often admire people who are famous, people who have a lot of money, and people who are beautiful and talented. But Jesus reminds us that God sees the world in a different way. God loves all people but gives a special place to the poor in spirit.

God of the poor in spirit, thank you for caring for those who need you so much. Give me eyes to see the world the way you see it. Give me hands and feet to help those who are sad, or lonely, or hungry. Amen.

FEBRUARY 16

•

"Blessed are those who are hungry and thirsty for what is right. They will be filled."

Matthew 5:6 NIRV

When you are really hungry or thirsty, all you can think about is food or drink. Your imagination "cooks up" your favorite food. You see yourself slurping down your favorite icy drink. But you don't stop there. Instead, you do whatever you can to make your wishes come true!

Jesus wants us to be "hungry" and "thirsty" for what is right. He wants us to spend our time imagining what it would be like if our home, our neighborhood, and our world were places where everyone were treated fairly. He wants us to do whatever we can to make our wishes for a better world come true.

In Birmingham, Alabama, a man named Fred Shuttlesworth was "hungry" and "thirsty." In the 1950s and 1960s, Mr. Shuttlesworth saw that African-American people in his city did not have nice schools, did not get fair treatment from police, and had to ride at the back of the bus. Seeing these things made him "hungry" for fair laws and "thirsty" for equal treatment of African-American people. And so he and many other people worked very, very hard to bring changes. Fred Shuttlesworth was often treated badly. But he wouldn't stop until changes came!

God, you have a better world in mind for us. Help me to be hungry and thirsty for that new world. Give me courage to help make those wishes come true! Amen.

FEBRUARY 17

•

"God blesses those people who make peace. They will be called his children!"

Matthew 5:9 CEV

The world is full of people and nations who are fighting with each other. You don't have to look very hard to see that this is so. The TV news people tell of it. The newspapers tell of it. Maybe you yourself have seen people fighting—using words or even weapons to try to hurt each other.

God wants us to be at peace with one another. Jesus said God blesses people who make peace. He didn't mean that we have to go around breaking up fights or even that we must keep others from getting into fights in the first place. We can be "peacemakers" in other ways. For example, we can keep cool and calm when someone doesn't treat us quite right. And we can search for ways to show patience, kindness, and loving care toward our family members, our friends and neighbors, and people in our school. The problem of fighting in our world is so big that these might seem like tiny steps to take. But they are big enough for God to notice and big enough to make a difference!

God, teach me to be a peacemaker! Help me to be patient and calm if others are rude or unkind. Help me to treat *all* your children with love and respect. Amen.

FEBRUARY 18

•

"God blesses those people who are treated badly for doing right. They belong to the kingdom of heaven."

Matthew 5:10 CEV

What are the rewards you get for doing the right thing? If you are kind to your brothers or sisters, they will probably be kind to you in return, and your mom or dad may give you praise. If you help someone who needs it, you may receive a word or a note of thanks.

But sometimes there is no obvious reward for doing what is right. Jesus said that you may even suffer for walking in God's way. For example, many people suffered during the Civil Rights movement in the United States, in the 1950s and 1960s. African-American people and white people too were working to change unfair rules and unfair ways of treating African Americans. One way they tried to bring change was by practicing "civil disobedience." That means that they refused to obey the unfair laws. When they did so they were sometimes beaten or sent to jail. Some children took part in the civil disobedience too.

When Jesus taught his disciples about the kingdom of heaven, he was speaking of a time and a place where all the rules are fair and where there is peace. Whenever you do what is right, you are helping to make earth a little more like heaven. And whether people reward you or punish you, God will bless you.

God of earth and heaven, make my spirit strong so that I can do what is right, even if people treat me badly for doing so. Help me to make my world more like heaven. Amen.

FEBRUARY 19

•

"You are the light of the world. A city on a hill can't be hidden. Also, people do not light a lamp and put it under a bowl. Instead, they put it on its stand. Then it gives light to everyone in the house. In the same way, let your light shine in front of others. Then they will see the good things you do. And they will praise your Father who is in heaven."

Matthew 5:14–16 NIRV

Can you remember a night, maybe during a thunderstorm, when the electricity went off in your home and you had to use flashlights? Perhaps a member of your family lit a candle. Having one or two lights at hand becomes very important when the whole apartment or house is pitch dark. Without those lights you might stub your toe or bump into the edge of a door!

Jesus said to his followers, "You are the light of the world. Let your light shine in front of others." He meant that when you serve God by doing good things for other people, the light of God shines through you. You become like a candle that is casting its glow of light into the darkened house. Your light helps other people to get along better. And they will praise God for working through you in such marvelous ways.

Father in heaven, make your light shine through me in all that I say and do. Help other people to see the light and to know that it comes from you. Amen.

FEBRUARY 20

•

"Do not think I have come to get rid of what is written in the Law or in the Prophets. I have not come to do that. Instead, I have come to give full meaning to what is written. What I'm about to tell you is true. Heaven and earth will disappear before the smallest letter disappears from the Law. Not even the smallest stroke of a pen will disappear from the Law until everything is completed."

Matthew 5:17–18 NIRV

Jesus' teachings started a new way of understanding and worshipping God. Today we call that new way Christianity and the people who follow it Christians. But Jesus himself was a member of another faith; he was a Jew.

The Jewish people believed (and still believe today) that God has given rules for how people ought to live. These rules are called the Law, and they are found in the Hebrew Scriptures, or Old Testament. Christians still follow parts of the Jewish Law as a guide to doing what is right and fair to others. Other parts of the Jewish law they do not follow, because they have a different understanding of how people should worship and serve God. But we should remember what Jesus taught: None of God's Law will change or disappear. Today we can honor the Jews for continuing to uphold the Law, even if we ourselves follow a different way.

God, we thank you that you have always shown such care for your people, teaching us how to worship you and how to live right. Help us to walk in your way and to respect all others who do so. Amen.

FEBRUARY 21

•

"You have heard that it was said, 'Love your neighbor. Hate your enemy. But here is what I tell you. Love your enemies. Pray for those who hurt you. Then you will be children of your Father who is in heaven. He causes his sun to shine on evil people and good people. He sends rain on those who do right and those who don't. . . . So be perfect, just as your Father in heaven is perfect."

Matthew 5:43–45, 48 NIRV

"No one is perfect." Maybe you've heard people say that before. And yet, Jesus told his followers to "be perfect," just like God in heaven. God gives sunlight and rain—the means of life—even to those who do wrong. God loves everyone, even those who are different from us, or who hurt us. God's love is too great for us to understand. But it is one of the things that makes God perfect.

You might think it seems just too hard to *love* your enemies. But you could *pray* for them, couldn't you? That is what Ruby Bridges did. Ruby was the first African-American child to go to an elementary school in New Orleans, Louisiana, where only white children had gone before. Many white grown-ups did not want her to go there. They stood outside and shouted angry words at her when she walked into the school each morning. But instead of shouting back, Ruby prayed for those people.

We can pray for those who are mean to us, and we can also pray for ourselves. We can ask God to make the love in our hearts to grow. Then we too can love one another with "perfect" love.

God, your love is so amazing! All people are your children, and you love each one. Let me feel your perfect love, and teach me to love others as you do. Amen.

FEBRUARY 22

•

"When you give to the needy, don't let your left hand know what your right hand is doing. Then your giving will be done secretly. Your Father will reward you. He sees what you do secretly."

Matthew 6:3–4 NIRV

We feel good when other people praise us for things we do. When your mother, your father, your teacher, or a friend says, "You did a nice job!" or "Excellent work!", don't you feel great? When people praise us, we want to try even harder!

Jesus taught that God sees everything we do—even the things that no one else sees. And God praises us when we do right! Jesus said we should always let God be the one who watches our good deeds. If we want to help people who need it, we shouldn't make a big show of it. Instead we should help people quietly or even in secret. By doing good deeds in secret, we give honor to God instead of trying to bring attention and praise to ourselves. And that pleases God very much!

God, you see everything I do. Please make me kind and generous toward people who need my help. Let me do good deeds quietly, as a way of bringing honor to you. Amen.

FEBRUARY 23

•

I think about the heavens.
I think about what your fingers have created.
I think about the moon and stars that you have set in place.
What is a human being that you think about him?
What is a son of man that you take care of him?
You made him a little lower than the heavenly beings.
You placed on him a crown of glory and honor.
You made human beings the rulers over all that your hands have created.
You put everything under their control.

Psalm 8:3–6 NIRV

Have you ever looked at a sky filled with stars or an ocean that stretches farther than you can see and felt very small? The stars and the ocean are so much bigger and older than you are! They were there millions of years before you were born, and they will be there long after you die. Maybe you wonder if your little life matters very much.

This psalm assures us that even though we are small, and even though we will die someday, God loves us and has given us very important work to do. God shows us the beautiful creation, full of birds and fish and other animals, and tells us to love and care for it. God values us enough to give us a big responsibility. We must be pretty important after all!

Maker of all things, thank you for creating me and caring for me. Thank you for trusting me enough to give me important work to do. Help me to take care of your beautiful world. Amen.

FEBRUARY 24

•

Lord, how long must I wait? Will you forget me forever?
How long will you turn your face away from me?
How long must I struggle with my thoughts?
How long must my heart be sad day after day?
How long will my enemies keep winning the battle over me?
Lord my God, look at me and answer me.

Psalm 13:1–3a NIrV

Have you ever been really sick and had to wait to get better? Have you ever been scared or hurt and had to wait for someone to comfort you? Have you ever been in danger and had to wait for someone to rescue you? In those situations, it is very hard to wait, isn't it?

The writer of this psalm was finding it hard to wait too. "How long, God?" he asked. He needed help desperately, and he wanted God to hurry up and help him right away. But he had to keep waiting.

Sometimes we pray to God for healing or peace or happiness, and God keeps us waiting. We want those things desperately, and we can't understand why God isn't answering us. "How long, God?" we ask. It is hard to wait. But if we trust that God loves us, we can find the strength to wait until God answers our prayers.

How long, God? Hear my prayers for help, and give me the strength to trust in you while I wait. Amen.

FEBRUARY 25

•

The Lord is my shepherd, I shall not want.
He makes me lie down in green pastures;
he leads me beside still waters;
he restores my soul.
He leads me in right paths for his name's sake.
Even though I walk through the darkest valley,
I fear no evil;
for you are with me;
your rod and your staff—
They comfort me.
You prepare a table before me in the presence of my enemies;
you anoint my head with oil;
My cup overflows.
Surely goodness and mercy shall follow me
all the days of my life,
and I shall dwell in the house of the Lord
my whole life long.

Psalm 23:1–6 NRSV

Psalm 23 is one of the best known and most loved psalms in the Bible. Can you see why? It is a very comforting psalm, because it assures us of God's loving care all through our life.

The psalm compares God to a shepherd who cares for his sheep. Sheep need someone to take good care of them, because they are easily confused. They tend to get lost. They are not very good at finding enough food to eat or protecting themselves from danger.

We are like sheep. We get lost and confused. We are often hungry, or hurt, or in danger. How comforting to know that God is our good shepherd!

Lord, you are my shepherd. Because you are with me, I do not have to be afraid. I am sure that your goodness and mercy will follow me all the days of my life. Amen.

FEBRUARY 26

•

Have mercy on me, O God,
according to your steadfast love;
according to your abundant mercy
blot out my transgressions.
Wash me thoroughly from my iniquity,
and cleanse me from my sin.
For I know my transgressions,
and my sin is ever before me.
Against you, you alone, have I sinned,
and done what is evil in your sight. . . .
Create in me a clean heart, O God,
and put a new and right spirit within me.
Do not cast me away from your presence,
and do not take your holy spirit from me.

Psalm 51:1–4a, 10–11 NRSV

Throughout life, we often have to say, "I'm sorry." We all do things that are wrong, things that hurt other people. But admitting that we're wrong is not always easy. It is much easier to pretend that we didn't do anything wrong or that our sins don't really matter.

But our sins do matter. They matter to the people we hurt, and they matter to God. The writer of this psalm is doing something very hard. He is admitting to God that he did something wrong. He is telling God how sorry he is. And he is asking God to give him a clean heart, so that he can become a person who does what is right.

If you are having a hard time telling someone you're sorry, try telling God first. Knowing that God loves you and forgives you may make it easier to say you're sorry to someone else.

God of grace, I'm sorry for all the wrong things I have done and for the ways I have hurt other people. Forgive me, and give me the strength to tell others that I'm sorry. Amen.

FEBRUARY 27

•

You are the King and the Lord. You have always been my hope.
I have trusted in you ever since I was young.
From the time I was born I have depended on you.
You brought me out of my mother's body.
I will praise you forever. . . .
My mouth is filled with praise for you.
All day long I will talk about your glory.
Don't push me away when I'm old.
Don't desert me when my strength is gone.

Psalm 71:5–6, 8–9 NIRV

You used to depend on others in many ways, but now you can do more and more things by yourself. When you were a baby, you needed someone to carry you. Now you can walk around by yourself. When you were a young child, you needed someone to read to you. Now you can read many things by yourself.

As you grow up, you will be able to do even more things by yourself, and others will depend on you more and more. But even as an adult you will never stop depending on other people for many things! When you are old, you may need help again with things you used to be able to do by yourself, like walking and reading. God wants us to depend on each other.

No matter how old we get, we will never stop depending on God! We depend on God for every breath we take. We live our whole life in God's presence, from the day we were born to the day we die. It is good to know that God will always be there for us.

Lord, you are my hope. Thank you that I can depend on you every day of my life. Amen.

FEBRUARY 28

•

"The Spirit of the LORD has filled me with power. He helps me do what is fair. He makes me brave. Now I'm prepared to tell Jacob's people what they've done wrong. I'm ready to tell Israel they've sinned."

Micah 3:8 NIRV

Standing up for what is right is hard, especially when it involves telling people they have done wrong. More than 2,500 years ago in Israel, God's Spirit filled the prophet Micah with power so that he would be brave enough to do that.

More than one hundred years ago in the United States, Frederick Douglass knew that slavery was wrong. Douglass was born a slave in Maryland. But he escaped slavery and spent his life helping other slaves escape to freedom. God's Spirit filled him with power and made him brave enough to tell white people in America and England that owning slaves was against God's will.

The good news is that God's Spirit is still filling people with power, so that they will have the courage to tell the truth in difficult situations.

Spirit of God, thank you for filling people from all different times and places with your power. Fill me, so that I will brave enough to stand up for what is right. Amen.

FEBRUARY 29

•

So teach us to count our days that we may gain a wise heart.

Psalm 90:12 NRSV

Today is Leap Day! Once every four years, we add a day to the month of February, so that it has twenty-nine days instead of twenty-eight. If you were born on February 29, you would have a birthday only once every four years. That means that you would miss out on a lot of birthday parties and presents unless you chose another "regular" day to mark the passing of the years.

Time rushes by, no matter when your birthday happens to be. Compared to the age of the world, our lives on earth are very short. The psalmist writes, "The days of our life are seventy years, or perhaps eighty, if we are strong" (Psalm 90:10a NRSV). For each of us our days at some point "run out," and then our life is over.

In saying that we should "count our days," the psalmist means that we should remember that the time God gives to us is very, very precious. We should not waste it but use it well. When we value each day and treat it as a gift from God, our hearts become wise.

Lord, you have always been God, even before you formed the mountains or created the world. All time is in your hands. Teach us to count our days and make us wise. Amen.

MARCH 1

•

Esther's words were reported to Mordecai. Then he sent back an answer. He said, "You live in the king's palace. But don't think that just because you are there you will be the only Jew who will escape. . . . Who knows? It's possible that you became queen for a time just like this." Then Esther sent a reply to Mordecai. She said, "Go. Gather together all of the Jews who are in Susa. And fast for my benefit. . . . Then I'll go to the king. I'll do it even though it's against the law. And if I have to die, I'll die."

Esther 4:12–16 NIRV

Queen Esther was a very brave person. A wicked person named Haman was planning to kill all the Jews in her country. Esther decided that to save her people she would risk going to the king and telling him about Haman's plan. This was a very dangerous thing to do, because the law said that anyone who went to the king without his invitation could be put to death.

One of the reasons Esther was brave enough to do this was because she had other people encouraging her. Her cousin Mordecai helped her see that being queen gave her special responsibility. The other Jews in her country came together to fast and pray for her.

The king listened to Esther and did not let Haman carry out his wicked plan. Because of her courage, the lives of the Jews were saved! But she would not have risked her own life without the help and encouragement of others.

God, I know that by myself I am often weak and afraid. When I need to be brave, send people to help and encourage me, so I can do what needs to be done. Amen.

MARCH 2

•

The days the Jews were celebrating were called Purim. Purim comes from the word pur. Pur means "lot." Now the Jews celebrate those two days every year. They do it because of everything that was written in Mordecai's letter. They also do it because of what they had seen and what had happened to them. So they established it as a regular practice. They decided they would always observe those two days of the year. . . . They and their children after them and everyone who joined them would always observe those days.

Esther 9:26–27 NIRV

The wicked Haman made a plan to kill all the Jews. But brave Queen Esther found out about it and, with the help of her cousin Mordecai, she saved the Jews. Every year, on the holiday called Purim, Jewish people remember this story and celebrate how the Jews were saved. Often they tell the story by putting on a play with Queen Esther, Haman, and Mordecai in it. Christians often do the same thing at Christmas, when they tell the story of Jesus' birth by having people play the parts of Mary, Joseph, and the shepherds.

We keep telling these stories, because we never want to forget the good things God has done. But these stories aren't just about people who lived long ago and what God did for them. These stories also tell us who we are and what God is doing in the world today.

God, never let me forget all that you have done for your people. Make me eager to set aside special days to celebrate your love and faithfulness. Amen.

MARCH 3

•

There in the desert they started complaining to Moses and Aaron, "We wish the LORD had killed us in Egypt. When we lived there, we could at least sit down and eat all the bread and meat we wanted. But you have brought us out here into this desert, where we are going to starve." . . . Moses and Aaron told the people, "This evening you will know that the LORD was the one who rescued you from Egypt. And in the morning you will see his glorious power, because he has heard your complaints against him. Why should you grumble to us? Who are we?"

Exodus 16:2–3, 6–7 CEV

Did you ever wish for more freedom or responsibility—and then wish you hadn't? Maybe you wished that your parents would let you stay home by yourself, and then you discovered that it was scary to be alone. Maybe you wished for the lead in a school play and then found out that you had stage fright.

The Israelites had wished for freedom. But when they got to the desert, they realized that freedom wasn't as easy as they had imagined. In Egypt at least they had food to eat! So they complained. Moses and Aaron told them that God would give them the food they needed. But they also told them that their complaints were really complaints against God. The people had not remembered that it was God who set them free! And yet, even when the Israelites complained, God was generous to them. God sent special kinds of food to keep them alive during their travel to the Promised Land.

God, sometimes when I get frightened I forget all the ways you have taken care of me in the past. Please help me to remember. Forgive me and teach me to trust you more. Amen.

MARCH 4

•

When the dew was gone, thin flakes appeared on the desert floor. They looked like frost on the ground. . . . Moses said to them, "It's the bread the LORD has given you to eat. Here is what the LORD has commanded. He has said, 'Each one of you should gather as much as you need. Take two quarts for each person who lives in your tent.'" . . . Then Moses said to them, "Don't keep any of it until morning." Some of them didn't pay any attention to Moses. They kept part of it until morning. But it was full of maggots and began to stink. . . . Each morning all of them gathered as much as they needed.

Exodus 16:14–16, 19–21a NIRV

If we save money, we will have it when we need it tomorrow, the next day, or years from now. But there are some things that we cannot store up. For example, our bodies cannot store up air for the future. Moment by moment we must breathe in the air that we need.

When the people of Israel complained that they were hungry, the Lord heard them and sent them food. Each morning when the people awoke, there was white, flaky stuff on the ground. It was a special kind of bread called manna—bread from heaven! But the Israelites couldn't store up manna for the future, because the leftovers would spoil. They had to trust the Lord to send manna each morning.

Like the Israelites, we depend on God for our life. We can't store up the life or the love that God gives us. We receive these gifts every day, moment by moment and breath by breath. That means we can never stop trusting in our generous God.

Giver of life and Giver of love, I praise you for your constant care! Help me to trust that there will always be enough life to enjoy and enough love to share. Amen.

MARCH 5

•

Once they camped at Rephidim, but there was no water for them to drink. The people started complaining to Moses, "Give us some water!" Moses replied, "Why are you complaining to me and trying to put the LORD to the test?" . . . Then Moses prayed to the LORD, "What am I going to do with these people? They are about to stone me to death!" The LORD answered, "Take . . . along the walking stick you used to strike the Nile River, and when you get to the rock at Mount Sinai, I will be there with you. Strike the rock with the stick, and water will pour out for the people to drink." Moses did this while the leaders watched. The people had complained and tested the LORD by asking, "Is the LORD really with us?" So Moses named that place Massah, which means "testing" and Meribah, which means "complaining."

Exodus 17:1b–2, 4–7 CEV

It is easy to love God when everything is going right for you. But what about when things are going terribly wrong? How do you act then? You may feel angry with God. You may even feel like giving God a test: "God, if you let my parents get divorced, I'll never trust you again."

The Israelites were dying of thirst. They were so angry that they forgot about all the ways God had blessed them and saved them before. They were so angry that they put God to the test. They wanted to see if God cared about them. Just like so many times before, God gave the people what they needed. But Moses named that place with Hebrew words meaning "testing" and "complaining." The names remind us of how the people failed to trust God.

God, help me to know that you are always with me and that you love me. Help me to trust in your care for me, even when things don't turn out just as I would like. Amen.

MARCH 6

•

After they started out from Rephidim, they entered the Desert of Sinai. They camped there in the desert in front of the mountain. Then Moses went up to God. The LORD called out to him from the mountain. He said, "Here is what I want you to say to my people, who came from Jacob's family. Tell the Israelites, 'You have seen for yourselves what I did to Egypt. You saw how I carried you on the wings of eagles and brought you to myself. Now obey me completely. Keep my covenant. If you do, then, out of all of the nations you will be my special treasure. The whole earth is mine. But you will be a kingdom of priests to serve me. You will be my holy nation.' That is what you must tell the Israelites."

Exodus 19:2–6 NIRV

What does it mean to be free? Some people think it means being free to run around all day and do whatever you want or go anywhere you please.

God set the Israelites free from slavery. But look at what God said next. Not, "Okay, now you can go and do whatever you want to do," but *"I brought you to myself."* After setting the Israelites free, God wanted to be in a covenant relationship with them. A covenant is when we make promises to one another. God promised to be present with the people and to treasure them. But the people in turn had to promise to obey all God's commands. If they did, they would be a people set apart, who would show and tell the whole world the news of God's good work and God's presence. Being "free" means being free to serve God!

God, thank you for freeing the people of Israel and bringing them to yourself, to be in a covenant relationship with you. Thank you for loving me also. Set me free to serve you! Amen.

MARCH 7

•

Don't let anyone tell you what you must eat or drink. Don't let them say that you must celebrate the New Moon festival, the Sabbath, or any other festival. These things are only a shadow of what was to come. But Christ is real! Don't be cheated by people who make a show of acting humble and who worship angels. They brag about seeing visions. But it is all nonsense, because their minds are filled with selfish desires.

Colossians 2:16–18 CEV

When you watch a movie with special effects, how do you know what is fake and what is real? Sometimes it is easy to tell. No matter how lifelike those dinosaurs look, you know that they are just a picture drawn by a computer! But at other times it may be hard to tell the difference between what is true and what is "just pretend."

The author of Colossians warned his readers about people who would try to trick them. Such tricksters might say that God loved the people only when they respected certain holy days, ate certain foods, or obeyed certain rules. Or they might claim that they had private visions of angels, or secret messages from God. "Be careful!" the author wrote. "What such people tell you could be fake. But Christ is real!"

Today too lots of people say that they have special knowledge about how God wants us to live. Some say that they are able to speak privately with angels or other spirits. It can be hard to know if what they say is true! But we can always trust Jesus Christ. We can always be sure that he is real.

Jesus, make me wise! When people try to tell me what I should believe and what I should do, help me to know the truth. Teach me always to follow you. Amen.

MARCH 8

•

You have been raised up with Christ. So think about things that are in heaven. That is where Christ is. He is sitting at God's right hand. Think about things that are in heaven. Don't think about things that are on earth.

Colossians 3:1–2 NIRV

As Christians we believe that after Jesus Christ was raised up from the dead on the first Easter Sunday he returned to heaven. But where is heaven? We know it isn't really in the sky, the way cartoon artists show it. Scientists have studied outer space, and heaven isn't out there. It's not a place you can get to in a spaceship.

When we speak of Jesus returning to heaven, it is a way of saying that the things that hurt or controlled him when he lived on earth do not do so any longer. When Jesus lived as a human on earth, he had a body that could be hurt and killed, but in heaven there is no more pain or suffering or death. While on earth Jesus needed food and drink to live, but in heaven he has perfect life with God that lasts forever.

The author of Colossians says that you have been raised up with Christ to heaven. At first this seems untrue. After all, you are still here in a world where there is pain and suffering and death. But if you have invited Jesus into your life, then you belong to him and his Spirit lives in you. You have begun to live tomorrow's heavenly life—today!

Jesus, I know you live in heaven, but please live in me also. Share with me the peace of heaven and set my mind on your ways. Amen.

MARCH 9

•

You have gotten rid of your old way of life and its habits. You have started living a new life. It is being made new so that what you know has the Creator's likeness. . . . You are God's chosen people. You are holy and dearly loved. So put on tender mercy and kindness as if they were your clothes. Don't be proud. Be gentle and patient. Put up with each other. Forgive the things you are holding against one another. Forgive, just as the Lord forgave you. And over all of those good things put on love. Love holds them all together perfectly as if they were one.

Colossians 3:9b, 12–14 NIRV

"Good as new," we sometimes say after we've fixed something that had been broken. When we look around at our world, we see a lot of things that are broken. We see families and nations fighting with each other. We see suffering and hatred and pain. Who can fix these broken things, and will it ever happen? Will our world ever be as "good as new"?

The author of Colossians tells us that God has already started to repair our broken world. God wants to make it even better than new! First, God raised Jesus Christ from the dead. Now Christ's Spirit is working to get rid of all the things that kill and tear down and destroy—things like jealousy, hatred, and lies. In their place the Spirit puts mercy, kindness, gentleness, patience, forgiveness, and especially love. The Spirit's love is like the glue that holds the whole world together.

Lord, please use me to help repair our world! Keep me from acting in ways that hurt any part of your creation. Instead make me tender, kind, and forgiving. Bind all things together with your love. Amen.

MARCH 10

•

Naomi then said to Ruth, "Look, your sister-in-law is going back to her people and to her gods! Why don't you go with her?"
Ruth answered,
"Please don't tell me to leave you and return home!
I will go where you go,
I will live where you live;
your people will be my people,
your God will be my God.
I will die where you die
and be buried beside you.
May the LORD punish me
if we are ever separated, even by death!"

Ruth 1:15–17 CEV

Nothing is going right for Naomi. First her husband died, and then her two sons died. Now she is very poor. Her name means "sweet," but she says that her life is very bitter.

All she has left are her two daughters-in-law, Orpah and Ruth. They both love her very much. When she tells them to go back to their own families, Orpah cries and kisses her good-bye. But Ruth won't go. She tells her mother-in-law Naomi that she will never leave her. Ruth promises that she will spend the rest of her life with Naomi. Ruth's words to Naomi are so beautiful that sometimes people who are getting married say them to each other at weddings.

When nothing is going right for someone you love, try to be like Ruth. You cannot fix all their problems, but you can promise them that you will never leave them.

God, sometimes our lives seem very bitter, and it feels as though your hand is against us. Send us someone like Ruth, who will stand by our side, and remind us that you still love us. Amen.

MARCH 11

•

Boaz went over to Ruth and said, "I think it would be best for you not to pick up grain in anyone else's field. Stay here with the women and follow along behind them, as they gather up what the men have cut. I have warned the men not to bother you, and whenever you are thirsty, you can drink from the water jars they have filled." Ruth bowed down to the ground and said, "You know I come from another country. Why are you so good to me?"

Ruth 2:8–10 CEV

Ruth is in a tough situation. She is in a strange country, she doesn't know anyone, and she is very poor. But in order to find food for her mother-in-law, Naomi, she has to take a chance. She goes to the fields of Boaz (one of Naomi's relatives) to gather grain.

Boaz could have been very mean to Ruth and told her to go away. But he isn't like that. He makes sure she gets grain for Naomi and water to drink. "Why are you so good to me?" Ruth asks. Boaz says it is because he has seen Ruth's goodness to Naomi. Don't worry, he tells her. You took a chance to help Naomi, but God will keep you safe and care for you.

God, thank you for caring people like Ruth and Boaz. Make me willing to take chances to help others, knowing that you will care for me. Amen.

MARCH 12

•

LORD, how long do I have to call out for help?
Why don't you listen to me?
How long must I keep telling you
that things are terrible?
Why don't you save us?
Why do you make me watch while
people treat others so unfairly?
Why do you put up with the wrong things
they are doing?
I have to look at death.
People are harming others.
They are arguing and fighting all the time.

Habakkuk 1:2–3 NIRV

"How long, God?" the prophet Habakkuk asks. He is waiting for God to fix all that is wrong and unfair in the world. God seems to be taking an awfully long time. Isn't God listening to his prayers? Doesn't God care about injustice?

Elizabeth Cady Stanton was a famous American woman who also asked, "How long, God?" She believed that God had created men and women equal. She thought it was unfair that men were allowed to vote but women were not. She worked most of her long life trying to convince men to let women vote.

When Elizabeth Stanton died in 1902, women were still not allowed to vote in America. But seventeen years later, the law was changed and women started to vote. They have been voting ever since.

Faithful God, sometimes justice seems to take an awfully long time to come. Help me to trust your vision of justice for the whole world. Even when I see injustice all around me, don't let me lose hope. Amen.

MARCH 13

•

Then Eliphaz the Temanite replied, . . .
"Here's something to think about.
Have blameless people ever been wiped out?
Have honest people ever been completely destroyed?
Here's what I've observed.
People gather a crop from what they plant.
If they plant evil and trouble, that's what they will harvest."

Job 4:1, 7–8 NIrV

When something terrible happens to someone, we want to know why. Sometimes we blame the person it happens to. She was hurt in a car accident, we say, because she wasn't wearing a seat belt. He got cancer because he smoked cigarettes.

Terrible things happened to Job: His possessions were destroyed, his children died, and he became very sick. Eliphaz, one of Job's friends, says that all the terrible things that happened to him were his own fault. Bad things never happen to blameless and honest people, he says. Bad things only happen to bad people.

But life is not as simple as Job's friend says it is. Often we can't understand why terrible things happen to people. It doesn't mean that they are bad people. Instead of blaming them, we should try to find ways to make them feel better.

Loving God, help me to comfort those who are suffering, instead of blaming them for what happened. When terrible things happen to me, let me know that you are with me and that you love me. Amen.

MARCH 14

•

"So I won't keep quiet.
When I'm suffering greatly, I'll speak out.
When my spirit is bitter, I'll tell you how unhappy I am.
Am I the ocean? Am I the sea monster?
If I'm not, why do you guard me so closely?
Sometimes I think my bed will comfort me.
I think my couch will keep me from being unhappy.
But even then you send me dreams that frighten me.
You send me visions that terrify me.
So I would rather choke to death.
That would be better than living in this body of mine.
I hate my life. I don't want to live forever.
Leave me alone. My days don't mean anything to me."

Job 7:11–16 NIRV

Have you ever felt so bad that you just wanted to be by yourself? Have you ever told everyone to go away and leave you alone? Of course, you didn't want everyone to leave you alone forever, just for a while.

That is how Job is feeling in this passage. He is so sad and miserable that he wants to die. He complains to God about how bad he feels. Then he tells God to stop bothering him and leave him alone.

When Job tells God to go away, he is being honest with God about how awful he feels at that moment. But he knows that God will never abandon him. Job still hopes that God will come back and comfort him later. And that is exactly what God does.

Sometimes I want everybody to go away, God, even you. But I know that you love me no matter what, and you will never desert me. Amen.

MARCH 15

•

Then Bildad the Shuhite replied, . . .
"But look to God.
Make your appeal to the Mighty One.
Be pure and honest.
And he will rise up and help you now.
He'll return you to the place where you belong."

Job 8:1, 5–6 NIRV

Sometimes you make a deal with someone so that you both get something you want. Your father says that if you clean up your room, he will let you watch a movie. You tell your friend at lunch that if she gives you her cookie, you will give her your potato chips. When you make a good deal, everyone is satisfied.

But we can't make deals with God. That is what Job's friend Bildad doesn't understand. He tells Job that if he does what is pure and honest, God will make him rich and happy. But it just doesn't work that way. Sometimes people who do the right thing suffer a lot. Sometimes those who do wrong things end up very rich.

We do what is right because we love God, not because it will get us what we want. And we know that God loves us and blesses us, even when we have trouble doing what is right.

Gracious God, I try to do what is right because I love you, not because we have made a deal. Thank you for all your blessings. And thank you especially for loving me even when I do what is wrong. Amen.

MARCH 16

•

Job replied,
"I've heard many of those things before.
You are terrible at comforting me!
Your speeches go on forever.
Won't they ever end?
What's wrong with you?
Why do you keep on arguing?"

Job 16:1–3 NIRV

When Job's three friends first came to visit him, they could see how much he was suffering. So they cried with him and sat with him for a whole week without saying anything.

But now they keep on talking, blaming Job for what happened to him, and giving him lots of advice about how to feel better. Job calls them terrible comforters. He liked it much better when they were quiet.

Sometimes when something awful happens to someone we know, we can't think of anything good to say. In those times, it is probably better to keep quiet and to comfort that person by just being there, not by our words.

God of comfort, keep me from saying things that hurt people. Show me how to comfort those who are suffering. Amen.

MARCH 17

•

Why do evil people live so long
and gain such power?
Why are they allowed to see
their children grow up?
They have no worries at home,
and God never punishes them.
Their cattle have lots of calves without ever losing one;
their children play and dance safely by themselves.
These people sing and celebrate
to the sound of tambourines, small harps, and flutes,
and they are successful,
without a worry, until the day they die.

Job 21:7–13 CEV

It's not fair! Have you ever said that? We know that God is a God of fairness. So why is the world so unfair? Why do people who cheat others get rich? Why do those who kill others live long, healthy lives? Why do some people never get caught for doing wrong, while others get punished for something they did not do?

Job was struggling with these questions. He had tried his whole life to be kind to everyone and faithful to God. But many terrible things had happened to him. Then he looked at the wicked people around him, people who were not even trying to be good. And they were rich and happy. It wasn't fair!

Many unfair things happen in our world. What can we do? We can pray that God's justice will come to our whole world. And while we wait, we can try our best to act fairly in our part of the world.

God of fairness, may your will be done on earth, as it is in heaven. Help me to be fair to others and to work for justice for everyone. Amen.

MARCH 18

•

From out of a storm,
the LORD said to Job: . . .
"Can you order the clouds
to send a downpour,
or will lightning flash
at your command?
Did you teach birds to know
that rain or floods are on their way?
Can you count the clouds
or pour out their water on the dry, lumpy soil?"

Job 38:1, 34–38 CEV

Job has been asking God a lot of questions and doing a lot of complaining. In this passage God answers back. God reminds Job that there is a lot about the world that Job does not know. There is a lot in the world that Job has no control over. God tries to show Job a much bigger picture.

Look, God says. I made the clouds and rain and lightning bolts. I feed the mother lions and the baby birds. I know the deepest parts of the ocean and the faraway stars. I tell the sun when to rise. I watch over the whole creation. Why do you act as if you know everything? When God is done speaking, Job admits how little he knows and promises to keep quiet.

Like Job, we can see only a tiny bit of what God is doing in the world. Instead of pretending we understand everything, sometimes it is best to keep quiet so we can hear God speaking to us.

God, all the wisdom I have comes from you. Remind me that there is much that I don't know. Help me put my trust in you. Amen.

MARCH 19

•

Deborah was a prophet. She was the wife of Lappidoth. She was leading Israel at that time. Under The Palm Tree of Deborah she served the people as their judge. . . . The people of Israel came to her there. They came to have her decide cases for them. She settled matters between them. Deborah sent for Barak. . . . Deborah said to Barak, "The LORD, the God of Israel, is giving you a command. He says, 'Go! Take 10,000 men from the tribes of Naphtali and Zebulun with you. Then lead the way to Mount Tabor. I will draw Sisera into a trap. He is the commander of Jabin's army. I will bring him, his chariots and his troops to the Kishon River. There I will hand him over to you.'" Barak said to her, "If you go with me, I'll go. But if you don't go with me, I won't go." "All right," Deborah said. "I'll go with you. But because of the way you are doing this, you won't receive any honor. The LORD will hand Sisera over to a woman."

Judges 4:4–9 NIRV

Before Israel had kings, God chose special leaders for Israel who were called judges. They led the Israelites in battle and helped them settle disagreements. Deborah was one of the famous judges of Israel. She was a wise and brave leader.

Some countries have queens or other women leaders. But most of the world's leaders are men. Most of the leaders of Israel were men. Why do you think this is? Some people say it is because men are stronger and braver than women. But in this story, Deborah is braver than Barak!

God, thank you for raising up strong women and men to lead your people. Make me wise and brave like Deborah. Amen.

MARCH 20

•

Jesus told his disciples: "Have faith in God! If you have faith in God and don't doubt, you can tell this mountain to get up and jump into the sea, and it will. Everything you ask for in prayer will be yours, if you only have faith."

Mark 11:22–24 CEV

About a hundred years ago, a woman named Mary McLeod Bethune wanted more than anything to start a school in Florida for poor African-American girls. She had only an old empty shack and $1.50, but she had faith in God and faith in her dream. Soon she had five students, and she convinced leaders from the town that they should help her build the school. And they did! The Daytona Educational and Industrial Training School opened in 1904. The first building was named "Faith Hall," to tell people of Mary's faith in God, which had made it possible. Now that school is a well-known college, called Bethune-Cookman College.

Jesus said, "Have faith in God." Our God is powerful and makes amazing things happen. Sometimes God does such things without any help from us. But often God works by giving us the strength and hope and patience we need to make dreams—even "impossible" dreams—come true. Having faith in God means trusting that your life is in God's hands. It means trusting that God will give you what you truly need when you ask for it in prayer.

Dear God, please give me faith. Help me to learn what it means to trust you with my life. Help me to come to you with all my needs. Amen.

MARCH 21

•

They brought the colt to Jesus. They threw their coats over it. Then he sat on it. Many people spread their coats on the road. Others spread branches they had cut in the fields. Those in front and those in back shouted,

"Hosanna!"
"Blessed is the one who comes in the name of the Lord!"
"Blessed is the coming kingdom of our father David!"
"Hosanna in the highest heaven!"

Mark 11:7–10 NIRV

When a very important leader comes to visit, people may show their respect by rolling out a red carpet for the leader to walk on. When Jesus rode into the city of Jerusalem, the people honored him by spreading clothes and leafy branches on the road. They welcomed him and sang praises to God. They shouted "Hosanna!", which means "save us!" They were rejoicing because they believed that God had sent Jesus to help them. They believed Jesus was the king for whom they had been waiting.

In church each year on the Sunday before Easter (called Palm Sunday) we remember how the people honored Jesus with palm branches and shouts of praise. It is a time to be glad, for God's servant has come!

Hosanna, King Jesus! I praise God for you! Help me always to welcome and honor you. Help me to understand what kind of king you are. Amen.

MARCH 22

•

Jesus was in Bethany. He was at the table in the home of a man named Simon. . . . A woman came with a special sealed jar of very expensive perfume. It was made out of pure nard. She broke the jar open and poured the perfume on Jesus' head. Some of the people there became angry. They said to one another, "Why waste this perfume? It could have been sold for more than a year's pay. The money could have been given to poor people." So they found fault with the woman. "Leave her alone," Jesus said. "Why are you bothering her? She has done a beautiful thing to me. You will always have poor people with you. You can help them any time you want to. But you will not always have me. She did what she could. She poured perfume on my body to prepare me to be buried. What I'm about to tell you is true. What she has done will be told anywhere the good news is preached all over the world. It will be told in memory of her."

Mark 14:3–9 NIRV

How would you feel if someone you loved planned to put himself in danger in order to make the world a better place? Would you tell him to go ahead? Or would you tell him to run away from danger?

Jesus' work to bring God's justice had made some people so angry that they were trying to kill him. Jesus' friends and followers wanted him to run away from danger. Even Peter, Jesus' close disciple, once tried to stop Jesus from walking on God's path. But the woman in this story did not try to stop Jesus. Instead, she poured costly perfume on him. Back then people did that to prepare someone's dead body for burial, but Jesus said she was preparing him even before he died. In that way she helped him on his path.

Jesus, help me to help you do your work—even when it will cost me a lot. When your path leads through dangerous places, make me brave, and use me to make others brave. Amen.

MARCH 23

•

Jesus went with his disciples to a place called Gethsemane, and he told them, "Sit here while I pray." Jesus took along Peter, James, and John. He was sad and troubled and told them, "I am so sad that I feel as if I am dying. Stay here and keep awake with me." Jesus walked on a little way. Then he knelt down on the ground and prayed, "Father, if it is possible, don't let this happen to me! Father, you can do anything. Don't make me suffer by having me drink from this cup. But do what you want, and not what I want."

Mark 14:32–36 CEV

It is the night before Jesus' death. He knows that he is about to suffer and that he needs God's strength. And so he goes to a quiet place to pray.

Jesus is not afraid to say what he is really feeling. He speaks of his terrible sadness. And he asks God not to let him "drink from this cup." Jesus isn't talking about a real cup but about the terrible suffering awaiting him. He asks God to take it away. But Jesus also knows that God plans for good things to come out of his suffering. That is why Jesus prays, "Do what you want, and not what I want."

We can pray the way Jesus prayed. It is always right to pray that God will keep us away from trouble and pain. But it is also right to pray the end of Jesus' prayer: "God, do what you want, and not what I want."

God, keep me away from sadness and trouble. Do not let me suffer. But if suffering should come to me, give me strength and comfort. Help me to see how some good may come out of my pain. Amen.

MARCH 24

•

Just as Jesus was speaking, Judas appeared. He was one of the Twelve [disciples]. A crowd was with him. They were carrying swords and clubs. The chief priests, the teachers of the law, and the elders had sent them. Judas, who was going to hand Jesus over, had arranged a signal with them. "The one I kiss is the man," he said. "Arrest him and have the guards lead him away." So Judas went to Jesus at once. He said, "Rabbi!" And he kissed him. The men grabbed Jesus and arrested him. . . . Then everyone left him and ran away.

Mark 14:43–46, 50 NIRV

What is one of the most joyous things that can happen to us? Loving people—really loving them—and receiving their love in return. What is one of the saddest things that can happen? Loving people—really loving them—and having them refuse our love, or even turn against us. When that happens we may feel ashamed or angry. We may feel deep pain and sadness.

Jesus truly loved his disciples. But the disciple named Judas turned Jesus over to the leaders who wanted to kill him. Judas kissed Jesus. It was a kiss of betrayal, not a kiss of love. And when Jesus was arrested, the other disciples all ran away. How do you think Jesus felt when those things happened?

When someone rejects our love, we can come to Jesus with our pain. We can tell him everything that is in our heart. The person or people who rejected us might not act any differently. But Jesus knows what we are going through. He listens to us and loves us. He won't ever betray us.

Jesus, thank you for caring about me when I feel very, very sad. Thank you for loving me always. Help me never to betray you. Amen.

MARCH 25

•

The chief priests and the whole council tried to find someone to accuse Jesus of a crime, so they could put him to death. But they could not find anyone to accuse him. Many people did tell lies against Jesus, but they did not agree on what they said. Finally, some men stood up and lied about him. They said, "We heard him say he would tear down this temple that we built. He also claimed that in three days he would build another one without any help." But even then they did not agree on what they said.

Mark 14:55–59 CEV

Most of the movies and TV shows you've seen and most of the books you've read have probably had "happy endings." The characters in the story had a problem, and by the end of the story they had solved it.

Jesus had a big problem, but he was not able to solve it by the end of Mark's story. God had sent Jesus to tell people how to change their ways. His words made some people very angry. Their anger and hatred led Jesus' enemies to bring him before the court. There, people said untrue things about him, so that they could find a reason to kill Jesus. Jesus was put on a cross and died a shameful and painful death.

God knew that Jesus was innocent, even if those around him did not. And God gave Jesus inner strength—the strength he needed to stay faithful to God, even to death.

God, when people were unfair to Jesus, you sent your light and truth to guide him. Send them to guide me also! Amen.

MARCH 26

•

The high priest stood up in the midst of them and asked Jesus, "Why don't you answer the charges they are making against you?" But Jesus kept silent and did not answer at all. Again the high priest asked him a question. "Are you the Christ, the Son of our Blessed God?" Jesus answered, "Yes, I am. And soon you will see the Son of Man sitting at the right side of Almighty God, and coming with the clouds of heaven." The high priest tore his robe and said, "Why do we still need witnesses? You heard the blasphemy! What is your decision?" They all judged him to be deserving of death.

Mark 14:60–64 AT

The high priest was the judge or leader of those who had put Jesus on trial. The high priest couldn't understand why Jesus stayed quiet when people said untrue things about him. Then the high priest asked Jesus if he was God's Christ. People knew that the Christ (also known as the Messiah) would be God's specially chosen leader.

Jesus said yes, he was the Christ. He also said there would come a day when all people would see and know that he was God's Chosen One. But the priest didn't like this answer. He thought it was "blasphemy"—when someone says something insulting to God. So the priest and the other members of the court decided that Jesus should be put to death.

Jesus spoke the truth. But sometimes people do not want to hear the truth. The high priest and those around him refused to hear the truth of Jesus' words, and so they decided that he should die.

God, give me ears to hear your truth! Give me courage to stand up for truth even if no one else does. Amen.

MARCH 27

•

Some of the people started spitting on Jesus. They blindfolded him, hit him with their fists, and said, "Tell us who hit you!" Then the guards took charge of Jesus and beat him.

Mark 14:65 CEV

The people who had been listening to Jesus began to spit at him and make fun of him. Others had said Jesus was a prophet—someone who knows and speaks the truths of God—but these people didn't believe it. So they played a cruel joke on Jesus. They put a blindfold on him, hit him, and then told him to say who was attacking him. Wouldn't a prophet be able to answer such a simple question?

Jesus wore the blindfold, but his enemies were the ones who were really "blind." They couldn't see that Jesus was the Holy One of God. They didn't know that, days before, Jesus had prophesied his own arrest, suffering, and death.

This story shows us how easy it is to be cruel to people whenever we think we have power over them. And it warns us to be careful whenever we are sure that we alone see the truth. We might just be the ones who are blind.

God, teach me to treat people fairly, even when I think they are wrong. Open my eyes to see things from your point of view. Amen.

MARCH 28

•

Peter was below in the courtyard. One of the high priest's women servants came by. When she saw Peter warming himself, she looked closely at him. "You also were with Jesus, that Nazarene," she said. But Peter said he had not been with him. "I don't know or understand what you're talking about," he said. He went out to the entrance to the courtyard. The servant saw him there. She said again to those standing around, "This fellow is one of them." Again he said he was not. After a little while, those standing nearby said to Peter, "You must be one of them. You are from Galilee." He began to call down curses on himself. He took an oath and said to them, "I don't know this man you're talking about!" Right away the rooster crowed the second time. Then Peter remembered what Jesus had spoken to him. "The rooster will crow twice," he had said. "Before it does, you will say three times that you don't know me." Peter broke down and sobbed.

Mark 14:66–72 NIRV

What kinds of things might make you cry? When you fall and hurt yourself? When someone is mean to you? When you lose something or someone you care about?

In this story Peter cries, but not for any of the reasons above. Earlier in the day, Peter had promised Jesus that he would always be a faithful friend to him, even if others turned away from him. Jesus answered that before the rooster crowed twice, Peter would tell people he didn't know Jesus. Later, when a woman started telling others that Peter was a friend of Jesus, Peter said it wasn't so. When the rooster crowed, it reminded Peter of what Jesus had said would happen. Peter cried because he had broken a promise to someone he dearly loved.

Lord, may I never be ashamed of my faith in you. But if I do break my promises to honor you, give me the courage to admit I have done wrong and ask for your forgiveness. Amen.

MARCH 29

•

"Do you want me to let the king of the Jews go free?" asked Pilate. He knew that the chief priests had handed Jesus over to him because they were jealous. But the chief priests stirred up the crowd. So the crowd asked Pilate to let Barabbas go free instead. "Then what should I do with the one you call the king of the Jews?" Pilate asked them. "Crucify him!" the crowd shouted. "Why? What wrong has he done?" asked Pilate. But they shouted even louder, "Crucify him!" Pilate wanted to satisfy the crowd. So he let Barabbas go free. He ordered that Jesus be whipped. Then he handed him over to be nailed to a cross.

Mark 15:9–15 NIRV

Sometimes when a bad thing happens, it is one person's fault. But sometimes many people are to blame.

After Jesus went before the high priest, the chief priests took him to Pontius Pilate. Pilate was a Roman ruler. Because the Romans controlled Jesus' country at that time, Pilate had the power to decide what should happen to Jesus. Mark's Gospel tells us that sometimes the Romans would free one prisoner. So Pilate asked the crowd if they wanted him to let Jesus go. "Crucify him!" was their answer.

Who is to blame for Jesus' death? The chief priests and other religious leaders plotted his arrest. They were to blame. Pilate decided to crucify Jesus, though he could have freed Jesus and knew he had done no wrong. Pilate was to blame too. The people—the same ones who had welcomed Jesus into their city—told Pilate to kill Jesus. They were also to blame.

God, show me when I am to blame for the sufferings of others. Do not let me go along with evil, but help me to resist it. Amen.

MARCH 30

•

They crucified two robbers with him. One was on his right and one was on his left. Those who passed by shouted at Jesus and made fun of him. They shook their heads and said, "So you are going to destroy the temple and build it again in three days? Then come down from the cross! Save yourself!" In the same way the chief priests and the teachers of the law made fun of him among themselves. "He saved others," they said. "But he can't save himself! Let this Christ, this King of Israel, come down now from the cross! When we see that, we will believe." Those who were being crucified with Jesus also made fun of him. At noon, darkness covered the whole land. It lasted three hours. At three o'clock Jesus cried out in a loud voice, "Eloi, Eloi, lama sabachthani?" This means "My God, my God, why have you deserted me?"

Mark 15:27–34 NIrV

When Jesus was dying on the cross, Mark tells us, he felt alone. His disciples had all deserted him. Those who stood on the ground looking up at him made fun of him. Even the robbers who were being crucified on each side of Jesus made fun of him!

But far worse than having friends leave him or hearing others mock him was Jesus' sense that God too had gone away. Jesus knew what it was like to be very close to God. But when he was dying, it seemed as though God were hiding. That is why Jesus cried, "My God, my God, why have you deserted me?"

There may come times in your life when you feel as though God has left you. When this happens, think of your brother, Jesus. Because of what he went through he knows just how you feel.

Jesus, even if I feel so sad or alone that I do not want to pray, stay near me. Give me hope for a better day. Amen.

MARCH 31

•

The Sabbath day ended. Mary Magdalene, Mary the mother of James, and Salome bought spices. They were going to apply them to Jesus' body. Very early on the first day of the week, they were on their way to the tomb. It was just after sunrise. They asked each other, "Who will roll the stone away from the entrance to the tomb?" Then they looked up and saw that the stone had been rolled away. The stone was very large. They entered the tomb. As they did, they saw a young man dressed in a white robe. He was sitting on the right side. They were alarmed. "Don't be alarmed," he said. "You are looking for Jesus the Nazarene, who was crucified. But he has risen! He is not here! See the place where they had put him. Go! Tell his disciples and Peter, 'He is going ahead of you into Galilee. There you will see him. It will be just as he told you.'" The women were shaking and confused. They went out and ran away from the tomb. They said nothing to anyone, because they were afraid.

Mark 16:1–8 NIRV

Some women who had been Jesus' friends and helpers wanted to put special spices and oils on his body. (That was the way people prepared bodies for burial in those days.) The women went to Jesus' tomb, which would have been an opening in a wall, like a cave.

But when they got there, the huge stone in front of the door to the tomb had been moved. A young man dressed in white—was it an angel?—told them that Jesus had risen from the dead. He commanded the women to go and tell others the good news. They would see Jesus again!

Mark writes that the women didn't tell anyone, because they were afraid. But somehow the news did spread! Soon many, many people were talking about how Jesus had risen from the dead.

God of the resurrection, thank you for the fantastic news! May I never be afraid to tell people that Jesus is alive. Amen.

APRIL 1

•

But when Jacob woke up in the morning—it was Leah! "What sort of trick is this?" Jacob raged at Laban. "I worked seven years for Rachel. What do you mean by this trickery?" "It's not our custom to marry off a younger daughter ahead of the firstborn," Laban replied. "Wait until the bridal week is over, and you can have Rachel, too—that is, if you promise to work another seven years for me."

Genesis 29:25–27 NLT

Happy April Fool's Day! Will you try to play a trick on someone today?

Jacob played a trick on his father, Isaac, in order to get the blessing that belonged to his twin brother, Esau. Isaac couldn't see very well. He could tell his two sons apart by touching them, because Esau was hairier than Jacob. But Jacob tricked his father by putting hairy goat skin on his hands and neck, so that his father would think he was Esau. (You can read this story in Genesis 27.)

Now it is Jacob's turn to be tricked. Laban had two daughters, Leah and Rachel. Jacob loved Rachel and agreed to work for Laban for seven years in order to marry her. But after the wedding celebration it was dark and Jacob couldn't see very well. Laban tricked Jacob by sending Leah to sleep with him. In the morning Jacob was very surprised to find out that Leah was his wife! He had to work seven *more* years to marry Rachel.

God, we can count on you not to play tricks on us. Show us how to have fun without hurting others. Amen.

•

The message of the cross seems foolish to those who are lost and dying. But it is God's power to us who are being saved. . . . Where is the wise person? Where is the educated person? Where are the great thinkers of this world? Hasn't God made the wisdom of the world foolish? God wisely planned that the world would not know him through its own wisdom. It pleased God to use the foolish things we preach to save those who believe.

1 Corinthians 1:18, 20–21 NIRV

Who is the smartest person you know? Is it one of your parents? A teacher? A friend? Perhaps you yourself are very smart. God gave us our good minds and wants us to use them. And yet, Paul teaches, some of God's most important lessons are ones that you can't figure out just by being smart. Some of the true things God wants us to know look silly to a lot of smart people in the world.

When Jesus died on the cross, many smart people thought that it meant God didn't care about Jesus or even that God was punishing Jesus. But it didn't mean that at all. God loved Jesus, and Jesus loved God! Jesus knew that we humans were far away from God because of sin, and he died to bring us close. He brought us close so that God might work in and through us. The cross looks silly to many smart people. But God used Jesus' death to give powerful new life to the whole world!

God, I know that you are very wise. But some of your wisdom is hard to understand. Please give me a mind and a heart to learn about Jesus. Amen.

APRIL 3

•

Because of what God has done, you belong to Christ Jesus. He has become God's wisdom for us. He makes us right with God. He makes us holy and sets us free.

1 Corinthians 1:30 NIrV

God is so wise. God knows so much more than any person can ever know. Compared to God's great universe we humans are so very small. How could we ever begin to know the things of God?

Paul wrote that Jesus "has become God's wisdom for us." We look to Jesus, and we see what God's wisdom looks like in a human life. Then we begin to share in that wisdom ourselves. We look to Jesus, and we see how enemies killed him for teaching about God's way. Then we begin to understand that people in our world do not always want to know the truth. We look to Jesus, and we see how God raised him from the dead. Then we begin to understand that our God is a God who wants life, not death.

There is so much more God wants to teach you. Get ready for a lifetime of learning!

God, thank you for sending Jesus to be your wisdom. Make me hungry for that wisdom. Make me want to learn more and more. Amen.

APRIL 4

•

The Spirit understands all things. He understands even the deep things of God. Who can know the thoughts of another person? Only a person's own spirit can know them. In the same way, only the Spirit of God knows God's thoughts. We have not received the spirit of the world. We have received the Spirit who is from God. The Spirit helps us understand what God has freely given us.

1 Corinthians 2:10b–12 NIRV

No one can read another person's thoughts. We may be able to guess what another person is thinking, if we know how she acts, or things she has said in the past. But we can never hear her thoughts as she is thinking them.

If it is so hard to read another human being's thoughts, how much harder it is to read God's thoughts! On our own, we cannot know God's thoughts. But God gives us the Holy Spirit. The Spirit helps us understand God and the wonderful gift God has given us, Jesus Christ.

The Spirit may not teach us everything we need to know all at once. But if we keep on listening, the Spirit will help us to understand more and more.

Spirit of God, speak to me. Help me to understand how and why Jesus is God's gift to the whole world. Teach me more and more as I grow. Amen.

APRIL 5

•

You are still following the ways of the world. Some of you are jealous. Some of you argue. So aren't you following the ways of the world? Aren't you acting like ordinary human beings? One of you says, "I follow Paul." Another says, "I follow Apollos." Aren't you acting like ordinary human beings?

1 Corinthians 3:3–4 NIRV

Did you or other kids you know ever invent a "club"? Maybe you made a chart showing all its rules. Clubs can help people come together to do fun things and to enjoy one another's company. But the trouble with clubs is that sometimes members start to think they are better than everyone who is not a member. Or they may start to argue with others, instead of cooperating with them.

Paul was worried that the people in his church were forming clubs. Some people were saying that you could only be in their club if you followed Paul as your leader. Others were saying you had to follow Apollos or someone else. All this arguing wasn't good, Paul told them. The people in the church were fighting against each other instead of working together to serve God!

If people in a church say that they are followers of Jesus Christ, then Christ should be the one whom they follow and obey. Jesus wants Christians to love and care for one another and work together. He wants peace.

Lord Jesus, keep your church from arguing and fighting. Help us to live and work together in peace and harmony. Amen.

APRIL 6

•

After all, what is Apollos? And what is Paul? We are only people who serve. We helped you to believe. The Lord has given each of us our own work to do. I planted the seed. Apollos watered it. But God made it grow.

1 Corinthians 3:5–6 NIRV

Farmers have to work very hard. They must prepare the soil, plant the seeds, water the fields if it doesn't rain enough, keep the weeds and bugs away, and harvest the crops. If farmers didn't do this important work, there wouldn't be food for the rest of us to eat. And yet, even though farmers work very hard, it is God who sends the sunshine to warm the earth and makes each seed sprout into a living, growing plant. Farmers deserve our thanks and praise. But God deserves our thanks and praise even more!

When we show and tell people the good news about God's love the way Paul and Apollos did, we are like farmers who plant and water seeds. The work of "planting" and "watering" is very important. But God is the one who fills a person's heart with faith and love. God is the one who makes a seed grow into a new and better life. God is the one who deserves thanks and praise!

God, thank you for making seeds to grow so that we have food to eat. And thank you for making love to grow and blossom in people's hearts! Teach me to plant seeds of love and kindness wherever I go. Amen.

APRIL 7

•

"Tell the people of Israel that on the tenth day of this month the head of each family must choose a lamb or a young goat for his family to eat. . . . Some of the blood must be put on the two doorposts and above the door of each house where the animals are to be eaten. . . . This is the Passover Festival in honor of me, your LORD. That same night I will pass through Egypt and kill the first-born son in every family and the first-born male of all animals. I am the LORD, and I will punish the gods of Egypt. The blood on the houses will show me where you live, and when I see the blood, I will pass over you. Then you won't be bothered by the terrible disasters I will bring on Egypt. Remember this day and celebrate it each year as a festival in my honor."

Exodus 12:3, 7, 11b–14 CEV

God saved the Hebrews from the terrible plague that came upon the land of Egypt. The firstborn male child in each family died. But God promised the Hebrews that their children would not die. Each family would eat a specially prepared lamb and put blood from the animal on their doorposts. The houses with the special marker would be passed over; the sons in those homes would not die. This tenth plague would finally force Pharaoh to let the Hebrew people go free.

Jews celebrate the Festival of "Passover" each year. They eat the same foods and do some of the same things as those people so long ago. The Festival is a way of remembering God's saving action. But even those of us who do not celebrate Passover can read and remember how God's people were saved. Remembering can help us to know, love, and trust God today and tomorrow.

God, thank you for rescuing your people from death and setting them free. Help me remember your saving actions in the past. And help me to look for your salvation now and in the future. Amen.

APRIL 8

•

Get rid of the old yeast. Be like a new batch of dough without yeast. That is what you really are, because Christ has been offered up for us. He is our Passover lamb. So let us keep the Feast, but not with the old yeast. I'm talking about yeast that is full of hatred and evil. Let us keep the Feast with bread made without yeast. Let us do it with bread that is honest and true.

1 Corinthians 5:7–8 NIRV

Yeast is what makes bread dough rise. The baker puts the yeast in the dough and waits a while for the dough to grow larger before she bakes it. But when God saved the Hebrew people from slavery in Egypt, they had to leave so quickly that they didn't have time to wait for the bread to rise. So they ate their bread without yeast. Now, every year when the Jewish people celebrate the feast of Passover, they get rid of all the yeast in their homes and share bread made without yeast. Doing this reminds them of that night so long ago when God set them free.

As Christians we believe that God sent Jesus to set us free from sin. We, too, have reason to feast and celebrate. But first God wants us to get rid of all the hatred and evil that are in our hearts, in our homes, and in our churches. Hatred and evil are like yeast. A little hatred quickly grows, till it is not so little anymore. That is why Paul says we must "get rid of the old yeast." We should celebrate our freedom by sharing honesty and truth with each other instead.

God, thank you for setting your people free. Help me and those around me to get rid of hatred and evil that are in us and among us. Teach us to share honesty and truth with one another. Amen.

APRIL 9

•

Elders, listen to me.
Pay attention, all you who live in the land.
Has anything like this ever happened in your whole life?
Did it ever happen to your people who lived long ago?
Tell your children about it.
Let them tell their children.
And let their children tell it
to those who live after them.

Joel 1:2–3 NIRV

When something terrible happens, we try to put it out of our minds. It is too painful to think about. But the prophet Joel tells the people of Israel to remember the disaster that has come upon them, and to tell their children and grandchildren about it.

Jewish people who are living now have a special Holocaust Memorial Day of Remembrance—Yom Hashoah—each year following the Passover celebration. On that day, they remember something terrible: the deaths of six million Jews and others in the Holocaust during World War II. They remember the children who were killed. They remember the mothers and fathers who died in concentration camps. They remember the people who died trying to protect Jews from the Nazis. And they tell their children and grandchildren what happened, so that it will never happen again.

Many Christians also remember the Holocaust every year. They mourn with their Jewish brothers and sisters. They feel sorry about the long history of Christian hatred toward the Jews. And they pray for a new future in which Christians and Jews will love and respect each other.

God, never let us forget what human hatred can do. Have mercy on all your children, and show us how to live together in peace. Amen.

APRIL 10

•

So here is what I ask. Did God turn his back on his people? Not at all! I myself belong to Israel. I am one of Abraham's children. I am from the tribe of Benjamin. God didn't turn his back on his people. After all, he chose them. . . . God does not take back his gifts. He does not change his mind about those he has chosen.

Romans 11:1–2a, 29 NIRV

Jesus and all his disciples were Jews. So was Paul, the author of the letter to the Romans. The only Scripture they knew was what Christians now call the Old Testament. In it, they found God's special promises to the people of Israel.

But Paul had a problem. The God of Israel he knew had come to him in a new way in Jesus Christ. Paul wanted to spread that good news to everyone, whether they were Jews or not. But he wondered whether this meant that God had taken back the special promises to the people of Israel. He wondered whether the Jews were still the people of God.

If you have ever played a game with a very young child, you know how they like to change the rules in the middle of the game. Paul tells us that God is not like that. God keeps promises. The Jews will always be the people of God, and they can trust the promises God made to them. Paul says the Jews are like the trunk of a big, strong tree. But in Jesus, God has made room for Christians to become branches on the tree of faith. That is why both Jews and Christians give praise to God!

God of the covenant, I know I can always depend on you to keep your promises. Thank you for sending us Jesus. Amen.

APRIL 11

•

I passed on to you what I received from the Lord. On the night the Lord Jesus was handed over to his enemies, he took bread. When he had given thanks, he broke it. He said, "This is my body. It is given for you. Every time you eat it, do it in memory of me." In the same way, after supper he took the cup. He said, "This cup is the new covenant in my blood. Every time you drink it, do it in memory of me."

1 Corinthians 11:23–25 NIRV

Every family has special days of remembering. Your birthday is one such day. You don't recall the day of your birth, but your mom certainly does! If you are adopted, you might remember the day you came to live with your family. There are other kinds of "remembering days." If a family member has died, the day of his or her death will often be a day to remember. On such days we may feel sad that people we loved have died. But, we can also feel great joy and thankfulness for the gift of having known them.

Paul here tells of the last supper Jesus ate before he died. Jesus had shared bread and wine with his disciples. He told them that his body would be broken and his blood would be shed for them. He also told them that after his death they should continue to share bread and wine with one another, as a way to remember how he gave himself for them.

Today in church we still share bread and wine (or grape juice) in a special time of remembering that we call "the Lord's Supper," or "Communion," or "Holy Eucharist." Even if we are quiet during Communion, we do not need to be sad. We remember what Jesus said at the table with his disciples because it shows us how much he loves us. Even his death was a way of giving himself to us. That is reason to be joyful!

Jesus, I know you love me so much. Thank you for giving yourself for me. Thank you for giving the church special ways to remember you. Amen.

APRIL 12

•

When you eat the bread and drink the cup, you are announcing the Lord's death until he comes again.

1 Corinthians 11:26 NIrV

What is it like at your house on days when you are going to have a very special dinner? Maybe the smells of good food cooking make you really hungry before it's time to eat! Perhaps your mom gives you a little snack. The snack isn't enough to fill you up, but it will help you wait until everyone can gather around the table for the great meal.

When we celebrate the Lord's Supper in church, we aren't just remembering. We are also looking forward. Jesus promised a time when all will feast with him in God's kingdom, a time when there will be no more hatred or death or pain and when everyone will have enough to eat. The Lord's Supper is like a snack before the great meal. It helps us to wait until that day when we can all gather around God's banquet table!

But we do not just sit around while we wait. When Paul reminded the Corinthians about Jesus' last supper, he was worried about how the members of the church were behaving. Some of the people in the church were feasting, but some people didn't have enough to eat and were going hungry. Paul wanted them to do a better job of sharing with one another. How can *we* do a better job of sharing with one another in this time of waiting?

Jesus, thank you for your promise of a better world. Thank you for giving us tastes of the banquet to come! Help us to do a better job of sharing with one another while we wait. Amen.

APRIL 13

•

My friends, I want you to remember the message that I preached and that you believed and trusted. You will be saved by this message, if you hold firmly to it. But if you don't, your faith was all for nothing. I told you the most important part of the message exactly as it was told to me. That part is:

Christ died for our sins, as the Scriptures say.
He was buried, and three days later
he was raised to life, as the Scriptures say.

1 Corinthians 15:1–4 CEV

Suppose that you have something very important to say. You want to be certain that your hearers listen well. What do you do? Do you wait until they're quiet? Do you raise your voice?

Paul has said many important things in his letter to the Corinthians. But now he has come to the most important thing of all—the good news that Jesus died for our sins and that God raised him up to new life. The Corinthians had heard Paul preach this good news before, when he first met them. They had believed and trusted it. But now Paul worries that they are forgetting, so he reminds them. He really wants them to listen!

The message of Jesus' death and resurrection is still the most important news there is. The Jesus whom we worship died for us. And now he shares God's life and power!

Lord Jesus, I have heard the good news of salvation in you. Help me to trust this good news and never forget it. Amen.

APRIL 14

•

Unless Christ was raised to life, your faith is useless, and you are still living in your sins. And those people who died after putting their faith in him are completely lost. If our hope in Christ is good only for this life, we are worse off than anyone else.

1 Corinthians 15:17–19 CEV

A role model is someone who shows you a good pattern for living your life. Are there people who have been important role models for you? It may be one of your parents, or a teacher, or someone in your church. Or it may be someone who lived a long time ago.

Jesus is a role model for Christians. We trust Jesus to show us the way to live our life. Some Christians even wear bracelets that say WWJD—What would Jesus do?

But Paul says that if we trust Jesus only as a good role model who lived a long time ago, we are missing out on the best part. Lots of people can be role models for us. But only Jesus was raised from the dead and offers us new life forever with God. Trust in Jesus as your role model. But don't miss out on the best part of God's promise!

Eternal God, my faith gives me hope for living each day. But don't let me ever forget that in Jesus Christ you have promised me new life with you forever. Thank you for that wonderful promise! Amen.

APRIL 15

•

But someone might ask, "How are the dead raised? What kind of body will they have?"

1 Corinthians 15:35 NIRV

Have you ever read a mystery? In a mystery story, there is something unexplained or kept secret. A character in the story asks lots of questions, searching for clues to help her to figure out the secret. As the story moves along, she puts the clues together like the pieces of a puzzle, till she finally solves the mystery. Mysteries can be very, very exciting!

Some of the truths that we learn from the Bible are also mysteries, but of a different kind. They are too big to be completely "solved." We get "clues" about these mysteries from the Bible, but we can never come to understand them completely.

Resurrection is one of the greatest mysteries of all. Paul said that Jesus was raised up from the dead and now shares in God's life and power. Jesus can give us new life with God beginning right now! But there is more to the mystery. Paul teaches that, someday and somehow, God will raise our bodies to a new and more perfect life, in the same way God raised Jesus' body. How could we ever understand that? The more we try, the more questions we have. But at least we know that God loves and saves every part of us, even our bodies.

God, thank you for the mystery of resurrection. Help me to trust that you have all the answers, even if I can never fully understand. Amen.

APRIL 16

•

Then what is written will come true. It says, "Death has been swallowed up. It has lost the battle."

> *"Death, where is the battle you thought you were winning?*
> *Death, where is your sting?"*

The sting of death is sin. And the power of sin is the law. But let us give thanks to God! He wins the battle for us because of what our Lord Jesus Christ has done.

1 Corinthians 15:54b–57 NIrV

Have you ever walked in a cemetery and seen all the stones marking where the bodies of dead people were buried? Have you ever wondered what will happen after you die? Some people think that death is the end of everything. No matter how good life is, they say, death wins at the end.

Christians believe that death doesn't win, because God's love is even stronger than death. Even after we die, we will still have life with God. It is hard to imagine what that life will be like, just as it is hard for a caterpillar to imagine what it will be like to be a butterfly. But God promises us that death is not the end of everything. It wasn't the end for Jesus, and it won't be the end for us. Next time you walk in a cemetery, give thanks that not even death can separate us from God's love in Christ Jesus!

Living God, it is hard to imagine what life after death will be like. Thank you for the promise that I will always have life with you. In Jesus' name, Amen.

APRIL 17

•

That same day two of Jesus' followers were going to a village called Emmaus. It was about seven miles from Jerusalem. They were talking with each other about everything that had happened. As they talked about those things, Jesus himself came up and walked along with them. But God kept them from recognizing him. . . . He joined them at the table. Then he took bread and gave thanks. He broke it and began to give it to them. Their eyes were opened, and they recognized him. But then he disappeared from their sight.

Luke 24:13–16, 30–31 NIRV

God raised Jesus from the dead. But that doesn't mean the risen Jesus was exactly like he was before. God raised Jesus to *new* life, and this new life was amazing to people but also mysterious and hard to understand. People who had known Jesus very well before he died had trouble recognizing him after he was raised up. He appeared and disappeared when no one expected it.

Jesus' followers thought that when Jesus died, he was gone forever. But God opened their eyes to see that Jesus was still present with them, in new ways. Today, when Christians share their food with a stranger or celebrate the Lord's Supper together, they discover that the risen Jesus is still present. How mysterious! How wonderful!

Risen Christ, thank you that you are still with me, sometimes when I least expect it. Give me eyes to recognize you in my daily life. Amen.

APRIL 18

•

Thomas was one of the Twelve. He was called Didymus. He was not with the other disciples when Jesus came. So they told him, "We have seen the Lord!" But he said to them, "First I must see the nail marks in his hands. I must put my finger where the nails were. I must put my hand into his side. Only then will I believe what you say." A week later, Jesus' disciples were in the house again. Thomas was with them. Even though the doors were locked, Jesus came in and stood among them. He said, "May peace be with you!" Then he said to Thomas, "Put your finger here. See my hands. Reach out your hand and put it into my side. Stop doubting and believe." Thomas said to him, "My Lord and my God!"

John 20:24–28 NIRV

Thomas knew that Jesus had died a terrible death on the cross. Jesus died with nail marks in his hands and a wound from a sword in his side. Could he possibly be alive again? Mary said so. The other disciples said so. But Thomas wanted to see for himself. Then Jesus suddenly appeared and let Thomas see for himself. After that, Thomas believed in Jesus.

We can't touch Jesus the way Thomas did. For almost two thousand years, Christians have believed in Jesus without being able to see him for themselves. The good news is that Jesus cares about all his disciples, not just the ones who saw him face-to-face. He promises all his disciples new life. Even if we can't see Jesus, we can see the new life that he gives us!

My Lord and my God, make my faith strong so I can see for myself the joy of being your disciple. Amen.

APRIL 19

•

Judas had betrayed Jesus, but when he learned that Jesus had been sentenced to death, he was sorry for what he had done. He returned the thirty silver coins to the chief priests and leaders and said, "I have sinned by betraying a man who has never done anything wrong." "So what? That's your problem," they replied. Judas threw the money into the temple and then went out and hanged himself.

Matthew 27:3–5 CEV

Judas is usually thought of as the bad disciple. He was the one who handed Jesus over to the people who wanted to kill him. But Judas was not the only disciple who had trouble being faithful to Jesus. Peter promised to be loyal to Jesus, but he denied him three times. Matthew says that both Peter and Judas felt really sorry for what they did. But their lives didn't end up the same way. Peter spent the rest of his life telling people about God's love in Jesus. Judas killed himself.

God loves everybody, even people who make terrible mistakes and do terrible things. But sometimes people feel so bad about who they are or what they have done that they can't feel God's love. They may want to kill themselves, like Judas did. Part of our job as Christians is to find people like Judas and tell them about God's love. God's arms are long enough to embrace everyone!

God, I know that I can always come to you and ask your forgiveness, no matter what I have done. Help me to reach out to people who can't feel your love. Amen.

APRIL 20

•

When I turned to see who was speaking to me, I saw seven gold lampstands. And standing in the middle of the lampstands was the Son of Man. He was wearing a long robe with a gold sash across his chest. His head and his hair were white like wool, as white as snow. And his eyes were bright like flames of fire. His feet were as bright as bronze refined in a furnace, and his voice thundered like mighty ocean waves. He held seven stars in his right hand, and a sharp two-edged sword came from his mouth. And his face was as bright as the sun in all its brilliance.

Revelation 1:12–16 NLT

In the Book of Revelation, a man named John describes a vision he had while he was alone on an island. This vision was much like a dream, though John wasn't sleeping. In his "dream" John saw many things that we can scarcely imagine—things in the highest heavens and at the farthest ends of the earth. He describes how God will judge the world and make all things new.

You might be surprised to learn that the one John describes in this passage is Jesus. John envisions Jesus not as he was when he walked with his disciples on earth but as he is after his resurrection from death. John chooses words and pictures to show us that Jesus shares in the full glory and power of God.

The Book of Revelation is hard to understand, because, like a poet, John uses many symbols—things that stand for something else. Here John says that Jesus has a sharp sword coming out of his mouth. That's hard to imagine, isn't it? But in other parts of the Bible, a "sword with two edges" is a symbol for the word of God. John is reminding us that God's first word to us is not a book but a person—our Lord Jesus Christ.

Thank you, God, for your Living Word, Jesus Christ. Teach me to know and to listen to this Word always. Amen.

APRIL 21

•

And I saw a strong angel, who shouted with a loud voice: "Who is worthy to break the seals on this scroll and unroll it?" But no one in heaven or on earth or under the earth was able to open the scroll and read it. Then I wept because no one could be found who was worthy to open the scroll and read it. But one of the twenty-four elders said to me, "Stop weeping! Look, the Lion of the tribe of Judah, the heir to David's throne, has conquered. He is worthy to open the scroll and break its seven seals." I looked and I saw a Lamb that had been killed but was now standing between the throne and the four living beings and among the twenty-four elders.

Revelation 5:2–6a NLT

You have probably read a book or seen a movie in which a lion was king. Lions make a good symbol for kings because they are strong and powerful animals. Not many other creatures want to tangle with a lion!

The Bible also uses lions to symbolize kings. When Jacob was about to die, he described his son Judah as a "lion" and foretold that one day a descendent of Judah would be king. King David was a descendent of the lion Judah. So was Jesus. In Revelation, when John says that "the Lion of the tribe of Judah has won the battle," he is speaking of Jesus.

But before Jesus died, he wasn't ferocious like a lion or powerful like a king. That is why John also describes him as a Lamb that has been put to death. In ancient Israel, lambs were sometimes sacrificed (killed) to bring good to the people. By describing Jesus as a sacrificed lamb, John reminds us that Jesus gave his life for God's people. Our king is the Lamb of God!

Lion of the tribe of Judah, I know that you are Lord and ruler of all creation. Lamb of God, you are worthy of all honor, glory, and praise! Amen.

APRIL 22

•

People call down curses on others. They tell lies and commit murder. They steal and commit adultery. They break all of my laws. They keep on spilling the blood of others. That is why the land is drying up. All those who live in it are getting weaker and weaker. The wild animals and the birds of the air are dying. So are the fish in the ocean.

Hosea 4:2–3 NIRV

The prophet Hosea said that when people break God's laws, awful things happen. When people act in violent and selfish ways, terrible things happen to other people. And terrible things happen to the earth. Our wickedness hurts other people and hurts the rest of creation. Can you think of some ways human violence and selfishness have hurt the earth and the animals in it?

Today is Earth Day, a day to celebrate the beauty of the earth and to remind ourselves to take good care of it. Lots of people celebrate Earth Day, but Christians have special reasons for doing so. We believe that we were created to obey God and to live in love and peace with human beings and the rest of creation. We show our love for our Creator by the way we treat everything God has made.

Creator of all, thank you for the beautiful world you made. Help me to live in a way that shows love and respect for you and for your creation. Amen.

APRIL 23

•

Here are all of the words God spoke. He said, "I am the LORD your God. I brought you out of Egypt. That is the land where you were slaves. Do not put any other gods in place of me."

Exodus 20:1–3 NIRV

God spoke to Moses and gave him rules to teach to the people of Israel. The rules would help them to live right. The first set of these rules we call "the Ten Commandments." The Ten Commandments are all about how we act with God and with one another.

The first commandment reminds us of who God is. God, who is also called the LORD, brought the people out of slavery in Egypt. How would you feel if you had been a slave or a prisoner and someone set you free? You would probably want to thank that person from the bottom of your heart. God told the Israelites to show their thanksgiving by serving no other masters. "Do not put any other gods in place of me," God said.

God set our ancestors in the faith free from slavery. And God is still setting us free from sin and from our wish always to put ourselves first. God rescues us from the slavery of serving other gods. Our God is a great God who sets people free!

God, you are wonderful! You have done great things. Set us free from all the things that keep us from loving you and serving you. Amen.

APRIL 24

•

"Do not make idols that look like anything in the sky or on earth or in the ocean under the earth. Don't bow down and worship idols. I am the LORD your God, and I demand all your love. If you reject me, I will punish your families for three or four generations. But if you love me and obey my laws, I will be kind to your families for thousands of generations."

Exodus 20:4–6 CEV

Sometimes when you are trying to talk to someone about something very important, she may become distracted by the telephone, by the television, or by something else. When that happens, you may feel like shouting, "Wait—stop—pay attention to *me* instead!" You don't want half of her attention—you want all of it.

"Idols" are those people and things that distract us and keep us from giving God our full love and attention. Idols can be many things: statues made of wood or silver or stone, or sports heroes, or movie stars. They can also be things like money or clothes or drugs. God gave the second commandment, telling us not to serve idols, so that we would not worship these other people or things. God loves each of us completely and expects our fullest love and honor in return.

God, keep us from idols. Help us to remember that you are the only one whom we should worship. Thank you for your steadfast love to us. Amen.

APRIL 25

•

"Do not misuse the name of the LORD your God. The LORD will find guilty anyone who misuses his name."

Exodus 20:7 NIRV

How would you feel if you found out someone was being nice to you only because he wanted to get something from you? Maybe he is friendly because he wants you to show him the answers to your homework. Or maybe he pays you compliments because you have something nice that he wants you to give to him. He doesn't care about you as a person; he only wants what you have. He is "using" you. Or, we could say that he is "misusing" you (using you in a bad way).

Sometimes people misuse God's name. They might tell a person that God will be angry with him if he doesn't do what they want. Or they might say a swear word that uses God's name. Or they might talk very loudly about how much they love God, just so that others will think well of them. When people act in these ways, they are showing that they do not love and respect God. Instead they try to control God, by using God's name to get what they want.

The third commandment God gave to Israel was not to misuse God's name. God gives us our life and all that we have and loves us completely. God wants our love and honor in return!

God, thank you for loving and caring for us because of who we are. Teach us to honor you and never to misuse your name. Amen.

APRIL 26

•

"Remember that the Sabbath Day belongs to me. You have six days when you can do your work, but the seventh day of each week belongs to me, your God. No one is to work on that day—not you, your children, your slaves, your animals, or the foreigners who live in your towns. In six days I made the sky, the earth, the oceans, and everything in them, but on the seventh day I rested. That's why I made the Sabbath a special day that belongs to me."

Exodus 20:8–11 CEV

Everyone wants you to work hard. Your parents and teachers want you to work hard at your schoolwork and other lessons. If you're on a sports team, your coach wants you to "work out." When you are a grown-up, your boss may be the one telling you to work, work, work at your job. And if you are lucky enough to find a job that you love, you may work very hard not because someone tells you to but because you want to!

Hard work is good for us, but work isn't all there is to life. We also need rest. In the fourth commandment, God set the seventh day apart from all the others and made it special. It is a time for us to take the rest we need. But when we "keep the Sabbath" we don't just sleep, or watch TV, or play computer games. Keeping the Sabbath means taking a day each week—or moments in each day—to stop doing all the things that usually keep us busy. Keeping the Sabbath means being still before God. Keeping the Sabbath means opening our minds and hearts to hear God's voice.

God, thank you for giving us minds and bodies that can work hard. But thank you also for calling us to times of rest. Help us to find our rest in you. Amen.

APRIL 27

•

"Honor your father and mother. Then you will live a long time in the land the Lord your God is giving you."

Exodus 20:12 NIrV

The first four commandments teach us how to love and honor God. But God wants us to love and honor other humans too. The rest of the Ten Commandments teach us the best ways to do that. Treating one another in these ways helps us to live together in peaceful community.

When you were a small child, did you think that your mom or dad knew everything? Perhaps you believed everything that he or she said. But now that you are older, you know that your parents make mistakes, just like everybody else. Maybe they even make a lot of mistakes. Whether they make few mistakes or many, God wants you to honor or respect them. That is the fifth commandment.

What does it mean to "honor" or "respect" your father and mother? Often it will mean that you should obey them. Always it means that you should listen to what they say and try to learn from them how to be the best person you can be. It means that you should help them when you can. There may even come a time when you can honor them by teaching them what *you* know!

God, thank you for the gift of life and for our parents who brought us into this world and care for us. Help us to honor them our whole life long. Amen.

APRIL 28

•

"Do not murder."

Exodus 20:13 CEV

Have you ever seen a priceless treasure? A priceless treasure is an object that is very, very valuable. It is so valuable that no price can be put on it. No amount of money would be enough to replace it. Usually when we speak of priceless treasures we mean things in museums—famous jewels, famous paintings, or things that are very old and rare.

But none of these things is as valuable to God as human life. In God's eyes, humans are the "priceless treasures." That may seem hard to believe, because many people in our world act in ways that hurt others' bodies or damage their spirits. Some movies, TV shows, and computer games give us the message that life is cheap. But to God each person is priceless. Each person is one-of-a-kind. No one can be replaced. That is why God gave the sixth commandment, telling us that we should not murder. To murder someone is to act as though his or her life doesn't matter. But it matters to God, and it should matter to us!

God, your love is so amazing. You know each one of us by name, and you care about our lives. Help us also to respect human life. Keep us from acting in ways that hurt or kill. Amen.

APRIL 29

•

"Do not commit adultery."

Exodus 20:14 NIRV

Have you ever been to a wedding? There are many different types of wedding ceremonies. Some take place in churches, some in synagogues, some in courtrooms, some in gardens, some in still other kinds of places. At a Christian wedding, the people who are being married stand before a minister and say their vows. A vow is an especially important kind of promise—a promise made to another person in the presence of God.

People who are marrying vow to trust one another, to care for one another, and to be faithful to one another. The seventh commandment, not to commit adultery, speaks of such faithfulness between married people. Married people can express their love for one another in many of the same ways that we all use. For example, they can help each other with work, listen well when the other speaks, and try to do nice things for each other. But there are certain bodily expressions of love that married people should save only for each other. When married people are faithful to one another and do not commit adultery, the love and trust between them can blossom and grow. That is the way God wants it to be.

God, thank you for creating our world in love and for helping us to love one another. Thank you for the special love that married people share. Whether I marry one day or not, help me to know what it means to be faithful and true. Amen.

APRIL 30

"Do not steal."

Exodus 20:15 CEV

Did you ever have anything stolen from you? Maybe it was money, a toy, a skateboard, or a bike. If this has happened to you, then you know how bad such an experience makes you feel. When someone steals from you, you may feel sad because you have lost something you cared about. You may feel angry because the thief acted as though your feelings didn't matter at all.

There are different ways to steal. Taking something that belongs to someone else or something that you haven't paid for is one way. But if you sneak into a movie or an amusement park without paying, that is stealing too. It is also stealing if you find something nice and keep it when you could have found the owner. Can you think of still other ways that people steal?

Whenever we steal—even if we only take something small—we are acting as though our own wishes are the only ones that matter, and as though other people are less important than we are. But God cares for all people and wants us to respect others and their property. That is why God gave the eighth commandment, instructing us not to steal.

God, forgive us for times when we act as if our wishes are the only ones that matter. Keep us from stealing. Amen.

MAY 1

•

"Do not give false witness against your neighbor."

Exodus 20:16 NIRV

Who gets hurt when a person lies?

The liar gets hurt. Often he has to tell still more lies in order to cover up the first one. He loses respect for himself and finds it harder and harder to tell the truth. And if people find out that he is lying, they will think badly of him and may not believe him even when he does tell the truth. He will lose their trust (think of the story of the boy who cried "wolf").

But other people get hurt by lying as well. That is why God gave the ninth commandment, telling us not to tell lies about other people. Why would someone say something untruthful about another person? Maybe she doesn't want to be blamed for something so she says that another person did it. Or maybe she puts the blame on someone just because she doesn't like him. But God wants us to care about other people's feelings as much as we care about our own.

At times it can be hard to tell the truth. The truth can hurt. But lies hurt even more.

God, please forgive us for the times when we have lied. Help us to respect ourselves and to care about others. Give us courage always to tell the truth. Amen.

MAY 2

•

"Do not long for anything that belongs to your neighbor. Do not long for your neighbor's house, wife, male or female servant, ox or donkey."

Exodus 20:17 NIRV

What happens when a garden goes untended? Weeds begin to grow. Soon they choke out the good plants by using up all the available space and air and water.

Our desires can be a little like weeds. When the wishes are small they don't matter too much. But desires can quickly grow from small wishes to great big ones that do not leave room or time for God or anything else. And what if we want something that belongs to another person? We may be tempted to treat that person badly in order to get what belongs to her.

The tenth commandment tells us not to long for things that belong to others. God doesn't want our lives to be taken over by desires for things, the way a garden is taken over by weeds. Instead, God wants our lives to be filled with other kinds of wants. For example, it is good to want to help your neighbor and to share the love of God with her. That kind of desire is not a weed but a beautiful plant that bears delicious fruit for all to eat!

God, forgive us for times when we let our desire for things take over our hearts and minds. Fill us instead with a longing to know you and to share your love with others. Amen.

MAY 3

•

The people trembled with fear when they heard the thunder and the trumpet and saw the lightning and the smoke coming from the mountain. They stood a long way off and said to Moses, "If you speak to us, we will listen. But don't let God speak to us, or we will die!" "Don't be afraid!" Moses replied. "God has come only to test you, so that by obeying him you won't sin." But when Moses went near the thick cloud where God was, the people stayed a long way off.

Exodus 20:18–21 CEV

What do you fear? Getting in trouble when you do something wrong? Getting hurt? Losing something or someone you love?

Sometimes the Bible tells of people fearing *God.* The people of Israel feared God when God gave them the Ten Commandments. They saw lightning and smoke and heard thunder and the sound of a trumpet—all signs that God was present there. But it wasn't the thunder and lightning that caused their fear. They were afraid because they understood the greatness of God. They felt small and helpless and sinful compared to God, who is so much greater than they could imagine.

The people were right: God *is* much greater and much more holy than we can ever imagine. But as Moses said to them, we don't need to be afraid. We can rely on God's love and goodness. We can trust that no matter what happens to us, God will be with us and care for us.

God, you are so great! When I think about your holiness and power, I feel very small. But I know that each person matters to you. Thank you for your never-ending love and care. Amen.

MAY 4

•

Our LORD, by your wisdom
you made so many things;
the whole earth is covered
with your living creatures.
But what about the ocean
so big and wide?
It is alive with creatures,
large and small.

Psalm 104:24–25 CEV

Do you have any favorite animals? Do you most like to see and learn about the massive and powerful creatures—the tigers, the hippos, and the elephants? Or do you prefer small animals—the colorful dart frogs, the flying squirrels, and the little meerkats (to name just a few)? Maybe your favorite animal isn't living in the forest, the desert, or the zoo but in your home as your pet!

The psalmist who wrote the passage above is amazed by the care with which God created the world. The land and the sea are alive with animals that God has made, and God planned how each one would live its life—what it would eat, where it would live, and how it would behave. We humans are animals too, and we are special to God. But God loves *all* the creatures on the earth.

Creator God, thank you for making so many animals to live in our world. Thank you for what they teach us about your care for the earth. Help me also to take care of your creation. Amen.

MAY 5

•

In the past, God spoke to our people through the prophets. He spoke at many times. He spoke in different ways. But in these last days, he has spoken to us through his Son.

Hebrews 1:1–2a NIRV

God has many ways of speaking to us. God can speak to us through beautiful music or a terrible thunderstorm or a newborn puppy. Everything in the creation can speak to us about God's love and power.

Often God speaks to us through other people. People who are given a message to speak from God are called prophets. The Bible tells us about many prophets, like Amos, Isaiah, Huldah, and Daniel. When we read the Scripture, these prophets still speak God's word to us.

There have been true prophets of God in every time. God is even speaking through people who are alive today. But Christians believe that the best prophet ever is Jesus Christ, the Son of God. Only Christ is "the exact likeness of God's being" (Heb. 1:3 NIRV). So we can be sure that God is speaking to us through Jesus Christ.

God, thank you for speaking to us through the prophets and especially through Jesus Christ. Help us to hear and follow your word. Amen.

MAY 6

•

The Son is the gleaming brightness of God's glory. He is the exact likeness of God's being. He uses his powerful word to hold all things together. He provided the way for people to be made pure from sin. Then he sat down at the right hand of the King, the Majesty in heaven.

Hebrews 1:3 NIRV

How many times have you had your picture taken? Quite a few? Some of the pictures were probably good, and some were probably bad—maybe your hair was sticking up or your eyes were half-closed.

The author of Hebrews says that we have a picture of God, and it is *perfect.* But it isn't a photograph you can hold in your hands—it is a person, Jesus Christ. When we look at the way Jesus lived and died, we see God's love, God's power, God's care for the weak and suffering, and God's desire that we live in faith and trust. When we look at how Jesus rose from the dead, we see God's glory and honor.

We cannot look at God's face. But we can learn about Jesus, the perfect picture of God, and know everything we need to know.

God, thank you for sending Jesus to show us what you are like. Help me to learn all about him so that I can know you better and love you more. Amen.

MAY 7

Jesus understands every weakness of ours, because he was tempted in every way that we are. But he did not sin! So whenever we are in need, we should come bravely before the throne of our merciful God. There we will be treated with undeserved kindness, and we will find help.

Hebrews 4:15–16 CEV

Some things you know by experience. If you have had the chicken pox, you know how itchy they are. If you have skinned your knee, you know how much it stings. If people have made fun of you, you know how that hurts your feelings. So when you see others having the same experience, you understand how they feel.

Jesus understands how we feel. He knows what it is like to be thirsty and hungry. He knows what it is like to be tempted to do the wrong thing. He knows what it is like to be made fun of. He knows what it is like to be in pain. He knows what it is like to die.

So whenever we are in need, we can come to Jesus in prayer. We don't have to be embarrassed or afraid. We know he will understand us and help us.

Jesus, it comforts us to know that you understand how we feel. Thank you for your mercy and kindness. Amen.

MAY 8

•

People who live on milk are like babies who don't really know what is right. Solid food is for mature people who have been trained to know right from wrong.

Hebrews 5:13–14 CEV

When you were a little baby, you lived on milk. It gave you everything you needed to be strong and healthy. Milk was also the only food that your body was ready for. As you grew older, you became ready for other foods: cereal, fruit, and vegetables. Now, after years of practice, you eat a lot of different foods. When you are a grown-up, you will probably enjoy even more foods than you do now.

In this Bible passage, the writer compares babies who drink only milk to people who are just getting started learning how God wants them to live. And just as babies grow up and start eating solid food, Christians also get better at knowing and doing what is good.

Learning how to tell right from wrong is something all Christians are still working on. You may even be better at it than some grown-ups! But just as you wouldn't want to spend your whole life drinking milk, you should not be satisfied with "baby faith." Let your faith grow along with the rest of you!

Send your Holy Spirit, God, to show me how to live. Help me practice doing what is good so that I may grow strong and wise in my faith. Amen.

MAY 9

•

Jesus is the high priest we need. He is holy and innocent and faultless, and not at all like us sinners. Jesus is honored above all beings in heaven, and he is better than any other high priest. Jesus doesn't need to offer sacrifices each day for his own sins and then for the sins of the people. He offered a sacrifice once for all, when he gave himself.

Hebrews 7:26–27 CEV

A sacrifice is a costly gift made to show honor and respect to someone. In ancient Israel, the high priests offered sacrifices to God in the great temple in Jerusalem as a way of showing that the people were sorry for their sins. The sacrifices didn't change God from being mad to being loving. Instead, the sacrifices were the way the Israelites showed their love for God and asked God's forgiveness.

The high priests of Israel were not perfect, just as priests and ministers today are not perfect. That is why they would first offer sacrifices for their own sins and then for the sins of the people. The sacrifices were gifts of things taken from God's good creation such as animals, grain, and oil.

The Bible compares Jesus to many things—a shepherd, a king, a mother hen—but the Book of Hebrews compares him to a high priest. Jesus is better than any other priest or minister. He is holy and innocent and faultless, so he doesn't need to ask God for forgiveness for his own sins. And instead of sacrificing a lamb from the creation, he sacrificed himself. That is why Jesus is sometimes called the Lamb of God.

Lamb of God, you take away the sins of the world. Have mercy on us. Amen.

MAY 10

•

Some people have gotten out of the habit of meeting for worship, but we must not do that. We should keep on encouraging each other, especially since you know that the day of the Lord's coming is getting closer.

Hebrews 10:25 CEV

When many black people in the United States were slaves, some of them were not allowed to worship God as they wished. Some would meet in secret to pray and sing. Others were allowed to go to church, but they had to sit upstairs in the balcony. If there were no stairs, the slaves had to climb an outside rope or a ladder to get up there!

Why, you might ask, would they or anyone else go to so much trouble to worship God? Because in worship, we feel the presence and the love of God, which give us hope and strength. In worship we say "thanks" to God for the life and the love that God gives us. In worship we learn how to be a follower of Jesus Christ.

Are you in the "good habit" of worshipping God? There are many places and ways to worship, but church is one of the best. If you don't go to church, talk to your mom or dad about it. Chances are, there is a church nearby whose members would love to have you.

God, help me form the worship habit! Lead me to others who love you and who can teach me well. Show me how to encourage others. Amen.

MAY 11

•

No training seems pleasant at the time. In fact, it seems painful. But later on it produces a harvest of godliness and peace. It does that for those who have been trained by it. So lift your sagging arms. Strengthen your weak knees. "Make level paths for your feet to walk on." Then those who have trouble walking won't be disabled. Instead, they will be healed.

Hebrews 12:11–13 NIRV

Does your mom or dad ever make you work hard at something you would rather avoid? At music lessons, or math homework, or something else? Parents do this because they know that your effort will be rewarded. Work hard at your music, for example, and you will enjoy the great pleasure of making music all your life.

Most of us—kids and grown-ups too—would rather avoid pain and sorrow. But those things are part of life, and most of us go through them at some time. It is easy to let the sad or painful times in our lives make us angry and bitter. It is much harder to look at them as lessons with something to teach us. But the author of Hebrews tells us that, if we try to learn from our suffering, our hard work will be rewarded.

God, when suffering comes to me, give me strength to stay on your path. Keep me from anger; instead, heal my sorrow and give me peace. Amen.

MAY 12

•

Remember the Lord's people who are in jail and be concerned for them. Don't forget those who are suffering, but imagine that you are there with them.

Hebrews 13:3 CEV

Being in jail is terrible. If you were in jail, you would hardly ever get to see your friends and family. You couldn't take a bike ride or go on a trip. Can you name five other things you love to do that would be impossible if you were in jail?

Many people are in jail because they did something wrong. Others were put in jail unfairly. But everyone in jail is suffering and needs our prayers. Many people who are in jail in our country are Christians. They trust in Jesus Christ just like we do, and so we have a special reason to be concerned for them.

It is hard to remember people in jail, because we can't see them. They don't live in our neighborhood or go to our church. We don't see them at the store or at the movies. But people we can't see are often the ones who need our prayers the most.

God, we know that you see and care for everyone in jail. Help us to remember them and to pray for them. Amen.

MAY 13

•

The day of Pentecost came. The believers all gathered in one place. Suddenly a sound came from heaven. It was like a strong wind blowing. It filled the whole house where they were sitting. They saw something that looked like tongues of fire. The flames separated and settled on each of them. All of them were filled with the Holy Spirit. They began to speak in languages they had not known before. The Spirit gave them the ability to do this.

Acts 2:1–4 NIRV

How do you celebrate your birthday? With a cake and candles? With presents and games? You celebrate that you are now a year older. But you also celebrate the day when you were first born.

Pentecost is like a birthday party for the church. We celebrate it every year and remember the way the church was born by the power of the Spirit. It happened in Jerusalem, and it was a very big party!

You probably invite friends your own age to your birthday party. But at Pentecost, just as the prophet Joel promised, God's Spirit was poured out on everyone, young and old. You probably invite friends who speak your own language. But at Pentecost the Spirit was poured out on people from every nation. That means there is room for every kind of person and every kind of language in the church. When the church has a birthday, everyone is invited!

God, thank you for the birthday of the church. Thank you that the church has room for a person like me. Fill me with the Holy Spirit! In Christ's name, Amen.

MAY 14

•

All the believers were together. They shared everything they had. They sold what they owned. They gave each other everything they needed. Every day they met together in the temple courtyard. In their homes they broke bread and ate together. Their hearts were glad and honest and true.

Acts 2:44–46 NIRV

In our society, private property is very important. One of the first sentences we learn to say is, "That's mine." We write our names on our books and sports gear to show that they belong only to us. But the Christians in the Book of Acts didn't behave this way. They shared everything they had. They made sure that everyone had what they needed. If you have ever been to a potluck meal, you know a little about this kind of sharing. At a potluck, everyone brings one dish and puts it on a big table to share with others. That way everyone gets lots of delicious food to eat.

The Christians in Acts shared this way because they knew that everything they had was a gift from God. They could be generous to others, because they had seen how generous God was to them. You can try to live that way too. There may be some things it is better not to share—your toothbrush, for example! But sharing your money, belongings, and time with others is a way of showing your love for God. Others will see your generosity and want to love God too.

Generous God, everything I have is a gift from you. Help me not to worry about my belongings and to be always ready to share with people who are in need. Amen.

MAY 15

•

In Joppa there was a follower named Tabitha. Her Greek name was Dorcas, which means "deer." She was always doing good things for people and had given much to the poor. But she got sick and died, and her body was washed and placed in an upstairs room. Joppa wasn't far from Lydda, and the followers heard that Peter was there. They sent two men to say to him, "Please come with us as quickly as you can!" Right away, Peter went with them. The men took Peter upstairs into the room. Many widows were there crying. They showed him the coats and clothes that Dorcas had made while she was still alive. After Peter had sent everyone out of the room, he knelt down and prayed. Then he turned to the body of Dorcas and said, "Tabitha, get up!" The woman opened her eyes, and when she saw Peter, she sat up. He took her by the hand and helped her to her feet. Peter called in the widows and the other followers and showed them that Dorcas had been raised from death. Everyone in Joppa heard what had happened, and many of them put their faith in the Lord.

Acts 9:36–42 CEV

Peter didn't heal Tabitha all by himself. He prayed to God, because he knew that God is the source of healing power. When Tabitha's friends and others living in Joppa found out that she was alive and well, they didn't put their faith in Peter. They put their faith in God.

We also should pray to God for healing. Sometimes God uses nurses and doctors and medicines to heal people. Sometimes people we pray for recover in a surprising way that even doctors don't understand. But whenever someone is healed, no matter how it happens, Christians give thanks to God.

Merciful God, thank you for answering our prayers for healing. Help us to trust in you, both in life and in death. Amen.

MAY 16

•

Peter had a vision. He saw heaven open up. There he saw something that looked like a large sheet. It was being let down to earth by its four corners. It had all kinds of four-footed animals in it. It also had reptiles of the earth and birds of the air. Then a voice told him, "Get up, Peter. Kill and eat." "No, Lord! I will not!" Peter replied. "I have never eaten anything that is not pure and 'clean.'" The voice spoke to him a second time. "Do not say anything is not pure that God has made 'clean,'" it said.

Acts 10:10b–15 NIrV

Imagine that you had a vision in which God commanded you to use God's name as a curse word. Wouldn't you be shocked? Most Christians are taught to use God's name with care and respect. Misusing God's name would be an offense to God and to other believers.

Peter's vision shocked him too. Peter was a Jew, and Jews showed their respect for God by not eating certain animals that the law said were "unclean." Jews also considered people who ate these animals unclean. Peter had always been faithful to the Jewish laws about unclean food. But God used this vision to change Peter's mind about which *people* were unclean.

Who are the people you consider unclean? Drug addicts? People with AIDS? People in prison? Peter's vision made him realize that God pours out the Holy Spirit on all kinds of people and makes them clean.

Generous God, all of us are unclean until your Spirit makes us pure. Don't let our ideas about other people keep us from seeing your grace to them. Amen.

MAY 17

•

He knocked at the door in the gate, and a servant girl named Rhoda came to open it. When she recognized Peter's voice, she was so overjoyed that, instead of opening the door, she ran back inside and told everyone, "Peter is standing at the door!" "You're out of your mind," they said. When she insisted, they decided, "It must be his angel." Meanwhile, Peter continued knocking. When they finally went out and opened the door, they were amazed. He motioned for them to quiet down and told them what had happened and how the Lord had led him out of jail.

Acts 12:13–17a NLT

You don't expect people who are in prison to knock at your door. Peter was supposed to be in prison, so when Rhoda heard his voice she was so surprised and excited she ran back without letting him in! When she told the others the good news, they didn't believe her and said she was crazy. But Rhoda was right: God had done an amazing thing and brought Peter out of prison.

You don't expect people who have died to rise again from the dead. So when Jesus appeared to Mary Magdalene, Joanna, Mary the mother of James, and some other women after his death, they were very excited too. When the women told the apostles the good news, the apostles didn't believe them and said the women were talking nonsense. But the women were right: God had done an amazing thing and raised Jesus from the dead.

God, thank you for Rhoda, Mary Magdalene, Joanna, Mary the mother of James, and all the other women who have told the truth about the amazing things you have done. Help us listen to them. Amen.

MAY 18

•

They had talked it over for a long time, when Peter got up and said: "My friends, you know that God decided long ago to let me be the one from your group to preach the good news to the Gentiles. God did this so that they would hear and obey him. He knows what is in everyone's heart. And he showed that he had chosen the Gentiles, when he gave them the Holy Spirit, just as he had given his Spirit to us. God treated them in the same way that he treated us. They put their faith in him, and he made their hearts pure. "Now why are you trying to make God angry by placing a heavy burden on these followers? This burden was too heavy for us or our ancestors. But our Lord Jesus was kind to us, and we are saved by faith in him, just as the Gentiles are."

Acts 15:7–11 CEV

Jesus was a Jew, and all his disciples were Jews. One of the biggest decisions faced by the followers of Jesus had to do with Gentiles—that is, people who were not Jews. Would Gentiles have to become Jews in order to follow Jesus? Would they have to obey all the laws God had given to Israel? Some Jewish followers of Jesus thought so.

But Peter disagreed. He said that God had given the Holy Spirit to the Gentiles. They too had put their faith in Jesus Christ. They didn't have to follow all the laws of Israel to join their Jewish brothers and sisters in trusting Jesus.

Even today, other followers of Jesus may have very different rules for how to dress and how to act in church than you do. They may be surprised at some of your rules! But you can still join them in trusting Jesus.

God of Israel, thank you for sending the Holy Spirit to the Gentiles so they too can hear and obey you. Amen.

•

About midnight Paul and Silas were praying. They were also singing hymns to God. The other prisoners were listening to them. Suddenly there was a powerful earthquake. It shook the prison from top to bottom. All at once the prison doors flew open. Everybody's chains came loose. . . . The jailer called out for some lights. He rushed in, shaking with fear. He fell down in front of Paul and Silas. Then he brought them out. He asked, "Sirs, what must I do to be saved?" They replied, "Believe in the Lord Jesus. Then you and your family will be saved." They spoke the word of the Lord to him. They also spoke to all the others in his house. At that hour of the night, the jailer took Paul and Silas and washed their wounds. Right away he and his whole family were baptized. The jailer brought them into his house. He set a meal in front of them. He and his whole family were filled with joy. They had become believers in God.

Acts 16:25–26, 29–34 NIRV

Have you ever gone to Sunday school at midnight? Have you ever had a feast at one o'clock in the morning? The jailer and his family did.

Paul and Silas had been whipped and thrown in prison for helping a slave woman. At midnight they were worshipping God when an earthquake freed them from prison. The jailer knew that only the power of God could have done this. He woke up his family. They listened as Paul and Silas told them about Jesus Christ, and then they were baptized. After that they invited Paul and Silas to eat with them. Sleep was less important than the joy of believing in Jesus Christ!

God, the joy of believing in Jesus Christ isn't just for Sunday morning. Let it shake up our lives night and day! In Christ's name, Amen.

MAY 20

•

In him we live and move and have our being.

Acts 17:28a NRSV

You were once in your mother's womb. There you lived for several months: sleeping, moving, digesting, growing. You were really dependent on her: Not only did she give you a place to live, she did all your breathing and eating for you! You had your being in your mother until it was time for you to be born.

Acts 17 says that we all live and move and have our being in God. We are dependent on God for giving us a place to live on earth, for providing us with food to eat and air to breathe. Without God, we wouldn't exist at all!

You don't depend on your mother as much now as you did when you were in her womb. As you get older, you may depend on her less and less. When your mother gets very old, she will probably depend on you.

With God, it's different. You will never stop depending on God. You will always live and move and have your being in God. The good news is that when you search for God, you will discover that God is always near.

Dear God, we know that we depend on you for everything. Thank you for giving us life and breath. Thank you for caring for us as a mother cares for her children. Amen.

MAY 21

•

"I have gone from place to place, preaching to you about God's kingdom, but now I know that none of you will ever see me again. . . . I now place you in God's care. Remember the message about his great kindness! This message can help you and give you what belongs to you as God's people." . . . After Paul had finished speaking, he knelt down with all of them and prayed. Everyone cried and hugged and kissed him. They were especially sad because Paul had told them, "You will never see me again." Then they went with him to the ship.

Acts 20:25, 32, 36–38 CEV

When you were a baby, you learned to wave bye, bye. And you have been saying good-bye to people ever since.

When you leave to go to school in the morning, it is not hard to say good-bye to your mom or dad, because you know you will see them again at the end of the day. But what about when someone you love moves far away, or dies? At those times, saying good-bye can be very, very hard. You may feel that your heart is breaking. Some friends of Paul felt that way when he had to say good-bye.

Paul told his friends that after he left they should remember all the things he had done with them and the message he had taught. Remembering those things would help them to live well after he was gone. "Remembering" will help you too when you have to say good-bye to someone you love. By remembering, you honor that person and you help yourself to live well.

God, keep me always in your care. When it hurts so much to say good-bye to someone, help me to keep the love and the memories of them in my heart. Comfort me in my sadness and help me to live well. Amen.

MAY 22

•

"About noon, King Agrippa, I was on the road. I saw a light coming from heaven. It was brighter than the sun. It was shining around me and my companions. We all fell to the ground. I heard a voice speak to me in the Aramaic language. 'Saul! Saul!' it said. 'Why are you opposing me? It is hard for you to go against what you know is right.' Then I asked, 'Who are you, Lord?' 'I am Jesus,' the Lord replied. 'I am the one you are opposing. Now get up. Stand on your feet. I have appeared to you to appoint you to serve me and be my witness. You will tell others that you have seen me today.'"

Acts 26:13–16b NIRV

Christians know the apostle Paul as someone who spread the good news of Jesus Christ to people living all around the Mediterranean Sea. Some of his letters to Christians in different cities became books of the New Testament. (To see some examples, look in your Bible for Paul's letter to the Romans and his two letters to the Corinthians.)

But Paul, also known by his Jewish name, Saul, didn't start out as a witness to Jesus Christ. In fact, he persecuted Christians, dragging them to prison and even watching them be killed. But one day, when Paul was on his way to the city of Damascus, God turned his whole life around. Paul was blinded by a bright light and heard the voice of Jesus telling him that God had chosen him to spread the Christian gospel. Paul's life was completely different after that.

People come to know Jesus Christ in many different ways. Some people come to know him very suddenly, the way Paul did. Other people are born and raised in the church. To them it may seem as if they have always known Jesus Christ. But whether we have known him a short time or all our lives, Jesus wants us to tell others about him.

Jesus, speak to me, and give me the courage to speak about you to others. Amen.

MAY 23

•

It was the first year of the rule of Cyrus. He was king of Persia. The LORD stirred him up to send a message all through his kingdom. It happened so that what the LORD had spoken through Jeremiah would come true. The message was written down. It said, "Cyrus, the king of Persia, says, 'The LORD is the God of heaven. He has given me all of the kingdoms on earth. He has appointed me to build a temple for him at Jerusalem in Judah. Any one of his people among you can go up to Jerusalem. And may your God be with you. You can build the LORD's temple. He is the God of Israel. He is the God who is in Jerusalem.'"

Ezra 1:1–3 NIRV

Cooks stir soups and sauces to get all the ingredients moving. God stirs up people to get them moving! God stirred up Cyrus to help the people of Israel rebuild the temple and start worshipping the Lord in Jerusalem again. Cyrus was the king of Persia. He was an outsider—he did not belong to the people of Israel. But Cyrus was kinder and more faithful than many of the kings of Israel.

Be on the lookout for people who are doing God's work in the world. God stirs up all kinds of people. They may not go to church; they may not even believe in God! When you see non-Christians being kind to Christians, give thanks that God has stirred them up. When you see people helping the poor, cleaning up the earth, or working for justice, praise God for them.

Whenever you see God's will being done, give thanks to God. It doesn't matter where it happens or who is doing it. God is busy stirring up goodness all over the world!

You've got the whole world in your hands, Lord. We praise you that you are at work in many places and in many people. Stir us up to do your will in the world. Amen.

MAY 24

•

And the LORD said, "Name him Lo-ammi—'Not my people'—for Israel is not my people, and I am not their God. Yet the time will come when Israel will prosper and become a great nation. In that day its people will be like the sands of the seashore—too many to count! Then, at the place where they were told, 'You are not my people,' it will be said, 'You are children of the living God.' "

Hosea 1:9–10 NLT

Choosing a name for a new baby is an important decision. You live with your parents' decision your whole life! Sometimes a baby is named after his father or another relative. Sometimes a baby is named after a quality her parents hope she will have: Grace, or Joy, for example. Do you know how you got your name?

The prophet Hosea's son got a terrible name. In Hebrew, his name means, "Not my people." God's greatest promise to Israel was "You will be my people and I will be your God." But Hosea said that Israel had broken God's laws and worshipped other gods. Hosea's son was a living reminder that Israel was acting as though they were "not God's people."

But God's love and faithfulness to Israel were stronger than Israel's sin. Hosea said that the people of Israel could look forward to a day when God would bless them and they would again be called "children of the living God."

Living God, whatever names our parents gave each of us, help us remember that our real name is "child of God." When we act as if we are not your people, call us back and show us again how to live in love and faithfulness to you. Amen.

MAY 25

•

"Listen to me, you priests! Pay attention, people of Israel! Listen, you members of the royal family! Here is my decision against you. You have been like a trap at Mizpah. You have been like a net spread out on Mount Tabor. You refuse to obey me. You offer sacrifices to other gods. So I will punish all of you."

Hosea 5:1–2 NIRV

Some people have more authority than others. A teacher has authority to make decisions for the whole class. A principal has authority to make decisions for the whole school. A king or queen or president has authority to make decisions for the whole country.

People with authority should act honestly and wisely. If a student in a classroom misbehaves, that is a problem. But if a teacher misbehaves, that is a really big problem, because she sets an example for the whole class!

Hosea said that those with the most authority in Israel—priests and members of the royal family—had been behaving terribly. They had not obeyed God, and the people of Israel had followed their leaders' bad example by disobeying God too.

Ruler of the universe, I know that sometimes people with authority are not good examples to follow. Help me respect your authority above all, and keep me from following bad examples. When I have authority, show me how to use it well. Amen.

MAY 26

•

Israel, the time has come. You will get what you deserve, and you will know it. "Prophets are fools," you say. "And God's messengers are crazy." Your terrible guilt has filled you with hatred.

Hosea 9:7 CEV

It is fun to bring others good news: "You won first place!" "Your new baby sister is strong and healthy!" It is much harder to bring bad news: "You failed your math test again." "Your dad has cancer." People don't like to hear bad news. Sometimes they refuse to believe it. Other times they get angry at the person who brings it.

Being a prophet is a hard job, because a prophet often has bad news to bring: "What you are doing is wrong." "Terrible things are going to happen." This is what Hosea told Israel. But they didn't want to believe him. They said everything was fine and that Hosea was crazy. But Hosea wasn't crazy; he was telling a truth that Israel didn't want to hear.

God, thank you for sending us prophets who dare to speak the truth. When someone has bad news to tell me, help me listen without getting angry. Help me hear the truth even when it sounds crazy. Amen.

MAY 27

•

"When Israel was a child, I loved him as a son, and I called my son out of Egypt. But the more I called to him, the more he rebelled, offering sacrifices to the images of Baal and burning incense to idols. It was I who taught Israel how to walk, leading him along by the hand. But he doesn't know or even care that it was I who took care of him."

Hosea 11:1–3 NLT

You probably don't remember very much about when you were a baby and a toddler. But you wouldn't be here today without the love and care you received then. At first, you were fed and carried and changed many times every day and every night. Later, someone taught you to walk and picked you up when you fell down.

When Hosea tried to explain how much God loved the people of Israel, he compared God's love to a mother's or father's love for a small child. God fed and carried Israel and taught Israel to walk.

But just as children sometimes grow up to be ungrateful and rebellious, so did Israel. The more God called to them, the more they ran away. Just as a mother would suffer if her children acted this way, so God suffered when Israel was unfaithful. God suffered because of this great love for Israel.

God, you are like a loving parent. Thank you for your tender care for us. You are the one who has loved us from the beginning. Help us always to trust in you. Amen.

MAY 28

•

Now they sin more and more. They use their silver to make statues of gods for themselves. The statues come from their own clever ideas. Skilled workers make all of them. The people pray to those gods. They offer human sacrifices to them. They kiss the gods that look like calves.

Hosea 13:2 NIrV

Most of the Book of Hosea is about the problem of idolatry. God's people were not being faithful to the true God. Instead they were serving false gods.

This wasn't just a problem for God's people a long time ago. Idolatry is still a problem for the people of God today. The false gods we worship may not be made of metal or stone. We may not actually bow down before them. But anytime we trust other things or other people more than God, we are showing idolatry.

What are some things that could become false gods for you? Money, good looks, music, being great at sports? Each of these is a good thing, as long as it doesn't become the most important thing in your life. It is good to love your family, to love your country, to love your friends. But even they can become idols. When you read God's message to Israel in Hosea's time, listen for what it may say to you now.

True and loving God, thank you for all the good things you have given me. But keep me from putting all my trust in them. Fill me with faithfulness and love, so that I will recognize you alone as God. Amen.

MAY 29

•

At that time Jesus came from Nazareth in Galilee. John baptized him in the Jordan River. Jesus was coming up out of the water. Just then he saw heaven being torn open. He saw the Holy Spirit coming down on him like a dove. A voice spoke to him from heaven. It said, "You are my Son, and I love you. I am very pleased with you."

Mark 1:9–11 NIRV

Have you ever been baptized or seen someone else be baptized? In ancient times, people being baptized would dip down under the water of a stream or river. The water of baptism shows how God washes away our guilt and shame and makes us able to start life fresh and new.

When Jesus was a young man, a holy man named John the Baptist began to travel around the countryside. He told people to ask God to forgive them for turning away from God, and he baptized them. John baptized Jesus.

Today, Christians practice baptism in several different ways. In some churches, people still dip all the way down under the water, while in other churches, the minister or priest sprinkles water on the person's head. In some churches, babies and small children are baptized, but in other churches, only grown-ups are. However it's done, baptism reminds us that God chooses us and makes our hearts clean.

God, forgive me for the wrong things I have thought, said, and done. Help me to live as your child and to remember how much you love me. Amen.

MAY 30

•

At once the Holy Spirit sent Jesus out into the desert. He was in the desert 40 days. There Satan tempted him. The wild animals didn't harm Jesus. Angels took care of him.

Mark 1:12–13 NIrV

After Jesus was baptized, he felt God leading him to a lonely place. While in that lonely place he found it hard to keep on living in God's way. The Bible teaches that the devil, who is sometimes known as "Satan," tried to get Jesus to serve him instead of God. But Jesus didn't give in to the temptations. He kept on obeying and honoring God.

Who is the devil? Do you need to worry about him? These are hard questions, and grown-ups disagree about the answers. Many people believe the devil is a wicked spirit who causes pain or uses tricks and lies to turn people away from God. Other people think the devil is a symbol—a way of talking about all the things that lead us away from God.

If you trust Jesus to help you, you don't need to be afraid of the devil. That is because Jesus will help you to honor and obey God, even when temptations come. It might not be easy, but with Jesus' help you can do the right thing! Jesus is stronger than any temptation.

Jesus, sometimes it is so hard to do what is right. But I know that even when I am weak, you are strong. Help me in times of temptation. Amen.

MAY 31

•

After John was put in prison, Jesus went into Galilee. He preached God's good news. "The time has come," he said. "The kingdom of God is near. Turn away from your sins and believe the good news!"

Mark 1:14–15 NIRV

Sometimes we wait and wait for something to happen. Then, when it finally does happen, it is not what we expect. It might not be as nice as we hoped. But, sometimes, what happens is far better than we imagined!

Many people in Jesus' land were waiting for God to send a leader to rescue the people from their enemies. Many hoped for a day when people from all over the world would come to Jerusalem and bow down to worship God as ruler over all the earth. Jesus told the people that soon God would answer their hopes and prayers for a better world. He said they should get ready for that day by turning away from their old, sinful lives.

Jesus was not the kind of messenger or leader that the people were expecting. He did not look like a powerful soldier or king. He did not seem to be rich and important. And yet, God chose him to bring the most important news of all—the news that God loves us, watches over us, and lives among us!

God, sometimes you speak to me in ways that I don't expect. Give me ears to hear your good news and eyes to see you working in people around me. Amen.

JUNE 1

•

One day as Jesus was walking along the shores of the Sea of Galilee, he saw Simon and his brother, Andrew, fishing with a net, for they were commercial fishermen. Jesus called out to them, "Come, be my disciples, and I will show you how to fish for people!" And they left their nets at once and went with him. A little farther up the shore Jesus saw Zebedee's sons, James and John, in a boat mending their nets. He called them, too, and immediately they left their father, Zebedee, in the boat with the hired men and went with him.

Mark 1:16–20 NLT

Someday you will probably want and need to get a job. What kind of job would you like to have?

Simon Peter, Andrew, James, and John already had jobs. They were fishermen. But Jesus gave them new jobs: They would be his followers, called "disciples." They would "fish for people." But Jesus didn't mean that they would catch people in nets! Instead, his disciples would tell people about how God is ruler over all the earth. They would tell about how God loves us. By sharing this good news, Peter, Andrew, James, John, and all of Jesus' other disciples would help bring more people to follow Jesus.

Following Jesus is a job you can do right now. You don't have to be a grown-up, because Jesus wants children also to follow him. Jesus wants children to "fish for people" by telling them about God's love. It is the best job of all, and you can keep it your whole life long!

Jesus, thank you for offering me the job of being your disciple. Help me to follow you all my life. Show me ways to tell others about how God rules over us and loves us. Amen.

JUNE 2

•

Suddenly a man with an evil spirit in him entered the meeting place and yelled, "Jesus from Nazareth, what do you want with us? Have you come to destroy us? I know who you are! You are God's Holy One." Jesus told the evil spirit, "Be quiet and come out of the man!" The spirit shook him. Then it gave a loud shout and left. Everyone was completely surprised and kept saying to each other, "What is this? It must be some new kind of powerful teaching! Even the evil spirits obey him." News about Jesus quickly spread all over Galilee.

Mark 1:23–28 CEV

Words and deeds ought to match. If someone promises to do something for you but doesn't do it, what good is the promise? Or if you tell someone that you love her, but don't act like you love her, what good are the words? In this story, Mark tells us about a time when Jesus had been teaching some people. His words impressed them very much. But then Jesus did something to show the people that his words and deeds matched.

What did Jesus do? In his day some people were said to have evil or "unclean" spirits living in them. These spirits made them do crazy and awful things. Everyone knew that a person who could drive such spirits away must be very powerful. Jesus made an unclean spirit go away from a man. Then the people knew that Jesus' deeds were as powerful as his words.

When we meet people whose deeds match their good words, we know we can trust them. We can trust Jesus when he teaches us.

Jesus, you are the Holy One of God. Teach me, as you taught people so long ago. Help me to trust in all your words and deeds. Amen.

•

Several days later Jesus returned to Capernaum, and the news of his arrival spread quickly through the town. Soon the house where he was staying was so packed with visitors that there wasn't room for one more person, not even outside the door. And he preached the word to them. Four men arrived carrying a paralyzed man on a mat. They couldn't get to Jesus through the crowd, so they dug through the clay roof above his head. Then they lowered the sick man on his mat, right down in front of Jesus. Seeing their faith, Jesus said to the paralyzed man, "My son, your sins are forgiven."

Mark 2:1–5 NLT

Have you ever seen the movie or read the book *The Impossible Journey*? It is about two dogs and a cat who get separated from their human family. The animals set out on their own to find the family. The journey is very hard for them. But they never give up. They know where they need to go, and they will do whatever they have to do in order to get there. Finally they arrive safely. Their family is amazed at the animals' determination!

Here Mark tells us a story about five friends. One of the five cannot walk, and the other four are carrying him. They want to take him to Jesus because they are sure that Jesus can help the man to walk. The house where Jesus is speaking is so crowded that the friends can't get through, so they make a hole in the roof and let the man down through the hole. Jesus is amazed at their determination!

Luckily, you don't have to take a long trip or dig through a roof to find Jesus. He is with you right now! If you pray, he will hear you.

Jesus, thank you for being so near to me. Help me to turn to you and to trust you, in hard times and in good times too. Amen.

JUNE 4

•

Jesus saw their faith. So he said to the man, "Son, your sins are forgiven." Some teachers of the law were sitting there. They were thinking, "Why is this fellow talking like that? He's saying a very evil thing! Only God can forgive sins!" Right away Jesus knew what they were thinking. So he said to them, "Why are you thinking these things? Is it easier to say to this man, 'Your sins are forgiven'? Or to say, 'Get up, take your mat and walk'? I want you to know that the Son of Man has authority on earth to forgive sins." Then Jesus spoke to the man who could not walk. "I tell you," he said, "get up. Take your mat and go home." The man got up and took his mat. Then he walked away while everyone watched. All the people were amazed. They praised God and said, "We have never seen anything like this!"

Mark 2:5–12 NIrV

Jesus was teaching people the good news about God. God rules over the earth! And God is working to set us free! When the Hebrew people were slaves in Egypt, God led them out. Now Jesus told them God wanted to set people free from all the other things that kept them down or held them back. When the friends of the man who couldn't walk lowered him through a hole in the roof, Jesus told the man his sins were forgiven. Jesus *set him free* from his sins.

But some other teachers didn't like what Jesus said. They thought that only God can forgive people's sins. Jesus wanted the teachers to see how he had God's power to set people free. So Jesus told the man to pick up the mat he had been lying on and walk. And the man did! Everyone was amazed and praised God.

Jesus first set the man free from sin and then he set his body free too.

God, I praise you! Thank you for caring about us so much and for working to set us free. Thank you for sending Jesus to forgive our sins. Amen.

•

John's disciples and the Pharisees sometimes fasted. One day some people came to Jesus and asked, "Why do John's disciples and the Pharisees fast, but your disciples don't fast?" Jesus replied, "Do wedding guests fast while celebrating with the groom? Of course not. They can't fast while they are with the groom. But someday he will be taken away from them, and then they will fast."

Mark 2:18–20 NLT

Have you ever been to a wedding? Weddings are happy times, when two people who love each other begin a new life together. After the wedding, there is often a party. Guests have good things to eat. There is music and sometimes dancing. People take pictures to remember the special day.

Some people thought that Jesus and his disciples were enjoying themselves too much as they traveled around the countryside. They thought they should be more serious. They thought Jesus and his disciples ought to "fast" (go without eating), like some other people did. But Jesus said that his time on earth was like the party after a wedding. It was a time of joy!

Being a follower of Jesus doesn't mean you have to be serious all the time. Jesus lives with us, and there are many reasons for parties and laughter and joy. So, go ahead and laugh!

Jesus, you knew the joy of living on earth, and you want us to know it also. Thank you for all the blessings in my life. Fill me with joy! Amen.

JUNE 6

•

Jesus' mother and brothers came and stood outside. They sent someone in to get him. A crowd was sitting around Jesus. They told him, "Your mother and your brothers are outside. They are looking for you." "Who is my mother? Who are my brothers?" he asked. Then Jesus looked at the people sitting in a circle around him. He said, "Here is my mother! Here are my brothers! Anyone who does what God wants is my brother or sister or mother."

Mark 3:31–35 NIRV

Many people didn't understand Jesus. Even his own mother and brothers sometimes didn't understand him. Once when Jesus was teaching and healing people, his family tried to stop him. They worried that Jesus was crazy. When someone told Jesus that his mother and brothers were looking for him, he didn't go to them.

It seems as if Jesus was being rude to his family, doesn't it? But Jesus wanted to serve God more than anything else. He knew that God wanted him to teach and to heal. So Jesus said that the ones who were trying to stop him were not his true family. He said his true "brothers" and "sisters" and "mother" are whoever does what God wants.

Jesus wants us too to love and serve God. It is wonderful when our families help us do that. But even if they do not help, we must go on doing what God wants.

Jesus, make me want to walk in God's way. Please give me the strength and help to serve you even when those close to me do not understand. Amen.

JUNE 7

•

And the LORD said to Moses, "Come up to me on the mountain. Stay there while I give you the tablets of stone that I have inscribed with my instructions and commands. Then you will teach the people from them." Then Moses went up the mountain, and the cloud covered it. And the glorious presence of the LORD rested upon Mount Sinai, and the cloud covered it for six days. On the seventh day the LORD called to Moses from the cloud. The Israelites at the foot of the mountain saw an awesome sight. The awesome glory of the LORD on the mountaintop looked like a devouring fire.

Exodus 24:12, 15–17 NLT

Have you ever gone to the Grand Canyon? Or the Rocky Mountains? Or Niagara Falls? These places are so big and so magnificent that the sight of them fills us with wonder. They help us to know the glory—the awesomeness—of God, their Creator.

When Moses went up on the mountain to speak with the LORD God, the people stayed at the bottom of the mountain. When they looked up, they saw something like a cloud and a fire, which told them that God was present there on the mountain. The cloud and fire filled the people with wonder and helped them to know the glory of God.

God is bigger than we can imagine. Moreover, the glory of God fills our world. But the most amazing thing of all is that we find our greatest happiness by living in obedience to God. That is why God spoke to Moses on the mountain—to teach us how to live.

Glorious God, I praise you for all that you are creating and doing in our world! And I thank you that you care so much about us that you show us how to live right. Amen.

JUNE 8

•

When Moses failed to come back down the mountain right away, the people went to Aaron. "Look," they said, "make us some gods who can lead us. This man Moses, who brought us here from Egypt, has disappeared. We don't know what has happened to him." So Aaron said, "Tell your wives and sons and daughters to take off their gold earrings, and then bring them to me." All the people obeyed Aaron and brought him their gold earrings. Then Aaron took the gold, melted it down, and molded and tooled it into the shape of a calf. The people exclaimed, "O Israel, these are the gods who brought you out of Egypt!"

Exodus 32:1–4 NLT

When you are waiting for someone who is taking a long time, the minutes and hours seem to move slowly. You may become cranky. You may lose hope that the person will ever get there.

Moses was on the mountain for forty days and forty nights. The Israelites grew very impatient, and they let their impatience make them forget all the things that God had done for them. They said, "Moses brought us up out of Egypt," forgetting that God was the one who made it all possible! Then they made a statue of a golden calf and said it was their god. They forgot all about the Lord—the one who really led them out of slavery.

Waiting for God can be even harder than waiting for people. God doesn't always answer our prayers as quickly as we want. But it would be foolish for us to give up on God or to treat other things as if they were gods. God has blessed us with life and freedom! We can trust God always—even when we have to wait.

God, forgive me for the times when I grow impatient with you or forget all that you have done for me. Help me to trust that you alone are the true and living God. Amen.

JUNE 9

•

As Moses approached the camp, he saw the calf. He also saw the people dancing. So he burned with anger. He threw the tablets out of his hands. They broke into pieces at the foot of the mountain. . . . He said to Aaron, "What did these people do to you? How did they make you lead them into such terrible sin?" "Please don't be angry," Aaron answered. "You know how these people like to do what is evil. They said to me, 'Make a god that will lead us. This fellow Moses brought us up out of Egypt. But we don't know what has happened to him.' So I told them, 'Anyone who has any gold jewelry, take it off.' They gave me the gold. I threw it into the fire. And out came this calf!"

Exodus 32:19, 21–24 NIrV

Can you fool God? That is what Aaron tried to do. Moses came down from the mountaintop, where he had been speaking with God. He found the people having a party, after they had worshipped the golden calf that they had made. It had been Aaron's job to lead the people, and he had failed. Moses asked him how it all happened. Do you remember? Earlier, we read that Aaron *made* the statue of a calf. He himself shaped it with a tool. But instead of telling the truth to Moses, Aaron said that the people put the gold into the fire, "and out came this calf."

In another part of the Bible, the Psalms, the writer asks these questions about God: "Does he who made the ear not hear? Does he who formed the eye not see?" (Psalm 94:9 NIrV). God is the one who created us and who formed our ears and eyes. Of course God also hears and sees everything that happens! God saw and heard what Aaron had done. Aaron could not fool God, and neither can we.

God, forgive me for times when I do something wrong and then do not tell the whole truth about it. Help me to remember that, even if I fool other people, I cannot fool you. Amen.

JUNE 10

Moses bowed down to the ground at once and worshiped. "Lord," he said, "if you are pleased with me, then go with us. Even though these people are stubborn, forgive the evil things we have done. Forgive our sin. And accept us as your people." Then the Lord said, "I am making a covenant with you. I will do wonderful things in front of all of your people. I will do miracles that have never been done before in any nation in the whole world. The people you live among will see the things that I, the Lord, will do for you. And they will see how wonderful those things really are."

Exodus 34:8–10 NIrV

Sometimes when people do something wrong, they try to "pass the buck." That means they try to blame it on someone else. Did you ever try to pass the buck to someone else when your parents or teacher were unhappy with you?

When the people of Israel sin by worshipping the golden calf, Moses doesn't try to pass the buck. He admits to God that he and his people have broken their promises. Moses humbly asks God to forgive them and to take them back. That is just what God does. Even though the people have acted very badly, God makes a new covenant—a new promise—to care for them.

God's answer to Moses shows us God's *grace.* Grace happens whenever someone forgives those who do not deserve it. Our God is holy and just and expects us to live right. But God is also full of grace and forgives those who are truly sorry for doing wrong. Accepting responsibility for our mistakes is one way we show God that we are sorry.

God, thank you for forgiving your people when they do not deserve it. Help me to remember your grace, so that I will be bold to confess my sins instead of blaming others. Amen.

JUNE 11

•

Moses came down from Mount Sinai. He had the two tablets of the covenant in his hands. His face was shining because he had spoken with the Lord. But he didn't realize it. Aaron and all of the people of Israel saw Moses. His face was shining.

Exodus 34:29–30a NIrV

Have you ever played with a glow-in-the-dark toy? If you have, then you know that it will glow much brighter if you hold it close to a lit bulb before you turn off the lights. The toy is made of a special material that soaks up energy from the light and then gives off a light of its own.

The Bible teaches that whenever Moses talked with God, afterward his face would shine. Being so close to God and talking to God made Moses become more like God. His face glowed with the light of heaven. Looking at Moses' face helped the people to know how glorious God is.

We don't speak to God face-to-face, the way the Bible says Moses did. But whenever we pray, we are spending time with God. Whenever we worship, we are opening ourselves up to God. Whenever we accept God's forgiveness for something we have done wrong, or enjoy the love and kindness of others, we are "soaking up" God's love. That love gives us great energy and power. Our faces may not glow like Moses' face, but we can still pass on the light and love of God to others. We can help people to know the glory of God.

God, thank you for listening to my prayers and for being present with me wherever I go. Thank you for your light and love. Help me to reflect them in my life. Amen.

JUNE 12

•

Then the cloud covered the Tent of Meeting. The glory of the LORD filled the holy tent. Moses couldn't enter the Tent of Meeting because the cloud had settled on it. The glory of the LORD filled the holy tent. The people of Israel continued their travels. When the cloud lifted from above the holy tent, they started out. But if the cloud didn't lift, they did not start out. They stayed until the day it lifted. So the cloud of the LORD was above the holy tent during the day. Fire was in the cloud at night. The whole community of Israel could see the cloud during all of their travels.

Exodus 40:34–38 NIRV

What is the most important thing to have with you on a long trip? Is it money? A map? Your suitcase? A good book to read? A keepsake from home?

The people of Israel were continuing on their journey to the land that God had promised them. They had followed God's instructions and built a very beautiful tent, the Tent of Meeting. It was not a tent to sleep in but a place where God could be present with the people. Just as when God was on the mountain with Moses, a cloud (which had fire in it at night) settled over the tent. The cloud meant that God was present with the people, dwelling in that tent.

We believe that God is present everywhere in heaven and on earth. And yet, there are times in our lives when we need and want to feel God with us in a special way. The wilderness journey was such a time for Israel. This story reminds us that God is with us in those times, just as God was with Israel. God isn't far off. God is right here with us, wherever we go. God is the one we should have with us on our journey!

Lord of heaven and earth, I know you are present everywhere. Help me to know you, and to know that you live with me. Be with me on my journey through life. Amen.

JUNE 13

•

Blessed is the one who finds wisdom.
Blessed is the one who gains understanding.
Wisdom pays better than silver does.
She earns more than gold does.
She is worth more than rubies.
Nothing you want can compare with her.
Long life is in her right hand.
In her left hand are riches and honor.
Her ways are pleasant ways.
All her paths lead to peace.

Proverbs 3:13–17 NIRV

What would make you really happy? Getting a certain toy, or having a big group of friends, or winning a special kind of prize or award?

This passage says that there is something that will make you even happier than being rich or popular or successful. It is having wisdom. The Book of Proverbs talks about God's wisdom as a beautiful, gracious woman. Everyone who listens to her and follows her ways finds the best happiness there is.

Following God's wisdom isn't the same thing as knowing a lot of information or being really smart. It's about knowing how to live a good life. Imagine a life of happiness and peace, a life of understanding and goodness. Imagine a life that brings joy to you, to other people, and to God. Doesn't that sound good?

God of wisdom, I know that being rich or popular or successful is not the key to true happiness. Help me to follow your wise path, and find the happiness that lasts forever. Amen.

JUNE 14

•

Let your eyes look straight ahead.
Keep looking right in front of you.
Make level paths for your feet to walk on.
Only go on ways that are firm.
Don't turn to the right or left.
Keep your feet from the path of evil.

Proverbs 4:25–27 NIRV

Have you ever walked on something really long and narrow, like a balance beam or a fallen log? Have you noticed that if you don't really concentrate on looking ahead and walking straight, you fall right off?

Life is like that too. It is very easy to get distracted from doing good things and end up doing bad things. Once you start going crooked, it is hard to get back on the right road.

Sometimes bad things tempt us. We know we shouldn't lie, but we may think that telling the truth will get us into a lot of trouble. We know we shouldn't steal, but there is a CD we really want. We know we shouldn't say nasty things about other people, but it's hard to resist.

No one is perfect. We all get on the wrong path sometimes. But if we keep our hearts pointing toward God, we won't lose our way.

God, do not let me go down the path of doing wrong and hurting other people. Keep my heart focused on what is good. Amen.

JUNE 15

•

You people who don't want to work, think about the ant!
Consider its ways and be wise!
It has no commander.
It has no leader or ruler.
But it stores up its food in summer.
It gathers its food at harvest time.
You lazy people, how long will you lie there?
When will you get up from your sleep?

Proverbs 6:6–9 NIRV

Have you ever seen an anthill swarming with ants? Have you ever watched a tiny ant carry a big piece of food back to its home to share with the others? Ants keep very busy!

People have to work hard too. We have a lot to do to make this world a better place and provide the things everybody needs to live. If we are lazybones and stay in bed all day, we will never get our work done. We will never learn anything or make a difference to others.

If we work hard all week, we will be ready for the Sabbath. Unlike the ants, we have a special day set aside each week for worship and rest!

God of the Sabbath, thank you for work to do. Help me to work hard and to use the gifts you have given me to help others. Amen.

JUNE 16

•

Foolish people are easily upset.
But wise people pay no attention to hurtful words.
An honest witness tells the truth.
But a dishonest witness tells lies.
Thoughtless words cut like a sword.
But the tongue of wise people brings healing.

Proverbs 12:16–18 NIRV

Have you ever heard someone say, "Sticks and stones can break my bones, but names can never hurt me"? It's not true! Proverbs says that thoughtless words cut like a sword—that hurts. We can hurt someone with our tongue just as much as with our foot or our fist. If you do hurt someone with your words, use words to say you're sorry too.

When someone hurts you with words, it is usually best to ignore it. Have you noticed that getting upset and saying something hurtful back makes the problem even worse? It is better to say nothing.

Instead, use your words to bring comfort and healing to others. Use your words to speak the truth to others. Your good words can make a big difference!

God, keep me from hurting others with my tongue. Help me to tell the truth. Let my words bring comfort and healing to those who need it. Amen.

JUNE 17

•

It is better to have respect for the LORD and have little
than to be rich and have trouble.
A meal of vegetables where there is love
is better than the finest meat where there is hatred.

Proverbs 15:16–17 NIRV

Money is important. Without money, you cannot have a place to live, or clothes to wear, or food to eat. Being very poor means you have to spend most of your time worrying about where you will sleep, what you will wear, and what you will eat. That is a very hard way to live. God doesn't want anyone to be that poor.

But money is not the most important thing. People can be happy with only a little bit of money. And people can be miserable with a lot of money. What is most important is trusting in God and being surrounded by love. The writer of Proverbs suggests that it is better to eat peanut butter sandwiches with people who love you than to eat in a fancy restaurant with people full of hatred. It is better to wear old clothes and rejoice in God's care than to wear expensive new clothes and spend all your time worrying about how you look.

Giver of all blessings, you want everyone to have enough. Help me remember that money is not what is most important; make me willing to share my money with those who need it. Amen.

JUNE 18

•

Listen to your father, who gave you life, and don't despise your mother's experience when she is old. . . . The father of godly children has cause for joy. What a pleasure it is to have wise children. So give your parents joy! May she who gave you birth be happy.

Proverbs 23:22, 24–25 NLT

Your parents and grandparents and teachers have high hopes for you! They want you to grow up and become wise and discover your gifts. They want you to live a life that is good for you and for others. So they give you lots of advice and help along the way. Sometimes it may feel like too much advice!

When their dreams for you actually come true, they will rejoice. *We are so proud of you,* they will say. *We are so glad that you found a way to make the world a better place. We are so happy that you are alive!*

God, thank you for giving me grown-ups who have high hopes for me. Help me to listen to them. Show me the way to wisdom and happiness. Amen.

JUNE 19

•

Don't visit friends too often,
or they will get tired of it and start hating you.
Telling lies about friends is like attacking them
with clubs and swords and sharp arrows.
A friend you can't trust in times of trouble
is like having a toothache or a sore foot.
Singing to someone in deep sorrow
is like pouring vinegar in an open cut.

Proverbs 25:17–20 CEV

Learning how to get along with other people is one of most important tasks of growing up. If you learn how to be kind and generous and fair to others when you are young, you will make a great adult!

The Book of Proverbs has a lot of advice about how to get along with others. It also gives lots of warnings about what *not* to do. For example, if you are always at your friends' houses, eating their food and playing with their things, but you never invite them to your house, they will get tired of having you over. If you tell lies about your friends, you hurt them as much as a sharp arrow. If you let your friend down when she is in trouble, you are like a toothache or a hurt foot to her. If you are happy and full of jokes when your friend is sad, you are like vinegar on a sore.

Try to come up with your own proverbs for getting along with people. Here's one: If you comfort a friend who is upset, you are like a bandage on a skinned knee. Can you think of others?

God, teach me how to get along with others. Thank you for all the kind, generous, and fair people in the world. Help me to be like them. Amen.

JUNE 20

•

Who can find a noble wife?
  She is worth far more than rubies.
Her husband trusts her completely.
  She gives him all the important things he needs.
She brings him good, not harm,
  all the days of her life.

Proverbs 31:10–12 NIRV

Some day you may choose someone to marry. But even if you don't ever get married, you will have to choose people to trust and be friends with. What will you look for? Will you look for someone who is beautiful or handsome? Will you look for someone who is famous? Will you look for someone who has a lot of money?

Proverbs says, don't look for someone with fame or beauty or riches. Those things don't matter very much. Instead, look for someone who is honest and kind. Look for someone who knows how to use money wisely. Look for someone who works hard at helping others. Look for someone who is generous to the poor. Look for someone who trusts God.

God, help me grow up to be strong and wise like the woman in Proverbs. And if I get married, help me choose a person like her. Amen.

JUNE 21

•

The Spirit and the bride say, "Come." Let each one who hears them say, "Come." Let the thirsty ones come—anyone who wants to. Let them come and drink the water of life without charge.

Revelation 22:17 NLT

In the Book of Revelation, Jesus promises Christians that he is coming again soon. But until then, they have to wait. Revelation compares Christians to a bride waiting for her husband to return. While Christians wait, they remember Jesus by celebrating communion, by reading stories about him in the Bible, and by treating others the way he did.

If we lived in a perfect world, waiting might be easy. But in our world, waiting is hard. We long for the time when there will be no more suffering or death. We long for the time when we will be in perfect relationship with God. That is why we pray for Jesus to come. "Come and fix our broken world," we pray. "Come and make us holy." As we pray for Jesus to come again, the Holy Spirit prays with us.

Other people hear us praying for Jesus to come. We invite them to pray with us. And we invite them to come and discover the new life that Jesus Christ offers to everyone.

Come, Lord Jesus! Our world is thirsty for the water of life you bring. Amen.

JUNE 22

•

We have been set free because of what Christ has done. Through his blood our sins have been forgiven. We have been set free because God's grace is so rich. He poured his grace on us by giving us great wisdom and understanding.

Ephesians 1:7–8 NIRV

Some people don't like to look at blood or even to hear the word. But in church you may have heard the minister talking about Jesus' blood. You may have noticed that some of the songs you sing there mention Jesus' blood. Have you wondered why?

The minister, the songs, and the author of this Bible passage are all talking about how Jesus bled when he was killed on the cross. Jesus died because of the hatred and cruelty of others. But Jesus' "blood" (his death) shows God's love for all of us, even when we are cruel and hateful. Jesus' death is proof that there is no place where the love of God can't go. Now even in our times of pain and sorrow, we can be sure of God's love.

But the blood isn't the end of Jesus' story. On Easter, God raised Jesus up to new life. Then a new sort of power came into the world. Now God freely pours out this power on us! It is not the kind of power that hurts or rules over others but power to live a new and rich life. It is power to live joyfully, because God has forgiven us for our sins and set us free.

Loving God, thank you that Jesus' blood has brought us closer to you. Thank you for your kindness and for giving us power to live as you want us to live. Amen.

JUNE 23

•

God has great wisdom and understanding, and by what Christ has done, God has shown us his own mysterious ways. Then when the time is right, God will do all that he has planned, and Christ will bring together everything in heaven and on earth.

Ephesians 1:8b–10 CEV

To construct a big building, you first need to draw up a plan. An architect's plan tells builders things like what size to make the foundation and where to put the walls. Once the plan has been made, it may take only a short time to finish the work, or it may take years. Some of the old churches in Europe took centuries to build!

God has drawn up a very big plan for our world. God plans for all the things that are divided in our world to be brought back together. When God's work is finished, all the forces or powers that work against God will serve God instead. All the people who are kept apart by hatred or jealousy will make peace with each other.

We know that all this will happen "when the time is right." That may be a long, long time from now! But by sending Jesus, God has already begun to carry out the plan. Jesus shows us how to serve God and how to make peace with each other. Jesus is the one who will bring all things together.

Wise and mysterious God, your plan is too big and too wonderful for me to understand! But I trust that in Jesus Christ you will bring together everything in heaven and on earth. Amen.

JUNE 24

•

Be humble and gentle. Be patient with each other, making allowance for each other's faults because of your love. Always keep yourselves united in the Holy Spirit, and bind yourselves together with peace. We are all one body, we have the same Spirit, and we have all been called to the same glorious future. There is only one Lord, one faith, one baptism, and there is only one God and Father, who is over us all and in us all and living through us all.

Ephesians 4:2–6 NLT

You have probably heard the song that says, "We are one in the Spirit, we are one in the Lord." But have you noticed that there are actually many different kinds of Christians in the world? There are Catholics, Methodists, Episcopalians, Lutherans, Presbyterians, Baptists, and others. There are even different kinds of Methodists, different kinds of Presbyterians, and different kinds of Baptists! Each of these ways of being Christian is called a "denomination."

People from different denominations sometimes argue about how to understand God and about what God expects of us. As a matter of fact, sometimes people from the same denomination—or the very same church!—argue about these things. But God doesn't want us to argue. Here the author of Ephesians tells us to be patient with each other, and to put up with each other in love. We must do this because we all worship one Lord! We have only one faith but many ways of practicing it. And there is only one God, who loves us all.

God and Father of all, forgive us when we forget that the whole church is your church and that you want all Christians to live as one. Teach us to be patient and loving even when we disagree with each other. Amen.

JUNE 25

•

Get rid of all hard feelings, anger and rage. Stop all fighting and lying. Put away every form of hatred. Be kind and tender to one another. Forgive each other, just as God forgave you because of what Christ has done.

Ephesians 4:31–32 NIRV

When a cartoon character becomes very angry, what happens? The character's face gets red, and steam comes out of his ears. Then the angry character acts—perhaps by throwing something or even by hurting the one who caused the anger.

Have you ever felt really, really mad? Your heart may have beat very fast, and maybe you wanted to scream or to hit something or someone. We get angry for many reasons, both good and bad. And when we do get angry, pretending that the anger isn't there will not make it disappear.

The Bible passage above reminds us that we can choose how to deal with our anger. We can choose to yell and curse or even hurt people. As a matter of fact, that is the choice many people—even grown-ups—make. But it is not the best choice. The best choice is to bring our anger to God and ask for the strength to forgive the one who did wrong to us. When we do this, God can help us turn the anger in our hearts to kindness and peace.

God, it is so very hard to choose forgiveness over anger. Sometimes I even *want* to stay angry! Give me the strength I need to deal with anger in a good way. Amen.

JUNE 26

•

Stand your ground, putting on the sturdy belt of truth and the body armor of God's righteousness. For shoes, put on the peace that comes from the Good News, so that you will be fully prepared. In every battle you will need faith as your shield to stop the fiery arrows aimed at you by Satan. Put on salvation as your helmet, and take the sword of the Spirit, which is the Word of God.

Ephesians 6:14–17 NLT

In some computer games, enemies face each other in combat. Some people find it exciting to see who is the better fighter. Who has the most strength? The best skills? The best weapons? The best strategies?

God wants us to be at peace, not to fight. Here the author of Ephesians tells us of a special kind of "armor" for Christians to use. Armor is never for attacking others but for protecting oneself. God's armor protects us against everything that might keep us from living the right way. The "belt of truth," the "armor of godliness," the "shield of faith," and the "helmet of salvation" will be your best protection whenever you are tempted to disobey God or to give up your trust in God.

There *is* one weapon mentioned in this passage, and that is the sword. The "sword" is God's word. But this sword doesn't injure or kill—instead it gives new life!

God, help me to stand firm when times are hard or when I am tempted to disobey you. Clothe me with your special armor and give me new life through your word. Amen.

•

Stop bringing offerings that do not mean anything to me!
I hate your incense.
I can't stand your evil gatherings.
I can't stand the way you celebrate your New Moon Feasts,
Sabbath days and special services. . . .
You might even offer many prayers.
But I will not listen to them.
Your hands are covered with the blood of the people you have murdered.
So wash your hands. Make yourselves clean.
Get your evil actions out of my sight!
Stop doing what is wrong!

Isaiah 1:13, 15b–16 NIrV

Some people think that faith is *only* about going to church on Sunday. So every week they put on nice clothes and go to church. They sing and say prayers and listen to sermons. They think God must be very pleased with them for going to church every Sunday.

Wait a minute, says Isaiah! Worshipping God is great, but God is also very interested in what we do during the rest of the week. Suppose that all week you have treated people unfairly. Suppose you have made life even harder for the poor. Suppose you have ignored the people who most need your help and protection. Do you think that God will be pleased with you just because you go to church?

If we don't show our faith in God all during the week by the way we treat others, going to church and offering many prayers won't mean anything to God. God hates it when what we do in church has no connection with the rest of our life. God wants to see our faith on Monday, Tuesday, Wednesday, Thursday, Friday, Saturday—AND on Sunday!

Holy God, teach me to do what is right. Help me to show my faith in you every day of the week, including Sunday. Amen.

JUNE 28

•

In the year that King Uzziah died, I had a vision of the LORD. He was on his throne high above, and his robe filled the temple. Flaming creatures with six wings each were flying over him. They covered their faces with two of their wings and their bodies with two more. They used the other two wings for flying, as they shouted,

"Holy, holy, holy,
LORD All-Powerful!
The earth is filled
with your glory."

As they shouted, the doorposts of the temple shook, and the temple was filled with smoke. Then I cried out, "I'm doomed! Everything I say is sinful, and so are the words of everyone around me. Yet I have seen the King, the LORD All-Powerful." One of the flaming creatures flew over to me with a burning coal that it had taken from the altar with a pair of metal tongs. It touched my lips with the hot coal and said, "This has touched your lips. Your sins are forgiven, and you are no longer guilty." After this, I heard the LORD ask, "Is there anyone I can send? Will someone go for us?" "I'll go," I answered. "Send me!"

Isaiah 6:1–8 CEV

God used a vision to call Isaiah to be a prophet. God wanted Isaiah to deliver a message to the people of Judah. But Isaiah's vision of the Lord made him afraid to say anything! How could a weak, sinful person deliver a message for a holy, all-powerful God? In the vision, one of God's creatures touches Isaiah's lips with a burning coal. You might think this would hurt Isaiah's lips and make it even harder for him to speak. But instead, the coal is a sign that God has forgiven Isaiah's sins. Now Isaiah is ready to speak God's word!

Send me, Lord, to speak and do what you say in your word. Forgive my sins and give me the strength I need to do what you want me to do. Amen.

JUNE 29

•

About that time Hezekiah became deathly ill, and the prophet Isaiah son of Amoz went to visit him. He gave the king this message: "This is what the LORD says: Set your affairs in order, for you are going to die. You will not recover from this illness." When Hezekiah heard this, he turned his face to the wall and prayed to the LORD, "Remember, O LORD, how I have always tried to be faithful to you and do what is pleasing in your sight." Then he broke down and wept bitterly. Then this message came to Isaiah from the LORD: "Go back to Hezekiah and tell him, 'This is what the LORD, the God of your ancestor David, says: I have heard your prayer and seen your tears. I will add fifteen years to your life, and I will rescue you and this city from the king of Assyria. Yes, I will defend this city.' "

Isaiah 38:1–6 NLT

The prophet Isaiah brought King Hezekiah bad news. God had told Isaiah that Hezekiah was going to die soon. Hezekiah could have given up hope for getting better. He could have accepted God's word from Isaiah and prepared himself to die. But he didn't.

Instead, Hezekiah prayed to God. He reminded God of how faithful he had been. Because of Hezekiah's prayer, God gave him fifteen more years to live.

It is right for us to pray when we get bad news. Sometimes we pray quiet prayers for God to comfort us. Sometimes we cry and argue with God in our prayers, like Hezekiah did. No matter how we pray, our prayers make a difference to God.

Lord God, help me to pray, even when things seem hopeless. Thank you for hearing my prayers. Thank you for using them to shape the future. Amen.

JUNE 30

"So who will you compare me to? Who is equal to me?" says the Holy One.

Isaiah 40:25 NIRV

The next time you are in a worship service, pay special attention to the songs you sing. What words do the songs use to address God? Do they call God *King, Father,* or *Shepherd?* Do the songs refer to God as *Lord* or *Master?* Make a list!

Our words for God are symbols that express what we believe God is like—God is like a shepherd and God is like a king. The Bible uses many symbols to help us understand what God is like. The Bible compares God to many more things than our songs usually do. It compares God to a mother comforting her child (Isaiah 66:13). It compares God to a mighty rock (Psalm 144:1). It compares God to a fierce lion (Isaiah 31:4). Each of these comparisons tells us something about God. But God is not *exactly* like any of these things.

God is bigger than all our symbols. Isaiah 40 asks, "So who will you compare me to?" The right answer is that nothing in the whole world truly compares to God. God is greater than any person or lion or rock. Nothing in the whole world is equal to God!

Strong fortress, loving father, fountain of blessing. Tender shepherd, just ruler, door to eternal life. You are all these things to me, God. Yet you are bigger and more wonderful than all the words I use to praise you! Amen.

JULY 1

•

The people of Zion said,
"The LORD has turned away and forgotten us."
The LORD answered,
"Could a mother forget a child who nurses at her breast?
Could she fail to love an infant who came from her own body?
Even if a mother could forget, I will never forget you."

Isaiah 49:14–15 CEV

Have you ever felt forgotten? Maybe no one picked you up after your soccer practice. Maybe no one at school remembered it was your birthday. The Israelites were feeling forgotten. They had been forced out of their own land and were living in exile in Babylon. "The LORD has turned away and forgotten us," they said.

We all need people we can count on to remember us. Many of us count on our mothers. Mothers give us birth (though sometimes the mother who loves you and cares for you is not the same one who gave birth to you). Mothers feed us and help us and worry about us. Yet even mothers sometimes forget. They get busy with other things and don't remember their kids' needs. They get sick or have too many problems to take good care of their children.

Even if your human mother forgets, God will never forget you. Like a loving mother, God feeds you and cares for you. You are God's child, and God will remember you forever!

When I feel forgotten, God, send your Spirit to comfort me. Help me trust in your promise that you will never forget your children. Amen.

JULY 2

•

He was hated and rejected;
his life was filled with sorrow
and terrible suffering.
No one wanted to look at him
We despised him and said,
"He is a nobody!"

He suffered and endured great pain for us,
but we thought his suffering was punishment from God.
He was wounded and crushed because of our sins;
by taking our punishment, he made us completely well.

Isaiah 53:3–5 CEV

God's people Israel were in exile in Babylon. Maybe they hoped that God would raise up a strong and handsome warrior to defeat the Babylonians. But God raised up the "servant" this passage talks about. He seemed like a nobody. Instead of conquering others, this servant of God suffered. We don't know who this servant was. The important thing is that God gave him a very special job to do. This servant brought healing and hope to sinful people, not through power and violence, but through suffering and obedience to God's will.

These verses from Isaiah also speak to Christians of Jesus Christ, even though they were written many centuries before Jesus was born. His life too was filled with sorrow and terrible suffering. Christ's death on a cross was not a punishment from God, even though it might look that way. Instead, Christ's death was for us, to make us completely well.

Loving God, you bring us hope and healing in ways we don't expect. Thank you for all the servants who do your will. Thank you for Jesus Christ. Amen.

JULY 3

•

"Wolves and lambs will eat together.
Lions will eat straw like oxen.
Serpents will not bite anyone.
They will eat nothing but dust.
None of those animals will harm or destroy
anything or anyone on my holy mountain of Zion," says the LORD.

Isaiah 65:25 NIRV

"It's a dog-eat-dog world." Have you ever heard people say that? They mean that the world is a dangerous, competitive place, in which everyone has to fight to do well. In a world like that, it is hard to feel safe and to trust others. It is hard to help others because you are too worried about your own safety. In what ways do you think you live in a dog-eat-dog world?

This passage from Isaiah shows us another kind of world. It is a world in which animals that are enemies now, like wolves and lambs, will live together in peace. Human beings will also stop harming each other. God's people will live long, happy lives together, free from sorrow and pain.

God is already at work creating this world! Whenever you see enemies living together in peace or people helping others, give thanks to God. You have seen a sign of the "new heaven and new earth" that God has in store for us.

Lord, we wait for the world of joy and peace you promise. Help us to see signs of it even now. Amen.

JULY 4

•

"Build houses and settle down. Plant gardens and eat what they produce. Get married. Have sons and daughters. Find wives for your sons. Give your daughters to be married. Then they too can have sons and daughters. Increase your numbers there. Do not let the number of your people get smaller. Also work for the success of the city I have sent you to. Pray to the LORD for that city. If it succeeds, you too will enjoy success."

Jeremiah 29:5–7 NIRV

The people of Israel didn't want to live in Babylon. The Babylonians forced them to leave Jerusalem and go there. But God told them to make Babylon their home. God wanted them to build houses and raise children in Babylon. God told the Israelites to work for the success of their new country and to pray for it.

Some people in the United States have lived here for many centuries. Others came to this country much later, because they wanted to. Still others were forced to come to this country as slaves. But no matter how we got here, we can claim this country as our home and work to make it a better place to live. Pray to God for our country's success!

God of all the earth, bless our country. Show us how to make it a good home for all its citizens. Amen.

JULY 5

•

Jesus replied: "I am the bread that gives life! No one who comes to me will ever be hungry. No one who has faith in me will ever be thirsty."

John 6:35 CEV

How many times do you eat every day? Three times? Five times? You have to eat so often because you keep getting hungry. The food you eat only satisfies you for a few hours. Then you have to eat again.

Jesus knows that we need food and drink. He gave people at a wedding lots of wine to drink. He gave a huge crowd lots of bread and fish to eat. But he knew that they would get hungry and thirsty all over again.

That's why Jesus says, "I am the bread that gives life." Jesus is a source of life that never runs out and will satisfy us forever. If we follow him, we will never be hungry for God's love or thirsty for God's peace again.

Lord Jesus, you are the bread of life. I give thanks that you offer life to the whole world. Fill me with the love and peace of God. Amen.

JULY 6

•

As Jesus was walking along, he saw a man who had been blind from birth. "Teacher," his disciples asked him, "why was this man born blind? Was it a result of his own sins or those of his parents?" "It was not because of his sins or his parents' sins," Jesus answered. "He was born blind so the power of God could be seen in him. . . ." Then he spit on the ground, made mud with the saliva, and smoothed the mud over the blind man's eyes. He told him, "Go and wash in the pool of Siloam" (Siloam means Sent). So the man went and washed, and came back seeing!

John 9:1–3, 6–7 NLT

Do you know someone who was born deaf, or blind, or unable to walk?

The man in this story was born blind. Jesus said it wasn't his fault or his parents' fault that he was born this way. Jesus healed him so his eyes worked again. The man could see everything now, but what he saw most clearly was the love of God in Jesus. Some people who had never been blind couldn't see this love!

Some problems we are born with never go away. But deaf people can still receive the good news of Jesus, even if they can't hear it with their ears. People in wheelchairs can still follow Jesus. Jesus wants all kinds of people to be his disciples!

Lord Jesus, your love has healing power. Fill us with your love, so that we can be your disciples. Amen.

JULY 7

•

Martha said to Jesus, "Lord, if you had been here, my brother would not have died. Yet even now I know that God will do anything you ask." Jesus told her, "Your brother will live again!" Martha answered, "I know that he will be raised to life on the last day, when all the dead are raised." Jesus then said, "I am the one who raises the dead to life! Everyone who has faith in me will live, even if they die. And everyone who lives because of faith in me will never really die. Do you believe this?" "Yes, Lord!" she replied. "I believe that you are Christ, the Son of God. You are the one we hoped would come into the world."

John 11:21–27 CEV

Sometimes it seems to us that God doesn't help us soon enough. We pray for a sick person to get better, but she dies before God answers our prayer. We pray for a marriage that is in trouble, but the husband and wife get divorced anyway. We pray for peace, but the war continues, and more people are killed. We wish God had answered our prayers sooner so those things would not have happened.

Martha and Mary were sad because their brother Lazarus died. They had sent a message to Jesus to come while Lazarus was still sick. But by the time Jesus arrived, Lazarus was already dead. Martha wished that Jesus had come sooner so that he could have healed Lazarus.

But even though Lazarus died, Martha still trusted Jesus. This story shows us that even when bad things happen, we can still have hope in the new life Jesus brings. If we believe in Jesus like Martha did, we can start living a new life today that will last forever.

God, I know that the life you offer us in Jesus is stronger than anything else. Help me trust in your love no matter what happens. Amen.

JULY 8

•

When Jesus saw that Mary and the people with her were crying, he was terribly upset and asked, "Where have you put his body?" They replied, "Lord, come and you will see." Jesus started crying, and the people said, "See how much he loved Lazarus."

John 11:33–36 CEV

If you have ever gone to a funeral, you probably saw people crying. Death is sad, because it separates us from people we love. Even if we have faith in God, we are still sad when someone we love dies.

Jesus loved Lazarus, and when Lazarus died, Jesus cried. But then Jesus did something that shows that God's love is stronger than death. He healed Lazarus even after he had been dead for four days. Because of what Jesus did, Lazarus had new life!

The new life Jesus offers is not just for Lazarus. It is for everyone! We will all die someday like Lazarus. But Jesus promises us that not even death will separate us from life with God.

God, when someone we love dies, we are sad. But the new life you offer in Jesus is stronger than death. Help me start enjoying this new life today. Amen.

JULY 9

•

Thomas said to him, "Lord, we don't know where you are going. So how can we know the way?" Jesus answered, "I am the way and the truth and the life. No one comes to the Father except through me."

John 14:5–6 NIRV

Have you ever cried when someone you love leaves you? Maybe your grandfather leaves to go home after a wonderful visit. Maybe your mother leaves to go on a long business trip. Maybe your best friend leaves to move to another city. It makes you feel sad, doesn't it? The disciples were feeling this way, because Jesus was leaving them.

But Jesus had some good news for the disciples. Even though he would no longer be there to walk beside them, he would still be their way to God. Follow me, he told them, and you won't get lost.

That's true for us today too. We can't walk beside Jesus. But Jesus shows us the truth of God. Jesus brings us God's gift of life. If we follow the way of Jesus, we will never be alone.

God our Father, thank you for giving us Jesus as the way, the truth, and the life. If we follow him, then we know we will never lose our way to you. Amen.

JULY 10

•

Jesus replied, "Those who love me will obey my teaching. My Father will love them. We will come to them and make our home with them. Those who do not love me will not obey my teaching. The words you hear me say are not my own. They belong to the Father who sent me."

John 14:23–24 NIRV

Think of someone you really love. It may be a person in your family or a friend. If you love them, then you want to show your love by being nice to them. If you love them, then you want to know them better.

But it also works the other way. If you get to know those you love better, and if you are fair and kind to them, then your love for them becomes deeper. Knowing and loving people and acting in a right way toward them are all connected. In fact, it can be hard to tell where loving stops and doing begins, or where knowing starts to become loving.

That's the way it is with God too. Loving God, knowing God, and acting according to God's teaching all belong together. We can't do one without the other two. When we do all three of them together, God is so close to us that it is like God making a home with us.

Father, Son, and Holy Spirit, come and make your home with me, so that I can spend my whole life loving, knowing, and following you. Amen.

JULY 11

•

After breakfast Jesus said to Simon Peter, "Simon son of John, do you love me more than these?" "Yes, Lord," Peter replied, "you know I love you." "Then feed my lambs," Jesus told him. Jesus repeated the question: "Simon son of John, do you love me?" "Yes, Lord," Peter said, "you know I love you." "Then take care of my sheep," Jesus said. Once more he asked him, "Simon son of John, do you love me?"

John 21:15–17 NLT

How do you show people that you love them? There are lots of good ways. You can say, "I love you." You can give them a hug or make them a present. You can be there when they need you.

Jesus was not going to be with his disciples much longer. How could they show their love for him once he was gone? Jesus gives Simon Peter a way. He tells Peter to feed his sheep. Jesus wants Peter to take care of the people that Jesus loves. Peter can show his love for Jesus by loving and caring for others.

When we pray by ourselves or worship God with others, we show God our love with words. Words are important, but we should also show our love for God by loving others. There's a song that ends, "And they'll know we are Christians by our love." What are some loving things you can do so others will know that you are a Christian?

Lord Jesus, I love you! Help me show my love for you by the way I love others. Amen.

JULY 12

•

Jesus also did many other things. What if every one of them were written down? I suppose that even the whole world would not have room for the books that would be written.

John 21:25 NIRV

Have you ever heard a good storyteller? Part of being a good storyteller is having a good story to tell. The other part is knowing *how* to tell it. When you tell a story, you have to decide what is interesting and important, and what you can leave out.

The New Testament has four books that tell the story of Jesus' life: Matthew, Mark, Luke, and John. They were all written by good storytellers, but none of them tell us every single thing that Jesus did. John said that if people tried to do that, they would write enough books to fill up the whole world. Think how long those would take to read!

But there is another reason John couldn't write down every single thing about Jesus' life. Christians believe that Jesus not only lived and died a long time ago but also is still living and present with us in a new way. That means the story of Jesus keeps on going. If you believe in Jesus Christ, you are part of that story. It is a story without an end!

Thank you, Christ Jesus, for making me a part of your story. It is the best story in the world. Amen.

JULY 13

•

That is why the LORD says, "Turn to me now, while there is time! Give me your hearts. Come with fasting, weeping, and mourning. Don't tear your clothing in your grief; instead, tear your hearts." Return to the LORD your God, for he is gracious and merciful. He is not easily angered. He is filled with kindness and is eager not to punish you.

Joel 2:12–13 NLT

You can usually tell when people are feeling very sorry about what they have done. Often they cry. They may stop eating. In Bible times they would tear their clothes. Those are all outward signs of how bad they feel on the inside.

The people of Israel were feeling sorry because they had disobeyed God and a terrible plague of locusts had devoured their land. But the prophet Joel brought them good news! God loved them and was waiting for them to come back. God told Israel to show on the outside how sorry they felt. But how they felt on the inside was even more important. If their hearts were broken, God would know that they were really sorry and ready to change.

Forgiving God, we know that you are slow to anger and full of love for us. When we do wrong, help us to show how sorry we are. Amen.

JULY 14

•

"Later, I will give my Spirit to everyone.
Your sons and daughters will prophesy.
Your old men will have dreams,
and your young men will see visions.
In those days I will even give my Spirit to my servants, both men and women."

Joel 2:28–29 CEV

Sometimes we try to divide people up into groups. "That's a man's job." "That's a girl's toy." "That's the way old people dress." Do you sometimes say things like that?

The prophet Joel promised that God's Spirit would be poured out on all people, male and female, young and old, rich and poor. Men and women would become prophets, speaking God's word to others. Everyone would have a vision of the truth. Joel's promise came true for the people of Israel.

Joel's promise has also come true for people who follow Jesus Christ! That means that no Christian has an excuse for not speaking God's word to others. No one can say, "I'm only a girl," or "I'm too old," or "I'm not smart enough." And no one has an excuse for not listening for God's word from every Christian he meets. No one can say, "He's only a kid," or "she never finished high school," or "he's in a wheelchair."

What kind of people is God's Spirit being poured out on? All kinds!

God, thank you for pouring out your Spirit on all kinds of people. Give me a vision of your truth, and help me listen for your word from everyone I meet. Amen.

JULY 15

•

The day of the L*ORD is near in that valley.*
The sun and moon will become dark.
The stars won't shine anymore.
The L*ORD will roar like a lion from Jerusalem.*
His voice will sound like thunder from Zion. The earth and sky will tremble.

Joel 3:14b–16a NIrV

There are a lot of things in the world that don't make sense. Some people live long healthy lives, and others die from war or starvation. Some people who do wicked things are punished, and others get away with it. Some people trust God with all their hearts, and others act as if God doesn't exist. Do you sometimes think that this mixed-up world will never change?

The prophet Joel said a time was coming when God would change the whole world. On the day of the Lord, God's justice and love would be so clear that everybody would see them. Evil would be punished and good would be rewarded. Even the earth and sky would know that God is God.

We don't have a calendar that tells when the day of the Lord is coming. But we can trust God now and work to spread God's justice and love in the world.

Lord, give me the wisdom I need to live in a world that doesn't make sense. Give me hope that one day you will make everything right. Amen.

JULY 16

•

Lord, I cry out to you for help.
In the morning I pray to you.
Lord, why do you say no to me?
Why do you turn your face away from me?

Psalm 88:13–14 NIrV

Sometimes talking to God feels like talking into a toy telephone. There does not seem to be any real connection. God does not seem to answer us. We wonder if God is even listening. The writer of this psalm is feeling this way. He is sad, frightened, and lonely. He thinks that he will die soon. He cries out to God, but he hears no answer.

Reading this psalm can help us when we think God is not listening to us. It lets us know that other believers have felt the same way we do. It reminds us that believing in God does not mean that we will always feel happy or that bad things will never happen to us. Most importantly, this psalm encourages us to keep praying, even when we are sad or angry, even when we wonder if God is listening to us. We can be honest with God when we pray, just like the writer of this psalm was. And one day, we will discover that God was listening the whole time.

Are you really there, God? Sometimes you seem far away, and I wonder if you hear my prayers. Help me to keep praying, even when it does not seem to be working. Help me to know that you do listen and that your love surrounds me, even when I cannot feel it. Amen.

JULY 17

•

Let the ocean and everything in it roar.
Let the world and all who live in it shout.
Let the rivers clap their hands.
Let the mountains sing together with joy.
Let them sing to the LORD.

Psalm 98:7–9a NIRV

You have seen people who are so happy that they can't help singing. And you have seen people clap their hands when someone does something wonderful. But have you ever seen mountains sing together for joy? Have you ever seen rivers clap their hands? Try to imagine what that would look like!

The writer of this psalm wants everybody and everything to give thanks for all the marvelous things God has done. He wants people everywhere to praise God with a lot of noise! But that is not enough. All created things, even the mountains and the rivers, have to join in the praise, because the whole world belongs to God.

The next time you hear the wind whistling through the trees, or see a beautiful sunset, or smell some sweet flowers, think about this psalm. Think about the trees whispering God's kindness, or the sun shining forth God's justice, or the flowers telling about God's love. The whole world will start to look different!

Creator of all, thank you for the beautiful world you have made. Help me to join with the whole creation in praising you. Amen.

JULY 18

•

The LORD is merciful and gracious;
he is slow to get angry and full of unfailing love.
He will not constantly accuse us,
nor remain angry forever.
He has not punished us for all our sins,
nor does he deal with us as we deserve.

Psalm 103:8–10 NLT

You'll pay for this! Has someone ever said that to you after you have done something wrong? It means that they want you to get exactly the punishment that you deserve. They want you to do something to make up for the wrong you have done.

Sometimes this is a good way to solve problems. If you break a neighbor's window with your ball, it helps to pay for a new one. If you don't do your chores when you are supposed to, you may "pay" by having to do them during your favorite TV program.

But if God treated us this way all the time, we would be in big trouble! We are always falling short of the life God wants us to live. The good news of this psalm is that God does not give us what we deserve. God doesn't pay us back for all the bad things we have done, or keep reminding us of them, but gives us another chance to do what is right. God is tender and kind to us, like a good parent is to his or her children.

Merciful God, thank you for being gracious to us. Give us strength to do what is right. Amen.

JULY 19

•

Our days on earth are like grass;
like wildflowers, we bloom and die.
The wind blows, and we are gone—
as though we had never been here.
But the love of the LORD remains
forever
with those who fear him.

Psalm 103:15–17a NLT

Life on earth is precious, because we never know when it may end. One bad accident or illness could end our lives. We try to protect our lives in many ways, by wearing seat belts and getting vaccinations for example. But we know that much of what happens to us is beyond our control and that someday we will die.

The psalmist compares our lives to flowers. One day they are alive and beautiful to look at, and the next day they are gone. But the psalmist says that God's love is different. God's love is not here today and gone tomorrow. It lasts forever.

It is scary to think that our lives are short and uncertain. But it is comforting to know that even when we die, God's love will still surround us.

God, make me be grateful for the precious life you have given me. And when I face death, help me trust in your everlasting love. Amen.

JULY 20

•

Happy are those whose way is blameless,
who walk in the law of the LORD.
Happy are those who keep his decrees,
who seek him with their whole heart,
who also do no wrong,
but walk in his ways.
You have commanded your precepts
to be kept diligently.
O that my ways may be steadfast
in keeping your statutes!

Psalm 119:1–5 NRSV

What makes you really happy? Is it celebrating your birthday with friends? Being able to stay home from school and play all day? Getting something you have wanted for a long time?

This psalm tells us that God wants us to be happy. What good news! But God is interested in the kind of happiness that lasts a lifetime, not just a day or two. How do we find that kind of happiness?

Some people try to find happiness by thinking only about themselves. Some people try to find happiness by surrounding themselves with lots of things. But this psalm shows us a better way. God has set up the world according to certain rules, rules about how to love and be fair to others. When we follow these rules, God promises that we will find real happiness. This doesn't mean that we will never feel sad, or that bad things will never happen to us. But when we keep God's rules we show our love for God, and we discover the happiness that comes from doing what is right.

God, you are the source of all true happiness. Help me to find my happiness in following you. Amen.

JULY 21

•

If the Lord had not been on our side
when people rose up against us,
they would have swallowed us alive
because of their burning anger
against us.
The waters would have engulfed us;
a torrent would have overwhelmed
us.
Yes, the raging waters of their fury
would have overwhelmed our very lives.

Blessed be the Lord,
who did not let their teeth tear us
apart!
We escaped like a bird from a hunter's
trap.
The trap is broken, and we are free!
Our help is from the Lord,
who made the heavens and the
earth.

Psalm 124:2–8 NLT

Be on my side! That is what kids say when they are picking teams to play a game. People on the same side work together to win. If there is no one on your side, you cannot win.

But the psalmist was not thinking about a soccer or basketball game. He was remembering Israel's struggle against a terrible enemy. If God had not been on their side, they would have been destroyed.

Think about an enemy you face: Maybe it is sickness, prejudice, violence, or drugs. Admit that you cannot beat your enemy all by yourself. Give thanks that God is on your side.

Maker of heaven and earth, I know that my help comes from you. When I am struggling against evil, be on my side. Amen.

JULY 22

•

Give thanks to the One who remembered us when things were going badly for us.
His faithful love continues forever.
He set us free from our enemies.
His faithful love continues forever.
He gives food to every creature.
His faithful love continues forever.
Give thanks to the God of heaven.
His faithful love continues forever.

Psalm 136:23–26 NIRV

This psalm says the same thing over and over again, twenty-six times: "His faithful love continues forever." Why say it so many times? Why not say that God's faithful love continues forever just once and then stop?

If God's love for us never stops, why should our praise to God ever stop? Every day of your life is a gift of God's love. By the time you are ten years old, you have lived 3,650 days! If you thank God for every day of your life, that is a lot of thank-yous! And every day we are reminded of God's love in a new way. We see God's love when we are sick and then get better. We see God's love when a baby is born. We see God's love when hungry people get food to eat. We see God's love in a meadow full of wildflowers. Everywhere we look we see signs that God's faithful love continues forever. So we have to say it over and over again!

God, I will never run out of reasons for praising you. Your faithful love continues forever! Amen.

JULY 23

•

You created the deepest parts of my being.
You put me together inside my mother's body.
How you made me is amazing and wonderful.
I praise you for that.
What you have done is wonderful.
I know that very well.

Psalm 139:13–14 NIRV

God knew you before anyone else did, before you were even born. That is because God made you. You are a special, wonderful creation of God. There is nobody else exactly like you.

Sometimes it is hard to feel that way about yourself. You may not like the way you look. You may think your body is too big or too small, or not graceful enough or athletic enough. Maybe your body gets sick a lot; maybe parts of your body do not work very well.

But if you remember that your body is a gift from God, you can learn to respect and honor it, no matter what it looks like. And you can learn to treat other people's bodies as wonderful works of God too.

Thank you, God, for giving me this wonderful body. Help me to love it and to take good care of it. Amen.

JULY 24

•

God, I wish you would kill the people who are evil!
I wish those murderers would get away from me! . . .
Lord, I really hate those who hate you!
I really hate those who rise up against you!
I have nothing but hatred for them.
I consider them to be my enemies.

Psalm 139:19, 21–22 NIRV

We all feel hatred in our hearts sometimes. You may read in the newspaper or hear on television about people who do terrible things to other people—killing them or hurting them on purpose. You find yourself getting very angry at those people, even hating them. There may be someone at your school or in your neighborhood who has hurt you, and you are full of hatred toward that person.

The psalmist feels this way toward some people he knew. He hates them. He does not pretend that he is too nice a person to feel this way. But he does not try to pay his enemies back for the bad things they have done either. Instead he brings his hatred before God. He tells God how much he hates the people who have done terrible things. He even wishes God would kill them. It is not a very nice prayer. But it is an honest one, and God cannot change our hearts unless we are first honest about our feelings.

God, when I am feeling angry and full of hatred, keep me from hurting other people. Help me instead to bring my feelings to you. Please send your Holy Spirit to fill my heart with your love. Amen.

JULY 25

•

From Paul, Silas, and Timothy. To the church in Thessalonica, the people of God the Father and of the Lord Jesus Christ. I pray that God will be kind to you and will bless you with peace! We thank God for you and always mention you in our prayers. Each time we pray, we tell God our Father about your faith and loving work and about your firm hope in our Lord Jesus Christ.

1 Thessalonians 1:1–3 CEV

Does your mom or dad ever have to take a trip away from home for a few days? While they are away they probably think about you and worry about you. If they talk to you on the phone, they may tell you how they can hardly wait to see you again.

Paul had to be away from his friends in the Thessalonian church. And just like a parent, he worried about them. So in this letter, he reminds them how much he cares for them and prays for them. He reminds them who they are and how God wants them to act. Paul praises them for having shown such great faith, love, and hope in all that they do.

Parents, teachers, and friends who worry about us and try to help us do right are a gift from God. They help us to live as God wants us to live. We can praise God for the love that they give to us!

God, I praise you for those who care for me and worry about me! Thank you for the love that I feel from them. Help me to show faith, love, and hope in all that I do. Amen.

JULY 26

•

When we told you the good news, it was with the power and assurance that come from the Holy Spirit, and not simply with words. You knew what kind of people we were and how we helped you. So, when you accepted the message, you followed our example and the example of the Lord. You suffered, but the Holy Spirit made you glad.

1 Thessalonians 1:5–6 CEV

Every family has its stories. The stories tell of times when parents and grandparents were growing up. They tell about hard times and suffering. They tell about things family members did to make one another proud. Our stories help us to know who we are.

Paul tells the Thessalonians the story about when he first met them. Back then Paul had told them the good news that Jesus Christ had died for them and given them new life with God forever. The Thessalonians had known that Paul was telling the truth and had turned to become followers of Jesus. Paul says that God's Spirit helped them do this. The Spirit had also helped them to feel joy and gladness—even during a time when they had to suffer for being followers of Jesus.

The Thessalonians' story is our story too. It can help us to know who we are! We too have heard the good news about God's love. And we can know the help and the joy that the Holy Spirit brings.

God, thank you for the good news about Jesus and for faithful people in times past. Give me the power and assurance that come from the Holy Spirit. Amen.

JULY 27

•

Everyone is talking about how you welcomed us and how you turned away from idols to serve the true and living God.

1 Thessalonians 1:9 CEV

"He's got the whole world in his hands." Did you ever sing that song? The song says there is one God who cares about everyone and who is in charge of all that happens in our world. But in times past people have thought that there are many gods at work in the world. They have made statues (or "idols") of those gods and have thought that worshipping the idols would bring good luck.

Before they became followers of Jesus, the Thessalonians worshipped idols. But when Paul came to town, he taught them that idols weren't real gods. He taught them about the "true and living God." When the people heard Paul's message, they gave up their idols and started to worship the true God instead.

In our world today, people in some places still worship statues of gods. Other people act as if friends, money, fame, nice clothes, and important jobs are gods who can bring a good life. But there is still only one God who deserves our worship and praise—the true and living God!

God, you are the one and only God. You are living and powerful. Thank you for holding the world in your hands. Help me to put all my trust in you. Amen.

JULY 28

•

They also tell how you are waiting for God's son from heaven. God raised him from the dead—Jesus, who saves us from the wrath that is coming upon us.

1 Thessalonians 1:10 AT

Who do you think of when you hear the word *power?* A hero from the movies? The president of the United States? The principal of your school? These answers are all correct. But there is a different and more important kind of power. It is not the power to make people do what you want them to do but the power to give new life. Only God has that kind of power!

The proof of God's power came when God raised Jesus from the dead. Now and then, other humans may "die" for a few minutes and then be revived, but one day they will die again. It was different with Jesus. When God raised Jesus, it was for all time. When we become followers of Jesus, we get to share in Jesus' new life. That is amazing!

When he said "the wrath that is coming upon us," Paul was talking about how we suffer when we are separated from God's presence because of our sin. But when we share in Jesus' new life, we don't stay separate from God any longer! God gives us the power to live in God's way, and to love people as Jesus loves them.

God, you alone have the power to give life. Thank you for giving new life to Jesus and for letting me share in that life now and forever. Amen.

JULY 29

But as apostles, we could have demanded help from you. After all, Christ is the one who sent us. We chose to be like children or like a mother nursing her baby. We cared so much for you, and you became so dear to us, that we were willing to give our lives for you when we gave you God's message.

1 Thessalonians 2:7–8 CEV

What is a church? Is it a building with fancy windows and an organ? Or something different?

In Paul's day the church didn't have special buildings or musical instruments. Members met in people's homes. What made the church special was the love and care and gentleness that were found there. Paul was gentle and kind when he first met the Thessalonians. He says that he had acted like a mother who loves her little children very much!

Churches today aren't perfect, any more than families are. Their members fight and make mistakes. But God loves the church. God wants the people in the church to treat one another with gentleness and respect—the way members of a family should treat one another. God wants the people in the church to share God's love with each other and with the world.

God, thank you for the church. And thank you for all the people who love and support me like a family. Help me also to care for other people and to show them how much I love them. Amen.

JULY 30

•

You belong to the light and live in the day. We don't live in the night or belong to the dark. Others may sleep, but we should stay awake and be alert. People sleep during the night, and some even get drunk. But we belong to the day. So we must stay sober and let our faith and love be like a suit of armor. Our firm hope that we will be saved is our helmet.

1 Thessalonians 5:5–8 CEV

Nowadays, there are plenty of people whose jobs keep them awake all night. Some people who work in grocery stores, hospitals, or factories have to work a night shift, for example. But before the days of electric lights, night was simply the time for sleeping, or maybe for getting drunk. Sleeping people and drunk people could not pay much attention to the things going on around them.

But Paul knew that Christians *should* be paying close attention to the new ways that God works in and among them! That is why Paul wrote, "Others may sleep, but we should stay awake and be alert." Paul doesn't really mean that our bodies should never sleep! Rather, he is telling us that we must always listen carefully to hear God speaking to us. "Stay alert"—God will help you to do what is right. "Stay sober"—you will discover the new power that God gives us to love one another. "Belong to the day"—you will live your life with faith, love, and hope. Now, those things are worth staying awake for!

God, keep my mind and heart alert to notice the ways you are leading me. Help me to live always in faith, hope, and love. Amen.

JULY 31

•

God is fair. He will pay back trouble to those who give you trouble. He will help you who are troubled. And he will also help us. All of those things will happen when the Lord Jesus appears from heaven. He will come in blazing fire. He will come with the angels who are given the power to do what God wants.

2 Thessalonians 1:6–7 NIRV

Jesus lived his life on earth as a human being much like us. But the New Testament teaches us that Jesus is different from all other humans. Here are two important differences: Jesus was raised up from the dead. And one day Jesus will return to earth to set all things right.

Jesus' expected return is called his "second coming." In this passage Paul teaches the Thessalonians that, when Jesus returns, he will help people who suffered. Other parts of this letter and other parts of the New Testament tell how to prepare for the second coming and what to expect when the time for it finally arrives. These teachings are hard to understand, and Christians sometimes argue about their meaning.

Though we don't know or agree on all the details, we can trust that when Jesus returns, it will be good news. Then God will act through Jesus to wipe every tear from people's eyes and to judge all people who ever lived. We can be hopeful and trusting as we wait for that day of judgment, because Jesus himself will be the judge. And we already know of Jesus' great love for us: He gave his own life to bring us close to God.

God, you see the suffering of those in trouble, and you promise to make all things right. Help us to know how to live as we await Jesus' return. Amen.

AUGUST 1

•

When anyone presents a grain offering to the LORD, the offering shall be of choice flour; the worshiper shall pour oil on it, and put frankincense on it, and bring it to Aaron's sons the priests. After taking from it a handful of the choice flour and oil, with all its frankincense, the priest shall turn this token portion into smoke on the altar, an offering by fire of pleasing odor to the LORD.

Leviticus 2:1–2 NRSV

In ancient times, the people of Israel honored God by offering sacrifices, which were special kinds of gifts to God. Sometimes the sacrifice was grain or choice flour mixed with oil and perfume. Other times the sacrifice was an animal—a goat, or a sheep, for example. The priest would kill the animal and then offer part or all of it to God by burning it on a table called an "altar." The altar was near the Tent of Meeting or, in later years, in the courtyard outside the Jerusalem Temple. The Book of Leviticus gives many instructions on how to offer sacrifices.

Jews do not offer sacrifices of animals or grain today, but they still read and study the Jewish Law. They obey the Law as best they can, as a way of showing the great honor and respect they have for God.

Whenever you work hard to give someone just the right gift, you show that person how much he or she means to you. In the same way, when the people of Israel gave God costly sacrifices, they showed how important God was in their lives. What are some of the ways that you show how important God is in *your* life?

God, what gift can I possibly give you? Everything that I have has come from you. Teach me how to live in a way that pleases you and that shows the world your greatness. Amen.

AUGUST 2

•

Aaron lifted his hands toward the people and blessed them; and he came down after sacrificing the sin offering, the burnt offering, and the offering of well-being. Moses and Aaron entered the tent of meeting, and then came out and blessed the people; and the glory of the LORD appeared to all the people. Fire came out from the LORD and consumed the burnt offering and the fat on the altar; and when all the people saw it, they shouted and fell on their faces.

Leviticus 9:22–24 NRSV

Aaron, the brother of Moses, was the very first high priest for the people of Israel. For seven days Aaron and his sons, who were also priests, had been preparing to serve the Lord.

But now it was time to begin their regular work as priests. The priests were the ones who burned the people's sacrifices on the altar. Aaron made three types of sacrifices on this day to show that the people wanted to live their lives for God. Then God's glory, like a cloud, appeared to the people. After that a burst of fire burned up the sacrifices. The glory and the fire showed the people that God truly was present with them.

Today, people of faith worship in different ways than the ancient people of Israel did. For example, Christians worship by singing songs of praise, by praying, and by reading and hearing the Scriptures. We also share bread and wine (or grape juice) as a way of remembering how Jesus gave himself as a kind of sacrifice for us. In worship we all celebrate God's glory and rejoice that God is always with us!

God, you are so great! Your glory fills not just the synagogues and churches but the whole world. Teach us to worship you in spirit and in truth. Amen.

AUGUST 3

•

"Suppose an outsider lives with you in your land. Then do not treat him badly. Treat him as if he were one of your own people. Love him as you love yourself. Remember that all of you were outsiders in Egypt. I am the LORD your God."

Leviticus 19:33–34 NIRV

Have you ever felt like you didn't belong? Like everyone around you knew each other and you were the only stranger? Perhaps you were the new kid in school or in your neighborhood. Being an outsider can be uncomfortable or even scary, and can make you feel very sad.

In Bible times, there were outsiders (people from other lands and cultures) living with the people of Israel. This passage teaches the Israelites that they were to treat each outsider just as they would treat one of their own people. After all, they themselves once lived as outsiders in the land of Egypt. So they knew how terrible it was to be treated like ones who didn't belong.

It is the easiest thing in the world to mistreat outsiders; it is much harder to love them before you get to know them. But God expects us to love others as much as we love ourselves! When we treat outsiders well, we are walking in the way of God instead of in the ways of the world.

Holy Lord, help me to remember what it is like to be an outsider. Teach me to love and embrace outsiders who come into my family, school, or neighborhood, just as you love me. Amen.

AUGUST 4

•

The LORD spoke to Moses, saying: Speak to Aaron and to his sons, saying, Thus you shall bless the Israelites: You shall say to them,

The LORD bless you and keep you;
the LORD make his face to shine upon you, and be gracious to you;
the LORD lift up his countenance upon you, and give you peace.

Numbers 6:22–26 NRSV

Have you heard these words before? Sometimes the minister in church will say them at the end of the worship service, in what is called the benediction. The minister is asking God to "bless" the people—to bring good to them and to let them see how much God cares for them.

In the Scripture passage, Moses tells Aaron to say these words to the Hebrews. Aaron is a "priest." A priest is someone who leads the people in serving God. But it is not only ministers or priests who can bless others. We can all do that!

How can we bless others? We can bless them through our kind words, thoughtful actions, cheerful attitude, or listening heart. Whenever we let others see how much God cares for them, we bless them. The surprising thing is, when we bless others, we ourselves are blessed!

Blessed are you, O Lord our God, ruler of the whole world! Make your face to shine upon us this day. Teach us to bless others with all that we say and do. Amen.

AUGUST 5

•

Moses heard people from every family crying. They were sobbing at the entrances to their tents. The LORD burned with hot anger. So Moses became troubled. He asked the LORD, "Why have you brought this trouble on me? Why aren't you pleased with me? Why have you loaded me down with the troubles of all these people?" . . . The LORD said to Moses, "Bring me 70 of Israel's elders. Bring men that you know are leaders and officials among the people. Have them come to the Tent of Meeting. I want them to stand there with you. I will come down. I will speak with you there. I will take some of my Spirit that is on you. And I will put the Spirit on them. They will help you carry the people's load. Then you will not have to carry it alone."

Numbers 11:10–11, 16–17 NIRV

God had led the people of Israel out of their slavery in Egypt and had cared for them as they traveled in the wilderness on their way into the Promised Land. God had even provided a special food called manna for the people to eat. But after a while the people grew tired of manna, and they complained and cried. The people's complaining angered God and made Moses think that being their leader was a weight too heavy for him to carry.

God saw that Moses couldn't go on leading the people all by himself. Moses needed some people to share the work with him. So God appointed seventy helpers for Moses. The Spirit of God was already with Moses, and now it would be with the seventy helpers.

Today also, God's work is much too great for one person to do it all alone. But God puts the divine spirit on many people so that they can help to carry the load. How about you? Are you helping out?

Thank you, God, for sharing your important work among so many people. I want to do my part. Please show me how I can help. Amen.

AUGUST 6

•

After exploring the land for forty days, the men returned to Moses, Aaron, and the people of Israel at Kadesh in the wilderness of Paran. . . . This was their report to Moses: "We arrived in the land you sent us to see, and it is indeed a magnificent country—a land flowing with milk and honey. Here is some of its fruit as proof. But the people living there are powerful, and their cities and towns are fortified and very large. We also saw the descendants of Anak who are living there!" . . . But Caleb tried to encourage the people as they stood before Moses. "Let's go at once to take the land," he said. "We can certainly conquer it!"

Numbers 13:25–26a, 27–28, 30 NLT

Long ago God had promised a land to the people of Israel: the land of Canaan. It was a land that would have everything the people needed—a land, the Bible tells us, that was flowing with "milk and honey."

Now the people were ready to enter the Promised Land. Moses sent twelve men in to see what the land was like. When those scouts came back, they reported that there was plenty of food. But there was a problem: People were already living in the land, and some of them were warriors. Most of the Israelites didn't want to enter the land because they knew they would have to fight those warriors. But Caleb was not afraid. The Bible says that God rewarded Caleb for trusting the promises of God.

Like Caleb, we too want to trust in God's promises and do what God desires, even when we are afraid. But we also think about those people who already lived in the land. We know that God wants us to live peaceably with others and not fight. It is sometimes hard to know what to do.

God, make us wise as we seek to serve you and to trust you. Help us to remember that you are a God who loves and cares for all people. Amen.

AUGUST 7

•

So the next morning Balaam saddled his donkey and started off with the Moabite officials. But God was furious that Balaam was going, so he sent the angel of the LORD to stand in the road to block his way. As Balaam and two servants were riding along, Balaam's donkey suddenly saw the angel of the LORD standing in the road with a drawn sword in his hand. The donkey bolted off the road into a field, but Balaam beat it and turned it back onto the road.

Numbers 22:21–23 NLT

Balaam was a seer—someone who could see and speak about what would happen in the future. The king of Moab wanted Balaam to say bad things against the people of Israel. But God didn't want Balaam to go with the king's people and so sent an angel to block Balaam's way. Balaam's donkey saw the angel, but Balaam could not. Balaam's donkey was a better "seer" than Balaam!

After the angel blocked the path two more times, Balaam lost his temper and beat the poor donkey. Then she spoke! She asked Balaam why he was beating her. Balaam told her she had made him feel foolish. After that, the Lord opened Balaam's eyes so he could see the angel. Balaam realized that he had sinned by going to curse Israel, and he said he was sorry.

When we read this story, we are amazed to hear of a talking donkey. But the greatest miracle in this story is that God made Balaam into a "seer" who could finally see!

God, forgive us if ever we mistreat those who try to help us. Heal our blindness so that we may see and follow your path. Teach us to look for your messengers in unexpected places. Amen.

AUGUST 8

•

Dear brothers and sisters, what's the use of saying you have faith if you don't prove it by your actions? That kind of faith can't save anyone. Suppose you see a brother or sister who needs food or clothing, and you say, "Well, good-bye and God bless you; stay warm and eat well"—but then you don't give that person any food or clothing. What good does that do? So you see, it isn't enough just to have faith. Faith that doesn't show itself by good deeds is no faith at all—it is dead and useless.

James 2:14–17 NLT

Sometimes people say things they don't really mean. "We can't wait to have you over," they say. But they never call and invite you. "You're my best friend," she says. But she ignores you when other people are around. Words mean nothing when they aren't attached to actions.

Christian faith is full of words: the words of Scripture, the words of hymns and creeds, the words of prayers and personal stories. But James says it is not enough to hear and say the words of faith. We have to *do* them. Our faith has to grow hands and feet!

Jesus gave us a law of love: Love God above all, and love your neighbors as yourselves. If we say that we are followers of Jesus Christ, we have to act like it by the way we treat other people, especially those who are not rich or popular or important. Then people will know that we mean what we say.

God, please give us living faith that makes a difference to others. Amen.

AUGUST 9

•

But no one can control the tongue. It is an evil thing that never rests. It is full of deadly poison. With our tongues we praise our Lord and Father. With our tongues we call down curses on people. We do it even though they have been created to be like God. Praise and cursing come out of the same mouth. My brothers and sisters, it shouldn't be that way.

James 3:8–10 NIRV

The tongue is a very small part of the body. But it can do a lot of good. It can tell the truth, encourage others, and praise God. Having a tongue is a great gift. On the other hand, the tongue can do a lot of evil. It can lie and curse others. Cruel or untrue words can poison your relationship with other people.

How you use your tongue says a lot about the kind of person you are. Try to control your tongue. When you are feeling calm and happy this may be easy for you. But controlling your tongue when you are impatient, frustrated, or angry is very difficult. Sometimes the best thing to do in those circumstances is not to use your tongue at all. Some people call this "biting your tongue." Ouch! But even if you don't really bite your tongue, find a way to keep your tongue from doing evil.

Lord, thank you for giving me a powerful tongue. Help me use it for doing what is good. Amen.

AUGUST 10

•

Look here, you people who say, "Today or tomorrow we are going to a certain town and will stay there a year. We will do business there and make a profit." How do you know what will happen tomorrow? For your life is like the morning fog—it's here a little while, then it's gone. What you ought to say is, "If the Lord wants us to, we will live and do this or that."

James 4:13–15 NLT

Do you have a planner? It is a calendar that helps you organize your time and remember things you have to do. Planners are useful for busy people, but they can fool you. They can make you think that you are the one in charge of your life. They can make you think that you can control your own future.

James says that it's foolish to think that way. Filling in little squares in your planner does not put you in control of your life. You don't even know what will happen tomorrow. Only God can see the full picture of your life.

Your life is uncertain. It is like fog that is around for a little while and then disappears. That doesn't mean you shouldn't plan for today and tomorrow. But when you plan, always remember that your life is in God's hands.

Lord of all time, thank you for giving me hours and days and months and years to live. Remind me that my life is in your hands, and show me how to live a life that is pleasing to you. Amen.

AUGUST 11

•

Are any among you sick? They should call for the elders of the church and have them pray over them, anointing them with oil in the name of the Lord. And their prayer offered in faith will heal the sick, and the Lord will make them well.

James 5:14–15a NLT

God gave us life. And God protects and supports our life every moment. So when we are sick, we should pray to God to heal us and make us strong again.

How does God heal us? In many ways! God gives us incredible bodies that can heal themselves. (Think of the way a cut turns to a scab and then to new skin.) God gives us medicines and nurses and doctors. And God gives us other Christians to pray for us. No matter how we are healed, we should give thanks to God.

Sometimes sick people do not get better. That doesn't mean that they didn't have enough faith or that people didn't pray hard enough. Whether we are sick or healthy, we know that God's love will never let us go.

Lord of life, thank you for healthy bodies. Hear us when we pray for those who are sick. Heal them and make them well again. Amen.

AUGUST 12

•

"Hear, O Israel! The LORD is our God, the LORD alone. And you must love the LORD your God with all your heart, all your soul, and all your strength. And you must commit yourselves wholeheartedly to these commands I am giving you today. Repeat them again and again to your children. Talk about them when you are at home and when you are away on a journey, when you are lying down and when you are getting up again. Tie them to your hands as a reminder, and wear them on your forehead."

Deuteronomy 6:4–8 NLT

Some people think that being a Christian means obeying a lot of rules. It is true that God wants us to behave in ways that are fair and generous and kind, and the Bible has rules that guide us to behave in such ways. But following rules is only important as a way of loving God with all our hearts.

Moses speaks the words above after he reminds the people of Israel about the Ten Commandments that God had given to them. God gave the commandments to show love for the people. Obeying them is a way the people can show love for God. Moses tells the people the commandments are so important that they should even write them down on paper and tie them to their bodies as a way to remember! When God's commandments are in their minds and hearts, they will be loving God with all their strength.

Lord, I love you! Teach me your ways and write them on my heart, so that I might obey you my whole life long. Thank you for loving me so much. Amen.

AUGUST 13

•

When you have eaten and are satisfied, praise the LORD your God. Praise him for the good land he has given you. Make sure you don't forget the LORD your God. Don't fail to obey his commands, laws and rules. I'm giving them to you today. But suppose you don't obey his commands. And suppose you have plenty to eat. You build fine houses and settle down in them. Your herds and flocks increase their numbers. You also get more and more silver and gold. And everything you have multiplies. Then your hearts will become proud. And you will forget the LORD your God.

Deuteronomy 8:10–14a NIRV

The people of Israel had been wandering in the wilderness for so long. In those forty years, they had to rely on God's care for them. They had to trust God to send the manna that they ate in the desert and to give them water to drink. Even so, sometimes they forgot God. They did not always follow God's law.

Now the people are about to enter into the Promised Land. Moses tells them that once they do, it may become even harder for them to obey and honor God. While they were in the wilderness, if they didn't trust in God's protection they would die. But once they move into the Promised Land and become wealthy, Moses says, they may forget God altogether. They may look around at all the things they own and think, "Look how good my life is. I guess I'm doing everything right!"

O Lord, my God, may I never forget you! Do not let me become too proud of the good things in my life, as if I alone had made them. May I always remember that all good things come from you. Amen.

AUGUST 14

•

So give freely to those who are needy. Open your hearts to them. Then the LORD your God will bless you in all of your work. He will bless you in everything you do.

Deuteronomy 15:10 NIrV

At Christmastime, you have probably seen people outside grocery stores and shopping malls ringing a bell and asking you to put money in a kettle to give to the poor. In the Christmas season, many people feel especially worried about those who do not have enough food to eat or enough money to buy presents for their children. Giving money is a way to help.

But Christmas isn't the only time that the poor need help. In all seasons, God wants us to give generously to those who are needy. Sometimes giving money is the way we can help the most. Other times, we help most by giving things money cannot buy: friendship, love, and kindness. Whatever and whenever we give, God wants the gift to come not only from our hands but also from our hearts. The Bible says that God will bless all those who freely give.

Generous God, so many of your children are in need. Some don't have enough food or money. Some don't have enough love and care. Make me a generous giver. Teach me to open my heart! Amen.

AUGUST 15

•

Then you will speak while the Lord is listening. You will say, "My father Jacob was a wanderer from the land of Aram. He went down into Egypt with a few people. He lived there and became the father of a great nation. It had huge numbers of people. But the people of Egypt treated us badly. They made us suffer. They made us work very hard. Then we cried out to the Lord. He is the God of our people who lived long ago. He heard our voice. He saw how much we were suffering. The Egyptians were crushing us. They were making us work very hard. So the Lord reached out his mighty hand and powerful arm and brought us out of Egypt. He did great and wonderful things. He did miraculous signs and wonders. He brought us to this place. He gave us this land. It's a land that has plenty of milk and honey."

Deuteronomy 26:5–9 NIRV

Did you ever ask your mom or dad about your ancestors? Perhaps they were pilgrims, immigrants, pioneers, or slaves. Perhaps your ancestors have always lived in your country. Knowing where you came from can change the way you think about who you are.

Moses tells the people of Israel to remember the story of those who lived before them. Each year the Israelites would give a special gift to thank God for God's care. And when they gave the gift, they would tell how their ancestors were made to work as slaves. They would speak about how God had freed them and brought them into the Promised Land. Telling the story would remind them of who they were: a people cared for by God.

Lord, you are the God of my people who lived long ago. When they suffered you heard their cries and rescued them. And you still care for us today! May we always remember what you have done and give you thanks. Amen.

AUGUST 16

•

I'm calling for heaven and earth to give witness against you this very day. I'm offering you the choice of life or death. You can choose either blessings or curses. But I want you to choose life. Then you and your children will live.

Deuteronomy 30:19 NIrV

The Hebrew people had been wandering in the wilderness for forty years. They were about to enter the land God had promised them. Moses told them it was time for them to make a choice. Would they love and obey God? Or would they turn away from the Lord to serve other gods instead? The first path was the way of blessings and life. The second was the way of curses and death. Which would it be?

Perhaps to you it does not seem like much of a choice. Wouldn't everyone choose life? But the truth is, for some people, life has become so hard that death looks better. They have no hope for a better future. The Hebrews must have felt that way after wandering in the wilderness for so many years. It must have seemed as though God's promises would never come true.

So, choosing life is not always as easy as you might think. Sometimes it takes great courage and strength to make that choice. But Moses says that God is faithful and will reward those who choose life.

Lord, my Creator, you are my very life! Help me always to choose you. Give me a heart to love you, obey you, and be true to you. Bless me with life, O Lord. Amen.

AUGUST 17

•

Then the LORD spoke to Moses. He said, "This is the land I promised with an oath to Abraham, Isaac and Jacob. I told them, 'I will give this land to your children and their children.' Moses, I have let you see it with your own eyes. But you will not go across the Jordan River to enter it."

Deuteronomy 34:4 NIRV

Some jobs are too big to be finished in a few years or even in a lifetime. Moses had the job of leading the people out of Egypt and into the Promised Land. But he died before the end of the journey. Just before Moses' death, God took him to the top of Mount Pisgah and let him see the Promised Land. Moses knew that things would be better there. But Moses himself would see that land only from afar.

On the night before he was killed in 1968, Dr. Martin Luther King Jr. spoke to a large church full of people in Memphis, Tennessee. He was there to help African-American workers get fair treatment from the city. In his talk, he spoke about how far black people had come in their struggle for freedom.

And yet, Dr. King said, so much work still remained. Himself might not see the "Promised Land" of full justice for African Americans. But he was happy, he said, because he had been to the mountaintop. Like Moses, Dr. King had looked over into that Promised Land. He knew that a better day was coming.

Thank you, God, for leaders who have eyes and courage to see beyond the end of their own lives. Thank you for their strength and patience in doing your work. May we too be so brave! Amen.

AUGUST 18

•

"Brothers and sisters, here is what I want you to know. What has happened to me has really helped to spread the good news. One thing has become clear. I am being held by chains because of my stand for Christ. All of the palace guards and everyone else know it. Because I am being held by chains, most of the believers in the Lord have become bolder. They now speak God's word more boldly and without fear."

Philippians 1:12-14 NIRV

What happens after you get in big trouble for doing something you weren't supposed to do? You probably feel ashamed for behaving badly. Chances are you won't make the same mistake again.

More than once Paul was put in jail for telling people about Jesus Christ. But he didn't feel ashamed. And he didn't stop spreading the good news about Jesus! In the passage above, he tells the Philippians how he had even told the guards right there in the jail about Jesus. Paul was so bold because he knew that God wanted him to keep telling people about how God raised Jesus from the dead.

God wants us, too, to spread the good news about Jesus Christ. We can tell people about how God loves us and sent Jesus to show us that love. People may not always understand. But we never need to be ashamed, and we must never stop trying to do what God wants us to do!

God, the news about Jesus is the best news there is! Make me bold to tell people how much you love us, and how you sent Jesus to show us your love. Amen.

AUGUST 19

•

"For me, life finds all of its meaning in Christ. Death also has its benefits. Suppose I go on living in my body. Then I will be able to carry on my work. It will bear a lot of fruit. But what should I choose? I don't know. I can't decide between the two. I long to leave this world and be with Christ. That is better by far. But it is important for you that I stay alive. I'm sure of that. So I know I will remain with you. And I will continue with all of you to help you grow and be joyful in what you have been taught."

Philippians 1:21–25 NIRV

Everyone dies—there is no way around it. But almost no one knows ahead of time just when he or she will die. Whether you are a young person or an old person, it can be scary to think about dying.

Paul was in prison and knew that there was a good chance he would die there, but he wasn't afraid. He knew that when he died, he would be with Jesus in a fuller and more perfect way than he could be in this life. Thinking about that filled him with joy. But Paul knew that the decision of whether to live or die was too hard for him to make, and was up to God. God might still have work for Paul to do before he died!

God has work for us to do, too. And God wants us to grow and to be joyful as we do that work. God wants us to know Jesus Christ right now! But we are promised that we will be even closer to Jesus when we die. So either way, God has great things in store for us.

God, I thank you for promising me Jesus' presence both now and forever. Help me to trust in your love and care for me. Help me to grow and be joyful! Amen

AUGUST 20

•

"No matter what happens, live in a way that brings honor to the good news about Christ. Then I will know that you stand firm with one purpose. I may come and see you or only hear about you. But I will know that you work together as one person. And I will know that you work to spread the teachings of the good news."

Philippians 1:27 NIRV

Have you ever watched a great ball team play? The members give each player a chance to use his or her strongest skills. No one tries to hog the ball. They always have a strategy—a careful plan—for getting the ball down the court or down the field or over the net. In order to win the game they have to work together.

The people in the Philippian church were not trying to play ball, but to serve the Lord. But Paul said that they must work together, just like a great athletic team. No one should try to get all the attention. Instead they should let the other team members use their strongest skills. That way they would play their very best game!

Whether you are in your church, or school, or family, God wants you to work together with those around you. Learn their strengths, and give each of them a chance to shine.

Lord, help me to remember that serving you is the most important goal there is. Teach me to be a good team member wherever I am, so that I can bring honor to Jesus Christ. Amen.

AUGUST 21

•

Strangers entered the gates of Jerusalem.
They cast lots to see what each one would get.
They carried off its wealth.
When that happened, you just stood there and did nothing.
You were like one of them.
That was a time of trouble for your brothers.
So you should not have looked down on them.
The people of Judah were destroyed.
So you should not have been happy about it.
You should not have laughed at them so much
when they were in trouble.

Obadiah 11–12 NIRV

When a friend or a family member is in trouble, you naturally want to help. But suppose the person in trouble is someone you don't like at all, someone who has been mean and unfair to you in the past. Then you may find yourself secretly glad that she is in trouble. You may even think of ways to take advantage of her problems.

Edom and Israel were neighbors who didn't like each other. Then something terrible happened to Israel. Enemies invaded their capital city, Jerusalem, killing many people, and stealing everything valuable. The people of Edom were glad! They watched and did nothing to help their neighbor.

The prophet Obadiah said that God was angry with Edom for acting that way. God wants us to try to help everyone who is in trouble, not just the people we like.

Your love is for all people, God, even people we don't like. When our neighbors are in trouble, make us ready to help them. Amen.

AUGUST 22

•

Assyria is like a lion.
Where is the lions' den now?
Where did they feed their cubs?
Where did all of the lions go? . . .
"Nineveh, I am against you,"
announces the LORD who rules over all.
"I will burn up your chariots with fire.
Your young lions will be killed with swords.
I will leave you nothing on earth to catch.
The voices of your messengers
will no longer be heard."

Nahum 2:11a, 13 NIRV

Lions are the most powerful animals in the jungle. The other animals fear them and try to stay out of their way. The prophet Nahum compared Assyria to a lion. Assyria was a very powerful country. All the other countries, including Nahum's country, Judah, were afraid of Assyria. But God was against the people of Assyria, and now it was their turn to be afraid. Nahum said their capital city, Nineveh, would be destroyed.

Nahum was happy that God was against Assyria, because he hated the Assyrians. But God doesn't hate any particular group of people—whether they are Assyrians or Americans or Australians. God hates wickedness, no matter who is responsible for it.

Lord, when our country acts like a proud, powerful lion, remind us that you rule over all. Show us how to turn from our wickedness before it's too late. Amen.

AUGUST 23

•

"How terrible it will be for the Babylonians!
They say to a wooden god, 'Come to life!'
They say to a stone god, 'Wake up!'
Can those gods give advice?
They are covered with gold and silver.
They can't even breathe.
But I am in my holy temple.
Let the whole earth be silent in front of me."

Habakkuk 2:19–20 NIRV

Doesn't it sound foolish to say to a wooden god, "Come to life!" or to a stone god, "Wake up!"? People made those gods. They aren't alive. They can't help anyone or give anybody advice. The prophet Habakkuk said life would be terrible for the Babylonians, because they foolishly trusted in those gods.

But we do foolish things too. We imagine that a new outfit or a new bike will give us perfect happiness. We pretend that having lots of money will keep us safe. We make gods out of things, just like the Babylonians did.

Meanwhile the real God, the God who made us and loves us and saves us and fills us with joy, is waiting. When will we stop being foolish and come in silence before God with humble and faithful hearts?

You alone are God! I come before you in silence. Give me the wisdom to trust and worship only you. Amen.

AUGUST 24

•

"So wait for me to come as judge,"
announces the L*ORD*.
"Wait for the day I will stand up
to witness against all sinners.
I have decided to gather the nations.
I will bring the kingdoms together.
And I will pour out all of my burning anger on them.
The fire of my jealous anger
will burn the whole world up.
But then I will purify what all of the nations say.
And they will use their words to worship me.
They will serve me together."

Zephaniah 3:8–9 NIRV

Anger is not the opposite of love. You can love someone and be angry at him at the same time. In fact, you only get angry about things or people you really care about.

The prophet Zephaniah talked about a time when God's anger would burn up the whole world. That's a very scary thought. But God's anger is not the opposite of love. God cares about all the nations of the world, and so becomes angry at their sins. God's hope is that all people will stop doing what is wrong and serve God together. Then God's anger will turn to joy!

Holy God, you love us enough to get angry at us when we do what is wrong. Purify us so that our words will worship you and our deeds will give you praise. Amen.

AUGUST 25

•

"But who will be able to endure it when he comes? Who will be able to stand and face him when he appears? For he will be like a blazing fire that refines metal or like a strong soap that whitens clothes. He will sit and judge like a refiner of silver, watching closely as the dross is burned away. He will purify the Levites, refining them like gold or silver."

Malachi 3:2–3a NLT

When miners take silver out of the ground, it isn't pure. It is mixed with other things. So before it can be used, the silver must be refined by fire to remove the impurities. Only then will it be beautiful and shiny. In the same way, clothes taken out of the laundry hamper aren't clean. They must be washed with soap to remove dirt and stains. Only then will they be fresh and ready to wear. The prophet Malachi compares God to fire and soap. He says God will cleanse and purify the priests who lead Israel, so that all the people of God will shine with holiness and goodness.

The problem is that we don't always want to get clean and shiny. "Leave us alone," we say. "We don't mind being dirty." Purifying our lives of bad habits is too hard. Cleaning out mean and selfish thoughts is too painful. That is why we would sometimes prefer to keep God's fire and soap out of our lives. When God appears and starts cleaning us up, lots of things will have to change!

Holy Lord, changing us into holy people is hard work. Make us willing to invite you into our lives to clean and purify us. Make us shine! Amen.

AUGUST 26

•

"Everything is meaningless," says the Teacher, "utterly meaningless!" What do people get for all their hard work? Generations come and go, but nothing really changes. The sun rises and sets and hurries around to rise again. The wind blows south and north, here and there, twisting back and forth, getting nowhere."

Ecclesiastes 1:2–6 NLT

Have you ever worked really hard at making something and then had it destroyed? Maybe you built a big sand castle, and the tide came in and washed it away. Perhaps you created a beautiful art project, and your little brother ripped it. What was the point of trying so hard, you say to yourself. All my work came to nothing!

The Teacher in Ecclesiastes looks around the world and sees people working very hard at lots of things. But time passes, and all their work comes to nothing. What is the point of all this hard work? "Everything is meaningless!" the Teacher says. Life is like chasing the wind. You run and run, but you never catch it.

There is nothing wrong with working hard. But working hard will not guarantee that we will be happy or safe or important. If we think it will, we are chasing the wind.

God, you are the one who gives meaning to my life. Help me look for happiness and safety in you. Amen.

AUGUST 27

•

I gave myself everything my eyes wanted.
There wasn't any pleasure that I refused to give myself.
I took delight in everything I did.
And that was what I got for all of my work.
But then I looked over everything my hands had done.
I saw what I had worked so hard to get.
And nothing had any meaning.
It was like chasing the wind.
Nothing was gained on this earth.

Ecclesiastes 2:10–11 NIRV

Have you ever heard the expression, "You can't take it with you"? Grown-ups sometimes say that to remind themselves of what is really important in life. Like everyone else, you will die someday. And when you do, you will have to leave behind the things that may seem very important while you're alive. Whatever it is—a great job, a new car, a huge video game collection, or a row of sports trophies—you can't take it with you!

That is what the Teacher is saying too. You can spend your whole life trying to have fun. You can spend your whole life making lots of money. But finally you have to leave it all behind. What might that mean for living your life now?

God our Creator, thank you for giving us life on this good earth. But help me remember that my life on earth will end someday, and that all I can take with me is your love. Amen.

AUGUST 28

•

There is a time for everything,
a season for every activity under heaven.
A time to be born and a time to die.
A time to plant and a time to harvest.
A time to kill and a time to heal.
A time to tear down and a time to rebuild.
A time to cry and a time to laugh.
A time to grieve and a time to dance.

Ecclesiastes 3:1–4 NLT

Ecclesiastes says that there is a time for everything. You already know that! There is a time to get up and a time to go to bed. There is a time to go to school and a time to go on vacation. There is a time to be with friends and a time to be by yourself. There is a time to be silly and a time to be thoughtful. There is a time to help others and a time to rest. Can you think of more examples?

Our lives have a rhythm or a pattern to them. We can never make our lives perfect and then keep them that way. They keep changing, just like the seasons of the year. You already know how to tell time with a clock. Learn to "tell time" with your life, so that you will always know what it is time to do.

Everlasting God, in all the different times of my life, I know that I can trust you. All the days of my life are in your hand. Amen.

AUGUST 29

•

I looked and saw how much people were suffering on this earth.
I saw the tears of those who are suffering.
They don't have anyone to comfort them.
Power is on the side of those who beat them down.
Those who are suffering don't have anyone to comfort them.
Then I announced that those
who have already died
are happier than those
who are still alive.
But people who haven't been born yet
are better off than the dead or the living.
That's because they haven't seen the evil things
that are done on earth.

Ecclesiastes 4:1–3 NIrV

The world can be a pretty terrible place. There are people all over the world who go to bed hungry. There are children whose parents are too poor to send them to school. There are people who cry themselves to sleep at night because of the terrible things others say and do to them during the day.

The world is full of so much suffering, the Teacher in Ecclesiastes says, that sometimes we wonder if it would be better to die than to suffer so much. Sometimes we wonder if it would be better not even to be born. That way we would never have to suffer at all!

When you suffer a lot and there is no one to comfort you, you might wonder whether life is worth living the way the author of Ecclesiastes did. But our life on this earth is a gift from God. Try to comfort those who are suffering, so that they will be glad they are alive.

God, I know that this world is full of pain. Show me how to comfort those who suffer. When I suffer, send someone to comfort me. Amen.

AUGUST 30

•

Here's something else on this earth that doesn't have any meaning. Sometimes those who are godly get what sinful people should receive. And those who are sinful get what godly people should receive. Here's what I'm telling you. That doesn't have any meaning either. So I advise everyone to enjoy life. People on this earth can't do anything better than eat and drink and be glad. Then they will enjoy their work. They'll be happy all the days of the life God has given them on earth.

Ecclesiastes 8:14–15 NIRV

What if you were in charge of the whole world? Would you make sure that only good things happened to good people? Would you make sure that people who did bad things always got punished?

You have noticed by now that the world doesn't work this way. Sometimes terrible things happen to those who love God and try to do what is right. And sometimes those who do terrible things get rewarded. Can you think of some examples?

The Teacher in Ecclesiastes reminds us that we are not in charge of the whole world. But we can still be happy to be alive. Even in a world that isn't perfect, we can still rejoice in the life God has given us and give thanks for food to eat and work to do.

God, I don't understand why the world is sometimes unfair. But I thank you for giving me life and joy. Amen.

AUGUST 31

•

Anyone who keeps on watching the wind won't plant seeds.
Anyone who keeps looking at the clouds won't gather crops.
You don't know the path the wind takes.
You don't know how a baby is made inside its mother.
So you can't understand how God works either.
He made everything.
In the morning plant your seeds.
In the evening keep your hands busy.
You don't know what will succeed.
It may be one or the other.
Or both might do equally well.

Ecclesiastes 11:4–6 NIrV

Do you ever wish you could predict the future? Wouldn't it be great if you could know exactly what is going to happen tomorrow, next month, or five years from now? It would make planning so much easier!

Part of being human is living with uncertainty about the future. We really can't predict what is going to happen. Sometimes things happen exactly as we planned. Sometimes they don't! But we still need to make plans and keep doing things.

The only thing we know for sure is that the future is in God's hands. God made everything, and if we have faith, we can learn to live with our uncertainty.

God of all time and space, there are many things in my life that I don't have control over. But I know that you love me. I don't know what my future will be like. But I know that you will be there. Amen.

SEPTEMBER 1

•

After the death of Moses the LORD's servant, the LORD spoke to Joshua son of Nun, Moses' assistant. He said, "Now that my servant Moses is dead, you must lead my people across the Jordan River into the land I am giving them. No one will be able to stand their ground against you as long as you live. For I will be with you as I was with Moses. I will not fail you or abandon you.

Joshua 1:1–2, 5 NLT

Parents, teachers, older friends, and people at church can all be good people to follow. You can trust good leaders to point you in the right direction and to help you make tough decisions. But one day, all these people will be gone, and you won't have them to follow anymore. Instead, you will be a leader, and there will be people following you!

This was Joshua's situation. He had followed Moses out of slavery in Egypt and into the wilderness. Now the people of Israel were ready to go into the land that God had promised. But Moses had died, and God wanted Joshua to be Israel's new leader. God gave Joshua a wonderful promise: "I will be with you, just as I was with Moses." You can count on that promise too!

Faithful God, it comforts me to know that you will never leave me or desert me. Make me a good leader. Amen.

SEPTEMBER 2

•

As Joshua approached the city of Jericho, he looked up and saw a man facing him with sword in hand. Joshua went up to him and asked, "Are you friend or foe?" "Neither one," he replied. "I am commander of the LORD's army." At this, Joshua fell with his face to the ground in reverence." "I am at your command," Joshua said. "What do you want your servant to do?" The commander of the LORD's army replied, "Take off your sandals, for this is holy ground." And Joshua did as he was told.

Joshua 5:13–15 NLT

While the Israelites were in the wilderness, God promised them a land to live in. The Book of Joshua tells the story of how they settled in that land. But first they had to take it away from their enemies, the Canaanites. That is why there is a lot of fighting in the Book of Joshua.

When Joshua, who was Israel's leader, met a man with a sword, he assumed that the man was either on his side or on his enemies' side. But the man was a messenger from God, and he told Joshua that he was not on either side.

When we are fighting with someone, we want God to be on our side. But God does not play favorites. God is on the side of what is holy and just and good.

God, show us how to be on your side in doing what is right. Amen.

SEPTEMBER 3

•

They completely destroyed everything in it—men and women, young and old, cattle, sheep, donkeys—everything. Then Joshua said to the two spies, "Keep your promise. Go to the prostitute's house and bring her out, along with all her family." The young men went in and brought out Rahab, her father, mother, brothers, and all the other relatives who were with her. They moved her whole family to a safe place near the camp of Israel.

Joshua 6:21–23 NLT

Rahab was a Canaanite woman who lived in Jericho. The Israelites were enemies of the Canaanites, and Israel's army destroyed every living thing in the city of Jericho. But Joshua told two Israelite men to protect Rahab and her family from being destroyed, because she had saved their lives when they had gone in to check out the land.

Rahab was kind to those Israelite men, even though they were her people's enemies. She believed that their God "rules over heaven above and earth below" (Josh. 2:11). The story of Rahab makes us wonder about all the other Canaanite people killed by the men of Israel. Were some of them people of kindness and faith like her?

God, when we feel hatred toward others, remind us that even our enemies can be people of kindness and faith. Amen.

•

Zelophehad didn't have any sons. He only had daughters. Their names were Mahlah, Noah, Hoglah, Milcah and Tirzah. The daughters of Zelophehad went to the priest Eleazar and to Joshua, the son of Nun. They also went to the other leaders. They said, "The LORD commanded Moses to give us our share of land among our male relatives." So Joshua gave them land along with their male relatives. That was in keeping with what the LORD had commanded.

Joshua 17:3b–4 NIRV

God had promised land to all the tribes of Israel, and it was very important that the land be divided up fairly among the twelve tribes. But the tribe of Manasseh had a problem. The usual way of dividing up the land was to give it to the male relatives in the family. But one of the families in the tribe didn't have any sons, only daughters.

Joshua did what God wanted. He gave the land to Zelophehad's daughters. Sons weren't the only ones who could keep the tribe going. Daughters could do it too.

In some places in the world, sons are valued much more than daughters. It was that way in Israel during the time of Joshua. But the daughters of Zelophehad were brave enough to stand up for themselves and ask for what belonged to them.

God, thank you for valuing your daughters as much as your sons. I know that you love all of us. Amen.

SEPTEMBER 5

•

One day the LORD told Joshua: "When Moses was still alive, I had him tell the Israelites about the Safe Towns. Now you tell them that it is time to set up these towns. If a person accidentally kills someone and the victim's relatives say it was murder, they might try to take revenge. Anyone accused of murder can run to one of the Safe Towns and be safe from the victim's relatives. The one needing protection will stand at the entrance to the town gate and explain to the town leaders what happened. Then the leaders will bring that person in and provide a place to live in their town."

Joshua 20:1–4 CEV

We usually think of our own homes as safe places. But sometimes our homes are not safe, and we need another place to live. Hurricanes and floods can make our homes unsafe. So can violence in our neighborhoods or in our families. What places of safety could you go to if your home became unsafe?

In the Book of Joshua, a person who killed someone by accident needed a place to go for safety. Even though the person didn't kill on purpose, the relatives of the dead person would be very angry with him. They might try to hurt or kill him to take revenge for what he did. The relatives' revenge might lead to even more violence. So God told Joshua to establish cities of safety, where a person could be protected until it was safe for him to go home again.

You are my protector and defender, Lord. When I am in danger, help me find a place of safety. Amen.

SEPTEMBER 6

•

"May Jael be the most blessed woman of all.
May the wife of the Kenite Heber be blessed.
May she be the most blessed woman of all those who live in tents."

Judges 5:24 NIRV

Jael was a war hero in Israel. She was praised for killing Sisera, who was a commander of the Canaanite army. Sisera had run away from Israel's soldiers. He thought he would be safe in Jael's tent, but Jael tricked him. She first pretended to be Sisera's friend. Then she killed him while he was asleep.

Christians disagree about killing. Some Christians think that it is sometimes right to fight in wars and kill people. Some Christians think it is right for the government to kill people who have murdered others. Other Christians think that killing is wrong, and that even enemies and murderers should not be killed. They think that we should not praise anyone for killing. What do you think?

God, it is confusing when Christians disagree about something important. Please give me wisdom. Amen.

SEPTEMBER 7

•

The temple was crowded with men and women. All of the Philistine rulers were there. About 3,000 men and women were on the roof. They were watching Samson put on a show. Then he prayed to the LORD. He said, "LORD and King, show me that you still have concern for me. God, please make me strong just one more time. Let me pay the Philistines back for what they did to my two eyes. Let me do it with only one blow."

Judges 16:27–28 NIRV

Samson was a leader of Israel who fought against Israel's enemies, the Philistines. Most of Samson's story would make a great cartoon! He was incredibly strong and had lots of adventures, just like the superheroes on television. Once he tore a lion apart with his bare hands. Another time he caught three hundred foxes and tied torches to their tails so they would burn up the Philistines' fields. He even killed a thousand of his enemies using the jawbone of a donkey!

In one way the story of Samson is not like a cartoon. Cartoon superheroes don't become weak or die, but Samson ended up weak and blind. Only God could help him. Samson prayed, and God answered his prayer. The temple fell, killing many Philistines. But it killed Samson too.

God, you are my only source of strength. When I am weak, show me that you have concern for me. Amen.

SEPTEMBER 8

•

Paul, a servant of Jesus Christ, called to be an apostle, set apart for the gospel of God. . . . To all God's beloved in Rome, who are called to be saints: Grace to you and peace from God our Father and the Lord Jesus Christ.

Romans 1:1, 7 NRSV

When someone calls your name, what do you do? You could ignore the person. But most likely you answer. You may say, "Yes?" or "What is it?" or perhaps, "Here I am."

In this passage, Paul speaks of a different kind of "calling"—the calling that comes from God. You don't answer this kind of calling with words alone. You answer with your life. Paul knew that God had chosen or called him to be an apostle. An apostle was a special servant sent by God to tell others about God's work in the world. Paul loved God very much, and so he answered God's call.

God is calling you too. You can answer the call by serving Jesus Christ. You don't have to wait till you grow up. And you don't have to become an apostle! There are many, many ways to show your love for God and to serve Jesus. Discovering the way that is right for you can bring you the greatest joy.

Here I am, Lord! I know that you are calling me to love you and to serve your Son, Jesus Christ. As I grow, help me to find the ways of service and love that are right for me. Amen.

SEPTEMBER 9

•

I do not understand my own actions. For I do not do what I want, but I do the very thing I hate.

Romans 7:15 NRSV

Thousands of years ago there was a famous teacher named Socrates. Socrates told a story about Leontius, a young man who happened to walk by a place where some criminals had been killed. When he realized that there were dead bodies lying there, Leontius suddenly felt confused. On the one hand he felt sickened by the thought of those bodies, and didn't want to look more closely. But part of him wanted badly to run over and stare at them! For a time Leontius wrestled with his thoughts, trying to make up his mind. But finally with eyes open wide he rushed over to the bodies and shouted, "There, you wretched eyes, fill yourselves up with the fine sight!" Leontius scolded his eyes as if he were speaking to another person, but he was actually angry at himself for not being able to stop himself.

Have you ever known in your mind that it would be better not to do something—but gone and done it anyway? The apostle Paul taught that this is often the way it is with people. But when we are weak, God's grace can help us to be strong. Next time you are having trouble doing the right thing, pray for God to help you in your time of need.

God, forgive me for the times when I know something is wrong and do it anyway. I need your help to do better! Please teach me to trust your Spirit for the strength I need. Amen.

SEPTEMBER 10

•

In the same way, the Holy Spirit helps us when we are weak. We don't know what we should pray for. But the Spirit himself prays for us. He prays with groans too deep for words. God, who looks into our hearts, knows the mind of the Spirit. And the Spirit prays for God's people just as God wants him to pray.

Romans 8:26–27 NIRV

Have you ever been "at a loss for words"? Different kinds of events may make it hard to know what to say to someone. Moments of great joy can take away our words, and so can moments of great sadness.

The same thing can happen when we try to talk to God in prayer. Sometimes we are so happy or sad or angry or afraid that words just won't come. But even when words come easily, they never fully express what is in our minds and hearts, or what God wants for us. That is why, Paul says, the Spirit of God helps us when we pray. The Spirit knows each of us very, very well and prays for us "with groans too deep for words." Even if we ourselves don't understand those "groans" or "sighs," God does!

The Spirit of God is always with us, in everyday times as well as in times of greatest joy and deepest sorrow. The Spirit searches our hearts and brings our prayers to God. And God always knows what we are trying to say.

Spirit, help me to pray! Give me words to say. And when the words won't come, then help me to pray with deep sighs and to know that God will understand. Amen.

SEPTEMBER 11

•

Who can separate us from Christ's love? Can trouble or hard times or harm or hunger? Can nakedness or danger or war? It is written,

"Because of you, we face death all day long.
We are considered as sheep to be killed" [Psalm 44:22].

No! In all these things we will do even more than win! We owe it all to Christ, who has loved us. I am absolutely sure that not even death or life can separate us from God's love. Not even angels or demons, the present or the future, or any powers can do that. Not even the highest places or the lowest, or anything else in all creation can do that. Nothing at all can ever separate us from God's love because of what Christ Jesus our Lord has done.

Romans 8:35–39 NIRV

When something terrible happens—something that causes people to suffer greatly through no fault of their own—they often ask, "Where was God?" Or, "Why didn't God stop this bad thing from happening?" Sometimes early Christians asked this question when others mistreated them for following Jesus. If they were mistreated for their faith, did that mean that God didn't love them?

The apostle Paul tells us that nothing ever stops God from loving us, not even death. Bad things do happen, but they don't keep God's love away from us. God cares for us the way a parent cares for a child; when we suffer, it brings God pain. But nothing stops God's love.

God, sometimes we wonder where you are! Help us to know that you are always here. Fill our hearts with sure knowledge of your love. Amen.

SEPTEMBER 12

•

We know that all that God created has been groaning. It is in pain as if it were giving birth to a child. The created world continues to groan even now. And that's not all. We have the Holy Spirit as the promise of future blessing. But we also groan inside ourselves as we look forward to the time when God will adopt us as full members of his family. Then he will give us everything he has for us. He will raise our bodies and give glory to them.

Romans 8:22–23 NIRV

When a woman is having a baby, she may groan or cry in pain. Her body has to work very hard. Some babies are born quickly, but others take a while to be born, and so the mother's pain may go on for many hours. It helps her if there is someone there to encourage her—to remind her that soon she will hold a sweet baby in her arms!

Paul writes that the whole world has been "groaning" like a woman who is having a baby. He is thinking about how humans, animals, and even the earth itself groan or cry out when they experience suffering or death.

God promises that one day all suffering and death will end. A more perfect world will be born! We do not know when. But while we wait, God's Holy Spirit is with us to encourage us and give us hope. The Spirit reminds us that God wants all suffering to end.

God, when the suffering world groans, teach us to listen and to give help where we can. May your Spirit give us comfort and hope. Amen.

•

But one night, Eli was asleep in his room, and Samuel was sleeping on a mat near the sacred chest in the LORD's house. They had not been asleep very long when the LORD called out Samuel's name. "Here I am!" Samuel answered. Then he ran to Eli and said, "Here I am. What do you want?" "I didn't call you," Eli answered. "Go back to bed." Samuel went back. Again the LORD called out Samuel's name. Samuel got up and went to Eli. "Here I am," he said. "What do you want?" Eli told him, "Son, I didn't call you. Go back to sleep." The LORD had not spoken to Samuel before, and Samuel did not recognize the voice. When the LORD called out his name for the third time, Samuel went to Eli again and said, "Here I am. What do you want?" Eli finally realized that it was the LORD who was speaking to Samuel. So he said, "Go back and lie down! If someone speaks to you again, answer, 'I'm listening, LORD. What do you want me to do?'"

1 Samuel 3:2–9a CEV

When someone's voice wakes you up, it is easy to get confused. Sometimes the voice becomes part of your dream, and you're not sure if you heard it or not! Samuel was a young boy who was living with the priest Eli so that he could learn how to serve God. Someone kept waking him up. He thought it was Eli. But it was really God who was calling Samuel! God had a special job for him to do.

How do you know when God is calling you? God calls people in many ways. Samuel heard a voice that woke him up. But God may also speak to you through a dream or through another person—maybe someone you never expected.

It is sometimes hard to recognize God's voice. Ask someone you trust to help you listen for it. Other people may hear God calling you even before you do!

I'm listening, Lord. What do you want me to do? Amen.

SEPTEMBER 14

•

When the Israelites saw the Ark of the Covenant of the LORD coming into the camp, their shout of joy was so loud that it made the ground shake! "What's going on?" the Philistines asked. "What's all the shouting about in the Hebrew camp?" When they were told it was because the Ark of the LORD had arrived, they panicked. "The gods have come into their camp!" they cried. "This is a disaster! We have never had to face anything like this before! . . . " So the Philistines fought desperately, and Israel was defeated again. The slaughter was great; thirty thousand Israelite men died that day. The survivors turned and fled to their tents. The Ark of God was captured.

1 Samuel 4:5–7, 10–11a NLT

The ark of the covenant was a wooden chest that contained the stone tablets on which Moses had written the law. The ark was a very holy thing to the people of Israel. It was a sign of God's presence with them.

The Israelites thought that taking the ark into battle would guarantee their victory over their enemies, the Philistines. If the ark was there, the Israelites believed, they were sure to win! But the people of Israel lost the battle, and the Philistines captured the ark. Having a holy ark did not mean that the Israelites could control God.

The Bible and the bread and wine at the Lord's Supper are holy things for Christians. They are a promise of God's presence with us, just as the ark of the covenant was for the Israelites. But our holy things do not guarantee that God will always be on our side when we oppose other people, and we cannot use them to make God do what we want.

God, forgive us when we think we can control you or when we think that we cannot be wrong because we know you. Amen.

SEPTEMBER 15

•

David was a success in everything that Saul sent him to do, and Saul made him a high officer in his army. . . . David had killed Goliath, the battle was over, and the Israelite army set out for home. As the army went along, women came out of each Israelite town to welcome King Saul. They were singing happy songs and dancing to the music of tambourines and harps. They sang:

"Saul has killed a thousand enemies;
David has killed ten thousand enemies!"

This song made Saul very angry, and he thought, "They are saying that David has killed ten times more enemies than I ever did. Next they will want to make him king." Saul never again trusted David. The next day the LORD let an evil spirit take control of Saul, and he began acting like a crazy man inside his house. David came to play the harp for Saul as usual, but this time Saul had a spear in his hand. Saul thought, "I'll pin David to the wall." He threw the spear at David twice, but David dodged and got away both times.

1 Samuel 18:5–11 CEV

Have you ever been jealous of someone who was smarter or better at sports or more popular than you? King Saul was very jealous of David, a young officer in his army. David had won many battles against Israel's enemies and had even killed the huge Philistine warrior, Goliath. People all over Saul's kingdom were praising David.

Saul became so jealous that one day he went crazy and tried to kill David with a spear. He tried to kill David other times too, but David always got away. Finally, the thing that Saul dreaded the most happened. David became king in Saul's place.

God, keep me from being jealous. Show me how to rejoice in the gifts and talents you give to other people. Amen.

SEPTEMBER 16

•

After the boy had gone, David got up from the south side of the stone. He bowed down in front of Jonathan with his face to the ground. He did it three times. Then they kissed each other and cried. But David cried more than Jonathan did. Jonathan said to David, "Go in peace. In the name of the LORD we have taken an oath. We've promised to be friends. We've said, 'The LORD is a witness between you and me. He's a witness between your children and my children forever.'"

1 Samuel 20:41–42a NIRV

King Saul hated David. But Saul's son Jonathan loved David. When David was hiding from Saul, Jonathan used arrows to send a message to David. If Jonathan's arrows fell in front of the young boy who was with him, that would mean David was safe. If his arrows went over the boy's head, that would mean David was in danger.

Jonathan was sad and angry that his father was putting David's life in danger. But he kept his promise to be friends with David. David and Jonathan's love for each other was stronger than Saul's hatred. After Jonathan died, David showed his love for Jonathan by taking care of his crippled son, Mephibosheth.

God, don't let hatred destroy love. Show me how to be loyal to the people I love, just as Jonathan and David were. Amen.

SEPTEMBER 17

•

The Lord was angry at what David had done, and he sent Nathan the prophet to tell this story to David: "A rich man and a poor man lived in the same town. The rich man owned a lot of sheep and cattle, but the poor man had only one little lamb that he had bought and raised. The lamb became a pet for him and his children. He even let it eat from his plate and drink from his cup and sleep on his lap. The lamb was like one of his own children. One day someone came to visit the rich man, but the rich man didn't want to kill any of his own sheep or cattle and serve it to the visitor. So he stole the poor man's little lamb and served it instead." David was furious with the rich man and said to Nathan, "I swear by the living Lord that the man who did this deserves to die! And because he didn't have any pity on the poor man, he will have to pay four times what the lamb was worth." Then Nathan told David: "You are that rich man!"

2 Samuel 12:1–7 CEV

King David did something very wrong. He made sure a good man named Uriah was killed in battle, so that David could marry Uriah's wife, Bathsheba.

God sent the prophet Nathan to David. Nathan told David a story about a rich man who stole a precious little lamb from a poor man. David could see that the rich man had done something wrong and selfish. But Nathan helped David see that he had acted as badly as the rich man in the story.

It is often easier for us to see other people's sins than it is to see our own. God sent many prophets to show the people of Israel the wrong and selfish things they had done. When you read the prophets' words in Scripture, ask yourself whether you too need help to see what you have done wrong.

Spirit of God, open my eyes to see the wrong things I have done. Give me the courage to admit my sins to others. Amen.

SEPTEMBER 18

•

David started trembling. Then he went up to the room above the city gate to cry. As he went, he kept saying, "My son Absalom! My son, my son Absalom! I wish I could have died instead of you! Absalom, my son, my son!"

2 Samuel 18:33 CEV

We can't get over grief—deep sadness—the way we get over a cold. When we catch a cold, we can usually count on feeling better after a few days. But sadness over the death of someone we love isn't like that. Our lives are never the same again.

King David's son Absalom wasn't a good son. He was plotting to take the throne away from his father. But David loved him. When he found out that Absalom had been killed in battle, he was filled with grief. He wished that he could have died instead of his son.

Death tears us apart from those we love. We can't hug them or talk to them anymore. When persons we love die, it is right for us to feel deepest sadness. After a while, we won't be trembling and crying all the time the way King David did when he first got the news of Absalom's death. But that doesn't mean that we should try to forget about what happened. Instead, we should remember the persons we grieve for and give thanks to God for their lives.

God, we know that when we grieve for people who have died, you grieve with us. Even in our sadness, give us faith in your promises of everlasting life with you. Amen.

SEPTEMBER 19

•

In a race all the runners run. But only one gets the prize. You know that, don't you? So run in a way that will get you the prize. All who take part in the games train hard. They do it to get a crown that will not last. But we do it to get a crown that will last forever. So I do not run like someone who doesn't run toward the finish line. I do not fight like a boxer who hits nothing but air. No, I train my body and bring it under control. Then after I have preached to others, I myself will not break the rules and fail to win the prize.

1 Corinthians 9:24–27 NIRV

In every sport the best players train hard. They practice, practice, practice. The very top players may even travel far away and live at a special training camp where they can get expert coaching and practice still more. Why do some athletes want to win so much that they will go to all that trouble? Because they love their sport. And because they wish for the glory and honor that the winners receive.

Paul says that he is like an athlete. But the race he is running isn't a footrace, and the prize he wants to win isn't a ribbon or a medal. Paul is striving to know and to be like Jesus Christ and to help others to know him too. But Paul can't do those things with just a little bit of effort here and there, and neither can we. We have to practice, practice, practice! Our practicing is sure to pay off. It will bring us the "prize" of joy in this life and forever.

God, remind me that I must practice knowing and being like Jesus. Show me the joy and the pleasure that come from working hard for you. Amen.

SEPTEMBER 20

There is one body. But it has many parts. Even though it has many parts, they make up one body. It is the same with Christ. We were all baptized by one Holy Spirit into one body. It didn't matter whether we were Jews or Greeks, slaves or free people. We were all given the same Spirit to drink. . . . The eye can't say to the hand, "I don't need you!" The head can't say to the feet, "I don't need you!" . . . You are the body of Christ. Each one of you is a part of it.

1 Corinthians 12:12–13, 21, 27 NIRV

Isn't it a good thing that all the parts of your body work with each other? Imagine if one part of your body tried to get rid of the other parts. What if your eye tried to get rid of your hand, or what if your head tried to go on without your feet? Luckily our bodies seem to know that we do best if all our parts cooperate. They know that if one part suffers, every part suffers with it. And if one part is honored, every part of the body shares in its joy.

The church is the body of Jesus Christ. We who are in the church do Jesus' work on the earth. And, just as your body has many parts, so does the church. There are preachers, teachers, worshippers, servers, and more. Every person is important. When anyone in our church suffers we all feel sad. When anyone is honored we all feel joy. All the parts of the body must work together!

Christ Jesus, thank you for your body, the church. Help me to find my place in the body of believers and to cooperate with others to do your work on earth. Amen.

SEPTEMBER 21

•

What if I could speak all languages of humans and of angels? If I did not love others, I would be nothing more than a noisy gong or a clanging cymbal. What if I could prophesy and understand all secrets and all knowledge? And what if I had faith that moved mountains? I would be nothing, unless I loved others. What if I gave away all that I owned and let myself be burned alive? I would gain nothing, unless I loved others.

1 Corinthians 13:1–3 CEV

This is the beginning of one of the most famous passages in the whole Bible. It is famous because so many people over the centuries have understood how true Paul's words about love really are.

Paul was talking about how we know that God is with us. People in Paul's church said that the Holy Spirit had given them unusual abilities. Some could speak in a heavenly language taught by the Spirit. Others could speak words of prophecy, telling of God's plan for days ahead. The people bragged that their unusual abilities were proof of God's special presence with them. But Paul said there was an even better way to know and show God's presence: the way of love.

Love is God's most precious gift to us. If we ask God in prayer, God's love will fill our hearts. And it makes us able to love others more completely. *Love* shows us that God is with us.

God, make our hearts overflow with your love. Teach us how to reach out to others in love. Let us feel your presence with us! Amen.

SEPTEMBER 22

•

Love is patient and kind. Love is not jealous or boastful or proud or rude. Love does not demand its own way. Love is not irritable, and it keeps no record of when it has been wronged. It is never glad about injustice but rejoices whenever the truth wins out. Love never gives up, never loses faith, is always hopeful, and endures through every circumstance.

1 Corinthians 13:4–7 NLT

What does love look like? Can you see it? What does it sound like? Can you hear it?

You *can* see love, and you can hear it too. You see and hear it in the way loving people act and speak. Love gives people the strength to be patient with one another. Love helps people to treat others with kindness. Love keeps people from being proud, boastful, or rude. When a person's heart is filled with love, she rejoices whenever she hears the truth. Is your heart filled with love? Can other people see the love in your life?

No one except God can love perfectly. Even people who are very loving fall far short of perfect love. But when our hearts are full of God's love, we do find it easier to act in all these good ways. The love spills over into all that we say and do.

God, sometimes I find it so hard to be loving and giving. Please fill me with your love so that others can hear it and see it in my words and deeds. Amen.

SEPTEMBER 23

•

So take this as a request from your friend Paul, an old man, now in prison for the sake of Christ Jesus. My plea is that you show kindness to Onesimus. I think of him as my own son because he became a believer as a result of my ministry here in prison. Onesimus hasn't been of much use to you in the past, but now he is very useful to both of us. I am sending him back to you, and with him comes my own heart. . . . Perhaps you could think of it this way: Onesimus ran away for a little while so you could have him back forever. He is no longer just a slave; he is a beloved brother, especially to me.

Philemon 9b–12, 15–16a NLT

Paul is writing to his friend Philemon about a man named Onesimus, who has lived as Philemon's slave. (In Bible times, it was not unusual for some people to have slaves.) Paul had been in jail for preaching the gospel, and Onesimus had come to Paul and helped him. During his time with Paul, Onesimus came to believe in Jesus as Lord.

Now it is time for Onesimus to return to Philemon. Paul writes this letter to ask Philemon to treat Onesimus well—perhaps even to set him free. The name Onesimus meant "useful," but Paul jokes that at one time Onesimus had not been a very "useful" slave. Onesimus, however, was changed as a result of the time he spent with Paul. God had transformed Onesimus into being useful just as his name said!

But Paul tells Philemon that God was transforming him too—from being the owner of Onesimus to being his brother. Philemon would have to treat Onesimus in a new way, with love and respect. We don't know whether Philemon listened to what Paul said. What do you think?

God of freedom, transform us so that we see all people as our brothers and sisters. Make us useful in showing others your love. Amen.

SEPTEMBER 24

•

I then saw what looked like a throne made of sapphire, and sitting on the throne was a figure in the shape of a human. From the waist up, it was glowing like metal in a hot furnace, and from the waist down it looked like the flames of a fire. The figure was surrounded by a bright light, as colorful as a rainbow that appears after a storm.

I realized I was seeing the brightness of the LORD's glory! So I bowed with my face to the ground, and just then I heard a voice speaking to me.

Ezekiel 1:26–28 CEV

Have you ever looked into a still pond and seen the reflection of the blue sky? The reflection is not the sky, but it shows you what the sky is like.

Ezekiel the prophet had a vision. It was like a dream, but Ezekiel wasn't asleep. In his vision, Ezekiel saw an awesome throne. On the throne was a being who looked somewhat like a human being—but far more glorious! Ezekiel was amazed. He knew that he was seeing the appearance of the glory of the Lord—like God's reflection in a pond or a mirror.

Most humans never have the kind of vision that Ezekiel had. But we can catch glimpses of God's glory all around us. The brilliant sun shining in the sky and the stars glowing at night all tell of it. The words of the Bible help us to see God's glory. Even good and loving people show us God's glory. And because Christians believe that Jesus reflects God's glory perfectly, when they read this vision of Ezekiel, they may think of Jesus.

Lord, teach me to see your glory all around me and to give you praise. Let the light of your glory shine in my own heart through Jesus Christ. Amen.

SEPTEMBER 25

•

"Ezekiel, I am sending you to the people of Israel. They are just like their ancestors who rebelled against me and refused to stop. They are stubborn and hard-headed. But I, the Lord God, have chosen you to tell them what I say. Those rebels may not even listen, but at least they will know that a prophet has come to them."

Ezekiel 2:3–5 CEV

Imagine yourself going to a lot of trouble to help someone and then having her ignore you or tell you to "get lost." Would you think that you had wasted your time?

God wanted the prophet Ezekiel to go to a great deal of trouble, to tell the people that they needed to obey God's laws. Instead of worshipping the Lord, the people had been worshipping idols. Ezekiel was supposed to tell them to serve the Lord. "Those rebels may not even listen!" God told Ezekiel. But even if they ignored him, God said, Ezekiel must not think that he was wasting his time. It is always right and good to speak God's truth.

If you hear someone telling us how we must change our ways, ask yourself, could this be a word from the Lord? And if you see something happening that isn't right, pray about it. Maybe God wants *you* to speak the truth to others!

God, thank you for sending prophets who show us your way. Teach me to listen, and make me brave enough to speak your truth. Amen.

•

"'They will throw their silver into the streets. Their gold will be like an 'unclean' thing. Their silver and gold will not be able to save them on the day I pour out my anger on them. They will not be able to satisfy their hunger. Their stomachs will not be full. Their silver and gold have tripped them up. They have made them fall into sin. My people were so proud of their beautiful jewelry. They used it to make statues of their evil gods. I hate those gods. So I will turn their statues into an 'unclean' thing for them."

Ezekiel 7:19–20 NIRV

When you were younger, did you have a blanket or a stuffed toy that made you feel safe? You trusted it to comfort you when you were sad or alone. Perhaps you still have it. Now that you are older, what or whom else do you trust to keep you safe in times of trouble? Your parents? Your friends? Your house? Your dog?

In Ezekiel's day, some people put all their trust in silver and gold. They thought that riches could solve all their problems. But God had Ezekiel tell them that their wealth—the very thing they thought would keep them safe—had actually led them away from God. They trusted and worshipped silver and gold instead of God. But money and fine jewelry can't help in a day of trouble; only God can do that.

God, thank you for all the people and things that help to keep me safe. Remind me that all these things come from you, and teach me to trust you with my life. Amen.

SEPTEMBER 27

•

A message came to me from the LORD. He said, "Son of man, you are living among people who refuse to obey me. They have eyes that can see. But they do not really see. They have ears that can hear. But they do not really hear. They refuse to obey me."

Ezekiel 12:1–2 NIRV

In the movie *Mary Poppins,* Mary tells the Banks children that some people cannot see past the end of their own noses. Jane and Michael's father cannot see the lady who feeds the birds on the steps of the great church, even though he passes her every single day on his way to work. He doesn't see her because he chooses not to use his eyes and ears when he is around her.

The people to whom Ezekiel was sent as prophet have eyes and ears, but they choose not to use them. God has been trying to tell them that they must stop worshipping idols and being cruel to one another. But they choose not to see or hear the bad things going on all around them.

In the movie, when Mr. Banks loses his job, he suddenly begins to see and hear all the things he was missing before. But you don't have to wait for something bad to happen to start using your senses! You can ask God right now to help you notice the world around you in a new and better way.

God, sometimes I choose not to hear what you are telling me or to see people who need your love and care. Heal my eyes and ears so that I might live the way you want me to. Amen.

SEPTEMBER 28

•

"The LORD and King says, 'I am against you prophets. Your messages are false. Your visions do not come true,' announces the LORD and King. 'Israel, my powerful hand will be against the prophets who see false visions. Their magic tricks are lies. They will not be among the leaders of my people. They will not be listed in the records of Israel. In fact, they will not even enter the land. Then you will know that I am the LORD and King. They lead my people away from me. They say, "Peace." But there isn't any peace. They are like people who build a weak wall. They try to cover up the weakness by painting the wall white.' "

Ezekiel 13:8–10 NIRV

Everyone likes good news. Sometimes we want to tell or hear good news so badly that we don't even care whether or not it is really true. But the truth matters! What if a teacher tells your parents that you are doing well in school when you aren't learning anything? What if a doctor tells you that you are healthy when you need an operation?

Some prophets were saying that there would be peace in the land. Everyone liked to hear that news! But it was a lie. Enemies would soon conquer Jerusalem, the city where the lying prophets lived. Because the prophets lied, they kept the people of Jerusalem from acting to protect themselves.

We don't like hearing bad news. But when there is bad news, God can strengthen us and help us to accept the truth.

God, help me to face the truth, even when it is painful. Give me the courage and honesty I need. Teach me how to help others when there is bad news to bear. Amen.

SEPTEMBER 29

•

The Lord took hold of me, and I was carried away by the Spirit of the Lord to a valley filled with bones. He led me around among the old, dry bones that covered the valley floor. They were scattered everywhere across the ground. Then he asked me, "Son of man, can these bones become living people again?" "O sovereign Lord," I replied, "you alone know the answer to that." Then he said to me, "Speak to these bones and say, 'Dry bones, listen to the word of the Lord! This is what the Sovereign Lord says: Look! I am going to breathe into you and make you live again! I will put flesh and muscles on you and cover you with skin. I will put breath into you, and you will come to life. Then you will know that I am the Lord.'"

Ezekiel 37:1–6 NLT

During the time when Ezekiel was prophet, terrible things happened to the people of Israel. The army of the king of Babylon took over the land. Many people were killed, and many were forced to leave their land and go to Babylon to live. These events caused the people to feel great despair. They were so sad that they felt like they were dead—as dead as dry bones.

Then the Spirit of God showed Ezekiel an amazing vision. Ezekiel saw a large valley full of bones dried up from the sun. But God told Ezekiel that there was hope for those bones. They would be put back into whole bodies and filled with the spirit of life. They would live again! The vision meant that the people of Israel should have hope too. Even though everything had gone wrong for them, God would bring them new life.

Lord, you are our Creator, and only you can bring hope of new life when all has been lost. Have mercy on those who suffer, O Lord. Amen.

SEPTEMBER 30

•

This is what the LORD says: "The people of Tyre have sinned again and again, and I will not forget it. I will not let them go unpunished any longer! They broke their treaty of brotherhood with Israel, selling whole villages as slaves to Edom. So I will send down fire on the walls of Tyre, and all its fortresses will be destroyed."

Amos 1:9–10 NLT

Do you know what a judge is? He or she is someone who loves justice and tries to see that everyone gets treated fairly. Do you know what judges do? They give judgments. First they find out whether someone has done something bad; then they decide whether that person deserves punishment.

The prophet Amos described God as a judge who knew all the bad things that the nations had done. One by one, God made a judgment against each country. The people of Tyre had broken their promise to be friends and had sold many people into slavery. They brought hardship and danger to other people, and God said now a fire would bring hardship and danger to them.

It makes us uncomfortable to think of God as a judge. It's easier to think of God as a gentle shepherd or a loving parent. But it is a comfort to know that God cares about the injustice in the world and wants everyone to be treated fairly.

God our judge, I am glad that you love justice. Help me to treat everyone fairly and help me work for justice in the world. Amen.

OCTOBER 1

•

The Lord says,
"I hate your holy feasts.
I can't stand them.
I hate it when you gather together.
You bring me burnt offerings and grain offerings.
But I will not accept them.
You bring your best friendship offerings.
But I will not even look at them.
Take the noise of your songs away!
I will not listen to the music of your harps.
I want you to treat others fairly.
So let fair treatment roll on
just as a river does!
Always do what is right.
Let right living flow along
like a stream that never runs dry!"

Amos 5:21–24 NIRV

Have you ever heard someone say "he is two-faced"? It's not a compliment! People who are mean and dishonest can fool you by sometimes appearing to be very kind and honest. We call them two-faced because they have two different faces that they show to the world.

Amos accused God's people of being two-faced. They showed one face to God in worship: There they sang songs of praise to God and gave God offerings. But they showed their real face in the unfair way they treated the poor.

We are sometimes fooled by two-faced people. But God isn't fooled. God hates dishonest worship. God wants to see our real face in worship and in everything else we do.

God of truth, help our faith show in how we treat others. Let our worship reflect who we really are. Amen.

OCTOBER 2

•

Then Amaziah said to Amos, "Get out of Israel, you prophet! Go back to the land of Judah. Earn your living there. Do your prophesying there. Don't prophesy here at Bethel anymore. This is where the king worships. The main temple in the kingdom is located here." Amos answered Amaziah, "I was not a prophet. I wasn't even a prophet's son. I was a shepherd. I also took care of sycamore-fig trees. But the LORD took me away from taking care of the flock. He said to me, 'Go. Prophesy to my people Israel.'"

Amos 7:12–15 NIRV

Amaziah was a very important person. He was the priest of the temple in Bethel where the king worshipped. He was in charge of everything that went on there. He didn't like what Amos the prophet was saying, and he wanted him to go back home.

But Amos said that God had told him to come to Bethel. God sometimes does surprising things! Amos was a shepherd no one had ever heard of before. But God told him to go prophesy in the temple of the king. He did, even though it made some important people upset.

Sometimes God works through important people like Amaziah. We need to listen to them and take what they say seriously. But important people are not the only ones we should listen to. We also have to be ready for God's surprises!

Lord of all people, thank you for leaders who speak the truth. Thank you for also using surprising people to speak your word. Use me! Amen.

OCTOBER 3

•

Every year Jesus' parents went to Jerusalem for the Passover festival. When Jesus was twelve years old, they attended the festival as usual. After the celebration was over, they started home to Nazareth, but Jesus stayed behind in Jerusalem. His parents didn't miss him at first, because they assumed he was with friends among the other travelers. . . . Three days later they finally discovered him. He was in the Temple, sitting among the religious teachers, discussing deep questions with them. And all who heard him were amazed at his understanding and his answers.

Luke 2:41–44a, 46–47 NLT

The Gospels—Matthew, Mark, Luke, and John—don't tell us very much about Jesus before he was a grown-up. Luke is the only one to tell a story from Jesus' childhood. It's a story with a scary middle and a happy ending.

Jesus' parents, Mary and Joseph, must have been very worried when they couldn't find Jesus—Jerusalem was a very big city, and Jesus was only twelve years old! But they finally found Jesus in a very safe place. He was in the temple, listening to the religious teachers. Even though he was young, he already knew a lot about God. As Jesus grew up, he learned even more, and many people came to him to learn about God.

God, as my body grows, help me grow in wisdom too. Help me to know you better and better, so that I can teach others about you. Amen.

OCTOBER 4

•

When he finished speaking, he turned to Simon. He said, "Go out into deep water. Let the nets down so you can catch some fish." Simon answered, "Master, we've worked hard all night and haven't caught anything. But because you say so, I will let down the nets." When they had done so, they caught a large number of fish. There were so many that their nets began to break. So they motioned to their partners in the other boat to come and help them. They came and filled both boats so full that they began to sink. When Simon Peter saw this, he fell at Jesus' knees. "Go away from me, Lord!" he said. "I am a sinful man!"

Luke 5:4–8 NIrV

Simon Peter was an expert on catching fish. When Jesus told him to put his nets into the water, he didn't think it was going to work. But he let his nets down anyway, and an amazing thing happened. The nets were so full of fish, they began to break. The boats were so full of fish, they started to sink. Simon Peter had never caught so many fish in his whole life!

Peter was so frightened that at first he told Jesus to go away, so that he could go back to his old life of catching fish. But Jesus had shown Peter a new and better way of life. Peter knew now that his life was about more than just catching lots of fish. He decided that following Jesus was what mattered more than anything else.

God, show me what my life is really about. Give me the courage to follow Jesus. In Jesus' name, Amen.

OCTOBER 5

•

"As a man was going down from Jerusalem to Jericho, robbers attacked him and grabbed everything he had. They beat him up and ran off, leaving him half dead. A priest happened to be going down the same road. But when he saw the man, he walked by on the other side. Later a temple helper came to the same place. But when he saw the man who had been beaten up, he also went by on the other side. A man from Samaria then came traveling along that road. When he saw the man, he felt sorry for him and went over to him. He treated his wounds. . . . Then he put him on his own donkey and took him to an inn, where he took care of him. . . . Which one of these three people was a real neighbor to the man who was beaten up by robbers?"

Luke 10:30–36 CEV

Often neighbors are a lot alike. They may live in the same kind of house, have the same color skin, or go to the same church.

Jesus shows us a different way to understand what it means to be a neighbor. We are neighbors not just to the people who are like us or live nearby. To be a neighbor is to show God's love to everyone around us, even if they don't look like us or worship God as we do, or live in the same kind of house. God wants us all to be neighbors to each other!

God, give me the grace to be a good neighbor to everyone around me, even people who are not like me. When I am in trouble, send someone to be a neighbor to me. Amen.

OCTOBER 6

•

Jesus and his disciples went on their way. Jesus came to a village where a woman named Martha lived. She welcomed him into her home. She had a sister named Mary. Mary sat at the Lord's feet listening to what he said. But Martha was busy with all the things that had to be done. She came to Jesus and said, "Lord, my sister has left me to do the work by myself. Don't you care? Tell her to help me!" "Martha, Martha," the Lord answered. "You are worried and upset about many things. But only one thing is needed. Mary has chosen what is better. And it will not be taken away from her."

Luke 10:38–42 NIrV

Jesus wanted his disciples both to hear the word of God and to do it (see Luke 8:21). To priests and other religious leaders, who spent a lot of time studying God's word, Jesus said, "Do what is right." To Mary and Martha, who were busy serving others all the time, Jesus said, "Take a rest from all you are doing and listen to God's word."

God has given us minds to listen and understand and hands and feet to do things. We can love God with our minds, and we can love God with our hands and feet. Whether you're young or old, male or female, poor or rich, you can use your mind and your hands and feet in God's service.

Lord Jesus, don't let me ever get so busy doing good that I forget to listen to you. But when I hear your word, make me ready to go out and serve others. Amen.

OCTOBER 7

•

"Jerusalem! Jerusalem! You kill the prophets and throw stones in order to kill those who are sent to you. Many times I have wanted to gather your people together. I have wanted to be like a hen who gathers her chicks under her wings. But you would not let me!"

Luke 13:34 NIRV

It's dangerous being a chick! A chick is small and fragile and can't protect itself from the foxes, wolves, and snakes that are just waiting to eat it up. That is why the mother hen protects her chicks by gathering them under her wing.

Jesus compared himself to a mother hen. In another place, the Bible compares God to a mother eagle that "hovers over its little ones," and "spreads out its wings to catch them" (Deut. 32:11). A mother bird is a good picture of the loving care Jesus and God have for us.

A real chick *wants* this care from its mother. But people often reject this care from God. We think we can keep ourselves safe without any help. We don't want to listen to the people God sends to us. Though Jesus wanted the people of Jerusalem to accept his care, they would not let him. Instead, they killed him, just as they had killed the other prophets God sent them.

God, gather me under your wings. I know that I need you to protect and care for me. Help me listen to the people you send me. Amen.

OCTOBER 8

•

"Or suppose a woman has ten valuable silver coins and loses one. Won't she light a lamp and look in every corner of the house and sweep every nook and cranny until she finds it? And when she finds it, she will call in her friends and neighbors to rejoice with her because she has found her lost coin. In the same way, there is joy in the presence of God's angels when even one sinner repents."

Luke 15:8–10 NLT

Everybody loses things. If you lose something that's not important, it probably doesn't bother you very much. Who cares about a lost piece of candy or a lost sock? But if you lose something you really need, or something that is very valuable to you, it's different. Then you probably stop what you're doing and search for it. When you finally find it, whether it's your dog that ran away or the report you worked on for school, you rejoice!

Jesus tells about a woman searching her house for a coin. She searches for the coin because it means a lot to her. When she finds it she throws a party to celebrate! This story tells us how much we mean to God. When we wander away from God and do what is wrong and hurtful, God doesn't give up searching for us. And when we are found, God rejoices.

God, thank you for reminding us that we matter to you. Help us spend our whole life rejoicing in your love and care. In Jesus' name, Amen.

OCTOBER 9

•

"The older brother was angry and wouldn't go in. His father came out and begged him, but he replied, 'All these years I've worked hard for you and never once refused to do a single thing you told me to. And in all that time you never gave me even one young goat for a feast with my friends. Yet when this son of yours comes back after squandering your money on prostitutes, you celebrate by killing the finest calf we have.' His father said to him, 'Look, dear son, you and I are very close, and everything I have is yours. We had to celebrate this happy day. For your brother was dead and has come back to life! He was lost, but now he is found!'"

Luke 15:28–32 NLT

Jesus told a story about two brothers. The younger one ran away and did terrible things and then came home again. The older one stayed at home and obediently worked for his father. Does either one of these sound like you?

The older brother didn't think that his younger brother deserved a big party after all the bad things he had done. The older brother didn't even want to celebrate. The reason the father gave his younger son a party was not because he deserved it; he gave a party because he was so happy his son came back. He wanted his older son to be happy about it too.

God my Father, you give me so much more than I deserve. Help me to rejoice when you give others more than they deserve. Amen.

OCTOBER 10

•

He broke open the fifth seal. I saw souls under the altar. They were the souls of people who were killed because of God's word and their faithful witness. They called out in a loud voice. "How long, Lord and King, holy and true?" they asked. "How long will you wait to judge those who live on the earth? How long will it be until you pay them back for killing us?" Then each of them was given a white robe. "Wait a little longer," they were told. "There are still more of your believing brothers and sisters who must be killed."

Revelation 6:9–11 NIRV

In a court of law, a witness is someone who has seen or who knows about something that happened—a traffic accident, for example. A witness is called on to tell others the truth about what he or she knows.

In Bible times, people were sometimes hurt or killed for speaking the truth about God. The prophet Daniel was thrown into a lions' den for saying what he knew about God. (See the entry for December 18.) And many early Christians were hurt or killed when they told others why they followed Jesus.

In his vision, John saw the souls of some people who were killed for being witnesses. (Sometimes we call such people martyrs, because the Greek word for witness is *martyria.*) These people were told that there would be more martyrs. And so it has happened: Over the centuries, good people have sometimes been hurt or put in prison or killed because they obeyed God and spoke the truth.

Lord, thank you for people who have been your faithful witnesses even when their lives were in danger. Help me to learn from their courage and their love for your truth. Amen.

OCTOBER 11

•

When the Lamb opened the seventh seal, there was silence in heaven for about half an hour.

Revelation 8:1 NRSV

Ancient Jews and Christians believed that heaven was filled with angels, who sang praises to God night and day. The Book of Revelation includes many examples of angel songs. Humans too use songs and music to express their love and praise for God. One famous hymn begins, "All creatures that on earth do dwell, sing to the Lord with cheerful voice!"

But there is another way to praise God: through *silence.* In the passage above, the author of Revelation tells how the inhabitants of heaven kept silent—made no noise at all—for half an hour. Other parts of the Bible tell us that we too can honor God by being very quiet. "The LORD is in his holy temple; let all the earth keep silence before him!" writes the prophet Habakkuk (Hab. 2:20 NRSV).

Perhaps you feel nervous when things are too quiet. Perhaps when you are alone, you play music or turn on the TV, just so you won't have to listen to the silence. Next time you are alone in the quiet, think about the angels who kept silent in heaven for half an hour.

Lord of Song and of Silence, I praise you! I thank you for words and for music. Let me use them well to express my love for you. But teach me also to keep silent before you. Amen.

OCTOBER 12

•

I saw a beast coming out of the sea. He had ten horns and seven heads. . . . The dragon gave the beast his power, his throne, and great authority. . . . The whole world was amazed and followed the beast. People worshiped the dragon, because he had given authority to the beast. They also worshiped the beast. They asked, "Who is like the beast? Who can make war against him?"

Revelation 13:1a, 2b–4 NIrV

In Bible times, people told many stories about beasts. Here John is using ancient stories about a sea monster to talk about the power of the Roman empire. In John's day, the rulers and armies of the Roman empire controlled many lands, including the one where John lived. The Roman armies were so mighty that no one could fight against them and win.

In John's vision, people are worshipping the dragon and the beast. John may be thinking about how people in his own day treated the Roman rulers as if they had all the power and glory in the universe. By comparing the Roman empire to the sea monster, John reminds his readers that no empire—no matter how great—is God. No ruler and no country deserve our worship; only God does.

We can be grateful that we live in a country where we are free to worship God. We can serve our country with our words, our money, and our time. And usually it is right to obey our country's leaders (see the entry for tomorrow). But John reminds us that it is possible for a nation to lead its people away from God.

Ruler of all nations, thank you for those who founded my country and for all who have protected it and kept it free. Help me to serve it well, but also to remember that you alone are God. Amen.

OCTOBER 13

•

All of you must be willing to obey completely those who rule over you. There are no authorities except the ones God has chosen. Those who now rule have been chosen by God. So when you oppose the authorities, you are opposing those whom God has appointed. Those who do that will be judged.

Romans 13:1–2 NIRV

In this passage Paul teaches that we should always obey those who rule over us. Our "rulers" today include lawmakers, judges, and police officers. Paul says that rulers are all chosen by God, and so when we oppose them it is the same as opposing God.

Sometimes, though, rulers act in ways that do not serve God. They misuse their power and treat people cruelly and unfairly. Another New Testament writer compares the authorities in his own time—a time of great trouble—to a beast who makes war against God's people (see yesterday's entry).

Still, we can't simply ignore Paul's instructions to obey our rulers. Usually we should do as Paul says. Most of the time it will be good and right to obey those who are in authority over us, even if we disagree with them! But if we love God, we have to be ready to disobey, if those rulers ever lead us down a path away from God.

God, thank you for giving us rulers who help to keep order in our world. Give them wisdom to lead us in ways that serve you well, and teach us to respect them. But remind us that our first loyalty is always to you. Amen.

OCTOBER 14

•

"My people have sinned twice.
They have deserted me,
even though I am the spring of water that gives life.
And they have dug their own wells.
But those wells are broken.
They can't hold any water."

Jeremiah 2:13 NIrV

Have you ever had a bucket or a cup with a hole in it? No matter how many times you fill it up, it never stays full. Have you ever tried to get a drink by using your own hands as a cup? That doesn't work very well either!

The people of Israel had deserted God and were trying to survive on their own. God was angry because what they did was both wrong and foolish.

It's wrong to turn away from God. God made us and loves us and deserves our worship and praise. But it is also foolish. God is the spring of water that gives life. Why would we ever want to turn away from that? If we think that we can survive on our own without God, we are drinking from a leaky cup. Without God's water of life, we would die of thirst!

God, you are the spring of water that gives me life. If I ever pretend that I can find life on my own, show me how foolish I am. Amen.

OCTOBER 15

•

The Lord says,
"Sing with joy because the people of Jacob are blessed.
Shout because the Lord has made them the greatest nation.
Make your praises heard. . . .
I will bring them from the land of the north.
I will gather them from one end of the earth to the other.
Even those who are blind and those who can't walk
will be among them.
Pregnant women and women having their babies
will be among them also.
A large number will return."

Jeremiah 31:7–8 NIRV

The prophet Jeremiah brought God's people a lot of bad news. He told them that they would experience great suffering, death, and destruction, and he was right. Their enemies, the Babylonians, destroyed Jerusalem and carried men, women, and children off to live in Babylon. The time when God's people were forced to live in Babylon is called the exile.

In this passage Jeremiah brings a word of comfort to God's people in exile: God is going to bring you back home! Even though they couldn't see any signs of this good news yet, Jeremiah tells them to count on it and start celebrating right away.

When you are surrounded by bad news, it is sometimes hard to believe that God has good things in store for you. But bad news is never God's last word to us. Part of faith is believing in good news before you can even see it.

God, I know that love is stronger than hate, goodness is stronger than evil, and life is stronger than death. When hate, evil, and death surround me, help me trust your good news. Amen.

OCTOBER 16

•

God built a fence around me
that I cannot climb over, and he chained me down.
Even when I shouted
and prayed for help, he refused to listen.
God put big rocks in my way
and made me follow a crooked path.
God was like a bear or a lion waiting in ambush for me;
he dragged me from the road, then tore me to shreds.
God took careful aim
and shot his arrows straight through my heart.
I am a joke to everyone—
no one ever stops making fun of me.
God has turned my life sour.
He made me eat gravel and rubbed me in the dirt.
I cannot find peace or remember happiness.

Lamentations 3:7–17 CEV

When terrible things happen, God sometimes feels like an enemy. The author of Lamentations had seen the destruction of Jerusalem by the Babylonians and the terrible suffering and despair of God's people Judah. How could a good and caring God let that happen?

The author says that God does not seem to be good and caring at all. He compares God to a wild animal that tears people to shreds. He says God has chained him down, put big boulders in his way, shot arrows into his heart, and rubbed his face in the dirt. Even our enemies are often nicer to us than that!

Sometimes God may feel like your enemy too. When you feel that way, you should tell God. Cry out to God and complain to God, just as this author did. God already knows how you feel and will listen to you, no matter what.

God, sometimes I get angry at you. Thank you that I can always come to you in prayer, no matter how I feel. Amen.

OCTOBER 17

•

Suppose we claim we are without sin. Then we are fooling ourselves. The truth is not in us. But God is faithful and fair. If we admit that we have sinned, he will forgive us our sins. He will forgive every wrong thing we have done. He will make us pure.

1 John 1:8–9 NIRV

There are probably many good things you can claim about yourself. Perhaps you are a good musician or have lots of friends. But you can't claim to be without sin. If you claim this, the Bible says, you are fooling yourself.

Sin includes bad actions like lying and stealing. But it also includes our failure to do good things, as well as our bad thoughts and attitudes. Sin is everything that keeps us from perfect love of God and our neighbors. If we say there is no sin in our lives, we are lying.

The good news is that we can stop pretending we are without sin. When we admit our sin to God, God forgives us and heals us. Once we stop fooling ourselves, the truth of God's word can shine through us!

God of light, in you there is no darkness at all. Give me the courage to bring my sin into the light, so that I can know the power of your forgiving love. Amen.

OCTOBER 18

•

Dear children, don't let anyone lead you down the wrong path. Those who do what is right are holy, just as Christ is holy. Those who do what is sinful belong to the devil. They are just like him. He has been sinning from the beginning. But the Son of God came to destroy the devil's work.

1 John 3:7–8 NIRV

When you are fighting with someone, you sometimes call him or her bad names. The author of this letter sure did! He called the people he was fighting with false prophets and liars and said they were of the devil. These people were Christians, just like he was. They used to belong to his community, but they had left it because of a disagreement about how to understand Jesus. Now the two groups refused to worship or eat together.

In the sixteenth century, Christians in Europe had a big fight, and a group who became known as the Protestants left the Catholic Church. For centuries these two groups fought and called each other names. The Protestants said the leader of the Catholic Church, the pope, was of the devil. The Catholics said the Protestants were false prophets. But now these two groups are realizing that even though they are different, they are both Christian. Catholics and Protestants are finding ways to worship and eat together again.

Both are showing that they are children of God by the way they love their Christian brothers and sisters.

Holy God, keep me from using my faith as a weapon to attack other people. Send the Holy Spirit to fill me and all of your children with truth and love. In Christ's name, Amen.

OCTOBER 19

•

Dear friends, do not believe every spirit. Put the spirits to the test to see if they belong to God. Many false prophets have gone out into the world.

1 John 4:1 NIrV

When you were little, your parents probably warned you not to talk to strangers. They did this because not every adult can be trusted. The same goes for people who claim to be filled with God's Spirit. Not every one of them can be trusted. Some of them are false prophets who spread lies instead of telling the truth about God.

How do you put the spirits to the test? How can you tell a true prophet from a false prophet? You can't believe people just because they are popular or bring a comfortable or familiar message. Sometimes God's true prophets will seem odd or even crazy to us. Sometimes they will bring a disturbing message.

Jesus Christ had a human body, and he suffered and died on a cross. The writer of 1 John thinks that anyone who believes this about Jesus has the Spirit of God. Jesus' death on the cross is a disturbing message. Some people will even think it's crazy. But Christians know they can trust it.

God, don't let me be fooled by false prophets, even when they tell me what I want to hear. Show me how to test the spirits, so that I can recognize the Spirit of truth. Amen.

OCTOBER 20

•

My dear friends, we must love each other. Love comes from God, and when we love each other, it shows that we have been given new life. We are now God's children, and we know him. God is love, and anyone who doesn't love others has never known him. God showed his love for us when he sent his only Son into the world to give us life. Real love isn't our love for God, but his love for us. God sent his Son to be the sacrifice by which our sins are forgiven. Dear friends, since God loved us this much, we must love each other.

1 John 4:7–11 CEV

When you look in a mirror, you see a reflection of your own face. If your face is tired or frowning, that is what the mirror will reflect back to you.

Jesus Christ is a mirror for seeing God's face. When we look at Jesus, we see that God is love. He is the perfect reflection of God's generosity and God's desire to be one with us. Jesus died for us, so that we can see God's love and become one with God just like he was.

Because of the new life Jesus gives us, we can be mirrors of God's love too. When we share this new life by giving ourselves to others, they can see in us a reflection of God's perfect love.

God, we love you! But we know that all love comes from you. Make our love a reflection of your perfect love. In Jesus' name, Amen.

OCTOBER 21

•

Suppose some people come to you and don't teach these truths. Then don't take them into your house. Don't welcome them. Anyone who welcomes them shares in their evil work.

2 John 10–11 NIRV

The Bible tells us over and over again to welcome strangers and to show them hospitality. Jesus showed hospitality to all different kinds of people, not just those who were nice and respectable.

But this passage tells us to be careful about whom we welcome, because we might become like them. Some people turn the truth about Jesus Christ into a lie and twist the Christian message of love into a message of hate. For example, there are groups who believe that only white Christians are the chosen people of God. They claim that people of color are less than human and that Jews are children of the devil. If you welcome people who hate into your home, you are sharing in their hatred and lies. It is better to stay away from them and to pray that God will change their hearts.

God, keep me from imitating people who teach violence and hatred. Help me stay away from those who would turn my heart away from your truth. Amen.

OCTOBER 22

•

I wrote to the church. But Diotrephes won't have anything to do with us. He loves to be the first in everything. So if I come, I will point out what he is doing. He is saying evil things about us to others. Even that doesn't satisfy him. He refuses to welcome other believers. He also keeps others from welcoming them. In fact, he throws them out of the church.

3 John 9–10 NIRV

There has always been fighting and arguing in the church. Even the disciples of Jesus argued about who was the greatest. In this letter the writer is complaining about a Christian named Diotrephes. Diotrephes wanted more power in the church. He was saying bad things about other church leaders and throwing out people who didn't agree with him.

Christians are still fighting about who should lead the church, how they should worship, and how they should spend their money. People who are not Christians look at all the fighting in the church and wonder why Christians don't act more like Jesus Christ.

Even when Christians disagree, they do not have to say bad things about each other. They do not have to throw each other out of the church. They can be ready to admit that they might be wrong, and they can pray that God will fill the church with wisdom and peace.

Christ Jesus, you are the vine, and we are the branches. All Christians draw their life and strength from you. Let your church be an example of your love and forgiveness to the world. Amen.

OCTOBER 23

•

The LORD gave this message to Jonah son of Amittai: "Get up and go to the great city of Nineveh! Announce my judgment against it because I have seen how wicked its people are." But Jonah got up and went in the opposite direction in order to get away from the LORD. He went down to the seacoast, to the port of Joppa, where he found a ship leaving for Tarshish. He bought a ticket and went on board, hoping that by going away to the west he could escape from the LORD.

Jonah 1:1–3 NLT

Have you noticed how little kids love to run away from their parents? When their parents say, "Come here," they often laugh and run in the opposite direction! You have probably also noticed that this game doesn't work for very long. Pretty soon parents pick their little kids up and carry them where they want them to go.

Jonah was acting like a little kid. God told him to go to Nineveh. Jonah didn't want to go, so he ran in the opposite direction toward Tarshish. But running away from God never works. There is no place in the world you can run to get away from God! Jonah went all the way to the bottom of the sea. But even there God found Jonah and sent something very surprising to pick him up!

God, running away from you never works. If I am running away from something you want me to do, put me back on track, and give me the courage to do it. Amen.

OCTOBER 24

•

But the LORD sent a huge fish to swallow Jonah. And Jonah was inside the fish for three days and three nights. From inside the fish Jonah prayed to the LORD his God. He said,

"When I was in trouble, I called out to you.
And you answered me.
When I had almost drowned,
I called out for help.
And you listened to my cry."

Jonah 1:17–2:2 NIRV

When people read the story of Jonah, they might think that being swallowed by a big fish was a punishment. After all, Jonah was running away from God when it happened. But Jonah didn't see it that way. He thanked God for saving him from drowning! Jonah recognized that God used the big fish to answer his prayers for help.

God doesn't always answer our prayers just the way we expect or would like. Sometimes God uses people we never would have picked. Sometimes God uses things we never thought of as an answer to prayer! When you are in trouble and pray to God, be on the lookout for God's answer. Sometimes it will come in surprising ways!

God, I trust that you hear my prayers for help and will answer me. Make me able to recognize your answer, even when it comes in strange ways. Use me to answer other people's prayers for help. Amen.

OCTOBER 25

•

When God saw that the people had stopped doing evil things, he had pity and did not destroy them as he had planned. Jonah was really upset and angry. So he prayed: Our Lord, I knew from the very beginning that you wouldn't destroy Nineveh. That's why I left my own country and headed for Spain. You are a kind and merciful God, and you are very patient. You always show love, and you don't like to punish anyone, not even foreigners. Now let me die! I'd be better off dead.

Jonah 3:10–4:3 CEV

We all like it when God shows love to us. But it is hard to be pleased when God shows love to our enemies. The people of Nineveh were Jonah's enemies, and Jonah was very angry at God for loving them. God sent Jonah to Nineveh to tell the people there to be sorry for the bad things they had done and to ask God for forgiveness.

Jonah didn't want to go to Nineveh. But he finally went anyway and gave the Ninevites God's message. They all listened! All the people of Nineveh showed God how sorry they were, and God forgave them. This made Jonah really mad. He said he would rather die than see God's kindness toward his enemies.

It makes us mad sometimes that God loves our enemies. But God is the Creator of the whole world. God has concern for everyone and everything, not just for us and the things that matter to us.

Creator of all, help us to remember that your love is as wide as the whole world. Help us rejoice in your love to all people, not just to us. Amen.

OCTOBER 26

•

Later Jesus was alone. The Twelve [disciples] asked him about the stories. So did the others around him. He told them, "The secret of God's kingdom has been given to you. But to outsiders everything is told by using stories. In that way, 'They will see but never know what they are seeing. They will hear but never understand. Otherwise they might turn and be forgiven!'"

Mark 4:10–12 NIRV

Did you ever hear a truly great storyteller? A good storyteller makes a story seem so real that you forget the world around you. All you want to do is listen!

Jesus was such a storyteller. All of his stories were about God. But to tell about God, Jesus filled his stories with common things, like seeds, sheep, workers, and children. People crowded around to hear Jesus. They wanted to hear more and more.

Even though the stories were about common things some people found them upsetting—so upsetting that they tried to stop Jesus from teaching. The stories can still upset people because God wants us to do things a certain way. God's way is the way of love and worship and giving. Those who aren't used to acting in such a way may find it hard to admit that they need to change. God is the only one who can open our minds to understand and our hearts to change.

God, thank you for all the stories Jesus gave us. Help me to understand them. Help me to know when I should change my ways. Amen.

OCTOBER 27

•

As evening came, Jesus said to his disciples, "Let's cross to the other side of the lake." He was already in the boat, so they started out, leaving the crowds behind (although other boats followed). But soon a fierce storm arose. High waves began to break into the boat until it was nearly full of water. Jesus was sleeping at the back of the boat with his head on a cushion. Frantically they woke him up, shouting, "Teacher, don't you even care that we are going to drown?" When he woke up, he rebuked the wind and said to the water, "Quiet down!" Suddenly the wind stopped, and there was a great calm. And he asked them, "Why are you so afraid? Do you still not have faith in me?" And they were filled with awe and said among themselves, "Who is this man, that even the wind and waves obey him?"

Mark 4:35–41 NLT

When you were younger, were you afraid of thunder and lightning? Your mom or dad probably told you that there was no reason to be afraid as long as you were safe inside. But what if you were on the sea in a small boat? In that case there really would be reason to be afraid. The boat could be turned over by the wind and waves or be struck by lightning.

The disciples were in a boat on the Sea of Galilee in a thunderstorm, and they were very afraid. It seemed to them as if Jesus didn't care at all about the danger. He was asleep! But he woke up and calmed the storm.

Sometimes when we find ourselves in trouble, it seems as if the Lord is sleeping. We worry about what will happen to us! This story reminds us that when we are in danger we should ask Jesus to calm our fears just as he calmed that storm so long ago.

Jesus, help me to trust you when I am afraid! In easy times and in hard times, remind me that you are with me and that you are in control. Amen.

OCTOBER 28

A large group of people followed. They crowded around him. A woman was there who had a sickness that made her bleed. It had lasted for 12 years. She had suffered a great deal, even though she had gone to many doctors. She had spent all the money she had. But she was getting worse, not better. Then she heard about Jesus. She came up behind him in the crowd and touched his clothes. She thought, "I just need to touch his clothes. Then I will be healed." Right away her bleeding stopped. She felt in her body that her suffering was over. At once Jesus knew that power had gone out from him. He turned around in the crowd. He asked, "Who touched my clothes?" "You see the people," his disciples answered. "They are crowding against you. And you still ask, 'Who touched me?'" But Jesus kept looking around. He wanted to see who had touched him. Then the woman came and fell at his feet. She knew what had happened to her. She was shaking with fear. But she told him the whole truth. He said to her, "Dear woman, your faith has healed you. Go in peace. You are free from your suffering."

Mark 5:24b–34 NIrV

Sometimes when people have a serious problem they are ashamed to go to anyone for help. Instead they try to hide their problem from other people. They might even try to hide it from themselves! Some people who take drugs or drink too much alcohol do that, for example. They hide their problem because they feel such shame and disgrace.

The woman in this story must have felt great shame. For twelve years she had been sick. Her sickness made people want to stay away from her. She could have been too broken in spirit to go to Jesus for help. But she did go to him. She wasn't shy about it either! She pressed hard to get through the big crowd of people around Jesus, until she was able to touch his clothing. Jesus knew immediately that she had come to him. He saw her faith and her courage. And he helped her.

Jesus, you know my problems even before I tell you! You understand when I feel ashamed. You forgive me when I feel bad for doing wrong. Help me always to trust in you. Amen.

OCTOBER 29

•

Herod gave a big dinner on his birthday. . . . Then the daughter of Herodias came in and danced. She pleased Herod and his dinner guests. The king said to the girl, "Ask me for anything you want. I'll give it to you." . . . She went out and said to her mother, "What should I ask for?" "The head of John the Baptist," she answered. At once the girl hurried to ask the king.

Mark 6:21b, 22, 24–25a NIRV

Herod was the ruler of Galilee, and Herodias was his wife. The wife hated John the Baptist, because she had done something bad, and John had told her that God was not pleased. Then, at a party, Herod told his daughter that he would give her whatever she wanted as a reward for her lovely dancing. The girl took her mother's advice and asked Herod to kill John the Baptist.

By telling us this terrible story Mark hints about what would later happen to Jesus. Like John, Jesus was a prophet—one who spoke the truth about how to live in God's way. And, like John, Jesus would be killed for doing so.

Today also, people sometimes risk their lives trying to put an end to evil ways. And today also, they are sometimes hurt or killed for doing that. When we see their courage to do what is right, it can make us brave too.

God, you want us to make your world a better place, but it is hard because we know how cruel people can be. Give me ears to hear your truth and make me brave to speak it. Amen.

OCTOBER 30

•

A vast crowd was there as he stepped from the boat, and he had compassion on them because they were like sheep without a shepherd. So he taught them many things. Late in the afternoon his disciples came to him and said, "This is a desolate place, and it is getting late. Send the crowds away so they can go to the nearby farms and villages and buy themselves some food." . . . How much food do you have?" he asked. "Go and find out." They came back and reported, "We have five loaves of bread and two fish." Then Jesus told the crowd to sit down in groups on the green grass. Jesus took the five loaves and two fish, looked up toward heaven, and asked God's blessing on the food. Breaking the loaves into pieces, he kept giving the bread and fish to the disciples to give to the people. They all ate as much as they wanted, and they picked up twelve baskets of leftover bread and fish.

Mark 6:34–36, 38–39, 41–43 NLT

When something we can't explain happens, we call it a miracle. God gave Jesus the power to make miracles happen. This story tells of one of Jesus' most famous miracles. He was teaching a great crowd of people. They grew hungry, but there was only a tiny bit of food there—five loaves of bread and two fish. Jesus blessed the food, broke it, and gave it to the people. And there was more than enough food for five thousand people!

Mark's story reminds us of some other famous bread stories. The Book of Exodus tells about when the people of Israel were wandering in the desert and didn't have enough food. Each morning God sent them a special kind of food called manna—bread from heaven. Another bread story happens later in Mark's Gospel. Mark tells how, when Jesus was having his last supper with his disciples before he was killed, he gave them bread and wine to eat and drink. Jesus told them that the bread and wine were his body and his blood, which would be broken and given for the people, to bring them new life.

God, you make miracles happen all around us. Thank you for giving us what we need to live. Amen.

OCTOBER 31

•

Jesus told the evil spirit, "Be quiet and come out of the man!" The spirit shook him. Then it gave a loud shout and left. Everyone was completely surprised and kept saying to each other, "What is this? It must be some new kind of powerful teaching! Even the evil spirits obey him."

Mark 1:25–27 CEV

November 1 was a holiday in England long before there were any Christians there. On this day people would carve lanterns out of turnips and watch out for the ghosts of people who had died that year. Christians in England later made November 1 a day to honor Christian saints who had died. (See the entry for tomorrow.) They called it All Hallows Day, and October 31 became All Hallows Eve, later known as Halloween.

On Halloween people still carve lanterns and expect visits from children dressed as ghosts, witches, and skeletons. Some Christians do not observe Halloween, because they think it celebrates evil spirits. Other Christians celebrate the holiday as a fun night to dress up and give out treats to others.

Christians disagree about Halloween. But they agree that Christ is Lord over all things. "Even the evil spirits obey him."

Lord Jesus, I know that you are more powerful than any ghost or monster. No evil spirit can separate me from your love. Amen.

NOVEMBER 1

•

What else can I say? There isn't enough time to tell about Gideon, Barak, Samson, Jephthah, David, Samuel, and the prophets. Their faith helped them conquer kingdoms, and because they did right, God made promises to them. . . . Such a large crowd of witnesses is all around us!

Hebrews 11:32–33a; 12:1a CEV

Some people of God are famous because of their great faith. The author of Hebrews reminds us of some of the famous people in the history of Israel who had great faith. Can you think of others? Christians sometimes put the word *saint* before the name of someone with great faith: Saint Mary, Saint Paul, Saint Francis, Saint Teresa.

But you don't have to be famous or have extraordinary faith to be a saint. All Christians are blessed by God and called to live as holy, loving people of God. You too are called to be a saint! On November 1, Christians celebrate all the saints, those who are famous and those who aren't. Who are the saints in your life? They could be people in your family, or neighbors, or friends at church. There are witnesses to God's holiness and love all around us. Celebrate them all today!

Holy Spirit, thank you for all the saints in my life who have been filled with your holiness and love. Thank you for making me part of your great crowd of witnesses. Amen.

•

That night the LORD appeared to Solomon in a dream, and God said, "What do you want? Ask, and I will give it to you!" Solomon replied, "You were wonderfully kind to my father, David, because he was honest and true and faithful to you. And you have continued this great kindness to him today by giving him a son to succeed him. O LORD my God, now you have made me king instead of my father, David, but I am like a little child who doesn't know his way around. And here I am among your own chosen people, a nation so great they are too numerous to count! Give me an understanding mind so that I can govern your people well and know the difference between right and wrong."

1 Kings 3:5–9b NLT

If you could have anything you wished for, what would you wish? King Solomon had to make that choice. He could have asked for more power and honor. But he had been king just long enough to know how hard a job it was. That is why he said that he was like a little child who needs help and why he prayed for God to give him wisdom to serve God's people well. Solomon's wish pleased God.

You too will have to make hard choices about what is important to you in life. You will have to choose how to spend your energy, your money, and your time. What choices will you make? God can help you to know what is truly valuable in life, so that you make good choices.

God, sometimes it is hard to know what choices to make. Give me a heart that understands and wisdom to know what is right. Amen.

NOVEMBER 3

•

[Two women] argued in front of the king. The king said, "One of you says, 'My son is alive. Your son is dead.' The other one says, 'No! Your son is dead. Mine is alive.'" He continued, "Bring me a sword." So a sword was brought to him. Then he gave an order. He said, "Cut the living child in two. Give half to one woman and half to the other." The woman whose son was alive was filled with deep concern for her son. She said to the king, "My master, please give her the living baby! Don't kill him!" But the other woman said, "Neither one of us will have him. Cut him in two!" Then the king made his decision. He said, "Give the living baby to the first woman. Don't kill him. She's his mother."

1 Kings 3:22c–27 NIRV

King Solomon was the son of King David. Solomon was famous for his wisdom. He showed wisdom in appointing government officials and meeting with foreign leaders.

Solomon also showed wisdom in dealing with people who weren't famous or important, like these two women. Each woman claimed that the living baby was hers. But Solomon knew that the woman who refused to let the baby be killed was the real mother. He gave the baby to her.

God, give me a listening heart like Solomon's, so that I will make wise decisions like he did. Amen.

NOVEMBER 4

•

"Go out and stand before me on the mountain," the LORD told him. And as Elijah stood there, the LORD passed by, and a mighty windstorm hit the mountain. It was such a terrible blast that the rocks were torn loose, but the LORD was not in the wind. After the wind there was an earthquake, but the LORD was not in the earthquake. And after the earthquake there was a fire, but the LORD was not in the fire. And after the fire there was the sound of a gentle whisper. When Elijah heard it, he wrapped his face in his cloak and went out and stood at the entrance of the cave. And a voice said, "What are you doing here, Elijah?" He replied again, "I have zealously served the LORD God Almighty. But the people of Israel have broken their covenant with you, torn down your altars, and killed every one of your prophets. I alone am left, and now they are trying to kill me, too." Then the LORD told him, "Go back the way you came, and travel to the wilderness of Damascus. When you arrive there, anoint Hazael to be king of Aram. Then anoint Jehu son of Nimshi to be king of Israel, and anoint Elisha son of Shaphat from Abel-meholah to replace you as my prophet. . . . Yet I will preserve seven thousand others in Israel who have never bowed to Baal or kissed him!"

1 Kings 19:11–16, 18 NLT

Being a prophet is very hard work, and Elijah was ready to give up. Jezebel, the wife of King Ahab, was trying to kill him. The people of Israel were worshipping false gods. Elijah thought he was the only faithful person left in Israel. He was feeling very sorry for himself.

God spoke to Elijah in a gentle whisper. God told him to go back home and gave him more work to do. God reassured Elijah that he wasn't the only faithful person left. There were 7,000 others in Israel!

God, when serving you is hard and I'm feeling sorry for myself, speak to me. Give me other faithful people to lean on. Amen.

NOVEMBER 5

•

One day the widow of one of Elisha's fellow prophets came to Elisha and cried out to him, "My husband who served you is dead, and you know how he feared the Lord. But now a creditor has come, threatening to take my two sons as slaves." "What can I do to help you?" Elisha asked. "Tell me, what do you have in the house?" "Nothing at all, except a flask of olive oil," she replied. And Elisha said, "Borrow as many empty jars as you can from your friends and neighbors. Then go into your house with your sons and shut the door behind you. Pour olive oil from your flask into the jars, setting the jars aside as they are filled." So she did as she was told. Her sons brought many jars to her, and she filled one after another. Soon every container was full to the brim! "Bring me another jar," she said to one of her sons. "There aren't any more!" he told her. And then the olive oil stopped flowing. When she told the man of God what had happened, he said to her, "Now sell the olive oil and pay your debts, and there will be enough money left over to support you and your sons."

2 Kings 4:1–7 NLT

A poor widow cried to the prophet Elisha for help. She needed money to pay her debts or her sons would become slaves. Elisha told her to take the little bit of oil she had and pour it into her neighbors' empty jars. She poured and poured. The oil didn't run out until all the jars were full! Now she could sell the oil to pay her debts and provide for her sons.

God wants life and well-being for everyone, and so shows special concern for the poor and weak. We rejoice when God sends people with special gifts to help those who are suffering. God uses those people to bring life-giving surprises.

God of the poor and the suffering, use me to bring life and healing to others. Amen.

NOVEMBER 6

Then, in a voice loud enough for everyone to hear, he shouted in Hebrew: "Listen to what the great king of Assyria says! Don't be fooled by Hezekiah. He can't save you. Don't trust him when he tells you that the LORD will protect you from the king of Assyria. Stop listening to Hezekiah! Pay attention to my king. Surrender to him. He will let you keep your own vineyards, fig trees, and cisterns for a while. Then he will come and take you away to a country just like yours, where you can plant vineyards, raise your own grain, and have plenty of olive oil and honey. Believe me, you won't starve there. Hezekiah claims the LORD will save you. But don't be fooled by him. Were any other gods able to defend their land against the king of Assyria? What happened to the gods of Hamath and Arpad? What about the gods of Sepharvaim, Hena, and Ivvah? Were the gods of Samaria able to protect their land against the Assyrian forces? None of these gods kept their people safe from the king of Assyria. Do you think the LORD your God can do any better?"

2 Kings 18:28–35 CEV

Whom will you trust? That's the question a commander in the Assyrian army asked God's people. King Hezekiah had told the people of Judah to trust in God. But the army commander reminded them that the gods of other nations had not been able to protect their people. If they wanted to be safe, the commander said, they should trust the great king of Assyria instead of God.

King Hezekiah trusted in God, and God delivered Judah from the Assyrians. Soon, though, the people of Judah were defeated by the Babylonians.

Trusting in God doesn't always guarantee a happy ending. But God is the only one worth trusting. God alone made us and forgives us and loves us. Trusting in God is always the right thing to do.

Lord God, show me how to trust in you, no matter what. Amen.

NOVEMBER 7

•

There was no king like Josiah either before him or after him. None of them turned to the LORD as he did. He followed the LORD with all his heart and all his soul. He followed him with all his strength. He did everything the Law of Moses required. In spite of that, the LORD didn't turn away from his burning anger. It blazed out against Judah. That's because of everything Manasseh had done to make him very angry.

2 Kings 23:25–26 NIRV

Josiah was the best king Judah ever had. He served God with all his heart and soul and strength. But the prophet Huldah gave Josiah bad news. She said that God was very angry with the people of Judah for all the bad things they had done when Manasseh was king. Terrible things would happen to them.

Josiah didn't give up trying to serve God. He hoped that his faithfulness to God would make a difference for Judah's future. But Josiah's good deeds didn't stop God's anger against Judah. Terrible things happened to them anyway.

Sometimes it seems that our good deeds don't make any difference. Maybe Josiah felt that way. But his good deeds did make a difference. Later generations of God's people remembered Josiah's faithfulness and tried to serve God like he did.

God, sometimes the good that I do doesn't seem to make any difference. Help me to keep serving you, even when I can't see the results. Amen.

NOVEMBER 8

•

Then Jesus left Galilee and went north to the region of Tyre. . . . Right away a woman came to him whose little girl was possessed by an evil spirit. She had heard about Jesus, and now she came and fell at his feet. She begged him to release her child from the demon's control. Since she was a Gentile, born in Syrian Phoenicia, Jesus told her, "First I should help my own family, the Jews. It isn't right to take food from the children and throw it to the dogs." She replied, "That's true, Lord, but even the dogs under the table are given some crumbs from the children's plates." "Good answer!" he said. "And because you have answered so well, I have healed your daughter." And when she arrived home, her little girl was lying quietly in bed, and the demon was gone.

Mark 7:24a, 25–30 NLT

If there were only a very small amount of food in the house, whom would the parents feed first: their children or their dog? Most parents would feed the children first; then, if there is food left over, they would feed the dog.

Jesus was a Jew, and he was preaching and healing among the Jews. He did not go to the Gentiles (those who were not Jews). But one day a Gentile woman asked him to heal her daughter. Then Jesus said something to her that surprises us: He said that the children had to be fed first and that it was not fair to throw the children's food to the dogs. He meant that he should be healing and helping Jews, not Gentiles such as she. But the woman was very brave. She didn't go away. Instead she reminded Jesus that dogs do eat whatever falls on the floor under the table while the children are eating. She meant that Gentiles should also receive the good gifts that Jesus gave—there was plenty to go around. Her words changed Jesus' mind. He healed her daughter.

Today many, many Gentiles are followers of Jesus. No one has to go without Jesus' love and care.

Jesus, thank you for giving your love and care to all who ask. Help me to be bold enough to come to you for whatever I need. Amen.

NOVEMBER 9

•

But the disciples discovered they had forgotten to bring any food, so there was only one loaf of bread with them in the boat. As they were crossing the lake, Jesus warned them, "Beware of the yeast of the Pharisees and of Herod." They decided he was saying this because they hadn't brought any bread. Jesus knew what they were thinking, so he said, "Why are you so worried about having no food? Won't you ever learn or understand? Are your hearts too hard to take it in? 'You have eyes—can't you see? You have ears—can't you hear?' Don't you remember anything at all? What about the five thousand men I fed with five loaves of bread? How many baskets of leftovers did you pick up afterward?" "Twelve," they said, "And when I fed the four thousand with seven loaves, how many large baskets of leftovers did you pick up?" "Seven," they said. "Don't you understand even yet?" he asked them.

Mark 8:14–21 NLT

The disciples weren't perfect! Mark tells us that they often did not understand Jesus' teaching. Once when this happened, Jesus seemed to get upset with them. "Won't you ever learn or understand?" he asked. Jesus had been trying to prepare the disciples for hard times ahead. He must have felt frustrated because they didn't get it. The disciples must have felt frustrated too—especially if they had been trying their best to do what Jesus wanted.

You don't have to be a perfect person to work for God. In his Gospel, Mark shows us that the disciples were slow learners. They didn't understand everything Jesus taught them, and sometimes they even annoyed him. But they could still be good workers for God. The same is true for you too. Even if you're not perfect, God can use you!

I thank you, God, that you have chosen me even though I am not a perfect person. Teach me what I need to know in order to serve you well. Amen.

•

Jesus and his disciples went to the villages near the town of Caesarea Philippi. As they were walking along, he asked them, "What do people say about me?" The disciples answered, "Some say you are John the Baptist or maybe Elijah. Others say you are one of the prophets." Then Jesus asked them, "But who do you say I am?" "You are the Messiah!" Peter replied. Jesus warned the disciples not to tell anyone about him.

Mark 8:27–30 CEV

Jesus caused quite a stir among the people! Many were talking about his powerful words and his amazing deeds. "Who is he?" they were asking each other. "How can anyone make the blind to see? How can anyone raise the dead to new life?"

Jesus asked Peter to tell him what the people were saying. Peter reported that some people thought Jesus must be John the Baptist or one of the great leaders of the past, come back to life. Then Jesus asked Peter the most important question of Peter's life: "Who do *you* say that I am?" What other people said was interesting to Jesus. But what he really cared about was Peter's own view.

Peter said, "You are the Messiah!" (Another word for *Messiah* is *Christ.*) Peter meant that Jesus was the one specially chosen by God to lead God's people. Peter spoke the truth! But Jesus told him it wasn't yet the time to tell others this truth. The right time would come later, after Jesus died on a cross and then rose from the dead.

Jesus Christ, help me to know you! People say so many things about you. Help me to know and to speak the truth of who you are. Amen.

NOVEMBER 11

•

The LORD will teach us his Law from Jerusalem, and we will obey him. He will settle arguments between nations. They will pound their swords and their spears into rakes and shovels; they will never make war or attack one another. People of Israel, let's live by the light of the LORD.

Isaiah 2:3a–5 CEV

On Veterans Day we remember all the people who fought and died in the wars of our country. We also celebrate that those terrible wars are over.

There always seems to be a war going on in our world. People fight over land. They fight over who should be in charge. Sometimes Christians decide that fighting in a particular war is the right thing to do.

But Christians also hope for a day when there will be no more war. They hope for a day when there will be no more guns or tanks or land mines because no one will be fighting. The prophet Isaiah tells of a day when all the people of the world will take their weapons and turn them into tools for growing food. Then, he says, we will be living the way God wants us to.

God of peace, help us remember all the people who have died in war. Show us how to make this world a peaceful place. Amen.

•

Then Jesus began to tell them that he, the Son of Man, would suffer many terrible things and be rejected by the leaders, the leading priests, and the teachers of religious law. He would be killed, and three days later he would rise again. As he talked about this openly with his disciples, Peter took him aside and told him he shouldn't say things like that. Jesus turned and looked at his disciples and then said to Peter very sternly, "Get away from me, Satan! You are seeing things merely from a human point of view, not from God's."

Mark 8:31–33 NLT

We know that each of us will die. But almost none of us knows just when or where this will happen. The time for our death is in God's hands. But Jesus did know when and where he would die. He knew that in Jerusalem people would kill him for saying things that they didn't want to hear.

Jesus told his disciples about the hard times that lay ahead for him—and for them. But when he said these things, Peter scolded Jesus! Peter didn't want to think about Jesus suffering and dying. When Peter scolded Jesus, Jesus answered, "Get away from me, Satan!" He meant that Peter was making it even harder for Jesus to do what God wanted. Peter was trying to pull Jesus off God's path instead of helping him on it.

Living as a follower of Jesus is not always easy. To serve God well we must follow Jesus wherever he leads and help others also to follow him on God's path. Sometimes Jesus will lead us into hard places. Will you follow Jesus where he leads?

Jesus, I know that I will need your help to follow you in hard times. Help me to stay on your path and to remember that you are always with me. Amen.

NOVEMBER 13

•

Brothers and sisters, we want you to know about the hard times we suffered in Asia Minor. We were having a lot of trouble. It was far more than we could stand. We even thought we were going to die. In fact, in our hearts we felt as if we were under the sentence of death. But that happened so that we would not depend on ourselves but on God. He raises the dead to life.

2 Corinthians 1:8–9 NIRV

This world can be a very mean place. Sometimes bad things happen to people—things so terrible that it makes them feel as if they are dead. They may feel so sad that it is as if they cannot hear or see or taste things anymore. They may feel as if they have been turned into a statue made of stone.

Here Paul tells about a time when something very bad happened to him. He was in Asia Minor, traveling on a mission to tell people about Jesus. We do not know exactly what took place, but Paul says that he was sure his life was at an end. His heart was in despair. But then, just when Paul had given up, God began to help. God saved Paul from the danger and put new hope and joy into his heart!

When terrible things happen to us, we may feel as if it is the end of everything. These are the times when we need God most of all. God can breathe the spirit of life into our hearts and make us live again.

Spirit of Life, be with me each day. Help me to hear and see and taste the goodness in your world. If ever I lose all hope and joy, breathe them into me once again! Amen.

NOVEMBER 14

•

Anyone you forgive I also forgive. Was there anything to forgive? If so, I have forgiven it for your benefit, knowing that Christ is watching. We don't want Satan to outsmart us. We know how he does his evil work.

2 Corinthians 2:10–11 NIRV

If you are carrying a bulky load of groceries, boxes, or books, can you tie your shoe at the same time? When someone does something wrong and we refuse to forgive her, we are "carrying a grudge." Carrying a grudge is a lot like carrying a big load in your arms. It is hard to do anything else at the same time. You may even trip and fall because you are paying so much attention to the load you are holding that you do not see what is right in front of you!

Paul forgave someone who had done something unkind to him, because he knew how carrying grudges can trip us up and make us fall. It can be hard to get rid of a grudge. But God can give you the strength to forgive!

God, make me forgiving and loving, the way you are. Let me feel the lightness that comes from letting go of a heavy grudge. Keep me from falling! Amen.

NOVEMBER 15

•

Some people need to bring letters of recommendation with them or ask you to write letters of recommendation for them. But the only letter of recommendation we need is you yourselves! Your lives are a letter written in our hearts, and everyone can read it and recognize our good work among you. Clearly, you are a letter from Christ prepared by us. It is written not with pen and ink, but with the Spirit of the living God. It is carved not on stone, but on human hearts.

2 Corinthians 3:1b–3 NLT

If you want to write a letter to someone, what do you need? You need paper, a pencil or pen, an envelope, and a stamp. Or you could type the letter on a computer and print it out or use e-mail. In Paul's day, people wrote with ink on a kind of paper called papyrus. In Moses' day, God once wrote to the people of Israel on tablets of stone.

Paul is talking about a special type of letter used to say good things about someone. Paul asks the Corinthians whether they think he needs such a letter to say good things about him. Then he answers his own question: No! The members of the Corinthian church are Paul's letter. Anyone who wants to know about Paul can simply look at what the Corinthians say and do. Paul was the one who first told them about Jesus as God's Son. They listened to Paul and began to worship and serve God. Their love for God and their care for one another were the very best proof of Paul's good work.

Spirit of the living God, write on my heart. Help me and those around me to love and care for others and to serve Christ. Help us to be a letter that the whole world can read. Amen.

NOVEMBER 16

•

The Scriptures say, "God commanded light to shine in the dark." Now God is shining in our hearts to let you know that his glory is seen in Jesus Christ. We are like clay jars in which this treasure is stored. The real power comes from God and not from us.

2 Corinthians 4:6–7 CEV

If you have something valuable, where do you keep it? If you have a special souvenir or other keepsake, you might put it high up on a shelf so that you don't break it or lose it. If you have money you don't need to spend right away, you might put it in the bank to keep it safe from thieves and from fire.

Paul says that we have the greatest treasure of all: the good news about Jesus Christ, who shows us the glory of God. God hasn't locked this treasure away in a bank or put it high up on a shelf where it won't break. God has put this good news right into our hearts. We humans are the place where God keeps the treasure!

But human bodies are a little like clay jars. They can crack and break. Because we break so easily, Paul says, we have to rely on God instead of on ourselves. It is God who makes the light to shine through us, and God who gives us power to show and tell others about Jesus Christ!

God, thank you for the good news about Jesus Christ, which shines like a light in my heart. Teach me to share that good news with others and to rely on you. Amen.

NOVEMBER 17

•

Anyone who believes in Christ is a new creation. The old is gone! The new has come! It is all from God. He brought us back to himself through Christ's death on the cross. And he has given us the task of bringing others back to him through Christ. God was bringing the world back to himself through Christ. He did not hold people's sins against them. God has trusted us with the message that people may be brought back to him.

2 Corinthians 5:17–19 NIRV

If you live in a cold climate you look forward to the coming of spring. You watch for the old, dirty snow to melt. You can't wait till it's warm enough to leave your coat at home. When the trees turn green and the flowers bloom, you know that spring is finally here. The world looks brand new!

Our hearts also need springtime. We all turn away from God. We all do things to hurt other people. We all sin. All our wrong attitudes and the wrong things we do pile up in our hearts like dirty snow on the side of the road.

But Paul says that when we love and honor Jesus Christ, God makes us brand new. All the old mistakes we made and all the things that kept us away from God are gone. It is springtime in our hearts!

God, thank you for the warm breezes and showers of springtime. Thank you for making all things new. Make my heart new too! Amen.

NOVEMBER 18

•

For he says, "At an acceptable time I have listened to you, and on a day of salvation I have helped you." See, now is the acceptable time; see, now is the day of salvation!

2 Corinthians 6:2 NRSV

Timing is important for many of the things we say and do. If you want to say something important to someone, like "I'm sorry" or "I love you," you won't do it while she is talking on the telephone. You'll wait for a better moment. And it would be strange to say "Merry Christmas" to people during the month of May or to say "Happy Valentine's Day" in October. Those words are meant especially for certain times of the year.

But Paul says you don't have to wait for the right moment to accept God's love and salvation. Every moment is the right moment to do that. Apart from God's salvation, we live our lives separated from God by sin. We disobey God by putting ourselves or other people or other things first. But God freely offers us the gift of salvation through Jesus Christ—all we have to do is receive it. When is the best time to do that? Now!

God, thank you for sending Jesus to show me your love and teach me your ways. Open my heart to receive your gift of salvation. Amen.

NOVEMBER 19

•

My friends, we want you to know that the churches in Macedonia have shown others how kind God is. Although they were going through hard times and were very poor, they were glad to give generously. They gave as much as they could afford and even more, simply because they wanted to. They even asked and begged us to let them have the joy of giving their money for God's people.

2 Corinthians 8:1–4 CEV

Opening presents is great fun, isn't it? It is fun to pull off the ribbons or bows and rip open the paper. And it is fun to enjoy the gift once it has been opened. But giving presents to other people is also great fun. Did you ever watch the expression of pride and delight on a toddler's face as he gives his mommy or daddy a gift that he made by himself?

In Paul's day, the Christians living in Jerusalem were very poor and needed help. Paul worked hard to collect money for them from Christians living in other places. Here he talks about how the Christians in a place called Macedonia gave very generously, not because they had to but because they wanted to. They were not rich. But they gave as much as they could, and then they gave some more. They did it because they had learned the joy of helping other people.

You have given me so much, God. Thank you for my many blessings. Fill me with love for others, and teach me the joy of sharing my money and my time with those who need help. Amen.

•

Three times I begged the Lord to make this suffering go away. But he replied, "My kindness is all you need. My power is strongest when you are weak." So if Christ keeps giving me his power, I will gladly brag about how weak I am. Yes, I am glad to be weak or insulted or mistreated or to have troubles and sufferings, if it is for Christ. Because when I am weak, I am strong.

2 Corinthians 12:8–10 CEV

Do you have a favorite superhero? In comics and cartoons, superheroes are always strong. They have big muscles, and often they have special powers.

Having large muscles or magical powers is not the only way to be strong. Paul was suffering from some kind of problem. He kept asking Jesus to make the problem go away. But, instead of fixing Paul's problem, Jesus said, "My kindness is all you need. My power is strongest when you are weak." Jesus knew that as long as Paul had that problem, Paul would keep on praying for Jesus' Spirit to give him strength. That is why Paul was able to go through all the troubles he did—because the Spirit of Jesus helped Paul get through hard times.

When we are suffering, it is good to pray that the Lord take our suffering away. And often the Lord will do so! But even if the suffering is not taken away, we can trust Jesus to help us through. We are weak, but he is strong.

Jesus, you have the power of God! Thank you for giving us the strength to do your work. Teach me to turn to you for strength in hard times and in good times too. Amen.

NOVEMBER 21

I'm afraid that when I come I won't find you as I want you to be. I'm afraid that you won't find me as you want me to be. I'm afraid there will be arguing, jealousy and fits of anger. I'm afraid you will separate into your own little groups. Then you will tell lies about each other. You will talk about each other. I'm afraid you will be proud and cause trouble.

2 Corinthians 12:20 NIrV

The Christmas Carol, by Charles Dickens, is a famous story about Ebenezer Scrooge. Scrooge was a mean old man who did not care about anything except himself and his money. But some unusual visitors came to see him on Christmas Eve, and because of what they showed him, he repented of his sin. That means he gave up his old, selfish ways. His stony heart became a heart filled with love and caring for others.

Paul worried about the Christians in the church at Corinth, because some of them had not repented of their sinful ways. He worried that when he came to visit he would be embarrassed by their bad behavior. They were insulting each other and arguing among themselves. But God wants church to be a place that is filled with love and caring for others. Church should be a place where people have given up their old, selfish, and sinful ways. Church should be a place where all the members help one another to be the best people they can be, for God and for one another.

Lord, send your Holy Spirit on the church, so that believers will repent of their selfish and sinful ways. Fill your church with love and peace. Amen.

NOVEMBER 22

•

May the grace shown by the Lord Jesus Christ, and the love that God has given us, and the sharing of life brought about by the Holy Spirit be with you all.

2 Corinthians 13:14 NIRV

The apostle Paul wrote this verse at the end of his letter as a blessing to the Corinthian church. Christians still use it today at the end of worship services to bless everyone who is there.

Did you notice that it has three parts? The blessing comes from the Lord Jesus Christ, God, and the Holy Spirit. That's because Christians have experienced God's blessing in more than one way. We are blessed by Jesus Christ, who is God-with-us (Emmanuel) in human form. We are blessed by God the Creator, who gives everything life. And we are blessed by the Holy Spirit, who makes us one with each other and with God.

Christians don't believe in three different gods. But Christians use the word *Trinity* to point to the different ways we know God's blessings. Trinity means three-in-one. Christians use Father, Son, and Holy Spirit as a name for the Trinity. Christians are baptized "in the name of the Father and of the Son and of the Holy Spirit" (Matt. 28:19). This tells you that they have joined all the other Christians who have received God's many blessings.

Father, Son, and Holy Spirit, we thank you for all your blessings. Amen.

NOVEMBER 23

•

Shout with joy to the LORD,
O earth!
Worship the LORD with gladness.
Come before him, singing with joy. . . .
Enter his gates with thanksgiving;
go into his courts with praise.
Give thanks to him and bless his
name.
For the LORD is good.
His unfailing love continues forever,
and his faithfulness continues to
each generation.

Psalm 100:1–2, 4–5 NLT

Thanksgiving is a day for being thankful. We thank God for family, for friends, and for homes to live in. We thank God for our beautiful world and for the good food that comes from it.

Thanksgiving is a feast day. On most days we don't mind eating a quick, simple meal, or even eating leftovers. But on Thanksgiving we usually take the trouble to make a big, special meal and spend a long time eating it. What is your favorite part of Thanksgiving dinner? We make more food than we really need to remind us that God gives us more than we need. Feasting is a way to celebrate God's generosity to us.

Another good way to celebrate God's generosity is to be generous to others. You can help serve a Thanksgiving meal to people who can't afford a feast. You can invite people who are far away from their homes to your feast. The more we share God's goodness with others, the more everyone on earth will shout to the Lord with joy!

Generous God, we give you thanks for all your good gifts to us. Your faithful love continues forever! Amen.

NOVEMBER 24

•

All eyes look to you for help;
you give them their food as they need it.
When you open your hand,
you satisfy the hunger and thirst of every living thing.

Psalm 145:15–16 NLT

Jesus gave thanks to God before he ate. It's a good habit for us too. Sometimes we're hungry or in a hurry at mealtime, and we don't feel like stopping to give God thanks. Sometimes we don't like what is for dinner, and it's hard to feel grateful. But meals are not only a time to fill our stomachs. They are also a time to fill our hearts, by reminding ourselves of how good God is to every living creature. So try to stop, even for a short prayer, before you eat.

When we pray at mealtime, we remember that all we have and enjoy belongs to God, not to us. We thank God for taking care of us. We thank God for the people who grow and sell and prepare food for us to eat. We remember the people in the world who are hungry and ask God to show us how to help them. We thank God for providing food for all living things, not just for people. Praying before we eat makes us more grateful for all of God's blessings.

Giver of all blessings, we thank you for providing food for us to eat. Help us receive what you give us with grateful hearts. Show us how to be generous with what we have, so that all your creatures will have enough to eat. Amen.

NOVEMBER 25

•

Don't put your trust in human leaders.
Don't trust in people. They can't save you.
When they die, they return to the ground.
On that very day their plans are bound to fail.
Blessed are those who depend on the God of Jacob for help.
Blessed are those who put their hope in the LORD their God.
He is the Maker of heaven and earth and the ocean.
He made everything in them.
The LORD remains faithful forever.

Psalm 146:3–6 NIRV

"Don't trust in people," the psalmist says. That is hard advice to follow! All of us live by trusting and depending on other people. We don't really have a choice. We cannot live all by ourselves. We cannot provide all the things we need. We cannot keep ourselves safe and happy. So we have to trust other people.

But we can't trust other people completely. Sometimes they let us down. Sometimes they have so many needs of their own that we cannot depend on them. No parent or minister or political leader or friend can ever give us everything we need or keep us safe from all dangers. If we put all our trust in them, we will be disappointed.

That is why this psalm tells us to put our final trust in God. God will never let us down. God watches over people whom everybody else has forgotten: prisoners, people with disabilities, the poor and lonely. We can trust God absolutely.

We praise you, God, because you remain faithful forever. We rejoice in the many ways you show your love for us. Help us trust you in all things. Amen.

NOVEMBER 26

•

Praise the Lord!
Praise God in his heavenly
dwelling;
praise him in his mighty heaven!
Praise him for his mighty works;
praise his unequaled greatness!
Praise him with a blast of the trumpet;
praise him with the lyre and harp!
Praise him with the tambourine and
dancing;
praise him with stringed
instruments and flutes!
Praise him with a clash of cymbals;
praise him with loud clanging
cymbals.
Let everything that lives sing praises to the Lord.
Praise the Lord!

Psalm 150 NLT

How many ways do you know to praise God? Here are some: praying silently when we are alone; praying aloud in a group; singing; playing a musical instrument; and dancing. Can you think of some other ways?

Christians all over the world praise God in different ways. They pray in many different languages. They use many different musical instruments. Some Christians dance or kneel or raise their hands when they praise God. Some hold hands with others.

It doesn't matter what language or musical instruments you use. It doesn't matter whether you are loud or quiet when you praise God, or whether you move around or sit still. God likes all kinds of praise! The important thing is to use your mind and your heart and your body to offer praise the best way you know how.

God, you are greater than anything else! As long as I live, I want to praise you. Amen.

NOVEMBER 27

•

Jesus called the crowd to him along with his disciples. He said, "If you want to come after me, you must say no to yourself. You must take your cross and follow me. If you want to save your life, you will lose it. But if you lose your life for me and for the good news, you will save it. What good is it if you gain the whole world but lose your soul? Or what can you trade for your soul?"

Mark 8:34–37 NIRV (1)

Have you ever heard or read about someone who saved a person's life? Maybe the hero entered a burning building and rescued someone trapped inside. Maybe he pulled a child who had fallen through the ice out to safety. The rescuer was not thinking about his own safety but about helping the one in need.

Jesus wants us to stop thinking just about protecting our own lives. He teaches us that if we think only about self-protection, we will lose out and our lives will be empty. Instead, Jesus wants us to give our lives to God. God will then show us the way to live: by loving others, even our enemies; by helping those in need; by spreading the news of God's love. When we give our lives over, God gives us new life in return! The new life is filled with God's love, God's Spirit, and God's joy.

Lord, help me to trust you so that I may give my life to you. Show me ways to serve you and fill me with your salvation. Amen.

NOVEMBER 28

•

Six days later Jesus took Peter, James, and John to the top of a mountain. No one else was there. As the men watched, Jesus' appearance changed, and his clothing became dazzling white, far whiter than any earthly process could ever make it. Then Elijah and Moses appeared and began talking with Jesus. . . . Then a cloud came over them, and a voice from the cloud said, "This is my beloved Son. Listen to him." Suddenly they looked around, and Moses and Elijah were gone, and only Jesus was with them.

Mark 9:2–4, 7–8 NLT

In fairy tales, people sometimes change in incredible ways—a wooden puppet is changed into a real boy, a servant girl becomes a princess. In this story Peter, James, and John see Jesus changed from an ordinary-looking man into someone with shining clothes, like an angel. They see him standing next to Moses and Elijah, two very famous leaders of the Jewish people.

The disciples did not know what they were seeing. Was it imaginary or real? Later, after Jesus was raised from the dead, the disciples would understand. Then they would know that Jesus has the most special place of all in God's plan. Jesus was a prophet and a leader, like Moses and Elijah. And at his resurrection Jesus was given heavenly glory, like the angels. But Jesus is more than a prophet or an angel—Jesus is God's Son. That is why we should listen to him.

Jesus, you are even wiser than the prophets! You are more glorious than the angels! Give me ears to listen to you and a heart to obey. Amen.

NOVEMBER 29

•

After they arrived at Capernaum, Jesus and his disciples settled in the house where they would be staying. Jesus asked them, "What were you discussing out on the road?" But they didn't answer, because they had been arguing about which of them was the greatest. He sat down and called the twelve disciples over to him. Then he said, "Anyone who wants to be the first must take last place and be the servant of everyone else." Then he put a little child among them. Taking the child in his arms, he said to them, "Anyone who welcomes a little child like this on my behalf welcomes me, and anyone who welcomes me welcomes my Father who sent me."

Mark 9:33–37 NLT

It's great to feel important, isn't it? When you get selected to do a special job at school or when people tell you how much they value your help, you feel good inside. But sometimes when people want to feel important they act badly toward one another. James and John were doing that. They were with Jesus on the way to Jerusalem, where Jesus would suffer and die. James and John should have been trying to help Jesus and to learn from him. But instead they were arguing about which of the two of them was more important.

Jesus showed them how silly their argument was. To be important in God's eyes, we should serve others instead of always trying to boss them around. Then Jesus held a small child before the disciples. In Jesus' day, children were not seen as very important. But Jesus said they were important in God's eyes. Jesus was showing that God's ideas about who or what is important are different from our ideas.

God, forgive me for times when I act badly so that I can seem important to others. Fill me with a desire to please you instead. Teach me to be your servant. Amen.

NOVEMBER 30

•

One day some parents brought their children to Jesus so he could touch them and bless them, but the disciples told them not to bother him. But when Jesus saw what was happening, he was very displeased with his disciples. He said to them, "Let the children come to me. Don't stop them! For the Kingdom of God belongs to such as these. I assure you, anyone who doesn't have their kind of faith will never get into the Kingdom of God." Then he took the children into his arms and placed his hands on their heads and blessed them.

Mark 10:13–16 NLT

When you were a toddler, you probably cried when your mom left the room. You were not old enough to understand that she was just around the corner and would be right back. But you did understand how much you needed her. You knew that without her help you would be lost.

When people brought children to Jesus so that he could bless them, the disciples tried to stop them. They thought Jesus was too busy and too important to spend his time with children. But Jesus ordered the disciples to let the children come. In fact, Jesus said that all people must become like children if they want to enter into God's kingdom. Jesus meant that people ought to know how much they need God, the way a young child knows that she needs her mom. Jesus meant that people ought to see how they would be lost without God's help. When we know these things, blessings will come.

Jesus, thank you for showing us how much we need God in our lives. Thank you for blessing children. Bless me! Amen.

DECEMBER 1

•

I heard a loud shout from the throne, saying, "Look, the home of God is now among his people! He will live with them, and they will be his people. God himself will be with them. He will remove all of their sorrows, and there will be no more death or sorrow or crying or pain. For the old world and its evils are gone forever."

Revelation 21:3–4 NLT

Advent is the time in the church year when Christians get ready to celebrate Christmas. The stores get ready by playing happy Christmas music and making everything look beautiful. We too sing carols and decorate our homes as we wait for Christmas.

But for Christians, sadness is also a part of waiting for the Christ child. We feel sad because there is so much death and pain in the world. Every year during Advent we long for the time when God will wipe away every tear from our eyes. We long for the day when there will be no more suffering and death.

The Advent season is a time of joy. But it is also a time of longing, as we realize how much our world needs the good news of Christmas—God-with-us in Jesus Christ.

Come, Lord Jesus! Come and make your home with us. Come and deliver us from suffering and hatred. Come and heal the whole creation. Amen.

DECEMBER 2

•

The Song of Songs, which is Solomon's.
Let him kiss me with the kisses of his mouth!
For your love is better than wine,
your anointing oils are fragrant,
your name is perfume poured out;
therefore the maidens love you.

Song of Solomon 1:1–3 NRSV

There are lots of different kinds of human love. There is love for friends. There is love for members of your family. You may feel love for your team, or for your school, or for your country. There is also romantic love between two people. That is the kind of love the Song of Songs is all about. It is a long poem about the love between a woman and a man. In the poem, they take turns talking about their love for each other.

Maybe reading this poem makes you feel a little embarrassed. It's a little like reading someone else's love letters! But having this beautiful poetry in the Bible shows us that we don't have to be shy or embarrassed about this kind of human love. It too is part of God's wonderful design of creation—a gift to be grateful for.

Fountain of love, pour out your love on all people. Help me to see reflections of your great love in every kind of human love. Amen.

DECEMBER 3

•

You are my dove
hiding among the rocks on the side of a cliff.
Let me see how lovely you are!
Let me hear the sound of your melodious voice.
Our vineyards are in blossom;
we must catch the little foxes that destroy the vineyards.
My darling, I am yours, and you are mine,
as you feed your sheep among the lilies.

Song of Songs 2:14–16 CEV

When two people love each other, they belong to each other. The love they share brings them together. Love that brings two people together has to go in two directions. When you love someone, you want that person to love you back. It hurts if they don't.

It is that way with the love between God and us too. God loves us. God is the greatest giver of love there is. But God also wants our love. When we love God back, the love we share brings us together. Our love matters to God!

God, I love you! Help me feel your great love for me and let my love for you grow stronger every day. Amen.

DECEMBER 4

•

"You are so beautiful, my love!
So beautiful!
Your eyes behind your veil are like doves.
Your hair flows like a flock of black goats
coming down from Mount Gilead.
Your teeth are as clean as a flock of sheep.
Their wool has just been clipped.
They have just come up from being washed.
Each of your teeth has its twin.
Not one of them is alone.
Your lips are like a bright red ribbon.
Your mouth is so lovely.
Your cheeks behind your veil
are like the halves of a pomegranate."

Song of Songs 4:1b–3 NIRV

When people are in love, they are always noticing great things about each other. They notice how beautiful, or how kind, or how brave and talented the other person is. And when they notice all these good things, they can't help telling each other. Do you like the way the man tells the woman how beautiful she is?

Prayer is one way we show that we are in love with God. That means when we pray we shouldn't spend all our time asking for things. Prayer is also our chance to tell God about all the great things we have noticed. Find your own way to say it!

Amazing God, your kindness is as deep as the ocean. Your justice is as big as the sky. Your goodness shines like the sun. Everywhere I look, I see how great you are! Amen.

DECEMBER 5

•

"You have ravished my heart, my treasure, my bride. I am overcome by one glance of your eyes, by a single bead of your necklace. How sweet is your love, my treasure, my bride! How much better it is than wine! Your perfume is more fragrant than the richest of spices. Your lips, my bride, are as sweet as honey. Yes, honey and cream are under your tongue. The scent of your clothing is like that of the mountains and the cedars of Lebanon."

Song of Songs 4:9–11 NLT

Have you noticed that when two people are in love, sometimes they don't seem to care about anything else? Their love for each other is more important to them than having good things to eat or nice things to wear. They don't seem to notice anything except each other.

It is a wonderful thing to be deeply in love with another person. The Song of Songs celebrates this romantic love between two people. But this kind of love can be a problem if it makes them forget their love for God and for other people.

The special love between two people doesn't have to be a selfish love. Instead, the love that they share can be a reflection of their love for God. And their love for each other can reach out to people who are in special need of love.

Loving God, don't let my love for anyone become a selfish love. Help my love for my friends and my family create a space for more love to grow. Amen.

DECEMBER 6

•

"For the time is coming," says the LORD, "when I will place a righteous Branch on King David's throne. He will be a King who rules with wisdom. He will do what is just and right throughout the land. And this is his name: 'The LORD Is Our Righteousness.' In that day Judah will be saved, and Israel will live in safety."

Jeremiah 23:5–6 NLT

What you believe about the future can change the way you act in the present. Suppose you think that this world will always be full of suffering and unfairness. It would make it hard to work to change things now, wouldn't it? But suppose you believe that a new day is coming, when no one will suffer and everyone will be treated fairly. Wouldn't you want to start getting rid of suffering and unfairness now?

During Advent we remember that we are still waiting for the new day God has promised. God has raised up Jesus Christ to be our King. He will fill the world with joy and fairness, and that makes us want to fill our lives with joy and fairness now.

Lord of the future, we wait for the new day you have promised. Help us get ready by treating people fairly and spreading your joy. Amen.

DECEMBER 7

Think the same way that Christ Jesus thought:

Christ was truly God.
But he did not try to remain equal with God.
He gave up everything and became a slave,
when he became like one of us.
Christ was humble.
He obeyed God and even died on a cross.

Philippians 2:5–8 CEV

The people in the Philippian church were not getting along very well. They kept arguing with each other and being selfish. Paul told them to think the same way that Jesus did. Paul reminded them that Jesus wasn't selfish; he trusted God and gave up his life for us.

Jesus lived almost two thousand years ago in Palestine. Of course, we don't live *when* Jesus lived and most of us don't live *where* Jesus lived. But when we read what the Bible tells us about Jesus' life, we see a pattern. It's a pattern of kindness and trust and unselfishness. If we try to think in the same way that Jesus did, our lives will start to show the same pattern. Even if we don't live when Jesus did, or where Jesus did, we can try to live how Jesus did.

Christ our Savior, help us think the same way that you did, so that our lives will be full of trust and love. Amen.

DECEMBER 8

•

Then God gave Christ the highest place
and honored his name above all others.
So at the name of Jesus everyone will bow down,
those in heaven, on earth, and under the earth.
And to the glory of God the Father
everyone will openly agree, "Jesus Christ is Lord!"

Philippians 2:9–11 CEV

Jesus spent his whole life saying yes to God. He spent his whole life obeying God's will and showing God's love. He was filled with God's power and wisdom.

But Jesus' life ended in a terrible way—on a cross. That was a very painful and shameful way to die. Was Jesus' whole life a waste? Did God abandon Jesus?

No way! says Paul. God said yes to Jesus, just as Jesus said yes to God. God raised Jesus from the dead. Now he will never die, because he shares in God's own life. Because of God's yes, everyone will know that Jesus Christ is Lord, and they will worship him.

I praise you, God, for raising Jesus from the dead. And I worship the one whose name is above every name. In the name of Christ, Amen.

DECEMBER 9

•

All I want is to know Christ and the power that raised him to life. I want to suffer and die as he did, so that somehow I also may be raised to life. I have not yet reached my goal, and I am not perfect. But Christ has taken hold of me. So I keep on running and struggling to take hold of the prize.

Philippians 3:10–12 CEV

Did you ever play "chase" with someone? It is a very easy game. You run, and the other person chases you and tries to catch you. "Gotcha!" she may shout when she grabs you.

Paul says that Jesus Christ grabbed hold of him, and when that happened, Paul's life was changed. When Christ took hold of Paul, Paul realized that he had been running in the wrong direction. He discovered that all the things he had thought were very important in life really were not. Paul learned that the one important thing—the one "prize" worth winning—was the prize of knowing Jesus Christ.

Jesus wants to take hold of you too. He wants you to know him and the power for loving and for right living that he brings. But if you decide to serve him, be ready for him to change your ideas about what is most important in life. Be ready for him to point you in new directions!

Christ Jesus, thank you for taking hold of my life. As I struggle to know you and serve you, keep pointing me in the right direction. Amen.

DECEMBER 10

•

Here is what I'm asking Euodia and Syntyche to do. I want them to agree with each other because they belong to the Lord. My true companion, here is what I ask you to do. Help those women. They have served at my side. They have helped me spread the good news. . . . Their names are all written in the Book of Life.

Philippians 4:2–3 NIRV

Even people who are trying hard to serve the Lord can disagree with one another. They may have different understandings of what God wants them to do or different ideas about the best plan of action.

That is the way it was with the women named Euodia and Syntyche. Paul says that they had worked like team members with him, telling people about Jesus. But now instead of working together they were working against each other. Paul doesn't say why they were arguing, but he asks them to work out their problem. He asks another person in the church (whom he calls his "true companion") to help them do so.

It is not wrong for us to disagree with other people. But God wants us to work out our disagreements. Doing that may not be easy. But we need to keep trying, because we serve God best if we are at peace with one another.

God of peace, it can be so hard to get along with other people, especially when I think that my way is best. Show me ways to work out my disagreements with other people. Amen.

DECEMBER 11

•

Always be full of joy in the Lord. I say it again—rejoice! Let everyone see that you are considerate in all you do. Remember, the Lord is coming soon. Don't worry about anything; instead, pray about everything. Tell God what you need, and thank him for all he has done. If you do this, you will experience God's peace, which is far more wonderful than the human mind can understand. His peace will guard your hearts and minds as you live in Christ Jesus.

Philippians 4:4–7 NLT

Have you ever been terribly afraid? Perhaps you got lost and weren't sure where to find your mom or dad. Or maybe someone you love was very sick. Whatever the reason, whenever we are afraid, it is hard to think straight. We can't get our worries out of our mind.

When Paul wrote the words you see above, his dear friends in the city of Philippi were afraid for him. He had been arrested for teaching about Jesus and was in jail. Paul knew that God would take care of him, and he wanted his friends to feel the same hope and joy that he felt. So he reminded them that they should (1) tell God all their worries, (2) ask God to help them, and (3) thank God for all the good things God had done. Paul did not promise his friends that God would make sure Paul got out of jail or take away the hard times. But Paul did promise them that God would answer their prayers by giving them peace in the midst of their troubles.

God, thank you for listening to me whenever I am afraid. Help me to remember all the good things you have done for me. Please fill my heart and my mind with your peace. In Christ's name, Amen.

DECEMBER 12

•

Finally, my brothers and sisters, always think about what is true. Think about what is noble, right and pure. Think about what is lovely and worthy of respect. If anything is excellent or worthy of praise, think about those kinds of things.

Philippians 4:8 NIRV

What grows in a garden? Perhaps flowers, perhaps fruits and vegetables, perhaps herbs to make food taste good. It depends on what you plant! If you want to grow daffodils, you plant bulbs for daffodils. If you want to grow blueberries, you plant blueberry bushes.

Your mind is a lot like a garden. Whenever you think about things that are excellent and true, you are planting in your garden. As you grow up, so do the plants. And sooner than you expect, they bloom into lovely and fragrant flowers, or they bear delicious fruit. But these "flowers" aren't the kind you can smell with your nose, and this "fruit" isn't the kind you can taste with your mouth. When you plant good thoughts, soon you will see love, kindness, patience, gentleness, and generosity growing in your life—all the "fruits and flowers" that make your life a joy to you and others!

God, help me to plant good thoughts in the garden of my mind. Help me to see and to remember the things that are true, noble, lovely, and worthy of respect, and to tell others about them too. Amen.

DECEMBER 13

•

With all my heart I wait for the LORD to help me.
I put my hope in his word.
I wait for the LORD to help me.
I wait with more longing than those on guard duty wait for the morning.
I'll say it again.
I wait with more longing than those on guard duty wait for the morning.

Psalm 130:5–6 NIRV

Advent is a season of waiting. If you have ever planted seeds, you know something about waiting. You put small, dry seeds into the soil, you water them, and you wait. You cannot see anything happening. You keep watering and keep waiting. You look eagerly each day to see if the seeds have sprouted. And then, one day, you see what you have been waiting for: a tiny green plant peeping through the soil.

People who believe in God wait for things that God has promised: for a day when sick people will be healed, when hungry people will be fed, when enemies will become friends, and when no one will be treated unfairly. It is hard to wait for these things. But while we wait we do what we can to make this world a better place, knowing that God is working even when we cannot see it.

Faithful God, help us to trust in you while we wait for the things you have promised. And help us to show others what we hope for by the way we love and care for them. In Christ's name, Amen.

DECEMBER 14

•

Then the angel told Mary, "Don't be afraid! God is pleased with you, and you will have a son. His name will be Jesus. He will be great and will be called the Son of God Most High. The Lord God will make him king, as his ancestor David was. He will rule the people of Israel forever, and his kingdom will never end." Mary asked the angel, "How can this happen? I am not married!" The angel answered, "The Holy Spirit will come down to you, and God's power will come over you. So your child will be called the holy Son of God."

Luke 1:30–35 CEV

Suppose an angel came to you and told you that God was pleased with you and wanted to give you a blessing. What might you hope for? Lots of friends? Wealth? Happiness and good health? Those are blessings that a lot of people would like to receive.

God gave Mary a very surprising blessing—she would have a special son, Jesus. It is easy to see how having a baby when you are married can be a blessing. But Mary wasn't married yet. Finding out that you will have a baby when you are not married often feels like a problem, not a blessing. Mary trusted God enough to accept God's special blessing. Through her, God came to us in Jesus and blessed the whole world.

God, help me trust you enough to accept the surprising blessings you may bring me. Send the Holy Spirit to fill me with faith and courage. Amen.

DECEMBER 15

•

Mary said,

> *"My soul gives glory to the Lord.*
> *My spirit delights in God my Savior.*
> *He has taken note of me*
> *even though I am not important.*
> *From now on all people will call me blessed.*
> *The Mighty One has done great things for me.*
> *His name is holy."*

Luke 1:46–49 NIRV

Have you ever seen books with the title *Who's Who*? They list all the people who are considered important in their field. There's the *Who's Who* of doctors and the *Who's Who* of professional athletes, for example. To get listed in one of those books, other people have to think you're very important.

Mary would never have been listed in a *Who's Who* book. She wasn't famous. She wasn't rich. She wasn't powerful. She was an ordinary person who was blessed by God to do an amazing thing: She gave birth to Jesus! In this song, Mary praised God for choosing her for something so important.

God takes our ideas about who's who in the world and turns them upside down! We've forgotten the names of most of the rich and famous people from Mary's time, but we still remember her name, because of what God did.

God my Savior, keep me from worrying too much about what other people think of me. I know that I will always be important in your sight. In Christ's name, Amen.

DECEMBER 16

•

[Joseph] went from the town of Nazareth in Galilee to Judea. That is where Bethlehem, the town of David, was. Joseph went there because he belonged to the family line of David. He went there with Mary to be listed. Mary was engaged to him. She was expecting a baby. While Joseph and Mary were there, the time came for the child to be born. She gave birth to her first baby. It was a boy. She wrapped him in large strips of cloth. Then she placed him in a manger. There was no room for them in the inn.

Luke 2:4b–7 NIrV

Every Advent, Hispanic Christians act out this part of the Christmas story during a nine-day celebration of Las Posadas. *Posada* is a Spanish word meaning shelter. Starting on the evening of December 16, children and adults form an outdoor procession, carrying lighted candles and statues of Mary and Joseph. Others play the role of innkeepers. When those in the procession stop at the innkeeper's door, they ask for shelter. But the innkeeper tells them rudely to go away. This happens for eight nights in a row. But on the ninth night, Christmas Eve, the innkeeper offers them all that he has left—a stable. There the baby Jesus is born, and everyone gathers for a big celebration.

Many Hispanic Christians in our country have traveled here from far away and know what it is like to seek shelter. Sometimes they have been rudely turned away because others say there is "no room." But sometimes, just like Mary and Joseph, they have been welcomed and given shelter.

God, help us to make room in our lives for Jesus. Help us make room in our lives for those who need our help. Amen.

DECEMBER 17

•

Shadrach, Meshach, and Abednego answered the king, "O Nebuchadnezzar, we have no need to present a defense to you in this matter. If our God whom we serve is able to deliver us from the furnace of blazing fire and out of your hand, O king, let him deliver us. But if not, be it known to you, O king, that we will not serve your gods and we will not worship the golden statue that you have set up."

Daniel 3:16–18 NRSV

If you read the rest of this story from the Book of Daniel, you will find out that Shadrach, Meshach, and Abednego were not burned to death in the furnace of blazing fire. The story has a happy ending, because God saved them in an amazing way!

But they didn't know about this happy ending when they talked to the king. If God is able to save us, they said, we will not die. But even if God does not save us, we still refuse to worship your golden statue.

Not every story of faith has a happy ending. Sometimes people end up suffering or even dying for their faith. Shadrach, Meshach, and Abednego did what was right, even though they didn't know if their story would have a happy ending. They showed true faith!

Giver of all things, give me true faith. Make me brave enough to do what is right, even when I don't know what will happen. Amen.

DECEMBER 18

•

So the two leaders and the royal rulers went as a group to the king. They said, "King Darius, may you live forever! All of the royal leaders, high officials, royal rulers, advisers and governors want to make a suggestion. We've agreed that you should give an order. And you should make sure it's obeyed. Here is the command you should give. King Darius, during the next 30 days don't let any of your people pray to any god or man except to you. If they do, throw them into the lions' den. Now give the order. Write it down in the laws of the Medes and Persians. Then it can't be changed." So King Darius put the order in writing. Daniel found out that the king had signed the order. In spite of that, he did just as he had always done before. He went home to his upstairs room. Its windows opened toward Jerusalem. He went to his room three times a day to pray. He got down on his knees and gave thanks to his God.

Daniel 6:6–10 NIRV

You already have lots of different roles to play: family member, friend, student, citizen. Sometimes it seems easy to trust in God and play all these roles at the same time. But sometimes it is very hard.

It was hard for Daniel. He was one of the king's top leaders. But he also trusted in God. The king signed an order that said that people in his land could pray only to him, not to God. If they disobeyed that order, they would be thrown into a den of lions. Even though Daniel was one of the king's leaders, he refused to obey the king's order. He kept praying to God.

Someday you may have to refuse to do something that some important person tells you to do, because you trust in God. Will you be ready, like Daniel was?

God, my family and friends and school and country are all important to me. But I know that trusting you is the most important thing of all. Amen.

DECEMBER 19

•

Then in my vision that night, I saw a fourth beast, terrifying, dreadful, and very strong. It devoured and crushed its victims with huge iron teeth and trampled what was left beneath its feet. It was different from any of the other beasts, and it had ten horns.

Daniel 7:7 NLT

Have you ever had an awful nightmare? If you have, you probably woke up scared. But then you were glad to realize that it was only a dream.

The prophet Daniel had a nightmare about four terrible beasts. But the angel told him that this was not just a bad dream. His nightmare was going to come true! The four beasts were four kingdoms. From these kingdoms, terrible rulers would frighten and hurt God's people. But that was not the end of the story. Finally all the rulers of the world would worship and obey God.

Daniel's dream warned him that awful things were going to happen to the people of Israel. But his dream also gave him hope that God had not forgotten them. One day, all God's children would be safe and the world would be the way God wanted it to be.

God of hope, when terrible things happen, don't let me get discouraged. Give me hope for a better future. Amen.

DECEMBER 20

•

"O Lord our God, you brought lasting honor to your name by rescuing your people from Egypt in a great display of power. But we have sinned and are full of wickedness. . . . O my God, listen to me and hear my request. Open your eyes and see our wretchedness. See how your city lies in ruins—for everyone knows that it is yours. We do not ask because we deserve help, but because you are so merciful."

Daniel 9:15, 18 NLT

When you want people to do things for you, sometimes you remind them of the good things you have done for them: "I cleaned up my room, Dad. Will you give me my allowance?" "I invited you to my party, Susan. Will you invite me to yours?"

Daniel didn't try this with God, because the people of Israel had been doing evil, not good. When Daniel asked God to help them rebuild the city of Jerusalem, he didn't say that Israel had loved and obeyed God. Instead, he said how sorry Israel was for the bad things they had done. He asked God to help them because God was merciful. God's love for Israel is so strong and steady that Daniel knew he could always count on it.

Lord our God, teach us to pray like Daniel. Help us to be honest about what we've done wrong. When we ask you to help us, give us trust in your perfect love. Amen.

DECEMBER 21

•

I heard what he said. But I didn't understand it. So I asked, "My master, what will come of all of this?" He answered, "Go on your way, Daniel. The scroll is rolled up. It is sealed until the time of the end."

Daniel 12:8–9 NIRV

Dreams are often hard to understand. Daniel's long dream is full of strange and puzzling things. There are terrible beasts and wise angels and numbers like 62 and 1,335. Many people have wondered what all these things mean. They have tried to figure out exactly when the awful suffering of the world will be over and God's promises for life and joy will come true.

Even Daniel had a hard time understanding his dream. "What will come of all of this?" he asks. But the answer he gets is to keep living and praising God, even though he doesn't know God's schedule for fixing everything. In the end, all will become clear.

What are the things you wonder about and wait for? Do you wonder when people will stop killing and hurting each other? Do you wait for the day when all creation will live together in happiness and peace? Do you wonder when you will get a clear answer to all the things you wonder about? Daniel's dream doesn't give us easy answers. It tells us to go on our way, trusting that one day all that God has promised us will come true.

God of the future, I look for signs of hope in dreams and visions. Help me to trust that all your promises will come true. While I wait, give me wisdom to do what is right. Amen.

DECEMBER 22

•

This is the beginning of the good news about Jesus Christ, the Son of God.

Mark 1:1 NIrV

The Gospels of Matthew and Luke tell us stories about Jesus' birth. Matthew tells about wise men from far away who followed a star to the place where Jesus was born. Luke tells about angels who spread the good news of Jesus' birth to the shepherds nearby. If you have a Christmas play at church, you will probably have wise men and shepherds!

But Christmas isn't really about shepherds and wise men. Christmas is about the good news that God's Son, Jesus, has come to be with us. The Gospel of Mark doesn't tell us anything about Jesus' birth. Mark begins with Jesus' baptism, when he was already a grown-up. But Mark also brings us the good news of Christmas. He tells us that Jesus, God's beloved Son, is here to save us.

Mark begins the story of Jesus' life with his baptism. We begin the story of our lives as Christians with baptism too. Some people are baptized when they are children, and some are baptized when they are adults. Either way, baptism is only the beginning for us. Once we are baptized, we can carry the good news of Jesus Christ into the world.

Thank you, God, for your Son, Jesus. Show me how to be a messenger of your good news at Christmas and all through the year. Amen.

DECEMBER 23

•

The angel said, "Joseph, the baby that Mary will have is from the Holy Spirit. Go ahead and marry her. Then after her baby is born, name him Jesus, because he will save his people from their sins." So the Lord's promise came true, just as the prophet had said, "A virgin will have a baby boy, and he will be called Immanuel," which means "God is with us."

Matthew 1:20b–23 CEV

God doesn't keep promises only once. God's promises are fulfilled again and again. The promises "God saves" (the meaning of the name *Jesus*) and "God is with us" (the meaning of the name *Immanuel*) came true for God's people many centuries before Jesus was born. The prophet Isaiah reassured King Ahaz that God would protect the people of Jerusalem and save them from their enemies. As a sign of this promise, Isaiah said that a young woman would have a son and call him Immanuel. (You can find this promise in Isaiah 7:10–17.) The Gospel of Matthew quotes God's promise from the Book of Isaiah, because it came true again in Jesus.

Jesus was a sign to the people of Joseph and Mary's time that "God saves" and "God is with us." And Jesus is our sign that God's promises are true for us too.

God of all times and places, thank you for keeping your promises to be with us. Thank you for giving us a Savior, Jesus Christ. Amen.

DECEMBER 24

•

The Word became a human being. He made his home with us. We have seen his glory. It is the glory of the one and only Son. He came from the Father. And he was full of grace and truth.

John 1:14 NIRV

When we think of the Christmas story, we usually think of Mary and Joseph, and baby Jesus in a manger. John tells the Christmas story in a different way. He says that the Word of God became a human being and made his home with us.

This shows how much God loves the world, because making a home with us isn't easy. Human life is full of weakness, confusion, and pain. When we read about Jesus' life in the Bible, we see that his life wasn't easy. He experienced everything other human beings experience, including death.

But at Christmastime, we focus on the birth of Jesus, not his death. In Jesus, the Word of God became a human being and made his home with us. What a wonderful gift!

Word of God, thank you for making your home with us. It is the best present I will ever receive. Amen.

DECEMBER 25

That night some shepherds were in the fields outside the village, guarding their flocks of sheep. Suddenly, an angel of the Lord appeared among them, and the radiance of the Lord's glory surrounded them. They were terribly frightened, but the angel reassured them. "Don't be afraid!" he said. "I bring you good news of great joy for everyone! The Savior—yes, the Messiah, the Lord—has been born tonight in Bethlehem, the city of David! And this is how you will recognize him: You will find a baby lying in a manger, wrapped snugly in strips of cloth!"

Luke 2:8–12 NLT

Merry Christmas! After weeks of waiting, Christmas is finally here. Christmas is probably not a terrifying or surprising day for you. But that's the way the day of Jesus' birth was for the shepherds. They were not expecting this good news!

We have been expecting to celebrate Jesus' birth today. But we can celebrate Christmas even more if we share some of the shepherds' fear and surprise. At Christmastime we tremble at God's nearness. The glory of God's love is so bright that we hardly dare to look at it. At Christmastime we are also astounded at the way God's good news comes to us. The Savior of the world doesn't come as a rich and powerful king. Christ comes as a little baby lying in a manger. What an amazing surprise!

God of surprises, the good news of Christmas is so big that we can never really be ready for it. Fill us with awe at the great joy of Jesus' birth. Amen.

DECEMBER 26

•

On that day large numbers of sacrifices were offered. The people were glad because God had given them great joy. The women and children were also very happy. The joyful sound in Jerusalem could be heard far away.

Nehemiah 12:43 NIRV

Happy Kwanzaa! Today is the first day of Kwanzaa, a seven-day African-American holiday that celebrates family and community life. During Kwanzaa, people light candles, tell stories, sing, and play music. Kwanzaa celebrates principles like unity, responsibility, and faith that keep families and communities strong.

The prophet Nehemiah tells about a community celebration too. The people of Israel had endured a terrible time of exile. The Babylonians had captured Jerusalem and destroyed the temple; many Israelites were captured and taken to Babylon. Now the community of Israel had returned to its land and was starting over. They rebuilt the temple and tried hard to obey God's law. They rebuilt the walls of the city of Jerusalem. After all this work, they had a big celebration that lasted several days. They played music, sang joyful songs, and gave thanks to God for their life together.

Matunda ya kwanzaa means firstfruits in the African language Swahili. Kwanzaa takes its name from African festivals celebrating the firstfruits of the harvest. Nehemiah tells that the people of Israel brought the firstfruits of their harvest to the Temple during their celebration too. It was a way of remembering that the harvest is God's gift.

God of the harvest, thank you for blessing our families and communities with many gifts. Your faithfulness fills us with joy! Help us always to stay faithful to you. Amen.

DECEMBER 27

•

But you are God's chosen and special people. You are a group of royal priests and a holy nation. God has brought you out of darkness into his marvelous light. Now you must tell all the wonderful things that he has done. The Scriptures say,

> *"Once you were nobody. Now you are God's people.*
> *At one time no one had pity on you.*
> *Now God has treated you with kindness."*

1 Peter 2:9–10 CEV

When you try hard, you can often make a big difference. Maybe your room was a mess, but you worked hard to make it clean. Maybe you used to be afraid of deep water, but now you swim with confidence.

This Bible passage is about a big difference that isn't the result of anything we did. It is the result of what God did for us. We didn't become the people of God by trying hard. God chose us. We didn't become a holy nation because we always did what is right. God brought us out of darkness into light by forgiving us.

Once we were nobodies. But now we are royal priests, a people who belong to God. God did all this. Is there anything left for us to do? Yes! We can tell others about the wonderful things God has done!

Gracious God, we love to tell of the wonderful things you have done. You are full of kindness. Thank you for choosing us to be your people. Amen.

DECEMBER 28

•

You don't gain anything by being punished for some wrong you have done. But God will bless you, if you have to suffer for doing something good. After all, God chose you to suffer as you follow in the footsteps of Christ, who set an example by suffering for you.

Christ did not sin or ever tell a lie.
Although he was abused, he never tried to get even.
And when he suffered, he made no threats.
Instead, he had faith in God, who judges fairly.

1 Peter 2:20–23 CEV

Rosa Parks was willing to suffer for doing something good. In the 1950s blacks and whites in the United States could not sit together on buses. When Mrs. Parks refused to give up her bus seat to a white man, the driver called the police, who arrested her and put her in jail. She lost her job and received threats from white people, but she kept working peacefully to change the unfair laws. God chose her to help make this country a better place for African-Americans. By her willingness to suffer for what was right, she followed in the footsteps of Christ.

But God doesn't want anyone to suffer for no reason. There is nothing good about suffering in itself. If you are suffering from violence at home or at school, you should ask someone you trust for help. Have faith in God, like Christ did, because God judges fairly and wants all suffering to end.

Christ Jesus, your suffering gives me courage when I have to suffer. Show me how to live in love, as you did. Amen.

DECEMBER 29

•

But make sure in your hearts that Christ is Lord. Always be ready to give an answer to anyone who asks you about the hope you have. Be ready to give the reason for it. But do it gently and with respect.

1 Peter 3:15 NIRV

You probably have friends in your neighborhood or at school who are not Christian. They could be members of another religious community or they may not be religious at all. They may question you about your faith: What do you do at church? Do you believe everything that is in the Bible? What's so special about Jesus?

Part of being a Christian is sharing your faith with others. So be ready to give an answer to their questions. Don't be embarrassed! Try to share your faith in simple words that people who are not Christian can understand. You may have some questions you want to ask about their faith too.

When you share your faith with someone, do it gently and with respect. Do not make fun of what other people believe. Do not pretend that you know everything there is to know about God. Spend time listening as well as talking. And remember that non-Christians will be watching to see whether your life matches your words.

Christ Jesus, you are Lord. Help me share my faith in you with gentleness and respect. I pray in your name, Amen.

DECEMBER 30

•

Dear friends, don't forget that for the Lord one day is the same as a thousand years, and a thousand years is the same as one day. The Lord isn't slow about keeping his promises, as some people think he is. In fact, God is patient, because he wants everyone to turn from sin and no one to be lost.

2 Peter 3:8–9 CEV

You have to be patient to go on a walk with a toddler. Her legs are short, so she takes small steps. Besides, she keeps seeing things she wants to stop and look at: a leaf, a worm, a fire hydrant. Going one block seems to take forever!

God is patient with us. God's will is for everyone to turn from sin. But our faith grows very slowly. We are easily distracted by things that don't really matter. The good news is that God doesn't give up on us or leave us behind. God patiently waits for us.

Because God is patient, we must try to be patient. We are in a hurry to see God's promises come true. We can't wait until the world is full of peace and justice, and everyone is filled with the love of God. We don't know God's schedule, and we often feel impatient. But we can trust God to keep these promises.

God, thank you for being patient with us. Give us the strength to wait for your promises to come true. In Christ's name, Amen.

DECEMBER 31

•

Jesus Christ never changes! He is the same yesterday, today, and forever.

Hebrews 13:8 CEV

Today is the last day of the year. If you think back to the beginning of the year, you can see many changes in your life. You have probably grown out of some of your clothes. You are in a different grade at school. Maybe you have made new friends or increased your skill in music or sports.

There may have also been some bad changes for you this year. Perhaps people you love have moved away, or gotten divorced, or died. Maybe someone or something you always counted on disappointed you.

Every year will bring changes. But in the midst of our changes, we have something to hold onto—Jesus Christ. Christ's love for us never dies and never disappoints us. This love surrounded us when we were babies and will be with us every day of every year of our lives. We can count on Jesus Christ forever!

Thank you, Christ Jesus, for being with me through all the changes of this past year. I know that nothing in the years to come will separate me from your love. Amen.

Subject Index

Scripture Index